P9-CQD-836

Praise for MONICA McCARTY
and her *New York Times* and *USA Today* bestselling Highland Guard series!

"Against a richly historical and violent backdrop, McCarty deftly weaves a surprisingly moving love story that demands a skillful writer's touch. Her exquisite prose makes this a book readers will treasure." —*RT Book Reviews*

"The characters leap off the pages and into your heart. With a stunning plot that has enough twists and turns in all the right places, McCarty has created yet another captivating story that is sure to please!" —*Fresh Fiction*

"Passion and politics abound in this exceptionally well-researched romance that skillfully interweaves fiction with history and sheds new light on a particularly fascinating and violent time." —*Library Journal*

"Readers who deplore 'wallpaper historicals' will appreciate not only the romance but McCarty's efforts to go beyond the superficialities of historical Scotland." —*Publishers Weekly*

"Spectacularly entertaining. . . . McCarty is a master of blending fact and fiction." —*Romance Junkies*

"One of those amazing books that captures your attention right from the get-go. . . . McCarty has written a tale fit for a king." —*Coffee Time Romance*

"Thoroughly enjoyable. . . . Cleverly interwoven plot twists . . . kept me on my toes!" —*The Romance Reviews*

MONICA McCARTY

The Striker

Pocket Books

New York   London   Toronto   Sydney   New Delhi

Pocket Books
An Imprint of Simon & Schuster, Inc.
1230 Avenue of the Americas
New York, NY 10020

This book is a work of fiction. Any references to historical events, real people, or real places are used fictitiously. Other names, characters, places, and events are products of the author's imagination, and any resemblance to actual events or places or persons, living or dead, is entirely coincidental.

First Pocket Books paperback edition December 2015

POCKET and colophon are registered trademarks
of Simon & Schuster, Inc.

For information about special discounts for bulk purchases,
please contact Simon & Schuster Special Sales at 1-866-506-1949
or business@simonandschuster.com.

The Simon & Schuster Speakers Bureau can bring authors to your live event. For more information or to book an event, contact the Simon & Schuster Speakers Bureau at 1-866-248-3049 or visit our website at www.simonspeakers.com.

Interior design by Leydiana Rodríguez

Manufactured in the United States of America

10 9 8 7 6 5 4 3 2 1

ISBN 978-1-5011-0870-9
ISBN 978-1-5011-0875-4 (ebook)

To Annelise, for your faith,
trust, and pixie dust!

ACKNOWLEDGMENTS

WHEN THE OPPORTUNITY came around to work with Lauren McKenna, an editor I have long admired from afar, I knew I couldn't pass it up. Still, change is never easy. Or at least that's what I thought. But, apparently, the folks at Pocket Books aren't in on that little truism. An enormous thanks to everyone at Pocket for making a mid-series transition to a new publisher unbelievably smooth, seamless, and yes . . . easy!

First and foremost, to Lauren—I am so excited to be working with you after years of hearing so many great things from mutual friends (which I'm happy to say are all true!). There is always a lot of anxiety in changing editors, but your insightful, spot-on comments immediately alleviated that stress. Here's to this being the first of many books to come!

A special thanks also to Elana Cohen for making sure that no beats were missed and for helping me to navigate through the new system. Your quick responses, great communication, and always friendly attitude have made the business part of the job a pleasure. I can't wait to meet you in person!

Thanks also to the art department for the fabulous Scottish eye candy—uh, I mean covers—and the production team (with a shout-out to production editor Nancy Tonik and copy editor Faren Bachelis) for getting this book ready for prime time and making sure no one finds out I can't spell.

And finally, last but not least, to the best-supporting crew in the business: Dave, Reid, and Maxine. I love you guys (most of the time).

THE HIGHLAND GUARD

TOR "CHIEF" MACLEOD: Team Leader and Expert Swordsman

ERIK "HAWK" MACSORLEY: Seafarer and Swimmer

LACHLAN "VIPER" MACRUAIRI: Stealth, Infiltration, and Extraction

ARTHUR "RANGER" CAMPBELL: Scouting and Reconnaissance

GREGOR "ARROW" MACGREGOR: Marksman and Archer

MAGNUS "SAINT" MACKAY: Survivalist and Weapon Forging

KENNETH "ICE" SUTHERLAND: Explosives and Versatility

EOIN "STRIKER" MACLEAN: Strategist in "Pirate" Warfare

EWEN "HUNTER" LAMONT: Tracker and Hunter of Men

ROBERT "RAIDER" BOYD: Physical Strength and Hand-to-Hand Combat

ALSO:

HELEN "ANGEL" MACKAY (NÉE SUTHERLAND): Healer

A NOTE FROM MONICA

THE TWELVE BOOKS of the Highland Guard series span the nine-year period from 1305 when William Wallace is killed to the Scot victory at the seminal battle of Bannockburn in 1314. One of the difficulties in writing a long series like this is that inevitably some stories will overlap in time. *The Striker* is one of those. The book opens in 1313, but quickly goes back to those days in the immediate aftermath of Wallace's death before Bruce makes his bid for the crown, giving new readers a chance to see what he went through, and previous readers a chance to fill in some of the gaps. As *The Viper* told the story of what happened to the women when Bruce was forced to flee, *The Striker* deals with what happened to the second prong of the attack in *The Hawk*.

FOREWORD

THE YEAR OF our Lord thirteen hundred and thirteen. After nearly seven years of warfare, Robert the Bruce has waged an improbable comeback from almost certain defeat to retake nearly all his kingdom from the English and Scot countrymen who have stood against him.

The final challenge from the English will come soon, but there are still pockets of resistance in Scotland to the man who would be called King Robert I. Foremost among them is the troublesome southwest province of Galloway, ruled by the most wanted man in Scotland: Dugald Mac-Dowell, the ruthless chief of Clan MacDowell.

Seeing Dugald MacDowell brought to heel is personal for Bruce, as it was the MacDowells who were responsible for one of the darkest moments in Bruce's quest for the throne.

To lead this important mission, Bruce calls on Eoin MacLean, one of the famed warriors of the elite secret fighting force known as the Highland Guard, who has reasons of his own for wanting the MacDowells destroyed.

But vengeance is never as easy as it seems, and Eoin will eventually have to face the past that haunts him and return to the days before Bruce made his bid for the throne.

1

St. Mary's Church near Barnard Castle,
Durham, England, January 17, 1313

IT WAS A damned fine day for a wedding. Eoin Mac-
Lean, the man who'd devised the plan to use it as a trap
to capture the most wanted man in Scotland, appreciated
the irony.

The sun, which had hidden itself behind storm clouds
for weeks, had picked this midwinter morn to reemerge
and shine brightly on the sodden English countryside,
making the thick grasses around the small church glisten
and the remaining foliage on the trees shimmer like trees
of amber and gold. It also, unfortunately, caught the shimmer of their mail, making it difficult to blend into the
countryside. The long steel hauberk was unusual armor for
Bruce's men, who preferred the lighter black leather *cotuns*,
but in this case, it was necessary.

From their vantage on the forested hillside beyond the
church, the small village on the River Tees in the shadow
of the great Barnard Castle looked pretty and picturesque.
A perfect backdrop for the equally pretty bride and her
knightly English groom.

Eoin's mouth fell in a hard line, a small crack revealing
the acid churning inside him. It was almost a shame to ruin

it. Almost. But he'd been waiting for this day for nearly six years, and nothing—sure as hell not the happiness of the bride and groom—was going to stop him from capturing the man responsible for the worst disaster to befall Robert the Bruce in a reign filled with plenty of them from which to choose.

They had him. Dugald MacDowell, the chief of the ancient Celtic kingdom of Galloway, the last of the significant Scots opposition to Bruce's kingship, and the man responsible for the slaughter of over seven hundred men—including two of Bruce's brothers. The bastard had eluded capture for years, but he'd finally made a mistake.

That his mistake was a weakness for the bride made it even more fitting, as it was Eoin's foolish weakness for the same woman that had set the whole disaster in motion.

He felt for the carved piece of ivory in his sporran by instinct. It was there—as was the well-read piece of parchment beside it. Talismans of a sort, reminders of another, but he never went into battle without them.

"You're sure he'll be here?"

Eoin turned to the man who'd spoken: Ewen Lamont, his partner in the Highland Guard, and one of the dozen men who'd accompanied him on this dangerous mission deep behind enemy lines. Though Bruce himself had led raids through Durham last summer, the king had had an army for support. If Eoin's dozen men ran into trouble, they were on their own a hundred miles from the Scottish border. Of course, it was his job to make sure they didn't run into trouble.

Opugnate acriter. Strike with force. That's what he did, and what had earned him the war name of Striker among the elite warriors of Bruce's secret Highland Guard. Like the striker who wielded the powerful blows of the hammer for the blacksmith, Eoin's bold, just-on-the-edge-of-crazy "pirate" tactics struck hard against their enemies. Today would be no different—except that this plan might be even bolder (and crazier) than usual. Which, admittedly, was saying something.

Eoin met his friend's gaze, which was just visible beneath the visor of the full helm. "Aye, I'm sure. Nothing will keep MacDowell from his daughter's wedding."

The information about Maggie's—*Margaret's*—planned nuptials had fallen into his hands by chance. Eoin, Lamont, Robbie Boyd, and James Douglas had been with Edward Bruce, the king's only remaining brother, in Galloway for the past month doing everything they could do to disrupt communication and the supply routes between the Mac-Dowell strongholds in Scotland's southwest province of Galloway and Carlisle Castle in England, which was provisioning them. During one of these "disruptions," they'd captured a bundle of missives, which included a letter from Sir John Conyers, the Constable of Barnard Castle for the Earl of Warwick, giving the date of Conyers's marriage to MacDowell's "beloved" daughter. Dugald had eight sons, but only one daughter, so there could be no mistake as to the identity of the bride.

Lamont gave him a long, knowing look. "I suspect the same could be said of you."

Eoin's lip curled in a smile that was edged with far more anger than amusement. "You're right about that."

This was one wedding he wouldn't miss for the world. The fact that it would lead to the capture of his most hated enemy only made it more satisfying. Two debts, long in arrears, would be repaid this day.

But bloody hell, how much longer was this going to take? He was always edgy before a mission, but this was worse than usual. For Christ's sake, his hands were practically shaking!

He'd laugh, if he couldn't guess why. The fact that she could get to him after all these years—after what she'd done—infuriated him enough to immediately kill any twitchiness. He was as cold as ice. As hard as steel. Nothing penetrated. It hadn't in a long time.

Finally, the appearance of riders on the drawbridge, one of whom was holding a blue and white banner, signaled the arrival of the groom.

Eoin flipped down the visor of his helm, adjusted the heavy, uncomfortable shirt of mail, and donned the stolen surcoat, which not coincidentally was a matching blue and white.

"Be ready," he said to his partner. "Make sure the others know what to do, and wait for my signal."

Lamont nodded, but didn't wish him luck. Eoin didn't need it. When it came to strategies and plans, no one did them better. Outwit, outplay, outmaneuver, and when necessary, outfight. MacDowell may have gotten the best of him six years ago, but today Eoin would even the score.

"*Bàs roimh Gèill*," Lamont said instead.

Death before surrender, the motto of the Highland Guard—and if they were lucky, of Dugald MacDowell as well.

She was doing the right thing. Margaret knew that. It had been almost six years. She'd mourned long enough. She deserved a chance at happiness. And more important, her son deserved a chance to grow up under the influence of a good man. A *kind* man. A man who had not been made bitter by defeat.

None of which explained why she'd been up since dawn, running around all morning, unable to sit still. Or why her heart was fluttering as if in a panic. Panic that went beyond normal wedding day anxiety.

She hadn't been nervous at all for her first wedding. Her chest pinched as just for a moment—one tiny moment—she allowed her thoughts to return to that sliver in time over seven years ago when everything had seemed so perfect. She'd been so happy. So in love and full of hope for the future. Her chest squeezed tightly before releasing with a heavy sigh.

God, what a naive fool she'd been. So brash and confident. So convinced everything would work out the way she wanted it to. Maybe a little anxiety would have served her better.

She'd been so young—*too* young. Only eighteen. If she could go back and do it all over again with the perspective of age . . .

She sighed. Nay, it was too late to change the past. But not the future. Her thoughts returned to the present where they must stay, and she focused, as she always did, on the best thing to come out of that painful time. The thing that had pulled her out of the darkness and forced her to live again. Her five-year-old son, Eachann—or as they called him in England, Hector.

Eachann had a small chamber adjoining hers in the manor house that had been their home in England for the past four years, since her father had been forced to flee Scotland. But she and her son would be leaving Temple-Couton for good this morning. After the wedding ceremony, they would remove to Barnard Castle with her betrothed—her *husband*, she corrected, trying to ignore the simultaneous drop in her stomach and spike in her pulse (two things that definitely shouldn't happen simultaneously!).

Instead, she forced a smile on her face and gazed fondly at her son, who was sitting on his bed, his spindly legs dangling over the side and his blond head bent forward.

The soft silky curls were already darkening as the white blond of toddlerhood gave way to the darker blond of youth. *Like his father's.* He was like his father in so many ways, looking at him should cause her pain. But it didn't. It only brought her joy. In Eachann she had a piece of her husband that death could not claim. Her son was hers completely, in a way that her husband never had been.

She smiled, her heart swelling as it always did when she looked at him. "Do you have everything?"

He looked up. Sharp blue eyes met hers, startling again in their similarity to the man who'd given him his blood if nothing else. Eachann nodded somberly. He was like his father in that regard as well, serious and contemplative. "I think so."

Stepping around the two large wooden trunks, Margaret glanced around the room to make sure. Just below his small booted heel, she spied the corner of a dark plank of wood.

Following the direction of her gaze, Eachann attempted to inconspicuously kick it farther under the bed.

Frowning, Margaret sat on the bed beside him. He wouldn't look at her. But she didn't need to see his face to know he was upset.

"Is there a reason you don't want to take your chessboard? I thought it was your favorite game?"

His cheeks flushed. "Grandfather said I'm too old to play with poppets. I need to practice my swords or I'm gonna end up a traitorous baserd like my father." The little boy's mouth drew in a hard, merciless line, the expression a chilling resemblance to her father. Why is it that she'd never noticed the negative aspects of her father until they appeared in her son? "I'm no traitor! I'll see that bloody usurper off the throne, and Good King John restored to his crown, if it's the last thing I do." Another chill ran through her. St. Columba's bones, he sounded exactly like her father, too. His head tilted toward hers. "But what's a baserd?"

"Nothing you could ever be, my love," she said, hugging the boy tightly to her. This was one word that she wasn't going to worry about correcting.

If she needed proof of why she was doing the right thing, she had it. She loved her father, but she would not have her son warped by his disappointments. She would not see Eachann turned into a bitter, angry old man who thought the world had turned against him. Who reveled in being the last "true" patriot for the Balliol claim to the throne, and the only significant Scottish nobleman who still had not bowed to the "usurper" Robert the Bruce.

Margaret understood her father's anger—and perhaps even commiserated with him about the source—but that did not mean she wanted her son turned into a miniature version of him. Despite Eachann's "traitorous bastard" of a father, Dugald MacDowell loved his only grandchild. Indeed, it was her father's mention of having Eachann fostered with Tristan MacCan—his *an gille-coise* henchman—so the lad could be close to him that gave Margaret the push to accept Sir John Conyers's proposal.

When the time came next year for her son to leave her care—God give her strength to face that day!—Sir John would see to his placement and not her father. Being a squire to an English knight was vastly preferable to being fostered by a man so completely under her father's influence, even one who was a childhood friend. Her son's safety came above everything else.

"Chess pieces are not poppets, my love." She pulled out the board etched with grid lines and the lovingly carved and painted wooden pieces. Some of the paint had begun to flake off on the edges, and the carefully painted faces had faded with use. She'd taught Eachann to play when he was three. He played against himself mostly, as despite prodigious efforts otherwise, she'd never had the patience for it. But he did. Her son was brilliant, and she was fiercely proud of him. "It's the game of kings," she said with a bittersweet smile. "Your father played."

That surprised him. She rarely mentioned his father, for various reasons, including that the memories pained her and mention of him drew her family's ire. They all tried to pretend that the "traitorous bastard" never existed around Eachann, but if the eager look on the boy's face was any indication, perhaps they had been wrong in that.

"He did?" Eachann asked.

She nodded. "It was he who taught me to play. Your grandfather never learned, which is why he . . ." She thought of how to put it. "Which is why he doesn't understand how useful it can be to a warrior."

He looked at her as if she were crazed. "How?"

She grinned. "Well, you could throw the board like a discus, or use the pieces in a slingshot."

He rolled his eyes. She couldn't get anything past him, even though he was only five. He always knew when she was teasing. "Don't be ridiculous, Mother. It wouldn't make a good weapon."

His expression was so reminiscent of his father's she

had to laugh so she didn't cry. If anyone needed proof that mannerisms were inherited, Eachann was it. "All right, you have me. I was teasing. Did you read the rest of the folio Father Christopher found for you?"

They'd been reading it together, but he'd grown impatient waiting for her. Like with chess, her son had quickly outpaced her hard-wrought reading skills.

He nodded.

She continued. "King Leonidas was a great swordsman, but that's not what made him a great leader, and what held off so many Persians at Thermopylae. It was his mind. He planned and strategized, using the terrain to his advantage."

A broad smile lit up Eachann's small face. "Just like you plan and strategize in chess."

Margaret nodded. "That was what your father did so exceptionally. He was one of the smartest men I ever knew. In the same way that you can look at the chessboard and 'see' what to do, he could look at an army on the battleground and see what to do. He could defeat the enemy before he even picked up a sword."

Though Eachann's father had favored a battle-axe like his illustrious grandfather for whom he'd been named: Gillean-na-Tuardhe, "Gill Eoin (the servant of Saint John) of the Battle-axe." He'd been good with it, too. But she didn't want to mention that. In spite of her son's auspicious name, harkening to one of the greatest warriors of ancient times, Hector of Troy, Eachann was small and had yet to show any skill—or love—of weaponry. Her father had begun to notice, which was another reason she had to get her son away. She wouldn't mind if Eachann never picked up a weapon and buried himself in books for the rest of his life. But Dugald MacDowell would not see his grandson as anything but a fierce warrior. Another MacDowell to devote his life to a war that would never end.

But she wouldn't let that happen. The constant conflict that had dominated her life—that had torn apart her life—would not be her son's.

She stood up. "Why don't you put your game in the chest, while I go to tell Grandfather we are ready."

He gave her a nod and hopped off the bed. She was almost to the door before she felt a pair of tiny arms wrap around her legs. "I love you, Mother."

Tears filled her eyes as she returned the hug with a hard squeeze. "And I love you, sweetheart."

Certainty filled her heart. She *was* doing the right thing.

∞

Three hours later, Margaret had to remind herself of it. As she stood outside the church door, her father, son, and six of her eight brothers gathered on her left, and Sir John on her right, flanked by what seemed like the entire garrison of Barnard Castle, it didn't feel right at all. Indeed, it felt very, *very* wrong.

Were it not for the firm arm under her hand holding her up, she might have collapsed; her legs had the strength of jelly.

Sir John must have sensed something. He covered her hand resting in the crook of his elbow with his. "Are you all right? You look a little pale."

She had to tilt her head back to look at him. He was tall—although not as tall as her first husband had been—and the top of her head barely reached his chin. He was just as handsome though. Maybe even more so, if you preferred smooth perfection to sharp and chiseled.

And Sir John liked to smile. He did so often. Unlike her first husband. Wresting a smile from him had been her constant challenge. But when she'd succeeded, it had felt like she'd been rewarded a king's ransom. Sir John's life also didn't revolve around battle—thinking about battle, planning about battle, talking about battle. Sir John had many other interests, including—novelly—*her*. He talked to her, shared his thoughts with her, and didn't treat her like a mistake.

Then why did this feel like one? Why did the very proper wedding, with the seemingly perfect man, feel so different from the improper one, with the wrong man that had come before it?

Because you don't love him.

But she would. By all that was good and holy in heaven, she would! This time it would grow, rather than wither on the bone of neglect to die. She was being given a second chance at happiness, and she would take it, blast it!

She drew a deep breath and smiled—this time for real. "I was too excited to eat anything this morning. I'm afraid it's catching up with me. But I'm fine. Or will be, as soon as we get to the feast."

Sir John returned her smile, she thought with a tinge of relief. "Then we must not delay another moment." He leaned down and whispered closer to her ear. "I don't want my bride fainting *before* the wedding night."

Her eyes shot to his. She caught the mischievous twinkle and laughed. "So I'm expected to faint afterward?"

"I would consider it the highest compliment if you would. It is every groom's hope to so overcome his bride on the wedding night that she swoons." He nodded to indicate the soldiers behind him. "How else am I to impress the men over a tankard of ale?"

"You are horrible." But she said it with a smile. This was why she was marrying him. This is why they would be happy. He made her laugh in a way she hadn't laughed in a long time. His humor was just as wicked as hers had been. Once.

Following the direction of his gaze, she scanned the large group of mail-clad soldiers. "Is that what you talk about when you are all together? Aren't you breaking some secret male code by telling me this?"

He grinned. "Probably. But I trust you not to betray me."

Not to betray me . . .

A chill ran down her spine. Her gaze snagged on something in the crowd. Her skin prickled, and the hair at the back of her neck stood up for a long heartbeat before the sensation passed.

It must have been Sir John's words, unknowingly stirring memories. Unknowingly stirring guilt.

Tell no one of my presence . . .

Pain that not even six years could dull stabbed her heart. God, how could she have been so foolish? The only good thing about her husband dying was that she didn't have to live with the knowledge of how much he would have despised her for betraying him.

"Margaret?" Sir John's voice shook her from the memories. "They are waiting for us."

The priest and her father, who had been talking, were both now staring at her, the priest questioningly, her father with a dark frown. Ignoring them both, she turned to Sir John. "Then let us begin."

Side by side, they stood before the church door and publicly repeated the vows that would bind them together.

If memories of another exchange of vows tried to intrude, she refused to let them. Of course it was different this time. This time she was doing it right. The banns. The public exchange of vows outside the church door. The only thing they wouldn't have was the mass afterward. As she was a widow, it was not permitted.

If she secretly didn't mind missing a long mass, she was wise enough not to admit it. *Now.* She wasn't the wild, irreverent "heathen" from "the God Forsaken" corner of Galloway anymore. She would never give Sir John a reason to be ashamed of or embarrassed by her.

When the priest asked if there was anyone who objected or knew of a reason why these two could not be joined, her heart stopped. The silence seemed to stretch intolerably. Surely that was long enough to wait—

"I do."

The voice rang out loud and clear, yet for one confused moment, she thought she'd imagined it. The uncomfortable murmuring of the crowd, and the heads turned in the direction of the voice, however, told her she hadn't.

Sir John swore. "If this is some kind of joke, someone is going to regret it."

"You there," the priest said loudly. "Step forward if you have something to say."

The crowd parted, revealing a soldier—an exceptionally tall and powerfully built soldier. Strangely, the visor of his helm was flipped down.

He took a few steps forward, and Margaret froze. Stricken, her breath caught in her throat as she watched the powerful stride that seemed so familiar. Only one man walked with that kind of impatience—as if he was waiting for the world to catch up to him.

No . . . no . . . it can't be.

All eyes were on the soldier wearing the blue and white surcoat of the Conyers's arms. She sensed the movement of a few other soldiers, circling around the crowd in the churchyard, but paid them no mind. Like everyone else, her gaze was riveted on the man striding purposefully forward.

He stopped a few feet away.

He stood motionlessly, his head turned in her direction. It was ridiculous—fanciful—his eyes were hidden in the shadow of the steel helm, but somehow she could feel them burning into her. Condemning. Accusing. *Despising.*

Her legs could no longer hold her up; they started to wobble.

"What is the meaning of this, Conyers?" her father said angrily, apparently blaming Sir John for the conduct of one of his men.

"Speak," the priest said impatiently to the man. "Is there an impediment of which you are aware?"

The soldier flipped up his visor, and for one agonizing, heart-wrenching moment his midnight-blue eyes met hers. Eyes she could never forget. Pain seared through her in a devastating blast. White-hot, it sucked every last bit of air from her lungs. Her head started to spin. She barely heard the words that would shock the crowd to the core.

"Aye, there's an impediment." Oh God, that voice. She'd dreamed of that voice so many nights. A low, gravelly voice with the lilt of the Gael. *Oh God, Maggie, that feels so good. I'm going to . . .* "The lass is already married."

"To whom?" the priest demanded furiously, obviously believing the man was playing some kind of game.

But he wasn't.

Eoin is alive.

"To me."

Margaret was already falling as he spoke. Unfortunately, Sir John wasn't going to get his wish: the bride would faint before the wedding night after all.

2

Stirling Castle, Scotland, late September 1305

A RE YOU SURE about this, Maggie?"
Margaret took that as a rhetorical question. She was sure about everything, as her oldest friend well knew. "Have you ever seen anything like this, Brige?"

Margaret's question was a rhetorical one as well. Of course her friend hadn't. Like Margaret, Brigid hadn't traveled more than twenty miles from her home in the Rhins of Galloway in the remote southwestern corner of Scotland. A place that was so far away it seemed almost another world. God's bones, it had taken them nearly two weeks to travel here with carts, and it wasn't a journey she was anxious to repeat anytime soon.

If she was successful—*when* she was successful—she might not be going back at all. Though the gathering at Stirling was an attempt to make allies of Scotland's rivals for the crown to form a unified force against England, her father had another purpose in being here. He intended to propose a marriage alliance between Margaret and young John Comyn, the son of John "the Red" Comyn, Lord of Badenoch. It was her job to win over the young lord and make him eager for the match. As winning over men was something she'd been doing since she could talk, she would probably be betrothed in a fortnight.

Margaret spun around. "Isn't it magnificent? Look how high the rafters are! The Hall is so large I'm surprised the ceiling does not come tumbling down. How do you think they built it to stay up there like that?" She didn't bother waiting for an answer, she was already racing across the room to examine the enormous fireplace. "I can stand up inside!" she said, ducking under the colorfully painted mantel.

Brigid laughed as she peeked back under. "Careful," her friend warned, suddenly sober. "The embers are still glowing from this morning. You'll light your skirts on fire."

"That would make an impression, wouldn't it?" Margaret said with an impish smile. "No one would forget me then. The girl who caught her skirts on fire."

"No one will forget you anyway," Brigid said with a fond—if slightly exasperated—shake of the head.

But Margaret wasn't listening; she'd already moved on to the next discovery. Since they'd arrived at Stirling Castle a few hours ago, it seemed every minute had been filled with them. She'd barely taken time to wash—in the finest tub she'd ever seen—change her clothes, and run a comb through her still damp hair before she'd dragged Brigid off to go exploring. They could rest tonight.

Margaret put her hand on one of the walls. "It *is* plaster! I wasn't sure. The painting of the arms is so exquisite I thought it might actually be a shield! Can you believe they painted the whole room with this brick and vine pattern? There isn't a surface that hasn't been decorated in here. I've never seen a more colorful room. And look at these curtains." She moved toward one of the windows and pulled the heavy scarlet velvet around her. "It's fine enough to make a gown." Glancing down at her plain dark brown wool kirtle, she grinned. "Actually it's finer than any of my gowns. What do you think? Will someone notice if we take it?"

Brigid shook her head with amazement. "Can you imagine using fabric as fine as that for curtains?" Suddenly, her face drew tight with consternation. "Do you think our gowns will be very different from the other ladies?"

"I should hope so," Margaret said with a proud squaring of her shoulders. "We are wearing some of the finest wool in all of Scotland. There are no finer weavers than from Galloway. I should think the other ladies will be very envious indeed."

Brigid bit her lip, not looking convinced. This time it was Margaret who shook her head. Her friend worried about the silliest things. They were just gowns, for goodness' sake!

Margaret walked past the wooden screen of the dais into an antechamber. "Look at this, Brigid. It's some kind of private solar. Holy cross! Do you see these candlesticks? They must be solid gold!" She plopped down on one of the benches around the edges of the room. "There isn't a chair without a pillow in this place. I believe I'm going to be busy when I return to Garthland Tower making cushions for all the benches."

"You shouldn't blaspheme, Maggie, and you don't sew."

Margaret replied to this minor detail with a stuck-out tongue. Leave it to Brigid to point out the realities. But maybe that's why they were such good friends. Brigid was the riggings to her sail. She didn't let her get carried away. Well, *too* carried away. As for the blasphemies, her brothers said far worse. If anyone was going to hell, it was them.

"Very well, I shall have Marsaili make them then."

"I don't think she likes to sew any more than you do."

"Well, at least she knows how," Margaret said, grinning.

She stood and walked over toward a table. On it was some kind of checkered board arranged with tiny carved pieces. She picked up one of the figures to examine it, noticing that it appeared to be made out of ivory. There were all kinds of different-sized figures in two colors. Some were arranged on the board, and some were off the board on opposite sides of the table. "Maybe this room is for the bairns," she said. "It looks like some kind of a game."

"That's a fine-looking game for a child." Brigid frowned when Margaret picked up another piece. "Do you think you should be touching that, Maggie? What if someone gets upset?"

Margaret looked at her friend as if she were daft. "It's just a game, Brige. Why would anyone care about that?" She picked up two of the biggest pieces. "Look at these—they are adorable. It looks like they have crowns. They must be a king and queen."

Brigid wrinkled her nose. "They look scary to me."

Margaret shook her head. "They should go in the middle." Realizing there wasn't a space in the middle in the checkerboard pattern, she improvised and put the queen in the center of the four spaces. "Well, the queen will go in the middle and the king will have to stand to her left." She grinned and moved the pieces around. "With all these men on horses around them."

"I take it the queen is you?" Brigid laughed. "Ruling over the men like you do at Garthland?"

"Well someone needs to," Margaret said matter-of-factly. "As much as my father and brothers are away, nothing would ever get done if I didn't take care of all those 'minor details.'"

They looked at each other and burst out laughing, knowing that Margaret handled far more than the "minor details" for which her father liked to give her credit.

Brigid picked up a few of the pieces to examine them, and then a small flat piece of wood that Margaret hadn't noticed before. It had something written on it.

"What do you think this says?" she asked.

Margaret looked at the lettering and shrugged. Like her friend she had no idea.

Not knowing how to play the game, they giggled as they took turns arranging the pieces in humorous formations.

"Do you hear something?" Brigid said. "I think someone is coming." She gasped in horror. "It can't already be time for the midday feast? We aren't ready!"

"I'm sure we still have plenty of time. It can't be that late—"

Margaret stopped, turning as a group of men walked into the antechamber. There were at least a half-dozen of them, but they seemed to be following one man. At least she assumed she must be following him, as he had the noble bearing of a king and was one of the most richly attired men she'd ever seen.

Probably a good ten years older than her eight and ten, he wore a dark green velvet mantle lined with fur, secured by an enormous jeweled brooch of silver. His surcoat was so richly embroidered it also looked jeweled. He was tall—about six feet—and sturdily built with dark hair and a neatly trimmed short dark beard.

"Friends of yours, Carrick?" one of the men asked with a speculative lift of his brow. He gazed at Margaret with unabashed interest, his eyes lingering over her hair. "Not the entertainment I was expecting, but I'm not complaining."

Margaret didn't realize what the man meant at first. She was too surprised to hear the identity of the young nobleman. This was the infamous Earl of Carrick and Lord of Annandale, Robert Bruce? From her father's description, she'd been expecting a forked tongue and devil's horns, not this impressive, handsome young man.

Entertainment? Her eyes narrowed back on the man who'd spoken. The man was older than the earl, shorter, and not nearly as handsome, although there was a brute strength to him. His eyes were fixed speculatively on her chest. He couldn't think . . .

He did! The man thought they were bawds! She almost burst out laughing. Wait until her brother Duncan heard this! He was always telling her she was as wicked as a French strumpet.

Carrick shot his companion a quelling stare and turned to Margaret and Brigid. "Are you lost, lasses? Did you become . . . uh, separated from someone? One of the ladies, by chance?"

Obviously the young earl was just as surprised to find them in here, but more subtle in his wondering of who they were. If she wasn't mistaken, he thought they were tiring women to one of the noble ladies in attendance—which offended her more than being thought a strumpet. The Mac-Dowells were one of the oldest clans in Scotland. They been ruling this country—at least the southwest part of it—before these Norman lords crossed the channel to England.

But she had to concede that Brigid might have had a point about their gowns.

She straightened her spine, lifted her chin, and met the young earl's stare with a bold challenge. "We are not lost, my lord. We were exploring the castle before the feast. We just arrived this morning with my father."

He quirked a brow, obviously surprised. "And who is your father?"

"Dugald MacDowell, Chief of MacDowell of Galloway," she said proudly, knowing exactly what kind of reaction that would provoke.

She wasn't disappointed. More than one man swore at the revelation that she was the daughter of their enemy. The earl hid his surprise well, though she could tell he was. "Lady Margaret," he said, with a short bow.

Margaret wasn't as adept at hiding hers. "You know of me?"

His mouth seemed to twitch, as if he were fighting a smile. "I suspect there are very few who haven't heard of the 'Fair Maid of Galloway.'"

Margaret frowned. She certainly hadn't. And why did she have the feeling there was more than beauty that he'd heard about?

The man who mistook her for a strumpet spoke. "Ah hell, Carrick. Look at that."

When he pointed in the direction of the game, and *all* the men started cursing, Margaret suspected Brigid had been right about something else, too.

She bit her lip. Perhaps touching the game *hadn't* been such a good idea.

I have him! Eoin knew just what he had to do to win.

He didn't smile much, but he couldn't prevent the one that lifted his mouth as he strode purposefully across the courtyard and into the Great Hall of Stirling Castle.

For two days he had been locked in a fierce battle of wits with Robert Bruce, the young Earl of Carrick, over a chessboard, but the answer had come to him last night, and victory would soon be his.

A victory that would bring him one step closer to the *real* reward.

He still couldn't believe it. His illustrious kinsman—his and Bruce's mothers were half sisters—was considering Eoin for an elite secret guard that Bruce was forming in the event he made a bid for the throne.

To have been singled out and chosen by Bruce was an honor for any young warrior, let alone the twenty-four-year-old third son of a Highland laird, as Eoin's father, Gillemore MacLean, Chief of MacLean, was quick to point out with a puff of pride.

But that wasn't why Eoin was so excited by the prospect. His kinsman hadn't given him many details, but those that he had were like holding out sweets to a bairn. A secret, highly specialized elite guard used for reconnaissance, intelligence, strategy, and special—in other words, the most dangerous—missions? For a man who had lived, breathed, even slept "pirate" warfare since he was seven years old and had helped his older brothers get back some fishing nets stolen by lads from a neighboring clan (*after* the lads had been good enough to fill it for them, of course), the prospect of bringing that style of warfare to a war against the most powerful army in Christendom was a challenge too great to resist. That Eoin would be fighting alongside a handpicked group of the most highly skilled warriors in all of Scotland was like sprinkling sugar on top of a trifle—heaping the sweet upon the sweet.

He was determined to win a position in the secret guard as a battle tactician, and besting his kinsman at chess—Bruce was known for his skill with the game—would help him in that regard. That the game was relatively new to Eoin, while Bruce had been playing for years, didn't concern him. Thinking two, three, or four steps ahead was something Eoin did all the time on the battlefield. Once he'd learned the rules, he could look at the board and see the moves played out in his head. Again, just like with battle—except that in the case of Highland warfare, there were no rules.

He smiled again.

"Satan's stones, Eoin, slow down!" His foster brother, Finlaeie MacFinnon, jogged up next to him. "I haven't seen a smile on your face like that since MacDonald fell into the cesspit." Eoin's smile deepened, remembering how he'd loosened the boards of the wooden seat over the barrack latrine just enough for the tyrant who'd been given the responsibility of training them by their foster father, Angus Og MacDonald—and who'd made every minute of two years miserable—to fall in. Almost better than seeing Iain MacDonald covered in shite was the fact that he'd never known it was Eoin who'd been responsible. "What are you so happy about?"

Eoin shook his head. "Nothing." The most difficult part about this group Bruce was forming was that it was secret. He couldn't even confide in his closest friend. He glanced over at Fin, taking in the red-rimmed eyes, tousled hair, and disheveled clothing. Eoin's nose wrinkled from the stiff stench of spirits. "Long night?"

Fin grinned. "You might say that. And an even longer morning. The lasses at court are quite welcoming. Not that it would interest you."

Eoin told him to do something that was physically impossible. He liked lasses as much as his foster brother did—when he had time for them. Right now he had too many important things on his mind.

"Maybe you're just saving yourself for that bride of yours?"

"Damn it, Fin, she's not my bride."

"Not yet, but don't tell me your father isn't working on it."

Eoin couldn't; it was true. His father was doing everything he could to secure a betrothal between him and Lady Barbara Keith.

"You're a lucky bastard, Eoin. I'd give my left bollock to have the Marischal of Scotland's daughter as my wife. With your skills and a marital connection to Scotland's top military commander, you'll be in a fantastic position if the war resumes."

When the war resumes, Eoin thought. For despite Edward of England's intentions, rather than end the Scottish "rebellion" with the brutal killing of William Wallace a few weeks ago, all he'd done was incite it.

That's why they were here. The great lords and magnates of Scotland had gathered at Stirling to "come together" to see what could be done to respond to this latest act by Edward.

But the likelihood of Bruce and Comyn (who represented his exiled uncle King John Balliol) coming together to agree about anything for any length of time was about as likely as the Mamluk sultan and the pope agreeing to share Jerusalem. Eoin knew the gathering was more about the two temporary allies gathering support and taking stock of potential allies when the next grab for power came. And it would come, there was no doubt about that. Hatred ran too deep between the two branches of the descendants of Prince Fergus to ever be reconciled.

The MacLeans were in a difficult position. Although Eoin's father had every intention of fighting alongside their kinsman Bruce, he was also trying to avoid more problems from the MacDougalls—the Lord of Argyll was technically their overlord for their lands in Lorn—who were firmly aligned with the Comyns, by appearing undecided.

"Lady Barbara is a lovely lady," he said. "Any man would be fortunate to have her as a wife."

The words came out as rote and unthinking as they were. But they were also true. Barbara Keith was pretty, well mannered, demure, and modest. A real lady, and everything he admired in a woman—just like his mother. Were it not for Rignach, daughter of the former Lord of Carrick, his father would never have become one of the most important and respected Highland chiefs. His father liked to jest that without her they'd be just as wild and uncivilized as those backward barbarian MacDowells, who were probably still living with their animals in long houses and worshipping pagan gods.

Having had the misfortune of crossing paths with Dugald MacDowell once, Eoin didn't doubt it. He could give the Vikings a lesson in ruthlessness and barbarity.

"Aye, I'm sure she'll make you a perfect wife," Fin said dryly.

Eoin's gaze sharpened. "What's that supposed to mean?"

Fin shrugged. "You don't want to be bothered, and she won't bother you. But you better wear a warm mantle when you bed her."

He shot him a look of warning. Eoin was used to his friend's talk about the women he bedded—or wanted to bed. Though distasteful, he usually ignored it. But speculating about the woman who might be Eoin's future wife was another matter.

Even if he was probably right. Lady Barbara was a bit . . . frosty.

Fin put his hand up. "Don't get all prickly. I don't mean anything by it. One can't have everything, I suppose. That's why so many men have lemans. A wife for money, position, alliances, and heirs, and a pretty mistress to fuck and suck your cock. Too bad the two never seem to go together."

Eoin winced. "Christ, Fin, do you have to talk like that?"

Fin just laughed and shook his head. "You are more of a prude than a nun in a harem, Eoin. If you ever relaxed long enough to sit around the fire at camp with us, rather than hunch over an oil lamp with those maps of yours, you'd know that is how most men talk."

He was focused, damn it, not prudish. "I'll relax when the war is over."

Fin made a sharp sound. "I doubt it. All you ever think about is battle. You'll just be planning for the next one."

His friend was probably more right than Eoin wanted to admit. He was saved from a response, however, when they passed from the Great Hall to the solar where he and Bruce were playing and he noticed a wall of men blocking the doorway. They seemed to be gathered around something protectively.

"Wonder what that is all about?" Fin asked.

Eoin frowned. "Let's find out."

They pushed past the first few men when Neil Campbell, one of Bruce's closest friends and advisors, said something to the earl and nodded in their direction. Bruce turned. There was a strange expression on his face; he seemed to be trying to prepare him for something.

"Cousin, I'm afraid . . ."

Eoin didn't know whether it was Bruce's expression or the fact that he called him cousin, which he didn't usually do, that caused him to turn and look to the left where the game was set up. Or at least where the game *had* been set up.

Bruce was saying something, but Eoin was too busy storming across the room to listen. "Bloody hell!" He looked in disbelief at the destroyed game. The pieces had been moved. His eyes narrowed. Not just moved, they'd been purposefully positioned into the design of a heart. He turned in outrage to his kinsmen. "By God, who did this? If this is some kind of joke . . ."

He'd kill them. Two days, damn it. And he'd been a few moves away from victory. He pictured the pieces in his head, trying to remember where they'd been placed.

"It was an accident," Bruce said.

"Accident?" Eoin picked up the piece of wood etched with the words Do Not Touch. "Did the idiot not read the sign?"

An uncomfortable silence fell across the room. Vaguely, Eoin was aware that someone had come up beside Bruce.

His gaze shifted, and he received the second blow of the morning. This one far more devastating. He felt like he'd been clobbered in the head with a poleaxe; stunned and more than a little dazed, as he stared—gaped probably—at one of the most sensual looking creatures he'd ever beheld.

She smiled, and that clobbered-by-a-poleaxe feeling dropped to his chest. "I'm afraid the idiot is me. I didn't see the sign until it was too late."

Ah hell. The discomfort in the room became clear. Although she did seem to be taking the offending words with surprising good humor. Most lasses he knew would be stricken with embarrassment. Instead it was he who felt the heat on his face. "I apologize for my ill-mannered words."

She waved him off with a deep, husky laugh that made

his bollocks tighten. "I've been called far worse by my brothers. I'd never seen the game before, and didn't realize it was so important."

Sensing she was amused by that fact, he frowned.

His cousin, always the gallant knight, rushed to reassure her. "And I was just assuring *Lady* Margaret that it was nothing."

Eoin hoped his eyes didn't widen as much as it felt like they had at the word "lady." From the look of her, he'd assumed something else entirely.

Very little about the lass conjured up the image of a lady. Her gown was plain, simple, and cut low and tight enough around the bodice to have made a tavern wench proud.

Her beauty wasn't quiet and restrained like a lady's, but bold and dramatic. *Too* bold and dramatic, the lass would draw attention, particularly masculine attention, wherever she went. Her lips were too red, her mouth too wide, her gold-hued eyes too seductively slanted, her breasts too big—not that he couldn't appreciate that particular excess—and her hair was red. A vibrant, dark red that wasn't plaited modestly behind a veil, but rather left loose to tumble around her shoulders in a wild disarray that was more appropriate to the bedchamber than the king's solar of a royal castle.

Aye, the bedchamber, which is exactly what he thought about when he looked at her.

But probably the most un-ladyish thing about her was the boldness in her gaze. There was no reserve, no modesty, and in a room full of important men, she was perfectly at ease, as if she belonged there. It was bloody disconcerting.

"Lady Margaret is Dugald MacDowell's daughter," Bruce added.

The Fair Maid of Galloway? Christ, that explained

everything. Eoin had heard of the lass, who was reputed to be every bit as wild, unruly, and outrageous as the rest of her clan. Despite her youth, she lorded over her father's lands when he was gone like a queen and had done so for years since her mother died. "Maid" was often said with irony, as the lass was reputed to be free with her favors.

Somehow he recovered enough to bow and mumble, "Lady Margaret."

"This is the young kinsman I was telling you about, my lady," Bruce explained.

She responded to Bruce with a wry grin, but her eyes hadn't left Eoin's. "I think the game was a little more serious than you let on, my lord Carrick."

Eoin was pretty certain his flush deepened. Bruce laughed. "*Everything* is serious to my young cousin here. Don't pay him any mind. Besides, he should be thanking you."

She broke the connection with Eoin and turned her slanted catlike eyes to Bruce. One delicately arched brow lifted. "Thanking me?"

Bruce flashed a broad grin. "Aye, for saving him from the embarrassment of losing. I had him beaten, although he didn't know it yet."

Lady Margaret laughed and turned back to Eoin. It felt as if every nerve ending in his body stood on edge as her eyes fell on him again.

"Is that so?" If he'd ever heard a more husky voice in a woman he couldn't recall it. "And do you agree, my lord?"

∞

Margaret didn't know what to make of the young warrior standing before her. She must admit, she'd been taken aback when he'd stormed into the room just as the other men had been doing their best to assure her that touching the game—the *chess*—pieces was "nothing." She didn't know whether it was his fury or his handsome face, but something had made her heart beat a little faster. All right, a *lot* faster.

He was dressed in a fine velvet surcoat like the other noblemen in the room, but he might as well have been wearing chain mail and wielding a long broadsword. Everything about this man bespoke warrior. It wasn't just his size, which was formidable (he was even taller and more powerfully built than the Earl of Carrick), but the fierce intensity that seemed to radiate from him. When he walked, it was with the long, powerful strides of a man ready for battle. With eight brothers, all of whom were or would be warriors, and a father who'd spent the better part of the last twenty years on the battlefield, she recognized the type well enough.

Men—even fierce, angry ones—didn't usually intimidate her. Usually. But something about seeing all those muscles bunch and the fury burning in his piercing blue eyes had made her pulse dance.

Although as she looked at him, waiting for him to respond, she realized the dancing could be a result of something else. Like maybe the surprisingly silky-looking honey-brown hair—streaked with enough sun-bleached chunks to recall what must have been the blondness of youth—that fell in careless waves to a clean-shaven, squared-off jaw with a slight dent, those striking eyes set below a seemingly perpetually furrowed brow (as if he were always concentrating), and sharp, carefully delineated features so finely carved they could have been chiseled from granite.

Lud, he's a handsome one. She'd always thought Brigid's brother, Tristan, the most handsome man she knew, but he'd never made her pulse race like this—even when Tristan was stealing a kiss, which had happened on more than one occasion. He'd also never made her skin prickle with a strange heat. Actually, her entire body seemed to have gone up a few degrees in temperature since he'd entered the room.

The young warrior seemed to be measuring his words carefully. Clearly, he didn't agree with the young earl's boast, but also wasn't going to contradict him in front of her and his men. "I agree the game was almost over," he finally said.

Dear lord, that voice! Deep and gravelly, it seemed to rub over her skin and sink into her bones.

Bruce laughed and clapped him on the back. "A very politic answer, cousin. But I suspect you know very well you had me trapped. I'd wager you are reconstructing the board in your head right now."

The young warrior—Eoin MacLean, Bruce had told her—simply shrugged.

Bruce laughed again and shook his head. "Do you know the truly appalling part, my lady? I've been playing chess since I was a lad, and MacLean here just learned. Still he's one of the best players I've ever competed against."

"I should like to know how to play this 'Game of Kings,' isn't that what you called it?" she asked Bruce innocently, although the hint of mischief in her gaze told him she knew exactly why he'd made that point to her earlier. Game of Kings—*he* being the king.

The Earl of Carrick was every bit as bold as she'd heard. She liked it, although she would never admit as much to her father. He would die before he saw a Bruce on the throne.

Bruce's equally mischievous smile told Margaret she was right about his intent.

She turned to MacLean. "Perhaps you would teach me one day?"

The surprise in those skin-prickling blue eyes, and the sudden silence in the room, told her that once again she'd done something wrong.

Devil take it, what is it this time? She'd barely been at Stirling Castle for a few hours, but already it was clear it was a long way from Garthland Tower.

No matter, soon enough she would find her footing. Margaret never doubted that for a moment.

3

"EVERYONE IS STARING at us," Brigid whispered as they entered the Hall a short while later.

Margaret had noticed the sudden silence in the bustling room and felt the eyes turned on them as well, but her reaction was the opposite of her friend's. Used to presiding over many tables at Garthland as hostess, she did not shy from attention. Actually, she rather liked it. Entertaining—*being* entertaining—was part of her duties as chatelaine, and she made sure no one left the castle without enjoying themselves. It helped that it came naturally to her.

Unfortunately, the same could not be said of her friend. Brigid was shy and reserved. Two words that weren't likely ever to be applied to her, Margaret thought with amusement.

After the initial pause, conversation had returned, so Margaret was able to reply to her friend in a normal tone as they wound their way through the crowd in search of her father and two eldest brothers, Dougal and Duncan. Given her clan's importance, she knew their seats would be near the dais.

Taking her friend's arm, she drew her tightly against

her side. "Of course they are! Isn't it wonderful? We have made an impression already. We are going to have such fun, Brige."

Brigid, however, did not share Margaret's ease at being the center of attention, and her friend's expression suggested that fun was definitely not something she was having.

Margaret gave Brigid's arm an encouraging squeeze. "Oh come now, Brige, smile. It's nothing to worry about. We are newcomers. It's only natural that they are curious."

Brigid didn't look like she believed her. "Perhaps we should have worn veils as Beth suggested?"

The serving girl who'd been assigned to help them dress for the feast had been shocked when Margaret had said they would just be wearing circlets.

Margaret hadn't paid her much mind. She only wore a veil to church, and even then she didn't like it. But gazing around the room, she saw what Brigid had: they were the only women who were bareheaded.

"So we can blend in with all the others?" Margaret gave her friend a cheeky grin. "What fun would it be if we were all the same? This way we shall stand out."

"I think we are doing that anyway with our gowns," Brigid said glumly.

Margaret had to admit, the finery of the ladies at court far exceeded her expectations. She'd never seen such an array of luxurious fabrics and fine embroidery. But they were just *gowns*. Pretty ornament was still just that: ornament.

"You look beautiful, Brige. You could be wearing a sack-cloth and you would still outshine everyone in this room. Whether garbed in velvet and jewels or in a woolen kirtle and plaid, it's what's inside that matters." Brigid gave her a look as if she didn't know where she got her strange ideas. "You will have your pick of suitors. Have you seen anyone that interests you yet?"

As soon as her father had told her of his plan to bring her to Stirling to secure an alliance with John Comyn, Margaret had begged him to let her bring Brigid along with her as her companion. Lord knew there were precious few men to choose from as potential husbands near their home. Except for Margaret's brothers, of course, but they didn't count. This was the perfect opportunity to find someone for Brigid, and Margaret wasn't going to waste it.

Heat rose to her friend's cheeks, and her gaze lowered. "We've only just arrived, Maggie."

"Yet we've met a dozen young men already." The image of a tall, dirty-blond-haired warrior rose to her mind, but she quickly pushed it aside. He might have attracted her attention, but her interest must be fixed elsewhere. "Although I hope you have not set your sights on the Earl of Carrick, as he is already wed."

Brigid let out a sharp laugh, which had been Margaret's intent. "You are horrible, Maggie. Can you imagine what Father and Tristan would say?"

Brigid's family was just as staunchly loyal to King John Balliol as Margaret's, meaning that none of the men they'd met today, assuming they were with Bruce, were suitable suitors.

"I imagine exactly what my father and brothers would say. 'Are you out of your wee mind, lass? I'd sooner see you marching down the fiery aisle of Hell to wed Lucifer himself,'" she said in a mock imitation of her father's voice.

As they neared the dais, she could see that she'd been right: her family was seated at the table just below to the left.

The girls were still laughing as the men rose to greet them. When her eldest brother, Dougal, asked what was so funny, Brigid couldn't seem to meet his gaze, but Margaret, knowing her humorless brother wouldn't understand, replied that it was nothing. She imagined her family would hear of their earlier encounter soon enough.

It was then that she noticed the young man standing next to her father. Fair of hair and coloring, he was gazing at her with an expression that could only be described as dazed. Slightly taller than her father, who stood a few inches under six feet, he was only a fraction of his width, with the long-limbed coltishness of youth. From the lack of significant stubble on his jaw, she guessed he was a year or two younger than her own eight and ten.

His identity dawned as her father was making the introductions. *John Comyn.* This was the Lord of Badenoch's son and heir, and the man to whom her father would see her betrothed. She'd known he was young, but . . .

Quickly covering any disappointment she might be feeling—so what if he didn't look much older than her sixteen-year-old brother, Uchtred? He was a fine-looking young man, and more important, the son of one of Scotland's greatest lords!—she took the seat that had been set out for her between the young lordling and her father, and spent most of the first course of the meal trying to make him relax.

He was shy, and seemed perhaps a little in awe of her, but Margaret was good at drawing people out. She asked him about his family. He had two sisters, Elizabeth and Joan, both of whom were here, and he'd served as a squire for his great-uncle King John Balliol before he'd been exiled to France, but now was with his father at Dalswinton Castle. She discovered that they shared a love of horses, and when he described the prized jennet that'd been his eighteenth saint's day gift (she hid her surprise at that), she found herself genuinely interested and enjoying herself.

It wasn't until the platters of roasted fowl were brought out for the second course that she felt the weight of a gaze upon her. Turning to the table directly opposite theirs—just below the dais to the right—she found herself looking into the penetrating blue-eyed gaze of Eoin MacLean.

She felt a jolt as if something had just taken hold of her. It raced up her spine and spread over her skin in a prickling heat.

It wasn't the first time Margaret had caught a man staring at her, but it was the first time she'd found herself flushing in response.

It wasn't embarrassment for what had happened earlier . . . exactly. At Garthland there was nothing wrong with a woman asking a man to teach her how to play a game. Lud, it wasn't as if she'd asked him to teach her how to swim naked! Yet that's how every man in the room had looked at her.

Although maybe naked wasn't something she should be thinking about when she was looking at Eoin MacLean, because she couldn't help wondering what his chest would look like when it wasn't covered in velvet and linen. He had such broad shoulders and his arms were very large. He must be exceedingly muscular.

The warmth in her cheeks intensified. She suspected it was wicked thoughts like that that had made her blush in the first place. It wasn't embarrassment, it was something more akin to awareness. Aye, definitely awareness.

And if the intensity of his gaze was any indication, he felt it, too.

The connection was so strong it seemed they did not need to talk to communicate. She smiled cheekily, lifted her brow, and shrugged her shoulders as if to say she didn't understand it either.

Unfortunately, Margaret had forgotten they were not the only two people in the room.

∞

Eoin noticed her the moment she entered the Hall. He wasn't alone. It seemed as if the entire room held its collective breath as the two young women appeared at the entrance. But it was the indecently sensual redhead to whom all eyes were turned. The pretty, pale blonde beside her seemed to fade into the background; she was just like every other woman in the Hall.

But Margaret MacDowell was different. Like a wildflower in a rose garden, she did not belong. And it wasn't just because of the soft tumble of hair that was streaming down her back rather than being covered by a veil, or because in a room full of ladies dressed in velvets and jewels she managed to look more regal in a simple wool gown and brightly colored plaid. Nay, it was far more elemental. She was carefree and unabashedly happy in a room of modesty and reserve. She was wild and untamed in a sea of constraint and conformity.

But either she was unaware of the attention or she did not care about it. She met the silence—half of which was admiring and half of which was condemning—not with a dropped gaze and maidenly blush of shyness at being the focus of so many, but with the confident, take-no-prisoners grin of a pirate captain seizing a ship, and the jaunty walk to match.

But if the comments he'd overheard so far were any indication, winning over this crew—at least the female half of it—wasn't going to be easy. Gossip about what had happened earlier already had made it's way through the Hall, and it was clearly disapproving. He'd had to fend off a half-dozen questions from his sister Marjory before the first tray of food arrived. Even his reserved and above-gossip mother had listened intently to his replies.

But he made it clear that the matter was over. He wasn't going to teach the lass to play anything. Although Eoin couldn't help admiring Lady Margaret's brash confidence, and undeniably her bold beauty held some appeal—all right, *a lot* of appeal—a lass like that spelled trouble. The kind of trouble he had no interest in pursuing, no matter how hard certain parts of him stirred.

That had been a surprise. His reaction to the lass was as fierce, primitive, and physical as it was unexpected. He usually had better control. He frowned. Actually, he *always* had better control. No lass he'd ever met had stirred his blood with a look and a smile that made him wonder whether she was as naughty as she looked.

But even if she weren't the daughter of a man who would likely be his enemy soon—which was reason enough to look the other way—Margaret MacDowell with her smile that promised mischief and devil-may-care attitude was undoubtedly a demanding handful, and Eoin's hands were firmly wrapped around his battle-axe.

Still, as the meal progressed he found his gaze sliding in her direction more than once. God, that hair was incredible. And her skin was flawless—so powdery soft and creamy it looked unreal. But it was those knowing, slanted eyes and sensual mouth that taunted him.

He'd been mildly surprised to see her seated beside young Comyn. It soon became apparent why, however, as the lass went out of her way to charm and dazzle the clearly uncomfortable and out-of-his element youth. Not that Eoin could blame the lad. Eoin was four and twenty—definitely not a stripling lad where lasses were concerned—and his bollocks tightened every time he heard that husky laugh all the way across the aisle.

But if her barbarian of a father thought the Lord of Badenoch, the most powerful man in Scotland, would tie his precious heir to a MacDowell, he was even more out of his mind than Eoin thought. Badenoch might hold the ancient clan in high regard on the battlefield, and value them as allies, but he would look for a bride for his heir among the highest nobility of Scotland—hell, probably of England.

If the half-in-love look on young Comyn's face was any indication, however, the son might be having other ideas. From the deepening frown on Badenoch's face as he looked down on his son from the dais, he appeared to have noticed it as well.

Eoin couldn't help wondering what they were talking about. The lass was speaking so animatedly, and that laugh was . . . damned distracting.

He didn't realize he was staring until their eyes met. He should have turned away. She should have turned away. And she sure as hell shouldn't have drawn attention to the exchange by giving him that adorable but too-intimate little shrug.

He knew exactly what she meant because he felt it, too, but others might misinterpret it.

Which they did.

"Did she just wink at you?"

Eoin looked harshly away from Lady Margaret to his younger sister, whose eyes had widened to extraordinary proportions.

"Of course not," he said. It was more of a lift of the brow and shrug.

"She did!" Marjory said with an odd mix of horror and glee. "That brazen creature is flirting with you from across the room! After she propositioned you. She must be every bit as wicked as they say."

"Keep your voice down, Marjory," Eoin said sternly. "I said it was nothing."

But it was too late, his mother had heard. She looked with barely veiled distaste at Lady Margaret, and then back to him with a hard look that he didn't need interpreted for him. *Watch it*, it said. *There is much riding on this.* A shift of her gaze to Lady Barbara, who was seated a few seats away next to his father, and who had thankfully missed the exchange, told him what she meant.

But he didn't need the reminder. Eoin's gaze didn't stray across the aisle again. Although with the growing crowd of men around Lady Margaret, he probably wouldn't have been able to see her anyway.

"Who in Hades are you looking at, daughter?"

Caught in the private exchange with Eoin MacLean by her father, Margaret was forced to explain how she'd come to meet him. Her description of how she'd accidentally disturbed the hotly contested, two-day-long chess match between the Earl of Carrick and his kinsman had her father and brothers laughing uproariously. They found it hilarious that men could put so much store in a child's game.

"God's breath, I should have liked to see their faces. It should be a lesson for Bruce in how easy it is to be defeated by a MacDowell."

John Comyn, who played the game but claimed to have

little patience for it (which Margaret took to mean he wasn't very good at it), chuckled as well, especially when she mentioned how they'd moved the pieces into the shape of a flower and then a heart.

Her father called over some of his friends—many of whom were new to her—and she was forced to repeat the tale a number of times during the meal. She didn't mind though, as entertaining was what she was used to, and it made the formal, foreign atmosphere of Stirling feel a little more like home. She was finding her footing.

At least with the men.

She was aware of the disapproving stares being directed her way by more than a few of the women, but it didn't bother her. They would take more time to win over, that was all.

In her retelling of the story, she left out the part about asking Eoin MacLean to teach her how to play, but she did take the opportunity while the servants cleared the trestle tables for dancing to ask her father about him.

Apparently, although Eoin was young and only the third son of the chief, he'd already made a name for himself as a brilliant tactician, leading a series of bold raids against the English in Carrick. He'd been educated in the lowlands, and despite his clan's Western Isles Norse background, he was reputed to be as learned as a monk. Margaret couldn't help but think that she hoped that was the only monk-like comparison.

A sharp look by her father made her wonder if her thoughts had been too transparent. He wasn't chiding her for her wickedness or her irreverence—neither of which he cared about—but for her interest.

The MacLeans were formidable warriors, he continued,

and despite their ties of kinship with the Bruces, they were still giving signs of indecision on whether they would fight for him if war came.

Her gaze might have turned too speculative. For although her father might not have much schooling and he had as much idea on how to play chess as she did, he was shrewd, and the look he subsequently directed to John Comyn reminded her of what was expected of her.

He need not have worried. Margaret knew her part. She liked the young nobleman well enough, and when the dancing began, she was surprised to discover that he was a good—if slightly stiff—dancer. When another man claimed her for the next dance, he was clearly reluctant to let her go, which Margaret took as a good sign.

Swept up in the dancing and three cups of wernage—the sweetened wine having gone to her head—it took her awhile to realize that Brigid was trying to get her attention.

When she could finally break free, her friend dragged her outside of the Hall into a small corridor.

Brigid looked like she was about to cry. "What is it?" Margaret asked.

"I heard them," Brigid answered, twisting her hands anxiously.

"Heard who?"

"All of them," her voice broke. "The ladies."

Margaret pursed her mouth. She might have thickened skin when it came to gossip, but Brigid did not. If someone had hurt her feelings, Margaret would see them regret it. "What did they say?"

"They called us *heathens*," she said in a hushed voice.

"Is that all?" Margaret laughed and shook her head. "That's ridiculous, Brige. You can't let people like that upset you."

Brigid shook her head. "That's not all. They are saying . . . horrible things."

Margaret frowned. Clearly those horrible things must be about her, as Brigid seemed reluctant to say more. "It's all right. You will not hurt my feelings."

Brigid chewed nervously on her bottom lip. "It isn't you . . . exactly. It's more your clan. The MacDowells do not have the, er, best reputation."

Margaret's frown turned sharper. Fiercely proud, she had been raised to think of the MacDowells as akin to royalty. They'd ruled over Galloway like kings—and queens—for hundreds of years. "What do you mean?"

"The MacDowells are thought to be . . . uh . . . a little uncivilized. A little *wild*."

Margaret was indignant. "Because we do not act like Englishmen? Because we hold true to our ancient Gàidheal culture and Brehon laws more than the feudal yoke of English kings?"

"They see it as backward."

"You mean *us* as backward."

Brigid shrugged indifferently, but Margaret knew it mattered to her. As much as she just wanted to dismiss it, she knew it wasn't so easy for Brigid to do so. "They have their ways and we have ours. Just because we do things differently doesn't make them wrong."

"I know that," Brigid said, her eyes swimming with tears. "It's just not as easy for me to ignore them as it is for you."

A wry smile turned her mouth. "It isn't always easy."

Brigid appeared shocked by her admission. "It isn't? But you always appear so confident. You never take anything from anyone—even your father."

Margaret had always thought her friend intimidated by

her father, but at that moment her voice held something more like fear.

"I am the only girl in a home of nine overbearing—or on their way to overbearing—men," she said. "How long do you think I would have survived if I'd shown any weakness? Appearing confident was a matter of survival. I learned early that if I didn't assert myself, I would be lost. I had to shout pretty loudly to be heard over all those male voices," she said with a smile. "But eventually I learned to make myself heard without raising my voice." She paused and said gently, "You can't let them intimidate you, Brige. People like those women, if they sense blood, they'll dive in for the kill. The trick is to not let them see that their words have wounded you."

Brigid eyed her skeptically. "And how might I do that? I'm not like you. I don't have a rebellious nature."

Did she? Margaret had never thought of it that way, but maybe Brigid was right. She was a MacDowell, and the MacDowells were always ready to fight. "By smiling in the face of their rudeness and remembering who you are," she replied. "A MacCan. A proud member of an old and respected clan. You are not ashamed of your family, are you?"

For the first time since they'd arrived, her friend showed a flash of the spirit Margaret knew was lurking underneath. She looked outraged by the mere suggestion.

Brigid straightened her spine and gave Margaret a long, proud look down the length of her nose. "Of course not."

Margaret grinned. "Hold that look, Brige, and smile. It's perfect. They won't stand a chance. And once we've shown them they can not intimidate us with their gossip, we'll slay them with our most powerful weapon."

A slow smile crept up her friend's delicate features, as she realized she'd been tricked. "What's that?"

Margaret linked her arm in hers. "Why friendliness, of course. Once they get to know us, they'll see we aren't all that different. We might not dress the same, and our customs might not be the same, but inside, where it counts, we are all alike."

Brigid shook her head and laughed. "All alike? You have the oddest ideas, Maggie. I don't know where you get them."

Margaret didn't know either. But her certainty must have convinced her friend. A moment later when they re-entered the Hall, Brigid was smiling every bit as broadly as Margaret.

4

A WEEK LATER, Margaret's smile had begun to falter. Discouraged, she was having a hard time following her own advice. Good gracious, these women were as judgmental as St. Peter at the pearl gates!

No matter how hard she smiled and tried to be friendly, her efforts were rebuffed. If anything, the disapproving looks had become less veiled and more outrightly hostile, and the whispers had grown louder and more cruel.

From her "idiotic" gaffe with the chessboard, to being mistaken for a servant and a wanton—which she'd unknowingly added to with her apparently forward attempts to "seduce" Eoin MacLean (first by asking him to teach her chess and then by "winking" at him—it wasn't a wink, blast it), to her gowns and uncovered hair, she'd apparently played into every ridiculous misconception they had about her and her clan.

But she refused to let them get to her. She had nothing to be ashamed of, and she would not pretend to be meek and mute for a bunch of narrow-minded, mean-spirited women. The MacDowells were not the unruly bunch of heathens everyone made them out to be. She might have been permitted more freedom than most women, being raised in a household of men so far from society—and after a week of being at Stirling with these women who made some nuns Margaret knew seem more fun, she could concede that was certainly true—but that didn't make her immoral.

Could they not see how ridiculous that was?

Apparently not.

Before every meal she had to practically get on her knees and beg to get Brigid to leave their chamber. She didn't know why she bothered, when they were met with such cold unfriendliness by half the guests at the castle. Even her own notorious good cheer had begun to wane.

Fortunately, if she hadn't made an impression (at least a good one) on the women, her ostracism didn't extend to the men. She never lacked for dance partners, and men crowded the benches at their table for every meal. They laughed at her jokes, listened to her stories, and did not seem to mind when she made a "misstep." Men were much more accepting of differences.

At least most seemed to be, but she wondered about the Lord of Badenoch. Her father told her not to worry, that the son was utterly "charmed," but Margaret did not think the same could be said of his sire. She had the sense that like his wife and daughters, the Lord of Badenoch did not approve of her. She hoped she was imagining it, but the more time John seemed to spend by her side, the more pinched his illustrious father's expression seemed to grow. Impressing him was going to be her true challenge.

Brigid had pled a headache for the midday meal, and Margaret was returning to the Hall after checking on her, when she stopped in her tracks at the sound of a voice. A deep voice that seemed to sink into her bones.

Despite the crowd gathered near the entry, she picked him out right away. As it had too many times over the past week, her gaze landed right on the familiar dark-blond head.

She felt that strange jarring in her chest—as if someone had gripped her heart and shook it—and then the blast of heat that illogically made her skin prickle as if she were cold.

Her attraction didn't make any sense. She liked men who smiled and jested—like Tristan. Not serious men who were as learned as a monk. But something about all that quiet, simmering intensity, something about those shrewd, nothing-gets-by-me eyes was wildly attractive. Viscerally attractive.

Holy Cross, this was ridiculous! It was getting worse. All she had to do was set eyes on him and her body reacted. Her senses suddenly heightened—the air seemed purer and the sounds sharper—and her pulse leapt with something that felt a lot like anticipation.

As there could be nothing *to* anticipate, however, she'd done her best to ignore both her reaction and him. The way he'd avoided her gaze when their eyes did happen to meet made her wonder if he were doing the same thing.

It was hard to tell. His expression was always so infuriatingly inscrutable. But something about the way the furrowed lines between his brows deepened when his gaze landed on her, and the way his eyes seemed to become a little darker blue right before he turned away, made her think he was fighting this attraction as much as she was.

Her reasons were clear, but what about his? Did they have something to do with Lady Barbara Keith?

She felt a strange pinch in her chest as she peered through the crowd and glanced at the pretty fair-haired young woman standing a few feet away who was so often in his company. Not his company exactly, but his mother and sister's, who were invariably nearby. Actually, the persons most often in his company were his foster brother, Finlaeie MacFinnon, and his brothers, Donald and Neil, but something about the way the marischal's daughter looked at him—properly, of course, out from under her lowered and demurely cast eyes—made Margaret suspect there was something between them.

And why that bothered her so much when she could have nothing to do with him, she had no idea.

Taking advantage of all the people standing around the edge of the room while the trestle tables were being put away for the dancing, she inched closer to where he stood to see if she could hear anything.

He was talking to Finlaeie—probably something about old battles, as the few times she'd overheard him talking it was about war—but she couldn't make out their words.

Unfortunately, his sister she could hear quite clearly. "Did you see that gown? I wouldn't have been surprised if she started brewing ale right in the middle of the meal."

Margaret stilled, and though she didn't want it to, her chest pinched. She had no doubt of whom they were speaking. She glanced down at what she thought was a pretty blue woolen gown. An ale wife? Although gossip and rumor might not bother her in the same way they did Brigid, that did not mean she was completely immune to their barbs.

"It wasn't as bad as all that," Lady Barbara said softly—almost kindly. Which she quickly ruined by laughing. "If that is the 'finery' of Galloway, then I should not like to see what the peasants look like. Perhaps they wear nothing but leaves and heather?"

Apparently the demure little kitten had claws.

"Maybe she just enjoys flaunting her body at anyone who will take notice," Marjory MacLean said. "I hope we are not forced to endure another few hours of watching her dance like a heathen at Beltane. I'm surprised she has found men willing to partner her and be the subject of such an . . . exhibition."

Margaret had heard enough, her hurt forgotten, her face heated with anger, no longer able to force a smile on her face. There was nothing wrong with her gown or the way she danced. And she was going to tell them exactly that.

$$\infty$$

"She was looking at you again," Fin whispered.

Eoin clenched his jaw and pulled his friend off to the side. He didn't need to ask who he meant. Fin and some of his other friends had picked up on the strange undercurrent running between Eoin and Lady Margaret and couldn't resist prodding him about it every time the lass looked at him—which was too bloody often!

But as he found himself doing the same damned thing, he could hardly blame her. Christ, his attraction to the lass was damned inconvenient, and Fin sure as hell wasn't making it any easier. "Shut the hell up, Fin. One of the ladies will hear you."

"I don't know why you are hesitating. If she were looking at me like that, I'd give her exactly what she was asking for and swive her senseless. It's not as if it's the first time . . ." His friend smiled wickedly. "For either of you."

Eoin didn't have a temper to lose, so when the flash of

rage sparked through him, tensing every muscle in his body and leaving him a hairbreadth from sinking his fist into Fin's gleaming white grin, it took him by surprise.

Fin as well. He stepped back instinctively, his brows shooting together.

"What the hell is the matter with you, MacLean? You're acting like a jealous suitor. Christ, you can't be seriously considering pursuing the lass."

"I'm not considering anything," Eoin said flatly. "But I'll not hear malicious gossip repeated about any lady." And no matter what he'd heard, he believed Margaret MacDowell was a lady.

The rage that had surged through him subsided just as quickly. Suddenly he was embarrassed by the display of emotion, which didn't make any sense, since he didn't get emotional. He must be going mad. Probably of boredom. Being locked away in long, tension-filled negotiations all day, trying to prevent Bruce and the Lord of Badenoch, John "The Red" Comyn, from killing each other, and then being forced to dance attendance on Lady Barbara and listen to his sister's prattle at the meals, was putting him on edge.

"I think I need that hunt more than I realized," he added. "The walls are beginning to close in on me."

Fin was still studying him too intently, but he accepted the explanation with a slam on the back. "I think I like it better when all you talk about is vanguards, ambuscade, and flanking."

Eoin managed a quirk of the mouth at that. His friend was right. That's what he should be focusing on. But he would have his chance to impress Bruce tomorrow. The hunt would be an opportunity to prove himself.

He turned back to the ladies just in time to hear his sister's snide remark about Lady Margaret's dancing.

His mouth flattened with distaste. The not-so-nice comments that he'd forgiven as girlish insensitivity when Marjory was six and ten, three years later were beginning to sound spiteful and mean. His sister needed to learn to curb that acid tongue of hers.

Unfortunately, Marjory's was not the only unflattering remark he'd heard about Lady Margaret over the past week. He felt bad, knowing that he was partly to blame for providing the fodder. She might have laughed off his unfortunate choice of words, but the rest of court had not. The gossip didn't seem to bother her though, and he couldn't help but admire the way she smiled in the face of their rudeness. His sister would be in tears were she subject to half the unkind words he'd heard spoken about Lady Margaret.

He was just about to admonish his sister when he noticed the lady in question moving toward them. The heightened color on her cheeks left him no doubt that Lady Margaret had heard what his sister had said, and from the determination in her expression, he sensed she was no longer of the mind to laugh it off.

Whether he was trying to protect his sister or Lady Margaret he didn't know, but without thinking he stepped in front of her. "Would you honor me with the first dance, my lady?"

He could hear his sister's gasp of surprise behind him. He hated dancing, and thus far had avoided it.

Lady Margaret stared at him, her sphinxlike golden eyes burning into his. For a moment he thought she might refuse. Clearly she wanted to give his sister a tongue-lashing. And though it was deserved, it wouldn't do for either of them.

The last thing Lady Margaret needed was more negative

attention to fuel the fires of the court gossip. Maybe she realized it as well. After a long, uncomfortable pause, she nodded.

His sister could thank him later, for he knew without a doubt that he'd saved her from a setting down she would not soon forget.

But the instant Lady Margaret's soft hand slid into his, Eoin knew he'd made a mistake. He should have let his sister take the public flogging. Instead, he'd opened Pandora's box, releasing something that would never be contained again.

The shock that ran through him at the contact was akin to a bolt of lightning. A *magnetic* bolt of lightning. It drew them together in a way that could not be denied.

Something jammed in his chest. His lungs seemed to have stopped working. But his heart made up for it with the frantic pounding. He was riveted—utterly spellbound. Eoin forgot that he was dancing—forgot that he didn't even like dancing—forgot the music, and forgot the other people around him. As he led her through the steps of the reel, he couldn't look away from her face. The delicate sweep of her cheek, the soft point of her chin, the slightly turned up nose.

The sensual curve of her mouth.

Damn it, she was so beautiful it almost hurt to look at her. Parts of his body *did* hurt. His chest, for one, and another part that had swelled with heat and was hard as a rock, oblivious to the fact that they were in a crowded ballroom.

But he was beyond all reason, caught up in an almost dreamlike trance. A *hot*, dreamlike trance of powerful attraction that sent fire racing through his veins.

Their bodies moved together as one. There was no need to talk. What was being said between them was in every glance, every touch, every heartbeat.

The bond held them together until the music stopped.

The music stopped. Damn it. He released her so suddenly she gave a small, startled gasp.

She stepped back, staring at him with a look on her face that was every bit as stunned as he was feeling. "Th-thank you," she whispered, her breath falling unevenly from beneath her softly parted lips.

God, they were so red and sweet looking. A fierce swell of desire rose inside him. The urge to cover them with his was so powerful—so elemental—he could think of nothing else. He lowered his head a few inches before a split second of sanity recalled his surroundings, and he stopped himself.

Bloody hell. He might have said it aloud. What had just happened? It wasn't a question the man who was supposed to be the smartest in the room found himself asking very often. But he couldn't think straight—or in any other direction, for that matter. His mind was reeling.

With a nod that was sharper than he intended, he walked away.

While he still could.

Margaret's heart was beating so fast she thought it might explode. She couldn't seem to catch her breath or stop shaking.

What had just happened?

Other than feel as if every one her senses had just come alive, she didn't know. It had left her rattled—almost panicked.

Needing to collect herself, she fled the Hall.

She felt close to tears, as if she'd just gone through a tremendous emotional upheaval. Which maybe she had. What she'd just experienced hadn't been a gentle awakening of emotion, it had been like a giant church bell going off in a small ambry. Loud, clamoring, reverberating . . . devastating.

The feelings had been so intense. So powerful. So overwhelming. She'd felt bound to him. Connected. As if they were the only two people in the world.

Her body still ached. Her stomach still flipped. Her pulse still raced. She could still feel the sensation of his hand resting on her waist, his fingers wrapped around her arm, his callused palm enveloping her hand. She could still feel the heat emanating from his body—the big, muscled body and broad-shouldered chest that had been so close, her body had strained to be pressed up against it. The tips of her breasts throbbed.

He'd smelled so good. The pine of his soap, the mint of his breath . . . His mouth had been so close. She'd thought . . .

She sucked in her breath with a small cry.

How could a man who said so little make such an impact?

She didn't know where she was going, she just knew she had to get away. Standing there she'd felt exposed—vulnerable—as if anyone looking at her would know just how she felt. Her confidence, her bravado, had seemingly deserted her.

She'd fled out the main entrance of the Hall and followed the corridor to the king's donjon away from the noise. She needed quiet. Though it was only a couple of hours past midday, the corridor was already shadowed. Reaching the old tower that had once served as royal accommodation for William the Lion, but was now in disrepair, she sought out the solitude of a small room on the far end of the building. It had probably served as a waiting chamber or private solar for the king but was now a library. She had no use for the books, only for the quiet.

Some of the men must have been enjoying the room earlier, as there were still embers in the brazier, although not enough to provide any warmth. What was in the flagon, however, would. Bringing it to her nose, she inhaled the slightly sweet but pungent scent of English brandy. She preferred good Scottish *uisge beatha*, but under the circumstances she could not afford to be discriminating. Pouring it into one of the goblets, she downed the contents in one long swallow. Almost instantly the calming effects of the spirits began to spread through her body.

Her heartbeat started to slow, air filled her lungs, and her hands steadied. Most important, her head cleared.

She'd overreacted. It was just a dance. He was just a man—an undeniably attractive one—but still just a man. She'd exaggerated the effect of his touch.

Then why could she still feel the imprint of his fingers on her skin? Why was her body still trembling?

She was bending over the brandy, gripping the edge of the table to steady herself, when she heard a noise behind her.

Turning, her heart sank, seeing who it was—and his expression. She'd never noticed a resemblance to his father before, but she could see the Lord of Badenoch now in the hardness of John Comyn's gaze and petulant twist of his mouth.

He didn't bother with politeness. "What is between you and the MacLean chief's son?"

Margaret straightened and looked him in the eye, her voice far steadier than she felt—even with the brandy. "Nothing."

She even meant it.

His eyes narrowed, and he took a few steps toward her. "That isn't what it looked like. I won't be made a fool of, my lady."

With eight brothers ranging in age from ten to one and twenty, Margaret knew well how sensitive a young man's pride could be and was quick to soothe it. "I've barely said more than a dozen words to the man. I told you what happened the first time we met." She smiled. "I hardly think him calling me an idiot is going to endear him to me."

She'd closed the gap between them, and either her words or her closeness seemed to have mollified him. Partly. He frowned. "Then why did you dance with him?"

I don't know. She bit her lip, considering how much to tell him. Deciding it was best to be honest, she answered, "I overheard his sister say something unkind. He asked me to dance to stop me from confronting her and making a scene."

The slight flush and discomfort told her he'd probably heard something of the gossip. "You should pay them no mind. They are only jealous."

Margaret gave him a long look, seeing beyond the youth to the man he would become. "Thank you. That is very kind."

He blushed harder, and shuffled his feet. Without the anger, he was back to his uncertain self. "I should go. We shouldn't be alone like this. I shouldn't have followed you, but I was jealous." His eyes met hers. "I thought he was going to kiss you, and I wanted it to be me."

"I'd like that, too."

She hadn't meant that as an invitation, but he'd taken it as one. With more deftness than she would have thought him capable, he cupped her chin in his hand and tilted her mouth to his. She barely felt the gentle warmth of contact before it was over.

The kiss was sweet and chaste. The look in his eyes was not. He wanted her, and although the kiss had not been unpleasant, she did not want to encourage another.

Fortunately, she was not inexperienced at putting the reins on a young man's passion.

She stepped back, wanting distance between them.

It was then that she glanced over to the mural chamber—the wide bench built into the thick wall of the castle that could be closed off with a curtain—and saw a boot.

5

At first Eoin thought she'd followed him. Sitting on the bench in the mural chamber with a flagon of whisky and a folio he'd grabbed without even looking at the title—*The Rules of St. Benedict* in Latin, for Christ's sake!—he'd heard her enter and been about to address her when young Comyn had shown up. Realizing he would likely make the situation worse if he let his presence be known, Eoin was forced to sit there half-hidden in the shadow of the alcove and listen to their conversation.

A conversation that was making his blood churn hotter and hotter, which to Eoin's already on-edge state was like tossing oil on a roaring fire. What the hell was she doing? Didn't she know that standing so close to Comyn like that, lifting her mouth to his, and telling him she wished he'd been the one about to kiss her was practically an invitation for him to do just that?

When the pup accepted, putting his hand on her chin and tilting her mouth to his, Eoin had felt a primitive swell of emotion unlike anything he'd ever experienced before. All he could see was red. His chest burned, his muscles flexed, and every instinct he possessed clamored to put his fist through the young lord's mouth for touching her.

But his anger wasn't reserved just for the lad. If anything, what he felt toward the *lady* was far worse. If he didn't know that she'd felt exactly what he did during that dance maybe it wouldn't have been so bad. But she had. And somehow, rational or not—forgetting that minutes before she'd entered the room he'd been denying the whole thing—it stung like a betrayal.

How much longer he would have been able to hold himself back, he didn't know. But he did know the moment she realized they were not alone.

Comyn mistook the startled gasp and sudden loss of color in her cheeks for maidenly shock at the kiss, which in Eoin's present state of mind, he thought, was ironic.

Maybe Fin was right. Maybe the rumors were true. Maybe she knew exactly what she was doing when she looked at Eoin like that. "*I'd give her exactly what she was asking for and swive her senseless.*"

Right now he was wondering what was stopping him.

"I probably should apologize," Comyn said upon stepping back.

She shot an anxious glance in Eoin's direction and quickly turned back to the lad, obviously distracted. "For what?"

"For taking advantage of your innocence like that."

Eoin saw a small frown gather between her brows before she seemed to realize what he meant. "Ah, yes, of course, the kiss." She bit her lip, and shifted her gaze down. "I think it's best if you leave now. It would not do for us to be discovered like this."

If Eoin heard the slight inflection in her voice, signifying a question, Comyn did not.

"You're right." He smiled. "Although maybe it would be easier if we were."

She frowned again, clearly not understanding. But Eoin did. The lad was obviously aware of his father's sentiments and looking for a way around them. Being caught in a compromising situation could suffice.

Although Comyn was not yet a knight, he had all the honor and nobility of one. Eoin, on the other hand, wasn't a knight and had no pretense of wanting to be to keep him in check.

With a short bow, Comyn left the room. As soon as she closed the door after him, Lady Margaret turned around and folded her arms across her chest. "I know you are there, you might as well come out."

She made it sound as if he were a bairn hiding or purposefully lingering in the shadows to spy on them. Neither of which were true, damn it. He'd just been sitting there when she'd come bursting into the room and headed straight for the brandy. But somehow, the lass had managed to put him on the defensive.

Though she wouldn't have been able to see his face from where he was seated with his back to the stone wall of the alcove, she didn't look surprised to see that it was him when he stood.

"Had I known what I would be interrupting, I would have made my presence known sooner."

"You speak!" she said with mock surprise. "I wasn't sure if dark, brooding stares were the extent of your communication skills."

Handful.

His eyes bit into hers unrelentingly. "I didn't realize we had anything to say."

She held his stare for a long moment before turning away. "Perhaps you are right."

Her voice held a note of sadness that made something inside him tug. Hard.

He should have left. He should have taken the opening she'd given him and walked away. Instead, he crossed the distance between them in a few strides. The soft scent of flowers that he'd noticed during their dance taunted his senses. But he was still too angry to heed caution. "Comyn isn't for you."

She lifted her brows, obviously taken aback by the adamancy of his tone. "You sound very certain of that."

He was trying to protect her, damn it. Badenoch would never let his son marry her. "I am. And letting him take liberties won't change anything."

"Liberties?" Her brows drew together. "You mean that kiss?" She laughed. "Lud, that hardly signifies."

He didn't know whether it was the laugh or the way she dismissed it as nothing that fanned the flames of his anger like a smith's bellows. "And you are so experienced as to know the difference?"

Something in his tone made her eyes narrow. "Have you never kissed a woman, my lord?"

"What does that have to do with anything?"

She looked at him for a long moment, as if willing him to see something, and then shook her head. "What I know or don't know is none of your business."

She was right, and yet she was so bloody wrong. "Not all men are pups like Comyn, my lady, to be so easily turned away when you are done with them. Some might see your kiss as an invitation for more."

The flush of pink to her cheeks told him she wasn't unaware of her reputation. He didn't realize how close they were standing until she straightened her spine and the dart of her nipples grazed his chest.

His knees almost buckled. He clenched his teeth against the guttural groan of pleasure that sent a flood of heat to his groin.

She lifted her chin, tilting her head back to meet his angry glare. "A man like you, you mean?"

Whether it was sarcasm or a challenge, he didn't know, but Eoin's control snapped. He wanted to punish her. He wanted to teach her a lesson. He wanted to prove to her that she played a dangerous game.

But most of all he wanted to kiss her so badly he couldn't see straight.

"Aye, that's exactly what I mean." He slid his arm around her waist and hauled her up against him. It was so bloody perfect he couldn't have pulled away if he wanted to. All of those lush, feminine curves molded against him felt incredible. He was hard against her. Pounding. Throbbing. Even when he was a lad he'd never felt desire like this so intensely. Need had reached up and grabbed him by the cock, stroking, licking, with more potency than a wanton's tongue.

He took advantage of her gasp and lowered his mouth to hers. The first touch, the first taste of her was like wildfire. Heat engulfed him. Pleasure tore through him in a scorching frenzy. Whatever rationality he might have still possessed went up in flames when she opened her mouth and kissed him back.

∞

Margaret had laughed when her brother Duncan caught her kissing Tristan in one of the caves below Dunskey Castle last year and warned her to be careful. She was playing with fire, he'd said. A kiss was one thing, but it could very easily end with something else. Beyond the fact that he referred to fornicating, she hadn't understood and thought he was exaggerating.

Out of control? Dangerous? What was he talking about? There was nothing that felt dangerous about kissing Tristan. It was pleasant and nice, but she was fully aware of what was happening. She wasn't going to end up with her feet by her ears, grunting enthusiastically, as she'd had the misfortune of witnessing more than once when visitors bedded down for the night in the very un-private Hall of Garthland.

But Margaret wasn't laughing now. If anything her brother had understated the danger. Curiosity and experimentation might not be dangerous, but passion certainly was. And the moment Eoin MacLean had pulled her into his arms she'd felt the difference to the bottom of her soul.

Desire practically exploded between them. All those sensations awakened and primed by their dance returned even more powerfully. A blast of heat poured over her in a molten wave. The strength of his arms and powerfully muscled body against her made her weak. She felt stunned—dazed—as if she'd fallen into a bog of sensation and couldn't pull herself out. Or rather didn't want to pull herself out because it felt too good. *He* felt too good.

She didn't want him to stop. Ever.

His mouth was hot and possessive. He kissed her as if he belonged there. And truth be told, it felt as if she did.

He tasted of an intoxicating mix of cloves and whisky, and she drank him in, opening her lips to taste him deeper. The deft strokes of his tongue weren't tentative and probing like she expected but fierce and demanding. The first powerful stroke licked all the way down between her legs and nearly made them collapse.

She felt a strange fluttering low in her belly that made her moan with pleasure. He answered with a harsh groan that sounded almost like a curse. Whatever restraint had existed between them in those first few moments was gone.

His hand plunged through her hair to cup the back of her head and his kiss turned punishing, ravishing, desperate. She understood because she felt it, too. She was kissing him back with passion that seemed to spring from nowhere, borne more from instinct than from experience. In the five or six times that she'd allowed Tristan to kiss her, she'd never felt a fraction of this kind of fervor. She'd never felt anything like this at all.

All that she knew was that she wanted him—more than she'd ever wanted anything in her life. Her fingers gripped the hard ridges of muscle on his shoulders as if she would never let go. He was even taller and bigger than she realized up close like this, making her feel oddly vulnerable.

She wanted to kiss him, to feel his tongue in her mouth, his hands on her body, and his big, battle-hard body wrapped around her. She wanted to inhale the delicious masculine scent of pine and soap. She wanted to feel her breasts crushed against his chest and her hips pressed against his. She didn't know how much she wanted that until she felt the thick club of him against her stomach. Good lord! And then she couldn't seem to think of much else.

Desire crashed over her in a drenching wave, dragging her under. She felt so heavy. Especially her breasts and the intimate place between her legs. She moaned at each new sensation as he kissed her deeper and harder, silently urging him to give her more.

He answered with a groan and more pressure. Their bodies seemed to be melded together. She could feel the hard flex of his arm muscles as he drew her in tighter and tighter. Their tongues circled and sparred, waging a desperate battle of desire and urgency. Yet she never felt threatened. Even in the midst of this fierce onslaught of passion, there was an underlying emotion she didn't recognize but trusted. It felt almost like tenderness, which seemed silly given the frenzy of the kiss. But it was there, squeezing her chest and hovering over her like a warm sentinel, silent and protecting.

His jaw scratched the tender skin of her chin, but she didn't care. Closer . . . Harder . . . She wanted to be consumed. She wanted to melt into him. To become one.

His hand was no longer in her hair. It was on her bottom, lifting her . . .

The floor dropped out of her stomach. A rush of liquid warmth flooded between her legs. She could feel him, the hard column of his manhood fitted intimately against her. It felt . . . *big*. Powerful. And really, really good.

Especially when he started to move his hips in insistent little circles. Her stomach dropped again, and the place between her legs grew even warmer and more needy. Her body trembled. She ached to press back. And she would have, had the sound of the door opening not torn them apart.

He released her so suddenly she stumbled and might have fallen had she not hit the stone support of the wall behind her.

"MacLean, are you—" The man stopped, and seeing them, he swore. Still in a lust-induced daze, it took Margaret a moment to recognize Eoin's foster brother standing in the doorway. "Oh hell, I didn't meant to . . . interrupt."

Though there was nothing overtly lascivious or suggestive in his tone, the way his eyes slid over her bruised mouth and still-heaving chest when he said the last made her stiffen.

Eoin recovered faster than she did. He stepped in front of her. The instinctively protective gesture—as if he could shield her from the embarrassment of being discovered in such an intimate embrace—was surprisingly sweet. She felt a strange swell of warmth fill her chest.

"I will join you in a moment, Fin," he said sharply.

Fin gave him a slow smile. This time there was no mistaking the suggestiveness. "Take as long as you need."

Margaret couldn't see Eoin's expression, but from how fast his friend left the room, she suspected it had been threatening.

By time he turned back to her, however, the look was gone, replaced by the inscrutable mask. "I owe you an apology. That never should have happened."

Looking at his hard, implacable features, it was hard to believe this was the same man who'd been kissing her so passionately a few minutes before.

What was it about Eoin MacLean that drew her? She'd known handsome men before, and even a few who were as tall and powerfully built. She'd also met serious men—although maybe none who were quite so intense. But she'd never met a man whose gaze could level on hers and make her feel as if he knew what she was thinking.

She tilted her head, studying him contemplatively. "What did happen?"

For one brief moment their eyes connected and she felt the force of it like a steel vise around her ribs. "I don't have any idea."

The blunt admission charmed her, and she couldn't

resist giving him a teasing smile. "Well, in case you were wondering, I think *that* signifies as 'liberties.'"

He surprised her with a sharp laugh, and then a smile—a crooked half-curl of his mouth that hit her square in the chest. The furrowed lines between his brows disappeared, and the smile transformed his features, making him look boyishly charming and so handsome she thought she might just be content to stare at him forever.

"Ah, yes, I can see the difference now," he said dryly.

"I thought you might. And I can see what you meant about pups." Her smile turned wry. "Although I didn't mean to offer quite that big of an invitation."

He sobered instantly. "I didn't mean what I said. I spoke out of anger. You did nothing wrong. What happened was my fault."

"What happened happened. It was no one's fault." She fought back a smile. "I'm glad to hear I didn't do anything wrong though. In case you are wondering, I don't have any complaints on your end either."

He bit out a sharp laugh and shook his head, as if he couldn't believe she was teasing him about something so intimate. "Good to know."

They shared a moment of silence that was surprisingly comfortable. She liked him, she realized. This quiet, serious, intense young warrior. She liked seeing the cracks in his reserve and the dry sense of humor that emerged. She liked making him smile, and seeing those lines between his brows disappear. She liked the way he looked, the keen intelligence in his eyes, the way he held her as he kissed her, and the way he'd jumped to protect her both on the dance floor and when Fin had interrupted them.

She liked him . . . a lot.

Maybe her thoughts were more transparent than she realized. His half smile fell, and his eyes softened almost imperceptibly. "Fault or not, it cannot happen again."

She wanted to argue, but how could she? He was right.

"You should go," he said. "Comyn is probably wondering why you haven't returned to the Hall."

If there had been anything in his voice to suggest he cared, she might have hesitated. Instead, she nodded and did as he'd bade. But her chest ached as she walked away. There was something about Eoin MacLean that called to her, that felt special, that made her want to hold on to him and never let go.

She told herself she was being as foolish as Annie, the thirteen-year-old butter girl, who'd followed the sixteen-year-old stable lad, Padraig, around moon-eyed for nearly a month last year, thinking she was in love.

Daughters of powerful lairds didn't fall in love.

She bit her lip. At least she hoped they didn't.

6

EOIN KNEW he should be trying to think of ways to impress Bruce, but he was too distracted. As the hunting party of a dozen men rode through the forested valley to the southwest below castle hill known as the King's Park on a cool, gray morning, he wasn't thinking about traps, strategies, terrain, or even the stag he'd just brought down. He couldn't think about anything but the kiss he was supposed to be forgetting.

What the hell had come over him? His physical weakness for the lass was unsettling. It wasn't like him at all. He'd never done anything like that in his life. He'd been moments away from pushing her back onto that bench in the mural chamber and doing something stupid. Something *very* stupid. Something that could have brought him a whole shite heap of trouble. From Bruce, from his father, and from MacDowell.

And she would have let him. *That* was what he couldn't get out of his blasted mind. He could have had her, and the knowledge taunted him—and tempted him—far more than it should.

He still didn't know how it had spun out of control

like that. One minute he'd been kissing her and she'd been responding—in a way that made it clear that it wasn't the first time she'd been kissed—and the next he'd had his cock wedged between her legs and they'd practically been swiving with their clothes on. The feel of that softly curved bottom in his hand and the press of her hip as she rode against him was not something he'd soon forget.

Hell, it was not something he'd ever forget. He'd probably go to his grave thinking about that kiss and those sweet little insistent moans.

He adjusted himself for what felt like the dozenth time as they'd ridden this morning as he swelled with the memory.

As the track through the forest widened, Fin rode up beside him.

"What's the matter with you?" his foster brother said in a low voice. "You've barely said a word all morning." He shot him a knowing sidelong glance. "Or maybe I don't need to ask. From your dark expression, I take it you didn't finish after I interrupted yesterday? The way the lass was moaning, I thought she wouldn't be able to wait."

Eoin's jaw hardened, his mouth clenching with anger and distaste. He sent Fin a dark glare. "I told you last night nothing happened. What you saw was a mistake."

Fin laughed. "It might have been a mistake, but if that was 'nothing,' I wouldn't mind a taste of it. Where do I get in line?"

If they hadn't been riding, Fin would have been on his back. As it was, Eoin contemplated leaning over and wrapping his hand around his neck. Instead, his fingers tightened around the reins until his knuckles turned white. "Stay away from her, Fin. I mean it."

Fin gave him a long look through narrowed eyes, as if he

knew how close Eoin was to striking him. "You're acting a little possessive for 'nothing.' Are you sure there isn't more to this than you are letting on? God's hooks, don't tell me you actually like the lass?"

Eoin's teeth hurt, his jaw was clenched so tight. He did like her. That was the problem. She was . . . different. Confident, good-natured, and charming with a wry, self-deprecating, slightly wicked sense of humor that made him wonder what outrageous thing was going to come out of her mouth next. "*I don't have any complaints on your end either.*"

The lass was incorrigible. And amusing. He couldn't remember the last time he'd laughed like that with a woman. Probably because he never had.

Fin must have guessed his thoughts. "She isn't for you, MacLean. I know you, and a brazen minx like Margaret MacDowell would drive you out of your mind with her antics. Do you really want to take the time to mold her into a proper wife—even assuming it could be done? You might be bold and inventive on the battlefield, but you are reserved and conventional about everything else. I'll give you, there's something different and enticing about the lass in all of her primitive splendor, but do you want a wife who runs around the countryside as wild as a heathen and looks like a ripe peach waiting to be plucked? She won't be content to sit waiting contentedly by the home fires while you do whatever the hell you want. A lass like that demands attention. Yours is fixed elsewhere and always has been. How long do you think it will take her to find that attention somewhere else?" He paused letting that sink in. "Do you think she'll share your intellectual pursuits? The lass probably can't even read and write her own name." Fin gave him a hard, unflinching stare. "Bed her if you want, but don't lose sight of what's important. You have a brilliant future ahead of you. The lass will hold you back. Have you forgotten about Lady Barbara?"

"Of course not," Eoin snapped. "I don't need a damned lecture, and you are well off the mark about my intentions."

"Am I?" Fin challenged.

Eoin slammed his mouth shut. His foster brother might be a crude arse at times, but he knew him too well. Eoin might have harbored a thought or two in Lady Margaret's direction after that kiss, but Fin was right in more ways than one. Lady Margaret was a temporary distraction—a beautiful one—but not the sophisticated, learned sort of woman who would content him in the long term.

For that he needed a woman like Lady Barbara. For an ambitious warrior there could be hardly better connection than with a Keith. Moreover, Lady Barbara knew what was expected of her. Demure and circumspect, she wouldn't draw attention wherever she went. She wouldn't make inappropriate jests or provide endless fodder for the gossipmongers at court. Fin was right. A man wouldn't have a moment's peace in his life with a wife like Margaret.

But there would never a dull moment.

And there would be fun.

And excitement.

And passion.

He'd never wanted that before, but she'd given him a taste of it, and he had to admit it was more enticing than he would have expected. Enticing *and* distracting.

Still furious with his friend, Eoin was saved from having to respond when Bruce called him forward. For the rest of the ride, Eoin concentrated on what he loved best—warfare—and on convincing his kinsman that he was the best man for the place in his secret army. This was his chance, and he wasn't going to bugger it up.

They were locked in a fierce debate about William Wallace as they reached the top of the steep hill and rode through the main gate into the outer bailey of the castle. Perched high on a rocky hill, inaccessible from three sides by sheer rock face, Stirling had not one but two walls protecting the towers and buildings within.

"Wallace failed because he could not rally Scotland's nobles behind him to stand as one against Edward," Bruce said, dismounting.

"Partly," Eoin agreed. Already off his horse, he handed off the courser to one of the stable lads who'd rushed out to meet them. "But he might have had a better chance had he stuck with his type of warfare and not relied on the nobles in battle."

Bruce stiffened, obviously sensitive about the subject, though Eoin hadn't been referring to him but to Comyn's desertion at Falkirk. The Lord of Badenoch's decision to have his cavalry retreat on the battlefield had left the infantry unprotected and led to Wallace's disastrous defeat. Even with Badenoch's cavalry, victory would not have been assured, but without him the loss had been all but guaranteed.

Eoin hastened to clarify. "Wallace was at his best when he avoided pitched battle, when he made the English fight on *his* terms. It was his unconventional warfare—the surprise attacks and ambuscade—that gave him a chance against the English militarily. Winning over Scotland—and its nobles—politically was another matter."

Bruce's mouth quirked. Eoin took that as a concession, as he followed his kinsman over to the wall that looked out over the town below. Most of the rest of the party did not follow them, retreating to the barracks or Hall, but Fin, Campbell, and a few others lingered.

"You speak of furtive 'pirate' tactics," Bruce said. "Yet here we are in the shadow of Wallace's greatest victory, and the one for which he will always be remembered." He pointed to the bridge in the distance below to the northeast. "The pitched battle of Stirling Bridge."

"Aye, it wasn't a skirmish or chance encounter, but even then he fought his war, using unconventional tactics—trickery of sorts. He took advantage of his position and lured the English into terrain of his choosing: a narrow bridge where he could trap them in a loop in the river and then cut them down as they came across to take away the power of their numbers. That's certainly a far cry from two armies meeting face-to-face and letting knights and strength of arms battle it out." Eoin paused. "I'm not saying that we can never fight a pitched battle and win. I'm saying we should not fight one unless it is a place and setting of our choosing where we can even the odds. Until then, many small victories can be every bit as demoralizing and effective as one big one. It isn't vanguards and formations, or longbows, cavalry, and schiltrons that will defeat the English, it's our knowledge of the terrain, our ingenuity, and our ability to outthink them by using all the weapons in our arsenal, be they trickery, deviousness, or fear."

Bruce smiled. "That's probably the longest speech I've ever heard you give, cousin. In fact, I don't think I've ever heard you speak so enthusiastically about anything."

"He lives for this shite, my lord," Fin interjected. "Don't let that serious, scholarly reputation fool you. MacLean might be smart, but he's also the most devious bastard I know on the battlefield. You don't know how glad I was to have him on my side when we were young. I almost pitied John of Lorn's sons, when we were all being fostered on Islay. I can't tell you how many times MacLean got the best of them after some prank they pulled. It's like a game to him. But he's the only one smart enough to play."

As the MacDougalls were shared foes, Bruce seemed to appreciate the example. He also looked very intrigued—as if this were exactly the type of information about Eoin that he'd wanted to hear.

Eoin was surprised by but grateful for Fin's praise after the near blows they'd come to earlier. He was closer to Fin than he was to anyone, and he didn't like to have discord between them. The way his foster brother spoke of women had always made him uncomfortable, but never had Eoin felt it so personally.

It wasn't just the crude comment about Lady Margaret, however, but also the cold, hard truth he'd imparted. Truth that Eoin didn't want to hear.

"Well, if he plays it half as well as he plays chess, I'd like to see it," Bruce said.

Before Eoin could ask him what he had in mind, Fin interjected, "Speaking of chess . . ." He nodded his head in the direction of the two women who'd just ridden through the gate behind him.

Eoin stiffened, almost as if he were bracing himself.

It wasn't enough to dull the impact.

God's blood, she was breathtaking. Gut wrenching. Knee buckling. The Fair Maid? What an understatement. Bold Enchantress, Seductive Siren, Brazen Beauty, those were more fitting.

What had Fin said? Primitive splendor? She certainly fit that description right now. Her fiery hair was streaming around her shoulders in wild disarray, her cheeks were rosy from exertion, and her eyes were bright and sparkling with laughter. Against the background of the burnished countryside and gray walls of the castle, she looked vibrant and alive. Like a part of life that he'd been missing. He wanted to breathe her in, let her wash over him, and bask in all that joyful radiance.

She might be trouble, utterly "wrong" for him, and show none of the restraint and modesty of a noblewoman, but she made him want to bother.

Their eyes met for one long heartbeat. He told himself he was relieved when she shifted her gaze away. But the hand that had wrapped around his chest wouldn't seem to let go.

He wanted her. So much that for the first time he didn't trust himself to do the smart thing.

She would have turned away, but Bruce had never met a woman he didn't want to charm—even one who was the daughter of his enemy. "Ah, it's your little *maid*," Bruce teased under his breath.

Christ, even his cousin had noticed?

Eoin tried to cover his embarrassment as Bruce gave the ladies a gallant bow. "Lady Margaret, Lady Brigid, I see that we were not the only ones to enjoy a ride this morning." He looked behind them and frowned. "But where are your escorts?"

Margaret and her friend looked at each other, clearly trying not to break out into fresh peals of laughter.

"Behind us," Margaret said. "*Far* behind us, I hope. Seeing as it was a race."

She gave the Lord of Carrick a cheeky grin as she dismounted with the help of one of the stable lads and walked toward them. Even her walk was enticing, the gentle sway of her hips a seductive promise. Eoin couldn't look away.

"With whom?" Fin asked.

"My brothers," Margaret replied with a glance in Fin's direction that seemed oddly cautious. "I even gave them a five-minute head start."

The two women exchanged glances again, and this time both of them burst into laughter.

Eoin could tell that Margaret was up to something, but Fin seemed confused. "You mean they gave *you* a five-minute head start."

Her gaze hardened almost imperceptibly. "Nay, I spoke correctly."

Fin didn't hide his incredulity. "And you won?"

"Well, I am a fast rider." Her mouth twisted. "We were on the road from Cornton a few miles from the ford at Kildean when we decided to race."

Eoin frowned. "But that ford isn't passable until low tide. You'd have to cross the Forth at Stirling Bridge to reach the castle from there."

She turned on him with pure mischief sparkling in her golden eyes. "Is that so? Now that I think about it, I do recall someone mentioning that. I wonder if my brothers know? I do hope they didn't ride all the way to the ford before realizing they would have to turn around."

He couldn't help it, he laughed. As did Bruce and the others. The lass wasn't just beautiful and outrageous, she was clever.

God help him.

∽

Margaret looked back and forth between the two kinsmen. Her heart was still thudding from that laugh. Deep and rough as if from disuse, it had swept over her skin like a callused caress, setting every nerve ending on edge. She thought it the most sensual sound she'd ever heard and feared she'd do almost anything to hear it again.

"Perhaps you aren't the only one good at this 'game,' cousin," Robert Bruce said. "Maybe I should ask the lass to play?"

"Game?" she asked.

Bruce explained what they'd been talking about, and she shook her head. She'd wondered why Eoin had appeared so animated when she and Brigid had first ridden up. She should have guessed. The older she got, the more she realized men were simply grown-up little boys content to play in the dirt, construct forts, and devise ways to kill each other.

She lifted her brow and turned to Eoin. "When I was young my brothers and I used to play a game called Christians and Barbarians. Perhaps you'd be interested in a contest?"

The slight lift of Eoin's mouth—only the hint of a smile—shot right to her heart. "We used to call it High-landers and Vikings."

She grinned back at him. "Same concept, I'd wager."

"And which side did you play, Lady Margaret?" the Lord of Carrick asked.

From the twinkle in his eye, she suspected he could guess her answer. Though her father would be horrified, Margaret had to admit, she liked the young nobleman. His sense of humor that was every bit as wicked as hers.

"Why a Barbarian, of course." She gave him a knowing smile. "They have much more fun."

He chuckled. "Better not let Father Bertram hear you say that or you'll be on your knees saying Hail Marys for the rest of the week."

Margaret gave a not-so-exaggerated shudder. From her brief exposure to the dour castle priest, she did not doubt it. "I must admit, I've spent more time on my knees than most."

There seemed to be a sharp moment of silence. The Lord of Carrick gave her an odd look, as if he wasn't quite sure he'd heard her correctly. She frowned and glanced at Eoin, who looked away uncomfortably. His face was slightly red, almost as if he were in pain or maybe embarrassed, she couldn't tell which.

She was about to ask what horrible gaffe she'd committed this time, when Dougal and Duncan came galloping through the gate.

She took one look at her brothers' disgruntled expressions and broke out into a broad grin. "Have a nice ride, laddies? Brige and I wondered what had happened to you. Hope you didn't have any problems . . . at the ford perhaps?"

Dougal, who never had much of a sense of humor, looked like he wanted to throttle her, but Duncan, who shared her more easygoing temperament, appeared more annoyed than angry. He prided himself on being the clever one in the family and didn't like being tricked.

Both men hopped down and came toward her. Though not as tall and with darker hair than Eoin, her brothers were both grim of visage, thick with muscle, had the rough and gritty look of brigands, and were undeniably formidable warriors. But she stood her ground, used to their attempts at intimidation. Which had worked until she'd been about five and realized they'd never hurt her.

"You aren't too old to be bent over my knee, Maggie Beag," Duncan said in a low voice. Wee Maggie. When she was young, she used to hate when he called her that. Now that she was older she didn't mind so much. Of all her brothers she was closest to Duncan.

"Try it and you'll feel my knee," she replied sweetly. As he was the one to teach her that particular method of defending herself, he knew it was not an idle promise and grimaced. "By the way that will be one shilling for each of us." She held out her hand. "And don't attempt to renege on our wager this time. I was careful with my wording. We reached the castle before you, so we won."

Duncan turned to Dougal for help.

"Don't look at me," their eldest brother said. "I told you not to accept the challenge—even with the horse and head start."

Duncan dug into his sporran, retrieved the coins, and with a look that promised retribution dropped them into her open palm.

Margaret turned to hand one to Brigid, but realized her friend was staring at Dougal with an odd look on her face, who in turn was glowering at the men behind her.

Margaret cursed silently, having forgotten that she was cavorting with the enemy—at least that's how her family would see it, despite this purported gathering of temporary allies.

She hastened to dispel some of the brewing tension. "The earl and his party returned to the castle from their hunt just before we did. I'm afraid Brigid and I interrupted them with our excitement over the race." She gave the Earl of Carrick a conspiratorial look. "Although fortunately the game we interrupted this time did not involve carved figures."

Robert Bruce smiled, which neither of her brothers seemed to appreciate.

"Game?" Dougal asked.

"A jest." She gave a dismissive wave of her hand.

Duncan looked back and forth between her and the earl a few times and seemed satisfied. He relaxed and faced Robert Bruce with slightly less outward hostility. Dougal, however, was looking at Bruce as if he couldn't decide whether to run him through with a sword or battle-axe.

"I wouldn't bet against her," Duncan said conversationally. "Not if you want to leave here with any silver in your sporran. Our Maggie Beag hasn't met a challenge she doesn't like. She took ten shillings off John of Lorn last time he was at Garthland."

"For what?" the Earl of Carrick asked, clearly impressed by the amount.

"He said a woman couldn't drink a tankard of ale faster than he could—he was wrong."

Margaret grinned. Although the MacDougalls were important allies of her father, she didn't much like John of Lorn and had enjoyed seeing him choke on his words—literally.

Although Robert Bruce lifted a brow in her direction, there was nothing impressed in Eoin MacLean's expression. Though inscrutable as usual, she sensed he did not approve of her wager.

She refrained from rolling her eyes . . . just. He really needed to relax and have more fun. Wagering was almost as much fun as winning.

"That's quite a . . . feat," Bruce said gamely.

She shrugged. "It's easy if you know how to open your throat."

For some reason, Duncan burst out into hysterical laughter, Dougal winced, and Bruce and Eoin had that pained, discomfited look again. She gazed at Duncan for explanation, but he just shook his head between guffaws, as if to say he'd explain later.

Duncan finally managed to get himself under control.

"It was my fault. I should have known better than to accept a challenge with horses involved."

"Why?" Finlaeie asked. "She won by trickery."

Duncan started to explain, but Margaret held him back with a look that told him to wait, this might be amusing. She turned to Eoin's foster brother. He was undoubtedly a fine-looking warrior. Tall and well built like Eoin, but with wavy, dark auburn hair and deep green eyes the color of emeralds. At first she'd even considered him as a possibility for Brigid. Brigid hadn't shown much interest—in anyone actually—and now she was glad. There was something about him that rubbed her wrong. She couldn't put her finger on why, but she didn't like him. "You do not think I could have bested him another way?"

There was a layer of steel beneath the lighthearted tone. Brigid recognized it, even if Finlaeie did not. She put her hand on Margaret's arm. "It's nearing time for the midday meal. Perhaps we should go—"

"Of course not," Finlaeie said, cutting off Brigid's attempt to pull her away.

"And why's that?" Margaret asked.

"You're a lass," he replied, as if the answer should be obvious.

She looked at Duncan and Dougal, both who seemed to be enjoying themselves, guessing where this was headed. "How kind of you to notice," she said with more amusement than sarcasm.

Eoin attempted to intervene, as if he, too, realized something was brewing. "Fin means you no disrespect, Lady Margaret. I'm sure you are an excellent horse-woman."

She was. But why did she have the feeling she was being

humored? She smiled, thinking the joke might end up being on them.

She forced her gaze from Eoin back to his foster brother. "It might surprise you to know that women can be just as good as men—even better—at some things."

"Maybe things like having babes, sewing, and making sure a man's meal is on the table," Finlaeie said with a patronizing smirk. "But at more uh . . . physical and mental tasks women are inferior."

She crossed her arms. "According to whom?"

"God. The church. The weaker vessel, you know."

This time she couldn't prevent her eyes from rolling. Not the "weaker vessel" and "the fall of man was Eve's fault" argument again? It was listening to things like this that was the reason she avoided church as much as she could, which admittedly was far harder to do here than at Garthland. It seemed that all women did at Stirling was go back and forth from the chapel.

"It seems to me that the weaker one wasn't the one who was deceived by Satan but the one who could be led into eating the apple." She grinned in the face of their shock. This time at least she didn't have to wonder at why. Irreverence was irreverence, even at Garthland. "But in the case of riding—and maybe sailing—I can say with certainty that they are wrong."

King Edward was reported to have a menagerie of animals at his tower castle in London, where his guests could stare and gape at the strange, exotic creatures from faraway lands. Margaret suspected she knew exactly how those animals felt right now. She wasn't sure whether it was her pronouncement itself or the heresy of questioning church doctrine, but the men in the earl's party, including Eoin, were undeniably gaping.

She shrugged unapologetically. It was the truth. "I've bested many men in a race."

Eoin's foster brother spoke without thinking. "Perhaps you've never faced adequate competition."

As Margaret could only pick one brother to step in front of she chose the more hotheaded one, Dougal. But both he and Duncan had made a low, threatening sound in their throats and instinctively gripped their swords.

Knowing she had to act quickly to prevent bloodshed, she said, "What a wonderful idea! I accept your challenge."

Finlaeie, who didn't seem to recognize the danger he was in from her brothers, whom he'd so casually slurred, looked at her as if she were mad. "*Me* race *you*?"

He sounded so appalled she had to smile. "Why not? It will be fun." She shot a pointed look at the brother she hadn't been able to block, who had taken a step toward him and was leaning forward ever so slightly as if ready to attack. "Don't you agree, Duncan?"

They exchanged a long look. Eventually she got through to him, and her brother eased back, releasing his sword. She could feel the threat behind her dissipating from Dougal as well. What she planned would more than adequately avenge the blow to the MacDowell pride, without disrupting the peace of the talks.

"Aye, I think that is a brilliant idea," Duncan agreed. "We could all use a little excitement around here."

Eoin seemed to be aware of the potential conflict she'd just avoided. He glanced at her brothers, as if making sure the threat was gone, before he returned his gaze to hers. "Fin meant no offense. He was only jesting. But I'm afraid he wasn't completely forthright with you—he's probably the best rider here."

She lifted a brow, eyeing the auburn-haired warrior speculatively. "Is he? Then this shall be even more fun than I thought. I like a challenge."

Finlaeie had obviously warmed to the idea. He smiled, a slow, smug smile that made her eager to see it wiped away. "When?"

"Now if you'd like. Unless you are too tired and would prefer to wait."

"Now is fine." His gaze grew calculating. "What should we wager?"

She shrugged indifferently. The win would be enough. "Whatever you'd like."

The lewd glint in his eye made her want to call back her words. It was clear what he wanted. He must have read her distaste because his gaze hardened. "The spirited black stallion your brother Duncan was just riding."

There were a few gasps of shock. The palfrey Duncan had been riding was worth what a knight made in a year.

Eoin looked like he was about to explode.

She stiffened, and Duncan started to object. "It's not my—"

"Fine," she agreed, cutting him off. Finlaeie didn't need to know that she and Duncan had switched horses before the race. The palfrey was hers. John Comyn wasn't the only one to receive a prized horse for his eighteenth saint's day. "And if I win, I shall claim the horse you ride in the race."

It was clear he didn't take the threat seriously; he smiled. "Whatever *the lady* wants."

Yes, she was going to enjoy wiping that smug smile off his face *quite* a lot.

∞

Eoin watched the preparations for the race with growing frustration. Bruce refused to intervene, claiming that Fin was lucky the lass had prevented her brothers from challenging him instead. Eoin also suspected his kinsman didn't mind seeing the MacDowells humbled, even if a lady was involved.

Fin wouldn't back down, intent on making some kind of point to Eoin about Lady Margaret and her unsuitability—something Eoin was well aware of even without the race. She was outrageous even when she didn't mean to be. "*On my knees*" and "*open your throat*" . . . God in heaven, was she trying to kill him?

And the lady herself seemed bent on a course of destruction from which nothing—and sure as hell not rationality—would intervene. Still, he had to try. The yard was already filling with gawkers as Eoin went in search of her. She'd claimed she needed something from her chamber and had gone racing into one of the towers, while her brother Duncan finalized the details of the race with Fin.

It would be a sprint of about ten furlongs on the road from the abbey at St. Mary's to the castle, starting on the flat, fertile grounds of the Forth riverbed, and finishing with the steep climb up castle hill. The first one across the drawbridge and through the portcullis would be the winner.

When Eoin reached the tower, he had to push his way through the crowd of people flooding out.

Bloody hell, it was already a damned spectacle! Word of the wager must have raced through the castle like the plague. The vultures unable to resist the scent of death. Lady Margaret's—though she seemed oblivious to the threat of condemnation—if she didn't put a stop to this.

He waited at the bottom of the stairwell for her to emerge. When she did, he feared his eyes were in danger of popping out of his head.

She stopped in her tracks when she saw him and quirked her mouth in a smile that managed to look adorable and enticing at the same time. The knot that formed in his chest whenever she was around tightened.

"If you are here to 'talk me into my senses' like you started to say earlier, you are wasting your time."

Eoin was too shocked by her attire to form a proper response. "You can't wear that!"

She glanced down at the snug brown leather breeches, a linen shirt stuffed into the waist, and the equally snug sleeveless leather surcoat that was fitted at the waist. She'd exchanged soft leather boots for the slippers she'd been wearing earlier, and for once her flaming locks were tamed in a thick coiled plait at the back of her neck.

She was dressed like a lad, but never had she looked more feminine. She was more slender than he'd realized, the fitted breeches and surcoat revealing the dips and contours of the curvaceous figure that were hidden by the full skirts of her gowns. Her legs were sleekly muscled and long, her hips gently curved, her bottom rounded, and her waist small. Her breasts were generous but well rounded and firm over the flat plane of her stomach.

He didn't need to imagine very hard what she would look like naked, and once formed, the image would not be dislodged.

Eoin was in trouble, and he knew it.

"I know it's unconventional, but you can't expect me to race in heavy skirts? They'll be in the way, and I'll fall and break my neck."

"You shouldn't race at all, and certainly not in that. You might as well be naked!"

She lifted a brow in amusement—probably because he sounded as flustered as he felt. "I didn't realize so many men walked around in such a state of undress. I will have to pay more attention."

She let her gaze drop from his eyes over the planes of his chest and down his leather-clad legs, lingering one cock-hardening instant on the heavy bulge between his legs. She might as well have stroked him, the heat enflamed every nerve ending in his body. He went as hard as a damned spike.

When she lifted those tilted golden cat-eyes to his, he felt caught in the seductive pull. He wanted to toss her over his shoulder and carry her upstairs to ravish her like one of his marauding Viking ancestors.

Where in Hades had that come from? What was it about her that made him feel so damned *primitive*? For a man who'd always prided himself on rationality, this base, unthinking reaction was a bitter blow. Not to mention confusing. She was a problem he couldn't solve, and for the first time he couldn't see a way around it in his head.

"And yet, you are wearing similar clothes and do not appear naked at all," she pointed out.

Was that a tinge of disappointment in her voice? God's breath she *was* trying to kill him!

"You're a lass," he said, as if the distinction should be obvious.

"As that's the second time I've had that pointed out to me today, I think it's been established." She laughed. "Now, if we are finished discussing my attire, I have a race to win."

She attempted to sweep past him but he caught her

arm. He wasn't fool enough to bring her closer than arm's length, but it was still close enough to wreak havoc on his senses. She might be dressed like a man but she sure as hell didn't smell like one. "That's just it, you can't win. Don't you see? Even if you beat him, you lose."

She frowned. "What are you talking about?"

"Ladies don't stage a public race with men and they certainly don't win. It isn't done."

Christ, he sounded every bit as prudish and uptight as the nun Fin had accused him of being. And she knew it, too. She seemed to be fighting back more laughter.

"Maybe not here, but I do it all the time at home and no one bats an eye. They'll get over it. It's a harmless bit of fun." She smiled up at him. "You take things too seriously. It's sweet, but I know what I'm doing."

Sweet? He wasn't sweet. "Do you?" Damn it, he didn't want to hurt her, but it needed to be said. "They will never accept you, if you do this."

Her smile turned wry. "I'm not sure that was likely to happen anyway. But really you are making too much of this."

Was he? Maybe. He was just trying to protect her because . . .

He didn't want to finish that thought.

"Look, even if I wanted to, my family wouldn't let me back out of it. It's too late."

Realizing the truth in that statement, and that her mind was made up, he stepped back and let her go. What else could he do? This wasn't his battle. She wasn't his.

She was already outside when he called out to her. "Fin is one of the best riders I've ever seen. Do you really think you can win?"

Her family must believe she could to let her go through with this.

"I wouldn't have made the challenge if I didn't."

He couldn't help smiling as the lass threw him a dimply grin before darting across the yard.

She sure as hell didn't lack for confidence. And damned if he didn't admire it.

7

MARGARET'S CONFIDENCE was well deserved. The race was over in less than five minutes. Barely had the shock died down from her unusual attire, than the crowd was stunned by her more-dramatic-than-she'd-intended finish through the portcullis gate.

First, thank goodness.

But it had been closer than she would have liked. Finlaeie had been ahead of her until the turn up the hill. He'd slowed at the sharp corner and she'd taken the straighter line by jumping across. She'd had to clear a few rocks to do so, but Dubh had been more than up to the challenge.

The horse was her secret weapon, and the reason she had been so confident. Dubh had never let her down (although he did require a set of steel nerves, as he liked to hang back until the end of the race). The skill of the *eochaidh*, or what the English called "eochy" or horseman, only accounted for a small part of a race.

Not that she wasn't a skilled rider—she was. Duncan had always said she had an eerie way with horses. Even spirited stallions like Dubh, which would have been thought unsuitable mounts for a woman, seemed to quiet when she drew near.

She smiled when she thought of Finlaeie's shocked expression as the "spirited black stallion" had been led out for her to ride. She must admit that she had suffered a moment of doubt or two when he'd brought out his own horse. Whatever the reason for her dislike of him, she couldn't fault his taste in horseflesh. The beast was every bit as magnificent as Dubh.

She also could not fault his riding. They were probably equally matched in that as well. But size was her other advantage, and one of the reasons she thought women could compete with men when it came to speed—especially against big, heavily mailed warriors. Since she was a foot shorter and probably half Finlaeie's weight—or more with all that armor—Dubh had much less weight to carry. Had Finlaeie MacFinnon been a smaller, slighter man, and removed his armor, he might have bested her.

She'd barely come to a stop before her exuberant brothers were pulling her off the horse and hugging her. "Hell's bells, Maggie Beag, what a jump!" Duncan said, spinning her around. "I wasn't sure you would clear."

Truth be told, she hadn't been either.

"You nearly stopped my heart, gel," her father said sternly, but with undeniable pride in his eyes. "I thought I told you to stop jumping or you were going to kill one of us."

"You did, Father, and I promised to stop." She dimpled. "I just didn't say when."

Brigid came over and gave her a quick hug. There were a few more congratulations from her father's men and some of his allies, but after the initial excitement wore down, Margaret realized it was rather quiet—especially compared to similar occurrences at Garthland. She frowned, glancing around the courtyard and realizing that the crowd had already dispersed.

She felt the first prickle of uncertainty, but quickly brushed it away. It was to be expected. The people were much more reserved at Stirling, and much less inclined to prolonged celebration. At Garthland something like this would send them feasting into all hours of the night.

She felt a pang in her chest, acknowledging only for a moment how much she missed her home and the life she knew. A life where she didn't feel as if she were treading on eggs all the time.

She supposed there was also the delicacy of the situation that could explain the lack of excitement, given the tendency of everything in Scotland to boil down to Bruce or Comyn. Though the race had nothing to do with that, some would see it as a victory for Comyn over Bruce. Finlaeie MacFinnon, like Eoin, might not be publicly aligned in Bruce's camp, but he'd been part of the earl's hunting party. Too much cheering for one side might be taken the wrong way at what was supposed to be a gathering to come together.

She finally glanced at the much less ecstatic group standing a short distance away. Finlaeie was staring at her with an expression on his face that chilled her blood. Dark, thunderous, and seething with resentment, it wouldn't be too fanciful to say that he looked as if he wanted to kill her. Eoin had his back to her and was clearly trying to say something to his friend, but Finlaeie wasn't listening. He was glowering at her too hard.

With what he'd said to her before the race, she shouldn't care. "*When I win, maybe you'll give me some of what you gave MacLean last night.*" She'd been furious and even more intent on seeing him humbled. But she would have been a fool not to be a little scared. She'd seen men angry at loss of pride before, but never had she been the recipient of such virulent animosity.

Whatever satisfaction and joy in victory she'd been feeling a few moments ago fled. She'd won, but she'd made a dangerous enemy in doing so. One she didn't want. She might not like Finlaeie, but he was Eoin's friend. And for some reason that mattered to her.

Finlaeie said something harsh to Eoin—if she read lips she might say it was a curse about what he could do to himself—and pulled away. Mouth white, he marched toward her, leading the magnificent chestnut palfrey behind him. When Eoin started after him, their eyes met. He looked upset, worried, and something else she couldn't identify.

Her brothers and father had seen Finlaeie's approach and instinctively formed a protective wall on either side of her. He stopped a few feet away from her and smiled, though it was the surliest smile she'd ever seen. "My *lady*." He had a way of drawing the word out that made it feel like a slur. "I congratulate you on your victory. It seems I underestimated your *riding* ability. I heard you were good. Lots of practice, I assume."

There was nothing specific in his voice, but something about what he said made the men at her side tense, and Eoin's face go white with fury.

"It was a close race," she said hastily. "Anyone could have won."

For some reason her attempt at graciousness was met with even more rage by Finlaeie. "But the victor was you," he said flatly. "Because of that jump."

Margaret thought there were other reasons as well, but

frankly she just wanted to have this conversation over. "Yes, I was quite lucky. Now, if you'll excuse me, I'm afraid we are frightfully late for the midday meal as it is, and I probably should change unless I want half the Hall to faint in shock."

No one smiled at the jest.

"Aren't you forgetting our wager?" Finlaeie said, pulling forward the horse.

Margaret caught Eoin's gaze and at that moment knew exactly what she had to do. "Wager?" she repeated, as if she didn't know what he was talking about. "Oh, you mean the jest about the horse. I will not hold you to that, of course." Her brothers exploded, voicing their objections, but she ignored them. "Had you won, I know you would not have taken Dubh from me."

They both knew he would have done exactly that. But she'd given him a way out. A way to keep the horse that he could ill afford to lose. The loss of such an animal would be a huge blow to a warrior trying to prove himself. God knows, the palfrey must have cost a small fortune.

Forced to agree, Finlaeie bowed his head as if acceding to the truth of her statement.

"Good," she said. "Then we will speak no more on the subject."

She knew she would have hell to pay with her father and brothers later. They would be furious at her refusing such a fine animal, but it would be worth it if the gesture dulled some of the sting of her victory.

A glance in Finlaeie's direction, however, told her that it may have—marginally—eased his anger, but it had increased his resentment.

Eoin, however, looked relieved. She caught his gaze

and wanted to hold on to it, but mindful of their audience, excused herself again.

Brigid was unusually quiet as they quickly washed and changed for the meal, but lost in her own thoughts, Margaret didn't press her for an explanation.

The crowd's reaction to the race bothered her more than she wanted to admit. She couldn't escape the twinge of apprehension that Eoin had been right. But what could she have done? Let a war break out between her brothers and Bruce's men in the midst of truce for the peace talks?

It was so blasted different here, with all these rules and conventions that seemed so silly. She told herself that the good opinion of these people didn't matter to her, but that wasn't completely true. Eoin's opinion mattered. And though she'd wanted to forget it, she was here for a reason. John Comyn's opinion should matter to her as well. There was also Brigid. She knew her friend had been having a difficult time here, and swore to do her best to try to make it better for her.

No more races, she vowed. And maybe once her father's anger cooled over losing the horse, he could be persuaded to lighten his sporran and buy them a few new dresses. Perhaps even a veil or two? That should make Brigid happy.

Indeed, as the girls made their way down to the Hall and Margaret confessed her plans, Brigid did seem a bit brighter.

Until they entered the Hall.

∞

It was worse than Eoin had anticipated. The condemnation and disdain toward Margaret MacDowell by some of the women had never been subtle, but now it fairly reverberated throughout the room.

The Hall had seemed subdued before she and her friend entered, but it had turned holy-week-in-the-abbey quiet the moment they did.

It wasn't just the race, but the alleged reason for it. It had taken Eoin awhile to figure out what people were buzzing about, but eventually his brother Neil filled him in. He seemed surprised Eoin didn't know. Margaret had been seen leaving the old donjon last night after Fin in a state of dishabille. She'd challenged Fin to the race (and then "cheated" by jumping) to retaliate at him for spurning her. By the time Eoin heard the story from Bruce again near the end of the meal, she and Fin had not just been seen leaving, they'd been seen in the actual act of fornicating.

Eoin hotly denied it and tried to dispel the rumors, but people seemed inclined to want to believe the worst of her. She was different—too bold, too confident, too indifferent to their approbation—and they were making her pay.

Eoin was furious, with the person who'd started the false rumor but also with himself. This was his fault. He was the one who'd kissed her. If she'd looked disheveled, it was because of him. Someone must have seen Fin leave the room after he'd discovered them, and then seen Margaret when she'd left before Eoin. He knew it could have just as easily been him rather than Fin who was the subject of the rumors.

Not that Fin seemed to mind. Eoin eyed his friend, whose temper seemed to improve considerably as the meal wore on and the rumor spread. Eoin understood his friend's anger at the blow to his pride over the race—Fin felt he'd been humiliated—but Eoin didn't understand the glee that Fin seemed to take in her shunning.

Especially after what she'd done with the horse. She'd had every right to claim Fin's palfrey as her prize. Despite the claim of "trickery" with the jump, she'd outridden Fin plain and simple.

Eoin had never seen anything like it. She seemed to sink into the saddle, to disappear into the beast until they'd been of one flesh. She was fearless. Light. Agile. Wild and unrestrained. It had been a sight to behold.

Although he could still feel the knot in his chest from where his heart had leapt out of his body when she'd jumped the corner over all those rocks.

The lass was wild. Outrageous. Too courageous for her own good.

And she was magnificent.

It was getting harder and harder to heed the reasons why she was so wrong for him.

He didn't realize how closely he'd been keeping an eye on her during the meal until it was finished and he couldn't find her.

Was something wrong? Had she heard something? Had someone been cruel to her?

He couldn't stand the idea of someone hurting her and wished to hell he could shield her from all this.

Thinking she might be with Comyn, Eoin looked for him to no avail. He was about to go in search of him when his sister raced up to the table.

She looked ready to burst. "Did you hear?"

Anticipating what she was about to say, he stood and pulled her off to the side. "I hope you aren't repeating gossip, Marjory."

She wrinkled her nose. "You should consider yourself lucky." She sighed. "Poor Fin."

His sister had a young maid's crush on his friend, but this was ridiculous. Fin wasn't the one who deserved sympathy. "Poor Fin?"

She nodded. "Aye, to have escaped that harlot's web. She seduced him and then tried to make him marry her!"

Eoin had had enough. He couldn't listen to this anymore. He took his sister's arm and forced her to look at him with a shake that he hoped knocked some sense into that pretty dark head. "Fin had nothing to do with it. It was me. I was the one in the room with her and nothing happened. Nothing. I will not hear you repeat any of this again. Do you understand?"

Eyes wide, she nodded. "You?"

"Aye, me. So if anyone is responsible for these rumors, it's me."

She looked horrified. But also contrite.

"Have you seen her?" he asked. Marjory shook her head. "How about young Comyn?"

She shook her head again. "I saw his sisters standing by the entry a few minutes ago."

Eoin grimaced. He didn't much like Comyn's sisters. Frankly, they reminded him too much of his own. Mean-spirited, judgmental, and gossipy. He and Marjory were going to have a long talk later. He could no longer pretend she was going to grow out of it.

There was a small, screened-off section of the Hall between the main entry and the corridor to the kitchens. With the garderobe nearby, the ladies tended to gather there to wait in groups. That was where he found them.

He stood near the entry and seeing no sign of Margaret was about to leave when he heard her name. He thought it was Elizabeth Comyn who spoke—John's eldest sister. In addition to Joan, Comyn's other sister, there were a few other ladies Eoin didn't recognize.

"Margaret MacDowell? You thought wrong! My brother would never consider marrying a woman like that. If her father is fool enough to think my brother would marry someone so utterly in lack of dignity, manners, and morals, that's his fault. Have you seen her? She might as well wear the yellow hood of a harlot with the way she dresses and looks; I wasn't surprised to hear she seduced Finlaeie MacFinnon." The woman who must have spoken first tried to put up some argument, but Comyn's sister shut her down. "They were seen. What more proof do you need? If there was any question before—which there wasn't," she emphasized, "there isn't now. My brother will not marry soiled goods."

If Eoin were the kind of man to strike a woman, Elizabeth Comyn would be in grave danger right now. Not trusting himself to listen to another minute of this shite without saying something to straighten these harpies out— something that would only worsen the gossip—he was about to leave when one of the women complained, "Who is taking so long in there?"

The door to the garderobe opened and a woman stepped out. "The soiled goods," Margaret said.

Shite. That was the moment Eoin knew what was wrong with him. He knew what he'd been trying to deny. He knew why instead of focusing all his efforts on impressing his kinsman for a job of which he could only dream, he was chasing down a woman to the garderobe.

His blood drained to the floor. The truth hit him square in the chest as she stood there like a damned queen, facing their condemnation with defiance and a look on her face that told them to go to hell.

I'm in love with her.

Bloody hell, how could he have let this happen? It didn't make any damned sense! He didn't want to believe that he could do something so completely and utterly stupid.

But he had. She was wild, outrageous, and didn't dress or act anything like a noblewoman should, but seeing her standing there, facing those women, with more pride and dignity in her tiny slippered foot than those women could ever hope to have, he knew he loved her.

God knows he didn't understand it, sure as hell wasn't happy about it, and didn't know what he was going to do about it, but neither could he deny it.

Regally, head held high, she walked across the small room. The women seemed stunned—and not a little shamed—and parted instinctively before her. Margaret's pride, her bravado, never faltered. Until she turned the corner of the partition and saw him.

Their eyes met, and he could see that she knew he'd heard every word. Her golden eyes widened. Her fair skin paled. And then her proud, beautiful face simply crumpled.

He glimpsed something he'd never thought to see in her expression: vulnerability, and it cut him to the quick.

He reached for her. "Margaret, I'm sorry—"

He didn't get to finish.

"Oh God, please . . . please, just leave me alone!" With a soft cry and sob that tore right through his chest, she twisted away from him and fled out the Hall as if the devil were nipping at her heels.

∞

He'd heard. He'd heard every horrible word, every lie they said about her.

Margaret felt the tears sliding down her cheeks as she ran across the yard. For the first time in her life she wanted to run away. She wanted to crawl in a hole and hide. Shame was a new emotion for her, but it burned through every limb, every bone, and every corner of her body.

They thought she'd seduced Finlaeie MacFinnon. They thought she dressed like a whore so she must be one? Is that what Eoin thought? God knows with what had happened in the library he had every reason to.

She heard him call her name, but it only made her run faster. She didn't know where she was going, only that she had to get away. She'd headed to the stables without even realizing it. A solitary stable lad sat at the entry. He took one look at her face and made himself scarce.

That was when Eoin caught up with her. He took her by the arm again. This time his grip was firm. When she tried to shrug away, he held fast. Blast it, he was strong, and right now, she hated all those muscles she so admired.

"Let go of me," she cried, in between sobs that tore through her lungs like fire.

"Margaret—Maggie—look at me."

She didn't want to, but there was something in his voice that would not be denied. *Maggie?* She lifted her gaze. Dark, velvety blue eyes met hers. Not with condemnation but with understanding. And something else. Something that looked like tenderness.

"I'm not going anywhere until we talk," he said in a voice that was both firm and gentle.

She didn't want to talk, she wanted to cry. She wanted to crawl into a ball and forget any of this had ever happened.

"Where were you going?" he asked.

"I don't know." She sniffled. "I just wanted to ride."

"I'll go with you."

She was too anxious to get away to argue with him. God knew her reputation couldn't suffer any more. And if he didn't mind being seen with the Whore of Babylon, she wasn't going to stop him.

He helped her saddle Dubh, and then saddled his own horse before lifting her up. They passed the guards at the gate without comment, and soon they were riding down castle hill to the flat stretch of land she'd raced over earlier that day. They rode past the abbey and continued along the banks of the River Forth until the castle on the rock, the narrow wynds of tightly packed stone and wattle-and-daub houses, and the town of Stirling fell behind them.

Only then did she slow, realizing how fast she'd been riding. Dubh had sensed her urgency to get away and responded.

It was late afternoon, which at this time of year meant the sun was already beginning to sink on the horizon. It was also, she realized too late, extremely cold and damp. Dark clouds hovered threateningly above them.

"Here take this."

They were the first words he'd spoken since the stable. She turned to find him riding beside her, holding out the plaid he'd had wrapped around his shoulders.

She shook her head to refuse, but he gave her a hard look that told her he was going to be stubborn.

"But it looks like it's going to rain," she protested. "Your fine surcoat will be ruined."

It looked to be a costly garment, a dark blue velvet edged with intricately embroidered scroll and leaf pattern in gold thread.

"Aye, well perhaps the next time you decide to take a ride before a storm, you could grab a cloak?"

The slight lift of one corner of his mouth gave him away.

"Are you teasing me?" she asked, unable to keep the surprise from her voice.

"Maybe." He shrugged, as if it surprised him, too. "Take the plaid, Lady Margaret. I'll survive."

"You called me Maggie before."

"Did I?" He gave her a sidelong look. "Very well then, take it, Maggie."

She did as he bid, wrapping the thick green and blue patterned wool around her shoulders. A feeling of warmth settled instantly around her. *He* settled around her, she realized, for the plaid still held the heat from his body. And it smelled of him, warm and cozy with just the faintest hint of heather. Drawing a deep breath, she sighed with contentment.

"Comfortable?" he asked dryly, as the first raindrops began to fall.

Their eyes met. She probably should have felt guilty, but something about his teasing made her happy. She sensed that he did not reveal this side of himself very often. So instead her mouth quirked. "Very."

He laughed and shook his head. "You might at least feign a little concern for my suffering."

She rolled her eyes. "And if you decide to play knight errant again, you should try not to whine. It rather ruins the effect."

"Not to mention a good surcoat."

This time it was she who laughed. It took her a moment to realize what he'd done. He'd made her feel better. "You're very clever, aren't you?"

His mouth quirked. "Not always apparently."

It took her a moment to realize he was referring to her, but she wasn't sure what it meant. Did he regret being here with her?

"We can return now, if you'd like," she said.

He shook his head, eyeing the dark clouds. "I think it's better if we get out of the storm." He pointed to a dilapidated stone building nestled along the river up ahead that appeared to be a fisherman's cottage. Long abandoned by the looks of it. "We can try in there. Half a roof is better than none."

It was actually more than half. Only the far corner of the roughly eight-by-eight-foot stone building had lost its turf. Enough to let in the chill and damp, but at least they would be relatively dry.

While Eoin tended the horses, Margaret did her best to sweep away some of the dust and cobwebs with an old straw broom that, although a tad moldy, was still service-able. There was little in the way of furniture. A table, a few stools, and a bed box stuffed with straw and covered by an old threadbare, dusty plaid. The floor was dirt and stone, but also covered by a thick, well-beaten-down layer of slightly moldy straw. She was grateful for it. Mold was vastly preferable to standing in mud.

Eoin entered not long after she sat on one of the stools. He stood in the doorway, scanning the small cottage. "I wouldn't call it comfortable, but it's better than I expected."

Closing the door behind him, he stepped into the room. Nay, he dominated the room. The already small cottage grew even smaller.

Chill? What chill? It felt like someone had lit a fire. Inside her.

The air seemed to shift, and every tiny hair on her arms and neck stood on edge. Her heart was pounding, and her stomach had that sink-to-the-floor feeling again.

She didn't know where to look, what to say, feeling sud-denly awkward—almost shy. What was it about this man that made her feel so . . . uncertain? So tumultuous? So confoundingly vulnerable?

He pulled up a stool and sat beside her. "Are you ready to talk?"

Her chest pinched. She didn't want to talk about it at all. "What is there to say? You heard them." She gave a harsh laugh. "But it must have come as no surprise to you. God knows after what happened in the library, I've given you no reason to think differently." Suddenly, her bravado vanished. When she looked at him it was with her feelings exposed. "But I don't want you to think that of me."

He looked almost mad at her. "I don't. Of course I don't. How could you think I could?"

"How could you not after what happened in the library? I let Brigid's brother kiss me a few times, but I swear I've never done anything like that before."

He held her gaze, his jaw seemed to clench a little tighter. "What happened was my fault."

Her mouth curved. "I thought we established that no one was at fault."

But this time she could not elicit a smile from him. His expression was painfully serious as he stared at her in the growing shadows. "Don't jest, Maggie, not about this."

She had to jest. What else could she do? God's mercy, what did he want from her? Hadn't she had enough blood drawn from her today? "Why are we here, Eoin?"

He seemed startled by her question. After a moment he shook his head. "I don't know."

"I doubt your family would approve." She paused. "Or Lady Barbara."

"Probably not."

She felt another pinch. This one deeper and more persistent. It wouldn't let go until her chest started to ache. Had a small part of her hoped he would disagree?

She looked away. "I think maybe you should go."

"That would be the smart thing to do."

The pinch was twisting now in pain. She stared at the

damp toes of her soft leather shoes that were peeking out beneath the edge of her grayish-blue gown, and waited to hear him push back the stool.

Instead she felt the rough calluses of his fingers on her chin as he tilted her face to his. "But that isn't what I want."

"What do you want?"

"You."

There was something warring in his eyes she didn't understand. Torment? Indecision? Resolve?

Whatever it was, it was lost when his lips touched hers.

8

EOIN KNEW this was a bad idea. If he hadn't had any control when he'd been a hundred feet away from a castle full of people, how the hell did he think he was going to find it when they were alone in a secluded cottage?

But as he was to discover, knowing and stopping were two very different things. He'd been wanting to take her in his arms since he'd caught her in the stables, and the moment he'd walked into this cottage and seen her sitting there, he'd known he was fighting a losing battle not to touch her.

He needed to touch her. Needed to show her how much he cared about her. And needed to let her know it would be all right.

So for the second time in as many days, he didn't do the smart thing. He didn't think. He let himself feel . . . and it was incredible.

The passion that had exploded between them in the library had not dulled; if anything it had only grown hotter. Their tongues knew exactly how to find each other, their bodies how to fit, and their hands how to touch.

Well, maybe not exactly how to touch, because if he

had his way, she wouldn't be gripping the hard muscles of his arms right now, she'd be gripping another hard part of him.

Just thinking about her hand wrapped around him made him throb, made him deepen the kiss, and bend her back into the curve of his body.

He loved the taste of her, the soft feel of her lips, and the passionate thrusts of her tongue circling against his.

She was a good kisser. He pushed that thought away before it could take hold, not wanting to think about what she'd said about Brigid's brother.

Still, a swell of possessiveness surged inside him, and his kiss grew a little fiercer. A little rougher. And a lot more carnal.

Was he trying to shock her? He didn't know, but with every suck, every nibble, every rhythmic thrust of his tongue—meant to mimic another rhythmic thrusting—he savored the soft gasps of surprise that told him this was new.

He ravished, he plundered, he claimed her mouth, and then he claimed a whole hell of a lot more. His mouth slid over her jaw, down her throat, and once he'd tossed the plaid off her shoulders, down the curved bodice of her gown.

She'd gone lax in his arms, her head falling back, her breath heaving, as if to offer the bounty of her breasts to gorge upon. And what a feast they were. Full and generous, yet firm and perfectly rounded, they were everything he'd dreamed about at night when he was an untried lad.

The pressure in his groin was growing unbearable. He groaned as he slid his hand up to cup her breasts, as his mouth slid over the creamy soft skin above her bodice. Just the weight of all that soft flesh in his hands sent a swell of heat deep in his groin that was nearly enough to drive him over the edge. When she arched her back and started pressing into the palm of his hand, he slid right over.

∞

Margaret didn't know what was happening, but she knew she didn't want it to stop. Eoin had taken control of her body, and she didn't want it back. Not when he could make her feel this good.

The feel of his hands on her breasts was unlike anything she'd ever imagined. Tristan had tried to touch her there once, but she'd kneed him in the bollocks so hard he hadn't been able to walk straight for a week—or so he claimed. But with Eoin . . . she wanted his hand there. And the lower his lips descended on her chest, the lower his tongue danced beneath the edge of her gown, the more she wanted his mouth there as well.

A fever had taken hold of her body. Her skin was hot, her breath uneven, her heartbeat erratic. Her limbs were so weak she could barely stand.

But he had her. The strength of his body was like a lifeline, an anchor to hold on to as the maelstrom lashed around them.

Still it wasn't enough. The maelstrom wasn't around them, it was inside her, and she needed to find a way to release it.

Instinctively she knew what she wanted, and the pressure of her body moving against his grew more insistent. More demanding.

And he responded. The heat of his mouth through the fabric of her gown as he covered her breast made her weak; the feel of his manhood wedged between her legs made her wet. She cried out in pleasure as his hands cupped the sensitive flesh of her breasts, as his mouth sucked, and as his hips thrust. She was falling apart. Melting. Surrendering to the pleasure racing through her veins.

But she wanted more.

Had she said it aloud?

She heard him swear, the sharp curse a guttural answer to her plea. The next moment she felt the rocky wall of the cottage against her back. He lifted her skirt, wrapped one of her legs around his hips and started fumbling with the ties at his waist.

She could have stopped him, but she didn't want to. She wanted this as badly as he did.

Yet as much as she wanted him inside her, it was still a shock to feel the tip of his manhood nestled at the cleft between her legs, and she gasped.

For one moment the haze cleared, and their eyes met in silent lucidity. From the firm grip she had on his shoulders, she could feel the tension reverberating through his body. He was shaking with it, every muscle in his body flexed with restraint.

"Tell me you want this," he said roughly, his blue eyes so dark they almost looked black.

He would pull away if she wanted him to. He was giving her a chance to change her mind. But she wasn't going to. "I want this," she said softly.

"Thank God," he groaned, "I'm sorry . . ."

She didn't understand the apology until she felt the jar of the wall as he thrust up inside her.

She cried out as a sharp pain sliced through her.

"I'm sorry," he murmured. "Oh God, *a leanbh*." Little one. "I'm sorry. It will be better in a moment."

She hoped that wasn't a note of uncertainty she heard in his voice. As it couldn't get much worse, she wasn't inclined to argue. Her body was pulled as tight as a bow. She couldn't breathe, let alone talk. But seeing the concern in his eyes, and the gentle pleading, she did all she could do and nodded.

He kissed her then. A slow, tender kiss like he'd never given her before. It was as if he was trying to soothe the sting—the hurt—with his mouth and tongue.

Nay, she realized. It was more than that. He was wooing her. Showing her with his kiss how much he cared for her.

She could feel her heart soften. Feel the love she now knew she felt for this man blossom inside her. It was the only explanation for what was happening. *I love him.*

She loved this serious, handsome young warrior with all his quiet intensity who was as learned as a monk but kissed with the raw, aggressive passion of a man who knew how to be wicked. She loved the dry sense of humor that seemed reserved just for her. She loved to tease him, loved to make him smile until the crease between his brows disappeared, and loved the unexpected gentleness and tenderness in his eyes when he looked at her.

Her body responded to that emotion. Relaxing. Releasing the tight hold she had on her pain.

It was then that she became aware of what the pain had prevented: the feeling of *him* inside her. Big, thick, and hard, filling her with his heat. Possessing her. They were connected, joined in a way she'd never imagined.

Not that she didn't know the particulars of fornicating, which she did. And she knew enough from her brothers (and those people in the Hall) to know that it could be enjoyable. But she'd thought it would be embarrassing and awkward. What she hadn't expected was the incredible closeness and bond that would be forged between them.

He lifted his head from her mouth. "Are you all right?"

Seeing the self-recrimination and silent apology in his eyes, her heart tugged. She would remember this moment for the rest of her life and cherish it.

She put her hand up to cup his stubbled jaw. "I'm perfect."

And she was. Margaret knew this was exactly where she was supposed to be. Joined with this man in the way God had intended. She didn't care what the priests said, this couldn't be a sin. It was heaven.

∞

Eoin's teeth clenched against the urge to thrust. The urge that was as primitive and powerful as anything he'd ever experienced.

He'd done this before. Maybe not as many times as Fin—he was focused on other things than chasing women—but enough to know that this was different.

And it wasn't just because Margaret was a maid (even if he'd had to keep reminding himself of that fact with the passionate way she responded to him). Christ, he hadn't expected that much pain. It had scared the lust right out of him. Though unfortunately only for a minute. It had come roaring back full force as he became aware of the tightness of her body squeezing around him.

What made this different wasn't just the sensations gripping his body, but the emotions gripping his heart. Eoin didn't believe in bards' shite like fate and destiny, but looking into those incredible golden eyes while seated deep inside her, the words came to mind. He felt something in his chest shift with the intensity of the emotion that rose inside him. He wanted to protect her, cherish her, and most of all love her with everything he had.

Unfortunately, the base instincts clamoring inside him like the drum had other ideas. The pressure pounding at the base of his spine warned him that he didn't have long. He'd just come up against the limits of his control.

As soon as he felt her relax, he couldn't hold back anymore. He had to move. Slowly at first, and then as her breath quickened, and soft cries filled the cottage, faster.

Her response drove him wild. Her back arched . . . the leg around his waist tightened, and he was lost. His hips thrust, circled, and plunged. Deeper, harder, faster, until the pleasure unwound inside him.

"Oh God, Maggie, you feel so good. I'm going to . . ."

He couldn't finish. He stiffened, shuddered, and cried out as the force of his release exploded from him in wave after wave of powerful bursts.

When it was over, it was all that he could do to stand. He collapsed against her and slowly let her slide from his body as he fought to regain some of his strength—and breath.

He was utterly drained. Spent. Wrung out of all his energy. When he was seven—just before he left to be fostered—he'd been swimming in the sea around Gylen Castle and become caught in the current. He'd nearly drowned, struggling for over an hour, before finally dragging himself to shore and collapsing in a dead heap in the sand. That was about how much energy he had right now.

Until her muffled voice penetrated the euphoric haze. "Eoin, uh, are you all right?"

Ah hell. He pulled back with a curse, realizing he'd probably been crushing her. He realized other things as well, like the fact that he'd just taken her maidenhead with little more finesse than an eighteen-year-old lad.

She was probably confused—worried—wondering what the hell happened now. In other words feeling the same way he was. Divesting young ladies of their virginity wasn't exactly something he had a lot of—*any*—experience with.

He didn't bother asking himself what the hell he'd just done, he knew exactly what he'd just done. Rather quickly. Against a wall, for Christ's sake.

"God, I'm sorry," he said, raking his fingers back through his hair. "I didn't mean it to happen that way. You deserved better."

She looked stricken. "You regret what—"

He stopped her. "Nay. God knows I probably should, but I don't."

It was too late for regret. Too late for self-recrimination. Too late to say he'd made a mistake. Too late to tell himself that he never should have brought her here.

Even if he wanted to be angry with himself for doing something so incredibly stupid (not to mention dishonorable), something guaranteed to cause them both a shite-heap of trouble, and something that could jeopardize his place in his kinsman's secret guard, he knew it wouldn't change anything. What was done was done. Whether she was right or wrong for him no longer mattered: she was his. And damned if that didn't make him happy.

Reaching down, he cupped her face in his hand, gently stroking the soft curve of her cheek with his thumb. She was so damned beautiful she took his breath away, and never more than now when she bore the stamp of their passion on her swollen lips and stubble-scraped skin.

Eoin was discovering that he hadn't left those Viking marauder roots as far behind as he thought.

"All I meant," he explained, "is that you deserved far

more than a wall in a fisherman's cottage for your first time, and had I any semblance of honor and control, I would have given it to you—along with far more pleasure."

Relief spread over her delicate features in a bright smile. "But you did bring me pleasure."

He had, he realized, as surprising as that was for a maid. From everything he'd heard, the first time for a lass was always horrible. But Margaret had liked it. Just thinking about the way her body had responded to him, how she'd pressed her breasts against his chest and tightened her leg around his hip, drawing him closer, did what he would have thought impossible. Defying every law of nature, he felt himself stir.

He looked into her eyes and continued to run his thumb over her bottom lip. "There's more, *a leanbh*," he said huskily. "Much more."

"Really?"

The spark of anticipation in her eyes went straight to his bollocks. She was still standing in front of the wall, and he was remembering too well how she'd looked pressed up against it. How her eyes had slitted, her breath had quickened, and her cheeks had flushed.

He had every intention of seeing that again, but this time, he was going to do it right. "Aye, really. But before I show you exactly what I mean, you must agree to one thing."

A small frown drew between her brows. "What's that?"

"To be my wife."

The look of shock on her face would have been amusing had it not been at the expense of what honor he had left.

"W-w-what?"

He frowned. Surely she knew as well as he what this meant. She was his, damn it. She'd given herself to him, and he had no intention of letting her go.

"I want you to marry me, Maggie. Right here, right now."

❧

Margaret's head was spinning.

Barely had she recovered from the fear that she might have killed him—the look on his face before he'd collapsed against her had been as close to a man glimpsing paradise as she'd ever seen—then she was reeling from the blow of thinking he regretted what had happened. Now he was proposing? And unless she was mistaken, what he was proposing was just as shocking.

"A clandestine marriage?" she asked.

He nodded grimly. "It's not ideal. And if there was another way, I wouldn't suggest it. But you know as well as I do that our families will not want an alliance between us. The church might not like informal ceremonies done without the banns, but it will be valid—and binding."

Their eyes met, and she knew exactly what he meant. Even if their families wanted to try to undo it, they would not be able to. If they agreed to wed right now, spoke their vows, and consummated them, in the eyes of the church they would be just as married as if they'd posted the banns for the next three Sundays and then exchanged vows before the church door with a priest.

"But once we explain to them what has happened . . ."

"Do you really want to take that chance? What do you think your father will say?"

Her father would be furious. She didn't want to think about what he would say, but it was what he would *do* that worried her. She wouldn't put much past her father when his pride was involved. He wanted her to marry the Lord of Badenoch's son—no matter how improbable that was now—he would not settle for a kinsman of Bruce's, and a third son at that. Her father loved her, but he would do whatever it took to keep them apart, virginity or not.

Eoin was right, if they didn't marry now, they might not have another chance.

But something was holding her back from saying yes. She tilted her head, studying this serious, handsome warrior who'd wound his way around her heart. "Why do you want to marry me, Eoin?"

He stiffened. "I would think that is obvious."

That was exactly the problem. Margaret wasn't a romantic. She hadn't thought her husband's feelings for her would matter to her when she wed. It was discomfiting to realize that they did. Honor should be enough, but in this case it wasn't.

"There is no reason for anyone to know what just happened," she said softly.

His jaw clenched angrily, his eyes darkening to midnight. He ground out each word. "I will know." His eyes scanned over her as if he were remembering every moment. An unmistakable thrill spread over her skin. "You gave yourself to me, Margaret, and if you think I'll pretend it didn't happen, you don't know me very well."

She didn't. That was part of the problem.

The dangerous glint in his eye made her shudder. Had she not been backed against a wall already, she might have taken a step back. But she wouldn't let him intimidate her. "You do not need to fall on your sword for the sake of my reputation, Eoin. I'm afraid it's rather too late for that. Marrying me won't change what they think."

His eyes narrowed. Holy cross, he could look menacing! "That isn't what I'm doing."

"Isn't it? I'm strong enough to weather the storm; I will not let them defeat me so easily. I don't care what they say. I know the truth." She gave him a wry smile. "Believe it or not, at home people actually *like* me."

He held her gaze for so long she didn't think he was going to say anything. But as usual, his expression held no hint of his thoughts. "I believe it. And that's why I want to marry you."

It took her a moment to realize what he meant. When she finally did, it felt like the sun had just broken out from behind a cloud. "You care for me."

He drew her up against him. "Aye, I care about you, lass."

The deep, rough huskiness of his voice sent tiny shivers racing across her skin. She looped her hands around his neck as if they belonged there. "I care about you, too."

As his hands already were moving possessively over her body, clearly he'd guessed as much.

"Good. Now, if you are finished with your questions, you have about five seconds to give me an answer before I carry you over to that bed. You can be my wife the second time I'm inside you or the third, but either way, I will be inside you, and you will be my wife."

Her eyes widened. This was a fierce, primitive side of him she'd never seen before, and something about it made her pulse quicken and her blood heat. Or maybe that was the feeling of him hard against her.

She arched a brow. "Is that the way of it, then?"

"It is." His hand was on her breast. She sucked in her breath as his thumb circled over the crest of her nipple. When he'd made it hard, he drew it between his fingers and gently pinched. She gasped as pleasure flooded her senses—and flooded somewhere else as well. She trembled with pleasure.

"And, Maggie?" His mouth was by her ear, his warm breath and silky tongue making her shudder.

She was in such a sensual daze it took her a moment to realize he was talking to her. "What?"

He lifted her up into his arms. "Your five seconds are over."

9

EOIN DIDN'T KNOW what had come over him, except that he knew he wasn't going to leave here without Margaret MacDowell as his wife.

The lass did something to him—besides turning him into a lust-crazed lad, that is. She brought out a fierce, possessive side of himself that he'd never exhibited before. He wasn't sure he liked it, and it sure as hell wasn't very civilized, but there was no denying that he was carrying her to the bed with every intention of ravishing her—again.

He held her gaze as he crossed the few steps to the small bed. He had to put her down to pick up the plaid he'd shoved off her shoulders and lay it down over the straw "mattress." Next time there would be feathers and silk bed linens, but for now this would have to do. At least it was an improvement over a wall.

With any other woman he wouldn't have considered asking what he did next. But Margaret was different. She was bold and confident, and not easily shocked. "I want to see you, *a leanbh. All* of you."

It took her a moment to understand what he meant.

Her eyes widened ever so slightly before meeting his with a challenge. "And if I should wish the same?"

He grinned. He was hoping she'd say that. He was realizing there were some good things about a wife who couldn't resist a challenge. "I could hardly refuse."

"You first," she said, her voice a little breathy.

He'd taken his clothes off in front of more than one woman, but never had he been so aware of the effect his nakedness had on another. She watched his every movement with the rapt attention of a hawk, not missing any detail as he quickly divested himself of his clothing.

With every inch of skin he revealed, her breath would catch then quicken, until eventually he pulled off the linen tunic to reveal his chest, and it stopped altogether. If the way her eyes seemed to devour his arms and stomach were any indication, she was one of those lasses who liked a lot of muscle.

As if the breathy sounds of her arousal weren't enough, he swore he could also feel her growing hotter. And that in turn made him hotter.

By the time he removed his braies, he was as hard as a spike. And growing harder by the minute as her eyes devoured that part of him, and egged on by a little gasp that parted her lips in a perfect little O that was too damned suggestive. It was too easy to imagine her soft pink mouth closing around him, sucking, milking, taking him deep down her throat.

"If you know how to open your throat . . ."

Ah Christ. He groaned, and her eyes flew to his. "You're big all over," she said almost accusingly. "No wonder it hurt."

He grinned; he couldn't help it. A big cock was sure as

hell something he wasn't going to apologize for. She was sure to appreciate it later, although he doubted she would believe that now. "It will feel better this time, I promise." He lifted a brow in silent challenge. "Your turn."

She took one more look at him, sniffed as if to say we'll see, and started to remove her own clothing. It was his turn to watch like a hawk. Hell, he couldn't have looked away if the English were kicking down the door.

Her movements were quick and unthinking with no hint of seductiveness, yet that is exactly what she did. There was a natural sensuality to her that could not be denied. It permeated the very air around her.

Each movement felt like a silent beckoning, a lure for him to touch her. His hands itched to rip the blasted garments right off her, but he forced his fists to his side.

She shimmied. She dipped. She reached and tugged. Tempting. Enflaming his desire with the skill of Salome and her veils.

When Margaret finally lifted the chemise over her head to reveal a body that would have made Venus weep with envy, he thought he was going to explode. Unconsciously, he'd fisted his hand around himself and was one hard pump away from doing exactly that. When her eyes followed the direction of his hand and widened with unabashed curiosity, he swore and released himself.

She definitely was going to kill him.

She was unreal. Her body more incredible than he'd imagined—and he'd done some pretty detailed imagining. Long, sleek limbs, curvy hips, a narrow waist, lush, round breasts with berry-pink nipples that jiggled enticingly as she shook out her long hair over her shoulders, and inch after inch of flawless, creamy white skin.

She stood there proudly, without an ounce of shame, as

he drank her in. Why shouldn't she? She had nothing to be ashamed about. She was perfect.

And she was his. His wild, wicked little enchantress.

Holding her gaze, he reached out to brush the back of his finger over a pearly nipple so exquisitely formed it didn't look real. "You are beautiful, *a leanbh*. Beautiful."

She grinned. "So are you." She reached up to loop her hand around his neck, bringing their naked bodies into contact for the first time.

He hissed at the sizzling shock of sensation, sliding his arm around her velvety-soft back to draw her closer. "Warriors aren't beautiful. You'll have to think of some other word."

She sucked in her breath as he started sliding his mouth down the side of her neck close to her ear. "Or what?"

His teeth closed around the tiny lobe. "Or I'll have to punish you."

He could feel the excited jump of her heart against his. "How?"

Naughty lass. "Like this." He nibbled on her ear and slid his hand around to take her nipple between his fingers and start to pinch. He could tell how much she liked it by the soft little moans and deepening imprint of his cock on her belly.

Carefully, he lowered her down on the narrow bed. As there wasn't much room, he had to prop himself on his side and lean over her. But since that gave him plenty of access to that gorgeous body, he didn't mind.

∞

Margaret was grateful to feel the straw of the mattress at her back, as it meant she no longer had to think about standing. She could concentrate fully on what he was doing to her.

Everything was so new and incredible. The way his mouth ravished her neck, his fingers plied her nipples, and even the feeling of his big, hard body stretched out against her. All the little details fascinated her. The warmth of his skin, how tanned it still was from the summer sun, the small V of golden hairs on his chest and the even more enticing trail that led from his stomach to his manhood.

She'd wanted to touch him. Especially after seeing the way he'd held himself in his hand, when he'd been watching her. It had made her curious. And aroused. Just looking at him made her aroused. He was wrong earlier: he *was* beautiful. Tall and broad-shouldered, his body was tightly packed with slab after slab of lean muscle so sharply delineated it could have been carved from stone. There was not a spare ounce of flesh on him. Good lord, his stomach was lined with so many bands the washwoman could have beat clothes against it!

When he leaned over to kiss her, she couldn't resist sliding her palm over some of those ropey bands before coming to rest on the big rock of muscle at the top of his arm.

She loved the feeling of him leaning over her. The solidness. The weight. The connection.

His kissed her mouth, her throat, and—finally!—her breasts. The warm, wet heat of his mouth closing over her and sucking made her cry out. She arched against him shamelessly, begging for more as he sucked harder, as his tongue circled her nipple and tugged it gently between his teeth.

A strange feeling was coming over her. Building. Intensifying. Her skin felt hot, her limbs weak, the place between her legs soft and achy.

She didn't know what she wanted until he touched her. Until his fingers found that warm place and started to caress it. Softly at first, with gentle little circles that made her body weep with pleasure.

But soon it wasn't enough. She started to shake. Her hips started to lift against his hand, pressing . . . begging for more.

He growled—maybe muttered some kind of curse—against her breast and sucked harder. Sucked until a needle of pleasure connected his mouth at her breast and his hand between her legs. Then finally, his finger slipped inside her and gave her what she hadn't known she wanted. Stroking. Plunging. Faster and faster. Harder and harder. The heel of his palm pressed against her, giving her the pressure she'd unconsciously craved. It felt so good . . .

She was writhing, moaning, lost in sensations she didn't understand. Her body seemed to be struggling, fighting against something.

Vaguely she was aware of the coolness of the air against her damp breast as he lifted his head to look her in the eyes. She would never forget the way he looked, his face a tight mask of restraint, his gaze as fierce and intense as she'd ever seen it.

"It's all right, sweetheart. Just let it go. I'll catch you."

Whether it was simply the sound of his voice, the look in his eyes, or that her body simply couldn't fight it anymore, his words snapped the last threads of resistance. She gave herself over to the sensations and felt her body lift and soar.

The flight of angels. For how else could she describe the catapulting into heaven, the shattering of stars, and then the gentle floating in the clouds as the wracked spasms of pleasure slowly ebbed.

And when she finally fell back to earth, he was there to catch her just as he'd promised.

∞

Watching the pleasure of her release play over her features was the most beautiful thing Eoin had ever seen—and also the most erotic. He had to be inside her.

Dropping a tender kiss on her mouth, he moved over her. Hands planted on either side of her shoulders, he looked into her eyes until the haze faded. "I need your vow, Margaret."

Her mouth curved into a slow smile that wrapped around his chest and squeezed. "I, Margaret, take thee, Eoin, to be my wedded husband, to death do us depart, and thereto I plight my troth to thee."

He repeated the vow, and with one purposeful thrust, consummated the vows they'd just spoken.

And then he stilled. Savoring the sensations. Savoring the moment of overwhelming completeness and of rightness.

It was done. They were married. Bonded by God as man and wife.

The poignancy of the moment was not lost on either of them. It seemed to be thick in the air—and in his chest.

She looked into his eyes, searching his face for a long time. He could see the emotion in her eyes and wondered if they reflected some of his own.

"No going back," she said.

"No going back," he agreed.

She smiled. "You were right."

"I was?"

She nodded. "It doesn't hurt as much the second time." She bit her lip. "You feel good."

"So do you, sweetheart," he groaned, "God, so do you."

He began to show her just how good with long, slow

strokes that gave voice to the emotions inside him. He loved her, and he told her that with every kiss, every touch, every thrust. And when he'd brought her to the peak and followed her over, he told her with words as well.

"*Tha gaol agam ort.*"

∞

It was a long time before either of them spoke. Eoin lay there with his new wife curled up against him—her soft cheek pressed against his chest, her hair spilled over his skin like a silken veil, his arm holding her close—feeling more content than he'd ever felt in his life, watching the room grow dark, and wishing they never had to leave.

But they had to go. The sun filtering through the hole in the roof was almost gone. As much as he wanted to stay here and delay what was bound to be an unpleasant return to the castle, they'd been gone for a couple hours and someone would have noticed their disappearance by now. People would be commenting on it, which was the last thing she needed. And soon someone—her family most likely—would come looking for them.

For her family to find them here like this would make an already precarious situation much worse. Eoin did not delude himself. Despite their marriage, he'd be lucky to come out of this without a dirk in his back. If not from Dugald MacDowell, then from one of her *eight* brothers. Though the youngest among them was probably still only a lad, they were a bloodthirsty bunch.

He didn't want to think about his own family's reaction.

Margaret propped her chin on his chest to look at him. "Did you mean it?"

He didn't pretend to misunderstand. He swept a few red

strands of hair that had tangled in her thick lashes to the side, but it was only an excuse to run his fingers over the curve of her cheek. He wondered if he'd ever get used to the baby softness of her skin. "Aye," he said. "I meant it."

The happiness shimmering in her eyes and the smile that lit her face warmed the chill that had crept into the darkening room with his thoughts of what was to come.

"I love you, too."

Though he'd guessed as much, hearing the words filled him with pleasure—and not a small amount of satisfaction.

"I'm glad of it, *a leanbh*." And he was. Their feelings would help to make the shite storm they'd just unleashed worth it.

He hoped.

But seeing her naked limbs entwined with his, her hair tumbling around her shoulders in wild disarray, and the boldly beautiful features turned to his, he couldn't help feel a twinge of doubt.

Fin's words came back to him. *Attention . . . Demanding . . . Wild.*

Nay. His friend was wrong. Margaret might speak and act a little outrageously at times, but that was simply because she didn't know any better. Despite the unusual freedom in how she'd been raised, there was something oddly sheltered about her—almost innocent.

She was ignorant of social mores, that's all, not wicked. Well, maybe a little wicked, but as he suspected that would keep him well satisfied in the bedchamber, he didn't mind.

With everything else, his mother would help. Once Margaret spent some time at his home with his mother and sisters, she would learn what was appropriate and expected of her as his wife.

If something about that didn't sit quite right, he pushed it aside. It would all work out.

She'd lowered her face back to his chest, and was tracing little circles through his chest hair with the tip of her finger. "I wish we could stay here like this forever," she said. He thought she might have picked up on some of his worry until she laughed. "Although as many times as I imagined what my wedding would be like, it was never like this."

"You wanted a big wedding?" Of course she did. Didn't all lasses? Damn it. "I'm sorry."

She shook her head. "That isn't what I meant. I just never thought my marriage would be so romantic—or that I could be this happy being so wicked." She grinned mischievously. "Although we might want to come up with a different story to tell our children." His heart jammed. *Children?* "I don't think 'Father ravished Mummy against a wall so he had to marry her' is exactly the kind of lesson in courtship we want to impart."

He couldn't help it; he laughed. She *was* outrageous, and damn if he didn't like it.

"Although I suspect I'd have a hard time convincing anyone of it," she added.

His brows drew together. "What do you mean?"

She rolled her eyes. "You hardly ever crack a smile, Eoin. I doubt anyone will think you've been swept away by passion."

"Looking at you right now they might," he said wryly.

She grinned unrepentantly. "Do I look as wonderfully and thoroughly debauched as I feel?"

"I think I should be the one who looks proud about it, but aye, you do."

"Ooh, I wish I had a looking glass."

He wished he could paint a picture. He would carry it with him forever, and never tire of looking at it.

Christ, she was turning him into a lovesick troubadour. Soon he'd be composing sonnets and singing songs about her beauty.

Sliding her up his body, he lowered his head and kissed her on the lips one more time, and then on the forehead. "We need to go."

Her gaze locked on his. "Must we?"

He nodded.

The sudden trepidation in her eyes made him think she wasn't as oblivious to the knowledge of what lay ahead of them than he'd thought.

"Will it be so horrible, do you think?" she asked.

He lied to her for the first time. "Once the initial shock is over, I'm sure it will be fine."

10

EOIN WAS WRONG. There was nothing fine about it. Even more than a week later, Margaret was still reeling from the aftereffects of their arrival back at the castle.

The dreamlike bliss of the cottage had been left decidedly behind the moment they'd ridden through the portcullis and been confronted by her brothers, who were preparing to ride out in search of her.

She didn't know what had been worse, watching her brothers coming to physical blows with the man she loved, or later, seeing the cold rage of her father and his, as she and Eoin—blood still running down his nose from the brawl with her brothers—stood before them in the king's solar and announced what they had done.

War between the two clans might have broken out right there had Eoin's mother not intervened. While the men shouted, issued threats and ultimatums, and exchanged names of relatives, hoping to find a connection that would provide an impediment to annul the marriage, Rignach MacLean had calmly told them it was too late for that. Margaret could already be carrying a child, and her first grandchild would not be branded a bastard. They would have to make the best of an "unfortunate" situation.

Despite her intervention, however, Margaret did not delude herself that Eoin's mother would be her champion. Lady Rignach could not hide her disdain as her gaze quickly swept over her—as if lingering too long might sully her. She looked at Margaret as if she were beneath her, as if she'd seduced her son, and forced him to do the only honorable thing.

Margaret wished she could say that once the initial shock and anger had passed it was better. But it wasn't. Her family's disappointment was just as bad—maybe even worse. No matter how far-fetched the idea of a betrothal with John Comyn might be, she felt as if she'd let her father down. She tried to make him understand, but he wouldn't hear her explanations. Indeed, he barely said three words to her in the days leading up to her departure.

Even Duncan looked at her as if she were a traitor, marrying "the enemy." But Eoin wouldn't fight against them now . . . would he? It was the one thing she hadn't fully considered in those dreamlike moments in the cottage, and the thought of being on opposite sides from her family were war to break out was too horrible to contemplate. She vowed to do whatever she could to convince him to fight with her clan and the Comyns if trouble came. The prospect of having her husband's considerable talents on their side had been the one thing to ever-so-slightly mollify her family.

Eoin's mother had thought it best that Margaret and Eoin remove themselves from court and return to Gylen Castle on the Isle of Kerrera as soon as possible to staunch the gossip. Margaret suspected it had more to do with his mother being unable to withstand the shame of Eoin marrying such a "backward," "heathen" creature from the godforsaken corner of Scotland.

Even though Margaret agreed it would be best for her and Eoin to go, it didn't make it any easier to say goodbye.

Only Brigid had tried to be happy for her. But something was wrong with her friend, and no matter how many times Margaret asked, she would not confide in her. She had a clue though when Brigid said she admired her for "following her heart" and "not letting anyone stand in the way when she loved someone."

Had Brigid fallen in love without Margaret realizing it? She wanted to be there for her friend, but instead she was saying goodbye, knowing that it would be some time before they saw each other again.

If they saw each other again.

The heartache of losing her family and best friend in one blow, of being sent far away from anything she'd ever known, might have been easier to bear had Margaret been able to share it with Eoin.

But since that day in the cottage they'd spent little time together. He'd been locked away most days with his father—and the Earl of Carrick, she couldn't help noticing. Nor did they share a bed at night. A private chamber at Stirling could not be arranged, and everyone—except apparently her—thought it better that they did not add to the "scandal."

Margaret didn't give a fig about the scandal. She just wanted to know that Eoin was all right, and that he did not regret marrying her after all.

Any hope that they would have time alone together on the journey west, however, vanished when she learned that his mother, sister, and foster brother would be accompanying them—along with half his father's household men for protection.

By the end of the third day of traveling, when it was clear that once again she would be forced to share a tent with his mother and sister—and not her husband, who was apparently bedding down by the fire with some of the other men—she didn't know whether to cry or strangle him. He was either the most uncaring of bridegrooms or the most obtuse. Whichever it was, she wasn't going to let it continue. She'd never felt so lost in her life and needed to know this hadn't been a horrible mistake.

Leaving his mother and sister to direct the servants with where to put their trunks in the canvas tent, which was bigger than the room she and Brigid had shared with a few of the other women in Stirling, Margaret excused herself to go in search of her husband.

Wrapping her cloak around her to ward off the autumnal chill in the air, she wound her way through the bustling clansmen as they made haste to set up camp in the falling light of dusk.

So far they'd endured long days in the saddle, rising just before dawn to be on the road as soon as the light broke and stopping shortly before dusk. The pace, however, was agonizingly slow—even slower than the journey from Garthland to Stirling. Dubh was going about as half-mad as she was, chomping at the bit to *ride*.

As carriages were rare and impractical on all but some of the old Roman roads, all the women were on horseback, but Eoin's mother and sister traveled with far more carts that she and Brigid. Margaret's two trunks seemed paltry to their four or five—each.

In addition to the trunks of linens and clothing, there were boxes for their jewelry, another for their veils and circlets, and another for their shoes. But it wasn't just clothing. Margaret had been shocked by the amount of household plate and furniture that had accompanied them. No doubt by time she returned to the tent, it would look as comfortable as a room at Stirling, replete with beds, fine linens, chairs, tables—one used solely for Lady Rignach's writing (Margaret had mistakenly asked if she traveled with a clerk, much to the amusement of Eoin's sister, who informed her that only the villeins at Kerrera didn't know how to read and write)—a huge bronze bath, and two braziers.

On the way to Stirling, Margaret and Brigid had slept on bedrolls and been content to eat with the men around the campfire. But even a night in the forest wasn't an excuse to deviate from "civilized" living arrangements, according to Lady Rignach. Margaret was sure the word had been for her benefit.

But Lady Rignach didn't need to remind her. Margaret was painfully aware of her inadequacies every time they took out a book to read or a piece of parchment upon which to write.

She just wished being civilized didn't take so much time. At this pace they wouldn't reach Oban, where they would ferry to Kerrera, for another week. In the Western Isles, travel by ship was usually much faster and far more efficient, but Lady Rignach did not like the sea.

She found Eoin on the opposite side of camp, gathered near the horses with a handful of his men—including Finlaeie MacFinnon. Eoin had his back to her, and the men seemed to be arguing about something.

Finlaeie glanced over and saw her first. She stiffened reflexively, but forced herself to smile. For Eoin's sake she was making an effort to forget what had happened at Stirling and befriend his foster brother. But it wasn't easy when Finlaeie looked at her as if she belonged in the lowest stews of London.

She would never forget what he'd said to her before the race, but she told herself she could try to forgive him. Of course, he had to *want* to be forgiven first, and thus far he'd given her no indication that he felt sorry for anything.

There seemed to be a coolness between the foster brothers though, and from the nasty-looking mottled bruise on Finlaeie's jaw, she suspected it had something to do with that.

From the intensity of the conversation, she could tell it wasn't a good time and would have backed away, but Finlaeie nudged Eoin, said something in a low voice, and nodded in her direction.

Eoin turned, saw her, and gave her a pleasant "my lady," but he was too preoccupied to completely mask that her interruption was not a welcome one.

It was a look that a good wife would have read, made some excuse, and scurried away. Unfortunately for him, she was not a good wife—actually right now she didn't feel like much of a wife at all—and the look only fueled her frustration, hurt, and anger.

She had left the only family she'd ever known behind three days ago, been "welcomed" into his with about as much enthusiasm as a leper, and he couldn't spare her a few minutes?

"Is there something you need, Margaret?" Eoin asked.

"I should like to speak with you. Alone, if you will."

"Can it wait? We were just about to ride out—"

"It's important," she said firmly, refusing to back down. She had to find out why he was avoiding her, and that look she'd caught left her with no doubt that he was doing exactly that.

Eoin told his men he would be back in a few minutes and walked to his wife, ignoring the snide glance from Fin that said "I told you so."

Just because she interrupted him didn't make her demanding and needing attention, damn it.

Fin was lucky Eoin was talking to him at all, after what he'd said about their marriage.

"Why the hell did you marry her? The lass probably wasn't even a virgin. I hope you checked for fresh cut marks when you saw the blood."

Eoin had struck him as hard as he'd ever struck anyone in his life. He'd laid him flat with that one fist to the jaw and had his hands around his throat a minute later. "If you ever say anything like that again," he'd sworn, "I'll kill you."

He meant it, too. Margaret was his wife, and Eoin wouldn't allow any man to speak ill of her—even the man who was like a brother to him.

He just wished Fin hadn't said what he'd said. Eoin hadn't even thought about blood—or the absence of it. Damn Fin to hell. Just because there hadn't been blood, it didn't mean anything. It had been obvious that she'd been a maid.

Why was he even thinking about this?

Taking her arm, he led her through the trees to the edge of the river, where some of the lads were fetching buckets of fresh water for the camp.

He pointed to a low rock for her to sit on, but she shook her head and turned to face him.

"Is something wrong?" she asked.

"It's nothing for you to be concerned about. One of the scouts discovered that a bridge has been washed out ahead of us. We are riding out to see what will be the best route for the carts."

"That isn't what I meant." He hadn't thought so but had hoped. "Are you upset with me for some reason?"

"Of course not."

"Then why are you avoiding me?"

"I'm not avoiding you." But even as he said it, he knew it was a lie. He had been avoiding her. Unconsciously maybe, but that wasn't an excuse. The promise he'd made to Bruce didn't sit well with him, and he regretted it. Even if it had been the only way to salvage the opportunity his kinsman was giving him.

The reaction from his family had been worse than he'd anticipated. The negotiations for a betrothal agreement with the Keiths had been much further along than Eoin realized, and his actions had impugned the clan's honor and pride. His father had been humiliated and forced to apologize and make amends. But Eoin had ruined any chance he had of working with the great Marischal of Scotland and would probably do best to avoid crossing paths with Robert Keith in the future.

Eoin suspected that his father's disappointment was worse because Eoin's actions had been so unexpected. Unlike his two elder brothers, Eoin never did anything rash or unwise. He was calculated. Thoughtful. *Smart*.

But not this time. His father couldn't believe he'd thrown away a bright future for a tumble with a lass. "*She'll hold you back*," he'd said, his words an eerie echo of Fin's.

The words had seemed all too prophetic when his father told him Bruce was refusing now to consider Eoin for the secret guard. The earl wouldn't risk a man so closely tied to the enemy—especially Dugald MacDowell. Losing the chance with Keith was bad enough, but the thought of missing out on a place in Bruce's secret guard was unthinkable.

It had taken days of discussion—pleading—but eventually Bruce had relented. Only, however, after he'd exacted a promise from Eoin to tell Margaret nothing about what he was doing, where he was going, or what he was a part of. She would be kept completely in the dark about that part of his life.

He would have to lie to her.

And maybe that was why he was avoiding her. It was almost as if he knew that the more time he spent with her, and the closer they became, the more of a betrayal it would be when she learned the truth. Although he would keep his vow to Bruce, Eoin had no doubt that if this progressed as they expected, one day she would find out.

His beautiful young wife, however, looked none to happy with him right now. She glared up at him through narrowed eyes. "Are we married or not?"

The question took him aback. "What are you talking about? Of course we're married."

"I wasn't sure, as I seem to be sharing a bed with everyone but you!"

Her voice had risen in her anger, and he pulled her away from a few of his men, who from their shocked expressions had heard what she'd said.

Still, his mouth quirked. "I don't think you meant it like that."

She thought for a moment, and then blushed. "Of course I didn't mean that. I simply meant that I just wanted . . . I just hoped . . ." Her eyes caught his, and he felt his chest squeeze. "I miss you," she said softly.

Eoin swore and pulled her into his arms. He was a thoughtless arse. He'd been so caught up in his own guilt about the promise he'd given Bruce that he hadn't considered what his avoidance was doing to her. She felt abandoned—understandably so.

And it would only get worse. But he pushed that troubling thought aside for now.

God knows the past week and a half had probably been just as hideous for her as it had been for him. None of this was her fault, but he was acting as if he blamed her. He didn't. He just cared for her too much and feared the toll joining his cousin's secret army was going to take on them.

But what Bruce offered him was the dream of a lifetime and a challenge he couldn't resist. It would give him a chance to test himself and operate at the highest, most elite level. He couldn't walk away from that. He'd been working toward this moment his whole life. And he was fighting for something he believed in—deeply. His cousin was the rightful king and Scotland's best—only—chance of seeing and end to Edward's overlordship. He couldn't walk away from that. Even for the wife he loved.

It wouldn't be easy, but he was determined to have both Margaret and a place in the Guard.

"I'm sorry, *a leanbh.* I've been . . . preoccupied."

It had been ten days since that day in the cottage, and his body was reacting to her closeness. She was soft and sweet and smelled like she'd just alighted from a steamy bath of wildflowers. He was probably responsible for the steam—his body heat had shot up about a hundred degrees just holding her—but how the hell her hair still smelled like flowers after a long day in he saddle, he had no idea.

She let her cheek rest against his dusty, leather-clad

chest for a moment before pushing back to look up at him. "So you have not changed your mind?"

"About what?"

"Having a wife."

What in Hades? "Of course not."

She scanned his face, as if looking for any hesitation. "Then why are we not sharing a bed?"

God have mercy, the things that came out of her mouth! "Christ, Maggie, it's not like there's a lot of privacy." He let her go, thinking that the heat must be getting too much for him. His face even felt hot. He couldn't be blushing, damn it. Jerking off his helm, he dragged his fingers through his hair and tried not to stammer. "I'm not going to kick my mother and sister out of their tent."

She studied him until he felt like a bug under a rock. "I'm not suggesting that. But there is no reason you can't sleep in the tent with us."

His face no longer felt hot. Actually it felt as if every drop of blood had drained right out of it as he stared at her in mute horror.

She held a straight face for as long as she could, and then burst into laughter. "I was only jesting. Good gracious, I wish you could have seen your face."

She shook her head and giggled a few more times, while he scowled forbiddingly at her. To no effect, he noticed. *Handful.*

"I know there isn't much privacy on the road," she explained, "but your mother's tiring woman sleeps near the fire with her husband—and a few of the married servants as well. We don't have to . . ." She didn't need to finish, the pink in her cheeks said exactly what she was thinking. She bit her lip a few times and looked up at him again. "It will be enough to sleep beside you."

The soft plea ate at him. "I was only thinking of your comfort."

She smiled. "Well, the tent is certainly that. I can't imagine there is much furniture left in your castle with all that is in those carts. But I don't need all that. I shall be perfectly comfortable beside you."

At least one of them would be. He couldn't think of anything more excruciatingly *un*comfortable than sleeping next to her night after night and not being able to touch her—or touch her in the way he wanted.

But she had a point about his mother. "I wish my mother and sister thought as you, it would make this trip a hell of a lot faster."

"It is rather *slow*, isn't it?" she said in exaggerated under-statement. "But perhaps we can use the time to get to know one another better?" Anticipating an objection he hadn't been about to make, she added, "I know you are busy, but I thought when you were done for the day, or had a little bit of time, you could do what you promised."

His brow furrowed. Had he made her a promise he'd forgotten about?

Seeing his expression, she grinned. "Maybe this will re-fresh your memory." She pulled something out of the purse tied to her girdle and placed it in his hand. "Unfortunately, I couldn't carry the full set. But the way this one was scowl-ing reminded me of you."

He was too shocked to object to the scowling com-ment. He stared at the finely carved ivory knight incredu-lously. "You stole one of the chess pieces from the set at Stirling?"

Christ, it had probably belonged to King William the Lion!

She grinned up at him unrepentantly. "Stole is rather

a harsh word for a child's game piece, isn't it? I simply wanted a remembrance of the first time we met. There was another one in this color, so I assumed it would be all right."

He didn't have the heart to correct her; she would find out soon enough. But Eoin had to smile thinking of the way his kinsman would be swearing the next time he sat down to play.

Eoin was still smiling when he rejoined his men and rode out in search of an alternate path through the forested hills of Callander. He was also—surprisingly, given the discomfort it was bound to cause him—looking forward to the coming night.

For the first time since the announcement of their marriage, he felt some of the hope for the future that he'd had in the cottage. It would be all right. What he and Margaret had was worth all the challenges they would face.

If only that first challenge wasn't coming so soon.

※

"Check . . ."

In disbelief, Margaret stared down at the makeshift board and finished for him, "Mate"—to which she then added a very crude oath.

Tempted to flip the entire table, she managed to exercise some restraint and glared at the handsome blighter instead.

Eoin just grinned. "Oh come on, Maggie, it's just a 'child's game.' You aren't upset are you?"

Her eyes narrowed. If he wasn't so infuriatingly big, she'd flip him instead. "It's the devil's game, that's what it is!" She shook her head, looking at him accusingly. "You let me think I had you this time."

He was wise not to say anything and merely shrugged—proving that even if they hadn't been able to make love, six nights of sleeping beside him by the campfire wasn't completely without effect in making him a proper husband.

But she would make him pay for that shrug. Tonight.

It hadn't taken her long to realize that her closeness at night was causing her husband a bit of *distress*. He wanted her. And if the size of the erection pressed against her bottom was any indication, he wanted her quite a lot. She couldn't resist teasing him. Lud, remembering how he'd blush with embarrassment at the word "privacy" still made her laugh. As had the muffled curse the first time she'd pressed back against that hardness.

But Eoin lived up to his brilliant tactician reputation. If the past week of chess lessons hadn't shown her that he had a devious mind, the torture he'd exacted on her body certainly had.

When she wiggled her hips against him teasingly the next night, he moved the hand that had been circled loosely around her waist up to her breast, where his finger circled her nipple ever so lightly—frustratingly lightly. The moment she made a sound, he stopped.

"Privacy," he whispered.

It had taken them both a long time to get to sleep that night. But waking up the next morning tucked in his embrace, feeling warm and safe and unbelievably happy, had made the frustration worth it.

The next night, however, when he didn't pull her into his arms as he had the night before, but turned the other way, she decided a little requital was in order. She'd slid her arm around his waist from behind and slipped her hand under the edge of his tunic, where she'd skimmed light swirls over the rigid bands of his stomach. Bands that she couldn't help noticing grew tighter and tighter the lower her hand dropped. When her thumb accidentally brushed the thick hood of his manhood and he made a sharp hissing sound, she stopped.

"Privacy," she'd reminded him smugly.

Unfortunately, she hadn't counted on how the rigid, aroused feel of his body against hers would affect her. Her heart had been beating just as fast as his. It had taken her even longer to get to sleep that night. But again, waking in his arms made it all worth it.

She wasn't as sure later that night, however, when the moment he slipped under the plaid behind her, his fingers slid between her legs. He stroked her until she'd been half-crazed with desire, stopping when she'd been unable to prevent herself from making a sound. She'd almost cried out anyway—in frustration.

It had been a long, restless night.

The following night he'd come to bed late—the coward—but she was ready. The moment he drew the plaid down on top of him, she found him with her hand, circling the rigid column of velvety steel with her hand the way she'd seen him holding himself that day in the cottage. He'd fisted his hand around hers and silently shown her how to stroke him.

She'd held his gaze in the darkness as she'd brought him to the very peak of pleasure. He was holding himself so taut she thought he might win the sensual battle that had sprung up between them. But he sucked in his breath—making a sound—and she'd stopped.

After nearly a week of stroking and touching, she was in as much torment as he. She couldn't wait until they could make love again. Tomorrow night, thank goodness! Eoin said they would reach the ferry at Oban late afternoon the following day. As less than a half mile separated Gylen Castle from the mainland just south of Oban, the quick boat ride would bring her to her new home well before nightfall.

Despite the promise of pleasure awaiting her, the tormenting nights, the plodding pace of travel, and spate of rainy weather that had hit them the past few days, part of her was sad to see the journey come to an end.

She was nervous about the new life that awaited her at Kerrera. She didn't know what to expect, how she would fit in, or what would be expected of her. Gylen Castle was the unknown; on the road she could pretend things would be the same.

She was also enjoying getting to know her husband. Since she'd confronted him a week ago, Eoin had made an effort to spend more time with her—and not just at night. He rode beside her when he could, and every evening after they finished eating, he brought out the thin piece of wood that he'd etched lines in with a knife and the piles of different colored stones to teach her to play chess.

She'd picked up the rules of the game quickly enough, it was losing—rather handily—that was the difficult part to accept.

"Who would have thought a child's game could exact such a blow to the pride?" she said. "Believe it or not, until I met you, I used to think of myself as relatively clever."

He grinned. "I think your pride is strong enough to weather the blow, and it isn't cleverness standing in your way."

She lifted her brow. "Then what is it?"

"You're too impatient for the game to end. You go on attack too soon. You need to bide your time."

She lifted her brow, surprised by the insight. He was

right. She was impatient and grew bored easily. Nor was she the lie-in-wait type; she liked the straightforward challenge. She suspected a two-day-long battle over a chessboard would never be in her future.

"Is that what you do?" she asked.

He shrugged. For a man who talked about battle so much with everyone else, he completely avoided the subject with her. She hoped there wasn't a reason. She'd yet to broach the subject of the war, but maybe now was the time.

She glanced around, seeing that as in previous nights, the others were giving them space. "What will you do if war breaks out again?" she asked in a low voice.

It might have been a trick of the torchlight, but she swore he stiffened defensively. "What do you mean?"

"My father wants you to fight with him. He said your abilities would be valued by those loyal to King John."

This time she was not mistaken: his expression went rigid. There was a steely glint in his eye she'd never seen before. "My duty is to my father."

"And his is to his overlord, Alexander MacDougall, the Lord of Argyll, and to his king. Not to his kinsman," she added, referring to Bruce.

She waited for a reaction, but there was none. His expression betrayed not a hint of his thoughts. He wore the same serious, intense expression on his face that he always did when he was with everyone else. But not usually her.

"My father knows well where his duty lies, Margaret."

Hope sprang in her chest. "Does that mean you will—?"

He stood. "It means this is a pointless conversation. When the time comes—*if* the time comes—he will do what he must. As will I."

He started to walk away, but she stood and stopped him

with a hand on his arm. "Wait, why won't you talk about this with me?"

"There is nothing to discuss, and it has nothing to do with you."

"I'm your wife! Of course it has something to do with me."

He held her gaze, saying nothing but challenging all the same. She didn't understand. Why was he doing this? Why was he shutting her out? Did he not value her opinion? She might not be as smart as he was, or know how to read and write, but that didn't mean she wouldn't understand.

"I have to go," he said impatiently.

She let her hand drop, not knowing or understanding how the conversation could have gone so wrong. "Where?"

"It's my night to be on guard duty." He paused. "I won't be to bed until midmorning. Perhaps it would be best if you slept in the tent the last night?"

She was stricken. "Why are you acting like this?"

His expression changed, and once again he was the man she loved. He drew her into his arms. "Ah hell, I'm sorry. But it is your fault." She looked up at him questioningly. "You have pushed me to the edge of madness. I can't take another night of it."

He was teasing her, but only partially. Suddenly, she scowled. "You volunteered for guard duty, didn't you?"

He winced, not bothering to lie. "It's only one more night."

Or so he thought. But the next night, after they'd *finally* retired to the private chamber that had been arranged for them (his mother had insisted on showing her every room of the beautifully decorated tower house), Margaret had a surprise for him.

"Your what?"

"Shhh," she said. "Do you want the whole castle to hear? My flux. It will only be a few days."

She thought he'd find the timing amusingly ironic, but apparently he didn't. He was strangely quiet, his expression almost pained.

Her brow furrowed. "I don't exactly have much control over these things, Eoin." She grinned wickedly and slid up against him, covering him with her hand. "Besides, there is plenty of *privacy* here, and no reason for you to be quiet."

He jerked her hand away. "Damn it, Margaret. Stop it. You don't understand."

More than a little hurt by the rejection, she moved back a few steps to look at him. "Then why don't you explain it to me," she said softly.

A strange sense of doom settled around her like a thick gray mist.

He moved to the glazed window, staring out for a few minutes before turning to answer her.

"I'm leaving."

For a moment she didn't think she heard him correctly. Her heart was beating too loudly in her ears. "You are what?"

"There is something I have to do. I must leave by Saturday."

Margaret just stared at him, dumbfounded. Saturday was in two days. "When will you be back?" she managed chokingly, a ball of hot emotion seeming to have stuck in her throat.

"I don't know."

She flinched as if struck. "What do you mean, 'I don't know'? A few days? Weeks?" He didn't say anything. "Christmas?" she could barely breathe.

"I hope so."

He hoped so? There were still almost two weeks until All Saints' Day! Christmas was more than two months away. This wasn't happening. Please let someone tell her this wasn't happening. The room seemed to be swaying as if they were still on the ferry. "Where are you going?"

"I . . ." He dragged his fingers through his hair, the way he did when he was anxious or uncomfortable. "I can't explain. It's just something I have to do, all right?"

"Of course it's not all right. How could it be all right? We have been married barely over a fortnight, have not yet shared a roof, let alone a bedchamber for the night, and you are leaving me in two days, telling me nothing about where you are going, what you are doing, and how long you will be gone, and it's supposed to be 'all right'?" Hearing the rising hysteria in her voice, she forced herself to try to calm. But how could she be calm? How could he do this to her? "How long have you known about this?"

He had the shame to look away. "Since the day before we left Stirling."

Her chest stabbed. "And you didn't think to tell me?"

"I intended to, damn it, just not like this."

"Then when? After you'd made love to me, until I was too exhausted to argue?" She gasped, her eyes widening at his guilty expression. "Good God, that's exactly what you intended, wasn't it?"

"Ah hell, Maggie, I know I should have said something earlier. But I knew you'd be upset, and . . ."

She straightened her spine, her anger the only thing that kept her from collapsing into a ball and sobbing. "And you thought it would be easier this way."

"Nay, that isn't what I was going to say. You were so happy. I didn't want to do anything to ruin that."

"And you thought this would be better?" He didn't say anything. She stared at him. "Please don't do this. Don't go."

"I have to."

"Then wait a few more days. At least give me that."

"I can't. I'm late already."

He reached for her, and for the first time, she flinched from him. Also for the first time, she didn't want him to touch her. "Then go, Eoin. Just go."

And to her utter despair and misery, two days later he did exactly that.

11

CHRISTMAS CAME and went. But Eoin was hopeful he'd be able to leave the Isle of Skye, where he'd been training with the other elite warriors recruited for Bruce's secret guard, and return to Margaret for a few days in January.

When he'd ridden away from her all those weeks ago, he'd had his anger to hold on to. For two days he'd tried to explain to her that this was what he did. He was a warrior. He went where and when his chief told him to. But she refused to listen to any explanations. When it became clear that he would not delay or change his plans—or explain them—she'd turned as cold as ice and would barely even look at him.

He'd expected tears and pleading, but maybe he should have known better. Margaret MacDowell might not be as refined and sophisticated as the noblewomen he knew, but she had the steel in her spine and iron in her blood of royal ancestors and generations of the proud Celtic chiefs who'd come before her.

Frustration at the situation, and her reaction, had turned to anger. But over the long weeks of training, including almost two weeks of hell that had been aptly named "Perdition," that anger turned to guilt. The hurt in her eyes—the look of betrayal—haunted him. He couldn't escape the feeling that each day they were apart, he was losing her more and more.

And then there were the tortured dreams of her turning to another man in his absence—Fin, his brothers, even the infamous Tristan MacCan whom he'd never met. She'd only let MacCan kiss her, damn it . . . hadn't she? It got so bad he didn't even want to close his eyes to sleep.

He'd heard nothing from his wife since the day he left. He'd written to her, but either she'd refused to avail herself of his father's clerk or had decided to ignore him. Only the occasional mention in the missives from his father or mother did he have word of her. "Margaret traveled to Oban again on Monday—borrowing your father's skiff without permission." He could hear his mother's disapproval all the way to Skye. It grew worse with, "Mathilda follows her all over the Isle." His sixteen-year-old sister was something of an imp; he supposed it wasn't surprising that she'd taken a liking to her new sister-in-law. It also wasn't surprising that his mother didn't approve.

No communication coupled with the frequent mention of trips to Oban to help the nuns at the convent (Margaret?) played on every doubt and fear he had in his head. But that was where he kept it.

Some of the other guardsmen, especially Erik MacSorley (whose personality reminded him quite a bit of Margaret's) and Eoin's partner, Ewen Lamont, were curious about his wife. But other than the fact that she was a MacDowell, from which they probably drew their own conclusions, he refused to speak of her. It wasn't just that he didn't want to give them a reason not to trust him—Bruce's caution around him was difficult enough—but how the hell could Eoin explain how a marriage could work between them, when he didn't even know himself?

By the end of Hogmanay, he was chomping at the bit to go home. But everything changed when Christina MacLeod was captured by the English and Tor MacLeod, the leader of the secret guard, launched an attack on the English garrison at Dumfries Castle to get her back.

It was Eoin's first opportunity to prove his place among the elite warriors, and his plan had been a resounding success.

It had also set off a chain of events no one could have seen coming. Within a month of freeing Christina MacLeod and taking the castle, John "The Red" Comyn, the Lord of Badenoch, was dead at Bruce's hand, and his kinsman had launched a bid for the throne.

After weeks of gathering support, and putting down skirmishes with Comyn supporters, by early March—March, damn it!—preparations were under way for Bruce's coronation in Scone. Edward of England had already ordered the arrest of Bruce for the slaying of Comyn, but every one of Bruce's men knew that the coronation would be an act of rebellion that would bring Edward and his army to their doorstep once more.

War was coming, and Eoin knew that if he didn't go home now, it could be months before he had another chance.

The problem was Bruce was refusing to give him leave. Eoin could not be spared this close to the coronation. And if the MacDougalls had noted his absence and suspected his involvement with Bruce, a trip to Kerrera in Lorn could be dangerous as well.

Eoin broke his silence where his wife was concerned

and took his case to the one man who might be able to change Bruce's mind.

There weren't many men who gave Eoin pause, but Tor MacLeod was one of them. Known as the greatest swordsman in Scotland—and probably the fiercest—he was as tall as Eoin with six years of added muscle on him, every pound of it earned on the battlefield.

If there was anyone more difficult to read than Eoin, it was MacLeod. As Eoin stood across the table from the proud island chief and presented his case, it was impossible to know what the other man was thinking.

"We did not part on the best of terms," Eoin explained. "My wife is young—only eighteen—and we'd been married less than three weeks before I left. A week is all I am asking. I will return before we leave for Scone."

"Do you intend to fly? It would take at least four or five days of hard riding to reach Oban from here."

They'd been at Bruce's Lochmaben Castle since the rescue of Christina MacLeod from Dumfries Castle.

"I'll find a ship."

"You'll also find the English navy," MacLeod said bluntly. "They are patrolling up and down the coast to Ayr."

Eoin's mouth clenched. "I'm an Islander—I'll manage."

MacLeod eyed him carefully. "This is that important to you?"

"It is." *She* is.

MacLeod seemed to understand—maybe better than he'd realized. Chief, too, had a young wife himself whom he'd nearly lost.

"I'll see what I can do."

Margaret's stomach dropped with dread as her small skiff drew closer to shore, and she made out the familiar form of the man waiting for her. After lowering the sail, she let the current take her safely into the dock, but she wished she could turn around.

While a couple of lads helped her with the moorings, Fin stood at the foot of the rocky path that led up to the castle watching. She couldn't avoid him, and her heart beat with not a small amount of trepidation as she walked toward him.

She had no reason to be frightened of him, and yet she couldn't deny that for the first time in her life a man made her uncomfortable, and yes, a little scared. She'd tried—truly she had—but in the five months since Eoin had abandoned her on this miserable rock, she could not force herself to like Fin MacFinnon.

He'd done nothing specific she could point to—maybe it would be easier if he had—but there was something in his eyes when he looked at her that made her skin crawl. Something that made her feel that he was just biding his time . . . waiting. For what she didn't know. She couldn't tell whether he hated her or lusted for her—maybe both.

He seemed to be always there, lurking in the shadows of the corridors, dark corners of the stables or outbuildings, and now, it seemed, by rocky cliff sides. She knew it was no accident that he stood in the perfect place to block her path, where she could not get around him without risking a fall down the rocks.

"Where were you?" he demanded.

Despite the trepidation thumping in her chest, she refused to let him intimidate her. He wouldn't dare to hurt her physically. She hoped. "It's none of your business."

He took her by the arm and drew her toward him. To anyone watching it would look like he was preparing to guide her up the path by the rocks. But his fingers gripped her just a little too hard, and he pulled her in just a little too close.

"I'm making it my business. Do you expect me to believe you really help the *nuns* at the convent?"

His gaze fell to her breasts as if their size somehow explained his reasoning.

Her heart was thumping in her throat now. "I don't care what you believe, it's the truth." Mostly. It was actually the nuns who were helping her. "How dare you touch me. Let go of me or . . ."

She looked to the men at the dock, but they were busy with the boat and turned in the other direction. As she was sure Fin knew. He wouldn't have touched her otherwise. Not that the men would come to her rescue. The entire isle seemed to look on her with suspicion and distrust.

She didn't belong here. She would never belong here. It was nothing like home. Everything she did was met with censure. She couldn't ride, sail, or walk anywhere without someone wondering where she was going or why she wasn't accompanied. There were no more challenges, no more whisky (apparently a man's drink), and no more bawdy jests with her brothers. What she wore, how she ate, even how she prayed—or rather how often she prayed—were all up for scrutiny.

God, how she hated it.

"Or what?" Fin sneered, but at least he dropped her arm. "Who are you going to run to? Lady Rignach? The laird? I think they'll be more interested in where you went after the convent, and what is in the purse at your waist."

She gaped at him in shock. "You were spying on me!"

He smiled. "I'm only doing my duty. You are my responsibility. Eoin left you to me."

Margaret suspected the wording was intentional, and it made her heart beat even faster.

Of all the grievances she had with her husband—and there were many—perhaps that was the worst. He'd made Fin swear to watch over her and protect her with his life. In other words, he'd put Fin in the position to torment her.

"I wonder what he'd make of his wife gallivanting all over town with another man, and then disappearing for hours together into a building."

Margaret's teeth were gritted together so hard with outrage she could barely get the words out. "With a man of the cloth into the rectory!"

The young priest had been kind enough to let her use his paints.

Fin gave a harsh laugh. "It would hardly be the first time a priest didn't hold to his vows."

Margaret had had enough. "I owe you no explanation. If my husband has questions when he returns he can ask me himself."

"After five months, I think it's safe to say your husband has found more important things to keep him busy."

The words were cruel and hurtful—especially because they were true—but something in Fin's voice told her that she wasn't the only one feeling the sting. Fin, too, was in the dark about Eoin's activities, and on that one point maybe they could commiserate.

Five months. How could Eoin have left her for five months with barely a word? The two short notes she'd received from him, which the nuns had been kind enough to read to her, had offered no explanation or excuse, only vague words of regret for how "soon they'd had to part," and even more vague promises that he would return to her "as soon as he could." Until then he hoped she would "make an effort" to "fit in" around Gylen with his mother's help.

Obviously Lady Rignach had been voicing her complaints.

Maybe if Margaret could have done so on her own, she would have responded. Maybe she would have poured out her misery, her anger, and her broken heart in dark blotches of ink all over that wretched piece of parchment.

But she would not ask the nuns to write about how much she hated it here. How she would never "fit in." How everyone treated her like a pariah so she had to escape to Oban to find someone to help her. How she had hoped to keep busy as she had at Garthland by helping with the household, but how his mother had made it very clear that her help was not needed or wanted.

Margaret still felt a pang at that disappointment. She might not know how to read or write, or how to dress or act like a noblewoman, but she knew how to run a castle, and she'd wanted him to see that. To know that he hadn't married an unaccomplished, backward barbarian, but a wife of whom he could be proud.

She'd tell him how she'd never felt so useless in her life. How the only thing that made his mother and Marjory's disdain about her "uncouth" upbringing and the endless comparisons to the saintly Lady Barbara bearable was Tilda. His youngest sister was the only person on the isle who didn't think he'd made a mistake—including her.

And that's what she would tell him last. How she feared she'd made a mistake. How all the happiness and love she'd felt for him in that cottage seemed very far away. How she looked around and wondered how she'd come to be here and how she could escape. How desperately she missed her home and being around people who actually *liked* her and weren't ashamed of her. How she didn't want to be a mistake anymore.

To say anything else to him would have been a lie.

So as the nuns patiently worked with her on her lettering, every so often asking if she wanted to try to respond to her husband's missive, Margaret declined. The rudimentary reading and writing skills she'd painstakingly acquired in the past few months—she wouldn't embarrass him with her lack of education—were no match for the maelstrom of emotion waiting to be unleashed when—if—he ever returned.

"Maybe you're right," she said to Fin. "Now, if you'll excuse me, I need to change before the evening meal."

God knows, Lady Rignach would not approve of her simple wool kirtle. But Margaret hadn't wanted to risk paint getting on one of her new gowns.

She shouldn't have been surprised when the day after Eoin left his mother had the dressmaker from Oban measuring her for new chemises, cottes, surcoats, cloaks—and veils, lots of them. Lady Rignach must have given instructions to Eoin's father as well, because when the MacLean chief arrived at Gylen Castle with Eoin's two brothers a few weeks after Eoin had left, his father was laden down with even finer cloth, fur trims, and embroidery from Edinburgh.

Fin let her pass with only a mocking bow but followed closely after her. At first she attributed the strange buzz that ran down her neck as they entered the bailey to him. But it was a different kind of awareness. One that she hadn't experienced in so long, she'd forgotten it.

She noticed a crowd of people standing near the gate. That was when Tilda saw her. The girl was the only bright spot in these past months. She was sweet and kind and didn't care that Margaret was a "wild" MacDowell.

"Oh, Maggie, there you are. I was looking for you everywhere, look who's . . ."

Margaret didn't hear the rest of her words, for at that moment a man stepped out of the crowd, and she froze.

He was dusty, grimy, more grizzled than she'd ever seen him, with a jaw thick with whiskers and hair down to his shoulders, and he seemed to have put on a good stone of muscle, but when those intense blue eyes riveted on hers, she knew him in an instant.

All the emotion, all the pain, all the misery of the past five months caught up with her in one lost heartbeat. Her chest squeezed. Her throat tightened. Her eyes swelled with heat. She made a sound that was a cry of half-pain, half-relief, and ran.

The next moment she was in his arms. Eoin was holding her, burying his face in her veil, murmuring soothing words against her ear, and then his mouth was on hers.

∞

Eoin would never forget the fear and uncertainty of the moment when his wife had first seen him and seemed to turn to stone. Nor would he forget the relief and happiness he'd felt when she launched herself into his arms an agonizing few moments later.

He wished he could forget what came next. How he'd started kissing her right there in the courtyard—heedless of the crowd around them, which included his mother and sisters, damn it!—and then, as if that wasn't bad enough, how he'd lifted her up and carried her to their bedchamber in the middle of the damned day.

No one in that bailey had seen what had come next, but he was sure every one of them had guessed. He'd barely taken time to remove his weapons and armor before he'd followed her down on the bed and made love to her with five months of built-up passion.

It hadn't been pretty. It had been hurried and frenzied and over far too quickly—although he had made sure she found her pleasure first. But it had been every bit as powerful as he remembered.

And maybe it had been just what they'd needed. A moment of physical connection before the questions and recriminations that his return would inevitably bring started to fly.

She'd collapsed in a heap on his chest and had remained quiet since. Her cheek rested against his shirt, but her face was turned away from him, and all he could see were the silky plaits of long red hair coiled neatly at the top of her head. She'd been wearing a veil when he'd first seen her, and it had taken him a moment to recognize her without the wild waves of vivid red that had tumbled over her shoulders like a silken cloud.

"Are you all right?" he asked.

She didn't answer for a long time. Finally, she lifted off his chest and out of his embrace to a sitting position where she could look down at him. Too late he remembered the words of their last conversation.

"No, Eoin, I'm not 'all right.' I haven't been all right since the day you left." Her golden eyes held his steadily. He'd forgotten the sensual tilt and catlike brilliance. How just the feel of those eyes on him could make his skin heat and blood race through his veins. "But if you are referring to the pleasure you just gave my body, then yes, I think I shall recover."

There wasn't one note of teasing in her voice, one wicked twinkle in her eye, or one naughty curve of her beautiful red mouth.

He hadn't expected to be greeted by the smiling, light-hearted, mischievous girl who'd stormed into the Great Hall of Stirling Castle—and into his life—five months ago, taking it over like a marauding pirate. But neither had he expected this serious, subdued young woman.

What had he done to her?

"I'm not sure I will," he said wryly. He took her hand, amazed at how soft and delicate it looked in his, and brought it to his mouth. "It's been too long."

"Has it?"

He frowned. "What's that supposed to mean?"

She shrugged, looking away. "I don't know. Something felt different."

Eoin swore inwardly, glad she couldn't see the guilt on his face. He hadn't even realized what he was doing until he pulled out at the last second. He couldn't believe he'd actually had the presence of mind to do so. But he knew it was the right thing. As much as he would like to leave her with his child, he knew it wouldn't be fair to her, knowing he might not survive to see it born.

But he knew that wasn't what she was alluding to. He reached up to cup her chin and turn her face to his. "I haven't looked at another woman since the day I met you, Maggie. There is, and has been, only you."

She held his gaze and must have been satisfied by what she saw there because she switched the subject. "You look different."

Unconsciously, he rubbed his jaw which hadn't seen a

razor in weeks. He knew he looked like hell—he'd been through it to get to her. "I didn't exactly have time to wash up after I saw you."

The girl he'd first met wouldn't have been able to resist teasing him about his eagerness and uncharacteristic public display, but she ignored it. "How did you arrive? I didn't see a boat down by the dock."

He hadn't wanted to draw that much attention to his presence. The ship and men who'd sailed with him were waiting in an inlet on the west side of Kerrera. MacLeod had come through for him, all right: he'd arranged to have the best seafarer in Scotland bring Eoin home. Without MacSorley's skills, Eoin would probably be dead—either from the English who'd chased them halfway around Ireland or from the storm that at first almost capsized them, and then forced them to take shelter on a small island for nearly two days until it passed.

The few days that he'd hoped for had been whittled down to less than twenty-four hours. How was he going to make her understand in under a day?

"I came in on the other side of the isle." Hoping to cut off more questions, he asked, "Is that where you were? Down at the dock? My mother said you go to Oban a few times a week to help the nuns at the convent?"

She stared at him as if trying to gauge whether there was something behind the question. There wasn't—except maybe curiosity.

"If you want to know what I've been doing for five months, Eoin—*five months*—just ask me. Because that is exactly what I want to know from you."

Eoin swore. Damn Bruce to hell for making him agree to that vow!

He would tell her what he could. She would learn part of the truth soon enough, when news of the coronation spread. "I will do my best to answer your questions, and I know we have much to talk about, but let me bathe and eat something first."

He also knew that his father, brothers, and Fin would be anxious for a report. When the call to battle came from Bruce, they would answer.

He could tell she wanted to argue, but she took pity on him. He must look more beaten up by the past few days than he realized. "Now that you are home, I suppose there is time. But I will expect answers."

He didn't know what he was looking forward to less: telling her he was leaving again or telling her why.

12

"IT WAS SO romantic—although I thought my mother was going to faint right there, she turned so red." Tilda giggled beside her on the bench. Margaret knew she belonged in the middle of the *hie burde* next to her husband, but she'd taken her usual seat below the high table beside Tilda instead. She thought it would be easier to sit next to someone she could talk to rather than someone she couldn't. His mother and father were only too happy to accept her offer to have their son to themselves, without their regrettable daughter-in-law in the way.

But for once Margaret wasn't in the mood for Tilda's cheerful chatter. She was too anxious about the coming conversation, and her husband's attempt to explain the inexplicable. She needed answers. But more important, she needed him to prove to her that she hadn't made the biggest mistake in her life.

She glanced down the table, and was glad to see that after the bath, shave, and meal, the dark circles under his eyes and the lines of weariness etched on his face had faded. But there was still something different about him—other than the added bulk and what looked to be one or two new scars on his face. He looked harder somehow. Fiercer. Darker. Even more intense than she remembered. Different from the man she'd married.

Tilda hadn't noticed her unusual quietness. She shook her pretty golden brown head. She had the same coloring as Eoin and Neil. The two other siblings, Marjory and Donald, were darker like their mother. "I've never seen Eoin do anything like that," she said. "I knew he must love you very much. He would have to turn his head away from the battlefield or one of those boring old folios for more than a few minutes. I hope one day I will marry a man that will take one look at me and carry me up to the bedchamber." She sighed dramatically. "You are so lucky."

Lucky? Margaret was lucky she wasn't drinking her sweet wine (the syrupy wernage was a suitable lady's beverage) or it might have been "uncouthly" spattered all over the pretty linen tablecloth. She mumbled something intelligible in response, which must have satisfied Tilda, because she resumed her soliloquy on the "romantic" events of earlier.

Margaret wished she could see it the same way as Tilda. But to her, the frenzied lovemaking had seemed more a cry of desperation and a release of pent-up emotion and pain than a romantic expression of love.

She would never deny the passion she felt for him, but lust wasn't romance. Romance wasn't sharing a bed, it was sharing a life. It was trusting someone. Having someone to share your thoughts. Knowing that the person lying next to you would do anything for you because you would do the same for them.

It wasn't disappearing for five months without explanation. It wasn't being kept in the dark. And it wasn't being left alone and miserable among people who thought you weren't good enough or smart enough for the "brilliant" young warrior with such a promising future.

Perhaps some of that misery showed on her face. Eoin caught her eye, said something to his father, and stood. Lady Rignach looked in her direction, and for once Margaret thought she detected sympathy.

She discovered why a short while later. Margaret sat on the edge of the bed, while the man she'd given her heart to stood before her and stomped all over it.

He calmly explained that he'd been at Lochmaben in Dumfries with the Earl of Carrick and turned her world upside down.

"But you said you were doing something for your father."

"I was," he said. "Am. Bruce is the rightful king of Scotland. My father believes that as much as I do."

"Rightful king of Scotland? Only because he rid himself of his rival by killing him in a church!" The news of the Lord of Badenoch's murder last month had spread across Scotland like wildfire. She'd been shocked—horrified—and sad for his son. John Comyn was too young to have such a weight on his shoulders. But ironically she'd thought the murderous act would help Eoin make the decision to fight *with* her clan. Never had she imagined Eoin . . . *Oh God!* "Please tell me you had nothing to do with it."

His mouth tightened. "I was not there when it happened. It was regrettable, but Bruce was provoked."

Margaret couldn't believe this was happening. The nightmare was only getting worse. Her absent husband had come home, but he'd done so in full-fledged rebellion. He'd chosen to fight not only against her family, but against the most powerful man in Christendom. How could he have kept this from her?

"You can't do this, Eoin. You have to reconsider. Think of what happened to Wallace. King Edward will do far worse to Robert Bruce—a man whom he trusted—and his followers. You will be hunted like a dog. And what of my family? There will be a civil war, and my father will never forgive you if you fight with Comyn's murderer. I thought you loved me. How can you choose Bruce over our marriage?"

He frowned. "This has nothing to do with you or our marriage. My decision was made long before I ever met you."

She stared at him wide-eyed. "But I thought . . . We discussed . . ." She looked up at him. "You let me think you would consider fighting with my family."

He shook his head. "You let yourself think that. I told you I didn't want to talk about it."

Was that supposed to be some kind of excuse? "So I'm to have no say in the matter? You will make enemies of my family, put your life at risk, and I'm allowed no choice?"

"You made your choice when you agreed to become my wife." He eased the harshness of his words by kneeling down before her and taking her icy hands in his. Big and warm, with more calluses than she remembered, they seemed to swallow hers up. "I know this is difficult for you, and I never wanted to hurt you, but you are my wife. Your loyalty belongs to me now."

Her heart wrenched in her chest, as if it were being twisted in two different directions.

But he was right. No matter how much she didn't want to hear it, she had made her choice when she married him. But she never realized what she would have to give up. With no discussion and no say.

"I love my family. You can't expect me just to forget them."

He shook his head. "I would never ask that of you. But I am asking for your support and loyalty. I'm asking for you to trust that I know what I'm doing. I truly believe this is the best thing for Scotland."

"More war is the best thing?"

"If it sees Scotland's rightful king on the throne and an end to Edward's overlordship."

"And you think Robert Bruce is that rightful king?" Half of Scotland—including her clan—would disagree.

"I do. I'm not asking you to believe in him, I'm asking you to believe in me."

Her heart squeezed. "I do."

The politics weren't what mattered to her, it was keeping all those she loved alive.

"I didn't know it would happen like this," he said in earnest. "I thought we'd have more time together before war broke out. Believe me, if I didn't have to leave—"

He stopped suddenly, as if realizing what he'd just said.

"Leave?" she repeated thinly, through lungs that had just had all the air sucked out of them.

His expression turned grim. "Tomorrow. I'd hoped to have longer, but we were unavoidably delayed. We will be racing across Scotland as it is to make it in time."

She was too shocked to question him about "we." She shook her head. "No." She shook her head furiously, panic rising in her chest. "You can't go. You can't leave me here alone."

"You won't be alone, my mother—"

"Your mother despises me. She and Marjory can barely stand to be in the same room with me. You don't understand how horrible it's been since you left. Everyone hates me here."

He looked genuinely taken aback. "I know it must be

difficult adjusting to a new home, and it might seem that way, but—"

"Don't tell me I'm exaggerating or imagining things, I'm not. They think I'm some kind of wicked strumpet who forced you into marrying me."

The circumstances of their marriage unfortunately had followed them to Kerrera—as had the disparaging stories of her clan and the fair "maid" of Galloway.

He frowned, clearly taken aback. "If someone has said something to offend you . . ."

"No one has said a thing. It's the way they look at me. The way they stop talking as soon as I come into the room. I'm a MacDowell, Eoin. To them I might as well be heathen dancing naked around the fires of Beltane. I can't even go to a convent without gossip and speculation. Half the people here, including your mother, think I'm doing something illicit. Do you know that Fin followed me today? He practically accused me of seducing a priest!"

Eoin frowned. "I'm sure you misunderstood. Fin told me what happened. He was only doing what I asked him to do. You shouldn't be going back and forth to Oban by yourself."

Margaret tried to rein in her temper, but it was quickly slipping through her fingers. "I did not misunderstand. I'm sorry, but I cannot like him, Eoin. I've tried, but there is something about your foster brother . . . he makes me nervous."

His eyes flared with the first real sign of anger. "If Fin has said something or done anything to hurt you, I'll kill him. Damn it, I thought that business with the race was forgotten. But if he's holding a grudge . . ."

"It's not like that. He hasn't done or said anything. I just don't trust him."

"He's my best friend, Maggie. I've known him since I was seven. I'd trust him with my life."

"And yet you told him nothing about where you were going either."

His mouth fell in a hard, grim line; he clearly wasn't happy to have that pointed out.

He was hiding something. She'd known it, and now she had proof.

"I will talk to him. But you do not need to worry about Fin."

"Why?"

"He will be leaving with my father and brothers as soon as war breaks out."

The look of relief on her face told him that maybe there was more than a young girl's loneliness and penchant for hyperbole at work.

Damn Fin to hell. Eoin suspected his foster brother had just as little regard for his wife as she did him. Maybe it had been a bad idea to have Fin watch over her, but he'd hoped they could become friends.

What a mess. Eoin had never felt so helpless in his life. Exaggerated or not—people didn't hate her, they just didn't know her—he could not deny that Margaret was miserable and believed it to be true.

He hated that he hadn't been here for her to help ease the transition. Hated that she'd had to go through her first few months at Gylen alone. But what the hell was he supposed to do? It was an impossible situation. He shouldn't even be here right now.

He took a chance and got up off his knees to sit beside her on the bed. When she didn't shirk away from him, he put his arm around her and drew her against him. She melted into his chest, wrapping her arm around his waist, and he felt the first flicker of hope.

"I wish I could make it easier for you," he said. "Tell me what I can do to make it better."

She looked up at him, her beautiful eyes glassy. "Don't go."

He was surprised how much the soft plea ate at him, and how much he wished he could stay with her. "If I didn't absolutely have to go, I wouldn't. But I'm needed."

"It's more than that though, isn't it," she accused. "You *want* to go."

The lass was too perceptive. "I would stay here with you right now if I could, but if you are asking whether this is something I want to do the answer is yes. You knew who I was when you married me. I'm a warrior, Maggie. Warriors fight. And this opportunity—" He stopped, realizing he was treading too close to the truth. "This is something I've been preparing for my whole life. There will be challenges and the chance to do something different—the chance to make a difference."

"So you are choosing war over me?"

Damn it, that wasn't what he was doing at all. It didn't have to be an either-or—not unless she made it that way. "I'm not choosing anything. What would you have me do? Ignore my duty? Would you ask your father or brothers to do the same? Would your mother have demanded your father stay with her rather than fight for King John?"

He could see the answer shimmering angrily in her eyes.

He took her chin, tilting it toward his. "Do you love me, Maggie?"

He didn't expect her to hesitate. When she did, he realized how close he was to losing her, his gut checked hard. Hell, it scared the shite out of him.

"Aye," she said finally.

"Then don't give up on me. I know it's been difficult for you, but if you could just try a little longer, I know you'll win them over." He smiled wryly. "Don't tell me all these new gowns and veils have made you soft."

A furrow appeared between her finely etched brows. "Soft?"

He shrugged. "I thought you didn't care what people said and would not be defeated so easily. What happened to the girl who donned lads clothing and bested one of the best horsemen I know in a race? Was all that MacDowell pride a bunch of bluster?"

He felt like he'd hung the damned moon when one corner of her mouth lifted. "Are you suggesting I wear breeches to break my fast tomorrow morning?"

He laughed. "Good God, no. I wouldn't want my mother to expire of shock." He sobered a little. "I know she can be difficult at times, but once you get to know her, you'll see that she just wants the best for my brothers and sisters and me."

"Which is exactly the problem."

"You are the best for me. She just hasn't realized it yet."

She smiled, and it wasn't like he'd hung the moon—it was like he'd hung the sun. Warmth spread over him like a bright summer day. *This* was why he loved her. She was fun and lighthearted, outrageous, knew how to make him laugh, and reminded him that not everything was the life-or-death stakes of war. This was why he needed her in his life. She was the light in a world that sometimes became too dark. The past months of doing—thinking—nothing but battle fell away.

"Really?"

"Really."

And he set about proving it to her. Slowly. With a kiss that told her exactly how much she meant to him. They had all night, and he was going to make damn sure she knew how much he loved her. He didn't want to think about how long this might have to last.

Following his lead, she responded to the long, slow strokes of his tongue with a deft tenderness of her own that made his chest ache. He'd never imagined a kiss could be filled with so much emotion—or express so much feeling. But he felt the longing, her desire, and love that matched his own, with every sigh, every stroke, and every soft caress.

When he'd finished worshipping her mouth with his lips and tongue, he went on to worship the rest of her. He kissed her jaw, her throat, the tender place below her ear, and finally, once he'd paused long enough to remove her clothes, the berry-pink tips of her nipples. Aye, he took plenty of time with those, circling his tongue around the puckered edges, flicking the rigid points, and sucking them deep into his mouth until she squirmed and moaned.

She tried to undo his surcoat, but he stopped her. "Not yet, sweetheart. If you touch me, it will be over too soon. I want to give you pleasure. Let me do this."

She nodded, and he went on exploring. Her body was a fantasy, and he took his time savoring every cock-hardening inch of it. He couldn't get enough. She was so soft and sweet, her skin dissolving against his mouth like honey. She tasted so damned good he wanted to taste all of her. He wanted to give her the kind of pleasure he'd never given another woman before. He wanted to put his mouth between her legs, slide his tongue inside her, and feel her come apart against his lips. And if the way she was pressing her hips against him was any indication, she was close.

He skimmed his hand over the slender curve of her waist to her hip. "Tell me what you want, Maggie."

Her half-lidded eyes met his in a sensual haze of passion so dark and deep it threatened to drag him under. God, she was beautiful. He'd taken the time to remove not just her veil this time, but the pins from her plaits, and her hair spread over the pillow behind her head like a fiery blaze.

"You. I want you, Eoin. Inside me."

A fierce swell of satisfaction surged through him; he loved the boldness with which she told him what she wanted. There was no false maidenly modesty with Margaret.

He brushed his fingers between her legs, feeling the silky dampness sliding between his fingers like warm honey. "Do you want my hands, my cock, or maybe my mouth?"

She gasped, the haze clearing from her eyes as they met his. She was clearly shocked, but she was also clearly aroused by the idea, if the fresh rush of dampness spreading through his fingers meant anything. So warm and silky. "Should I kiss you right here?" She gasped again when he pressed against her mound. "Should I slide my tongue inside you like this?" She cried out when his finger plunged and circled. "Shall I do that, Maggie?"

She was no longer looking at him. Her eyes were closed, her head moving side to side on the pillow. "Yes. Oh God, please, yes."

He gave her what she wanted. What her body was weeping for. But he took his time, teasing out every sensation, every drop of pleasure, as he kissed a slow trail down her stomach.

When he reached the delicate place between her legs, he lifted her hips, wrapped her legs around his neck, and brushed feathery kisses along the inside of her thighs until she started to shake. Finally, he nuzzled her softly with his mouth, applying the lightest amount of pressure where he sensed she needed it most. Only when her thighs started to tighten and her heels dug into his back did he give her the pressure she wanted. Gently at first, and then harder as her pleasure peaked. As her body started to quiver and contract.

She tasted so good he couldn't get enough. His tongue plunged deeper and deeper, his mouth sucked harder, and finally he had his reward when he felt the hard spasms of her release against his lips.

But he gave no quarter, bringing her to the peak again and again. All through the night and following day, in between short periods of rest and food, he made love to her—with his hands, his mouth, and his cock. The only time reality intruded was when he removed his shirt, and she noticed the bandage he'd wrapped around his arm to cover the new tattoo that he must hide from her, and when he slid out and moved between her legs instead of inside her as he took his release.

Shortly before he had to go, he woke her for the final time. She looked like a debauched angel, with the sheets snaked around her bare limbs, her fiery hair streaming around her shoulders, and her skin rosy—all over—from the scrape of his beard, and was clearly exhausted, but he didn't have time to wait. God knew how long they would be apart, and now that she knew pleasure, he had to make sure she knew how to find it without him.

Taking her hand, he moved it between her legs and told her what he wanted her to do.

Her eyes widened. She shook her head and tried to pull her hand away. "I couldn't." She blushed. "It's wrong."

"It's not wrong," he said firmly, keeping her hand where he wanted it. "I want you to think of me. Pretend it's my hand that is touching you. My fingers that are stroking you." Gently, he moved her fingers under his, showing her what he wanted. "That's what I'll be thinking about."

She looked surprised—and maybe a little intrigued. "You will?"

He nodded. "It will drive me crazy thinking about you touching yourself. Please, sweetheart, let me watch. Give me something to remember."

Slowly, he removed his hand.

She stared at him self-consciously, a soft blush staining her cheeks. "I don't know what to do."

"Whatever feels good. Close your eyes." She did as he bid and he nearly groaned at the first tentative strokes of her dainty fingers against those pretty pink lips. He only realized that he'd taken himself in his own hand when she opened her eyes, and her gaze followed him there.

Slowly, he started to stroke himself, matching the rhythm of the tentative fingers moving between her legs. "That's it, sweetheart. A little faster now. Rub yourself a little harder." He tightened his own grip and started to pump faster. "God, doesn't that feel good? Look what you are doing to me." He was big, red, and straining in his fist. "Are you wet yet? Are those soft pink lips quivering?"

He was rewarded with a soft moan and the gradual lowering of her lids as the heavy veil of desire began to descend. He felt it, too, the erotic intimacy of the moment wrapping around him. He wove the sultry web tighter, talking her through every moment of the awakening as she took control of her desire—as he gave her the power of knowing her own pleasure.

"When you close your eyes, I want you to remember how my mouth felt on you. How my tongue felt inside you." The strokes were intensifying now. Her body was straining toward release, her back arching, her hips grinding hard against her hand. "Think of my hand on your breast." He groaned as her hand followed his unconscious bidding, cupping her own breast and squeezing. "Pinch your nipple, sweetheart. Oh God, just like that." He felt the pressure at the base of his spine and couldn't hold back. His teeth clamped down as his arse clenched and the muscles in his stomach went rigid. "I'm going to come. Oh God, Maggie, I'm going to come."

He felt the first spurt right as she broke apart. She shattered right alongside him, her body contracted in spasms that matched his own.

When it was over he took her in his arms and held her until the sunlight streaming through the shutters softened.

Slipping out of bed, he started to put on his clothes.

She rolled onto her side to watch him, bringing the bedsheet up to tuck under her chin. She didn't say anything. She didn't need to. Her eyes swam with a heart-wrenching combination of longing and despair.

By the time he'd finished strapping on his armor, the guilt was so intense it felt like a rock was sitting on his chest. Damn it to hell, why did this have to be so damned hard? Why couldn't they have had more time?

He bent down to give her one last kiss. For a moment her arms latched around his neck and held so tightly he didn't know if she'd let him go. But she did.

He smoothed a tear that slid from the corner of her eye, wishing it were as easy to erase the acid eating its way through his chest. He tipped her chin to look at him. "I'll be back as soon as I am able."

She was fighting to control her emotions and could only manage a nod.

God's blood, how could he leave her like this? "It will get better, Maggie. Trust me. Just give it a chance. Promise me you'll try. Can you do that for me?"

"I'll try," she whispered. "If you promise to come back to me. No matter what happens, just come back to me."

It was a promise they both knew he could not make. God and the battlefield might have other ideas. "I will do everything in my power to return to you as soon as I am able."

It was the best he could do, and she seemed to understand that. With one last glance that would carry him through the long months ahead, he left.

13

MARGARET TRIED. The first few weeks after Eoin left were harder than anything that had come before. The relief and joy of seeing him, however briefly, made the contrast of when he was gone even sharper. All the love that she'd felt for her new husband had come rushing back in a torrential wave, and his departure had left her feeling crushed by it all over again. But she'd given him her promise and faced the clansmen of Kerrera with renewed determination to win them over.

She smiled in the face of their rudeness, pretended she didn't hear the whispers, and made an effort to be helpful and friendly. She made sure to wear a veil wherever she went, she held her opinion at meals, even when the conversation turned to the war and the bold-faced lies about her clan and its allies threatened to choke her, and she didn't argue when Lady Rignach suggested she take a guard to accompany her when she rode around the isle or traveled by skiff to Oban.

She even tried to enjoy embroidery, joining Marjory, Tilda, Lady Rignach, and some of her attendants in the afternoons to work on the MacLean banner that would accompany the men into battle. But when she noticed the tiny holes in the fabric in the sections where she worked and realized that many of her stitches were being taken out at night and restitched, she used the afternoons instead to finish the project that had kept her busy during those first five months. But the last piece had been carved, the paint had been applied, and the chess set that she'd made as a gift for her husband sat gathering dust on a table waiting for his return—much like herself.

But nothing she did could chip through the wall of prejudice against her. She was a "wild, wicked" MacDowell. An outsider—and worse, after war broke out and her family allied with the Comyns and Edward of England against Robert Bruce, she was the enemy. To disdain, distrust, and contempt, she could now add hatred.

Margaret spent more and more time in Oban. She would never be a scholar like her husband, but she was no longer illiterate. She could read a smattering of Gaelic and French and even a few words of English and Latin. Her writing was no doubt crude by Lady Rignach and Marjory's standards, but she could compose a simple note.

What impressed the nuns, however, wasn't her reading and writing, but her memory and facility with numbers— skills that she'd honed when her father had left her in charge. When she'd overheard one of the tradesmen who was making a large delivery of victuals read off a long string of numbers making an error in calculation, and corrected him without glancing at the accountings (she hoped he wasn't trying to cheat the brides of Christ!), the abbess had been stunned. She'd welcomed Margaret's assistance with the stewarding of the convent. Not only had it given her something to do, it had given her a way to pay back the nuns for all their help.

But as much as she appreciated all the nuns had done, they were not a substitute for the friendships she had known at Garthland. She missed Brigid desperately. She missed laughing. She missed jesting. She missed lively conversations that went long into the night. And she missed having someone to confide in, someone to share her joys, and someone to share her heartaches. God knew there had been so many of them.

Nor was the convent a substitute for a home. It was quiet and peaceful, but the subdued atmosphere was nothing like the lively, raucous Hall at Garthland, where there were always visitors to entertain or brothers to bicker with and reprimand. She missed the noise, the excitement, and the energy of the life she'd known.

But maybe most of all she missed the freedom. She missed galloping across the countryside with the wind tearing through her hair. She missed being able to go where she wanted and say what she wanted without having to worry about offending someone or doing something wrong.

She *was* wild, she realized. And now she felt caged. Margaret didn't know how much more of this she could take. She was dying on this island. Each day she was losing more and more of herself.

Her only escape was at night. At night she held tight to the memories of her husband and the love she felt for him, as she touched her body as he had. At that moment he seemed closer. But when she woke, the loneliness was even worse.

The only bright spot in the weeks that followed after Eoin left was the day not long after May Day, when Fin rode out with Eoin's father and brothers to join the call to rally to Bruce's banner. He hadn't followed her again since the day Eoin had come home, but she was still relieved to see him go.

Marjory, on the other hand, was heartbroken. Thinking that perhaps their shared grief and fear over the men who'd gone off to battle might bring them closer, Margaret had made yet one more overture to her sister by marriage. But it was harshly rejected. It seemed Margaret wasn't the only one aware of Fin's unwanted attention toward her. Marjory, however, suffered under the illusion that the attention was solicited. She accused Margaret of "flirting" and "toying" with Fin in her boredom and "need to have all the men fawning over her."

Margaret had protested and gently tried to warn her about Fin, but Marjory was blinded by love and refused to countenance any criticism of the handsome young warrior. Margaret left her to her illusions, but hoped for Marjory's sake that she learned the truth before tying herself to a man who Margaret was certain would only bring her heartbreak.

Even Tilda seemed different. Margaret found out why about a week after Eoin left, when she asked Tilda if she wanted to go out on the skiff—the girl loved sailing almost as much as Margaret did—and she'd shaken her head without meeting her gaze. Eventually she'd squeezed an explanation from her. "My brother said well-brought-up young ladies don't sail boats by themselves."

Margaret argued with her, until she realized it wasn't Neil or Donald, but *Eoin* who'd spoken to her. Apparently,

Lady Rignach had threatened to marry Tilda to the son of a nearby laird if she continued in her "wildness."

It shouldn't have hurt so much, but it did. Was Margaret such a bad influence that Tilda had to risk being sent away rather than spend time with her? Is that what Eoin thought, too?

But by far the worst part of intolerable weeks that passed was not knowing what was happening, and the constant fear that came from knowing that her husband was in danger. With no word from him since he left, she had no idea where he was, what he was doing, or whether he was lying somewhere injured—or, God forbid, worse.

He'd told her nothing about his plans, and if Lady Rignach knew more, she did not share it with her son's MacDowell bride. News of "King" Robert's movements was sparse and took an interminable time to reach them. It was early July by time they heard of Bruce's disastrous defeat at Methven two weeks before. Bruce's forces had been decimated, crushed under the mighty English king, Edward I, the self-described Hammer of the Scots. And it was another agonizing week of waiting and imagining before Lady Rignach received word from her husband telling her that they had all survived, although Neil had suffered a serious arrow wound to his shoulder.

For weeks Margaret stared out the window, looking for a ship, praying that Eoin would see the uselessness of Bruce's cause and return to her. No one—not even the charismatic knight she'd met at Stirling—could defeat Edward of England. And certainly not with only half of Scotland behind him.

It wasn't until late August that she saw a *birlinn* of warriors approaching from Oban. She ran down the stairs of the tower house into the bailey just as the men started stumbling through the postern gate from the dock like the walking dead. Although not all were walking. Some were limping, some were being helped by marginally more able men, and a few were being carried on litters.

Heart in her throat, Margaret scanned the grimy, bloodied faces of the men for someone familiar. But it wasn't until she saw the bloodied face of the man speaking to Lady Rignach that she recognized one of the laird's captains. He'd lost part of his arm, which was wrapped in a bandage that was bloody and dirty enough to make Margaret's stomach lurch.

But it was her heart that lurched a moment later, when Eoin's mother paled and gave a pained cry that rose above the din of chaos.

Margaret reached her just as Lady Rignach's legs gave out. The look on the proud lady's face was not one Margaret would ever forget. Her formidable mother-in-law looked shattered and suddenly very fragile.

Margaret helped Lady Rignach inside, called for wine, and sat her on a bench in the Hall. Marjory and Tilda joined them at some point. Eoin's sisters stood to the side, looking as anxious and scared as Margaret felt. For once, Marjory was happy to let her take charge.

As soon as the housekeeper brought the wine, Margaret asked her to gather the servants and start preparing beds, food, and to send for anyone with knowledge of healing. The men flooding the bailey would need to be cared for.

By the time she returned to Lady Rignach, the other woman had stopped shaking and looked marginally more composed. Steeling herself, Margaret forced herself to ask the question. "What has happened?"

Tears seeped from the corner of Lady Rignach's eyes. "It's over. My nephew's cause is lost." She drew a deep, shaky breath. "Bruce's army was all but destroyed yesterday at Dal Righ by the MacDougalls."

Tilda and Marjory cried out in despair, as Margaret fought to steady her wobbly knees. *Oh God, Eoin! Please don't say . . .*

Her chest, her eyes, her heart burned.

"Father? Our brothers?" Tilda asked.

Lady Rignach shook her head. "Connach isn't sure. He believes they escaped with the king, but it was chaos as they were forced to flee the battlefield and disappeared into the hills. The men who were too injured to follow were left to make their way home. The army has been disbanded, and the MacDougalls and their allies are hunting for what is left of Bruce and his supporters."

"Fin?" Marjory asked breathlessly.

Lady Rignach shook her head. "I don't know."

Something in Marjory seemed to snap. She turned on Margaret, her eyes blazing fury. "I hope you are happy. You and your traitorous family have won. Maybe your father is dancing on my brother's grave?"

Margaret gasped, looking at the girl in horror.

"Marjory, that's enough!" Lady Rignach said. "Margaret is your brother's wife. It is not her fault her clan chose to side with our English enemies."

The subtle dig masking as a defense snapped the last threads of her control. "My father chose to fight for *his* king—the rightful King John—and not for the man who murdered his kinsman." She turned from a stunned Lady Rignach to her daughter. "I love your brother, and when I married him I gave him my loyalty. Have you ever thought for one moment how difficult this is for me? Can you imagine what it is like to know that my husband is fighting my father and brothers, and the torture I live with every day wondering if they are meeting across some battlefield? I chose none of this, and I'm doing the best I can under difficult circumstances. I know you hate me and think I'm not good enough for Eoin, and maybe you're right, but he chose *me*. He *wanted* to marry me, whether you want to accept that or not, and maybe if you can't give me the benefit of the doubt, you should give it to him."

They stared at her in shock, even Tilda.

Margaret knew she'd probably made a mistake, but she could not stand there another minute and hold her tongue. She was never going to fit in here anyway. No matter what her husband wanted to think.

Without another word, she turned and walked away. The men in the bailey needed her, and it would help her keep her mind off Eoin and the uncertainty of knowing whether he lived or died.

She was done trying. She just prayed her husband kept his promise better than she.

"I hope you know what you're doing. Chief is going to be furious, when he discovers you've gone."

Eoin stared at the man who'd been his partner in the Highland Guard since the first day of training on the Isle of Skye over nine months ago. He and Lamont—known by the war name Hunter—had been through hell and back the past three months. They'd saved each other's lives more times than he'd like to recall. There was no one he trusted more, which is why he'd confided in him.

Tor MacLeod wasn't just going to be furious, he was

going to kill him. The leader of the Guard would never grant Eoin leave at this time, which is why he hadn't asked permission. But Eoin couldn't leave Scotland for God knew how long without telling his wife. Except for MacLeod—who's wife was privy to everything and safe on the Isle of Skye—Eoin was the only guardsman who was married. At times like this, he could understand why. It gave him a responsibility the others didn't have.

"I'll be gone two days—no more. I will catch up with you at Tarbert. Chief will barely have time to notice I'm gone."

Neither of them believed that. Chief would be cursing him to Hades as soon as he woke and discovered Eoin was gone. He didn't want to think about his punishment when he returned.

"Assuming you can make it past the MacDougalls. They'll be patrolling every inch of waterway between here and Dunaverty."

After the loss at Dal Righ at the hands of the Mac-Dougalls, Bruce and what were left of his men were on the run. After fleeing the battlefield, they'd taken refuge in a cave on the northern shore of Loch Voil in Balquhidder—MacGregor country. But with the MacDougalls hunting them from the west, the Earl of Ross from the north, and the English closing in from the east and south, there was no place safe for them to hide. They had to leave Scotland. From here they would make their way to Dunaverty on the southernmost tip of Kintyre, where they hoped Erik MacSorley, the best seafarer in the West Island kingdom of seafarers, would be able to slip a ship past the English blockade.

"That is why I plan to swim the short distance from

Oban to Kerrera tomorrow night. I'll cross back before dawn, and make my way through Argyll. They won't be looking for one man on a horse."

Lamont didn't look convinced but nodded. "*Bàs roimh Gèill*," he said in parting.

Death before surrender—the motto of the Highland Guard, and Lamont's way of wishing him good luck.

The words were with Eoin on the treacherous journey over fifty miles of rough terrain, filled with more sightings of war parties than he'd anticipated. But less than twenty-four hours later, he was trudging up the shore of Kerrera. Soaking wet and cold, but he'd made it.

Not sure what he would find, he approached the postern gate of the darkened castle cautiously. The MacDougalls would come here eventually, but for now, he hoped they were too busy trying to catch Bruce.

The bell for curfew would have been rung hours ago, and the castle gates were locked. But recognizing the guards on watch, Eoin took a chance and approached. The man called for the porter, and a short while later the gate was unlocked. Eoin was home.

He woke his mother first. After she recovered from the shock and he'd assured her of their well-being, she found him some dry clothes while he told her what he could of their plans. Knowing his time was short, he asked her to bid farewell to his sisters and went to wake his wife.

The sob of relief that tore from Margaret's throat, and the feel of her in his arms a moment later, made the risk he'd taken in coming to her worth it.

"Thank God, you are alive," she sobbed against his chest. "I was so scared. But the nightmare is over. You are back. I missed you so much. I didn't know how much more I could take."

He cursed the words that he must speak, knowing how hard they were going to be for her to hear. She'd sat up to throw her arms around his neck, and now he gently pushed her back so that he might look at her. "It's not over, Maggie. But I couldn't leave without letting you know I was alive—without saying goodbye."

She blinked, as if she'd misunderstood him. "What do you mean goodbye? Of course it's over. Bruce has been defeated. His cause is lost."

Eoin shook his head. "It's not over. Bruce has been defeated, aye, but he has not lost. We will regroup and return when we are ready to fight again."

She looked at him as if he were mad. "Regroup? You can't be serious. Bruce can't have but a handful of supporters left. His army has been disbanded. Those who were not killed in battle have renounced their loyalty to Bruce and surrendered either to John MacDougall, the Earl of Ross, or the Earl of Buchan."

Eoin's jaw hardened; he was well aware of the men deserting the king. His own foster brother was among them. The betrayal stung, but he was trusting Fin to protect his family. "I haven't. Nor will I."

"But you have to!" There was a wild, panicked looked in her eye that he'd never seen before. "You can't stay with him, you'll be hunted like a dog and executed. Everyone knows what happened to William Wallace—do you want to die like that?" Her hand clutched at his arm, as if willing him to listen. "My father will help. If we go to him now, he'll see that you aren't punished."

He carefully detached her hand. "I'm not going to your father, Maggie. Not now, not ever. My place is with Bruce, and it will be as long as there is a breath of freedom in his lungs."

"Which won't be long when King Edward gets ahold of him. There is no rock big enough to hide under for Bruce and his men. King Edward will have every man from Ross to the Borders looking for you." Which is why they were fleeing the mainland, taking refuge in the hundreds of isles in the western seas. "Where will you go?"

He looked at her mutely.

"You won't tell me?" she said, the hollowness of hurt echoing in her voice. "Of course not."

He cursed, raking his fingers through his hair frustratingly. Damn his kinsman to hell for doing this to them. "I can't, Maggie. It's not just my secret. I took a vow."

"And it has nothing to do with my being a MacDowell?" When he didn't deny it—couldn't deny it—her expression hardened. "Don't be a fool, Eoin. Don't do this. Don't give your life to a lost cause."

Eoin tried to keep a rein on his temper. He hadn't expected her to understand, but neither had he expected to be called a fool. After fighting beside his cousin for months, Eoin's belief in Bruce's cause had only grown stronger. But Eoin knew that was the last thing his wife wanted to hear. She only wanted him safe. "I didn't come here to argue with you, Maggie. I came to say goodbye. I don't know how long it will take, but I will be back."

She shook her head frantically. "No, you can't leave me here. If you will not listen to reason then take me with you. I can't stay here any longer without you."

His chest tugged, hearing the desperation in her voice. "I would if I could, but it's impossible. Where we are going is no place for a woman." Bruce had sent his own wife, sister, and daughter away. Lachlan "Viper" MacRuairi was leading them and the Countess of Buchan east to Kildrummy Castle.

"I don't care. I swear I will not be a burden. Just don't leave me here alone. Please," she cried. "I can't bear it."

Coming here had been a mistake. He was only making the situation worse. Her voice was verging on hysterical. He tried to soothe her panic by taking her in his arms, but she was stiff and unyielding.

"I would if I could. You have to believe that."

She wrenched out of his arms with a hard jerk. "I'm tired of *believing*. I'm tired of waiting here, while you disappear for months without telling me anything. We've been married almost a year, and we've spent less than three weeks of that together and shared a bed but one night. *One night*, Eoin. You can't leave me here. I won't allow it. Either stay or take me with you or . . ."

Eoin knew she was upset, and he was trying to be understanding, but he didn't like ultimatums. "Or what, Maggie? What choice do you have? This is the way it must be."

Her mouth pursed stubbornly, and she turned her head from him in the candlelight. He could almost hear what she was thinking, and it infuriated him. Fin's words of warning came back to him. Why did she have to be like this? This wasn't easy for him either. Couldn't she at least try to understand without making demands? Lady Barbara would have known her duty. This was war, damn it.

But she was young and impatient—he'd known that.

Taking her chin, he forced her gaze back to his. "You are my wife, Margaret. You will stay here and wait for me—where you belong."

"I don't belong here! Not without you. I can't do this anymore."

His chest pounded from the blow. She didn't want to be married to him. His jaw was locked so hard, he could feel the pulse in his neck ticking. "Maybe so, but as it's too late for second thoughts, I suggest you do your best to live with it. Who knows, maybe you'll get lucky, and King Edward will put you out of your misery."

She gasped, staring at him with a stricken look on her face. Tears filled her eyes, but he was too angry to offer her comfort.

"How could you say something like that? The fear of something happening to you has haunted me every hour of every day that we've been apart. I love you, it's just that I can't . . ."

But she had to. They both knew that. She was his wife.

She gazed at him helplessly, tears streaming down her cheeks.

The anger seeped out of him. He drew her into his arms again, and as he could say nothing to comfort her, he just held her as she sobbed. They made love almost out of desperation, but it only seemed to widen the chasm between them.

When he left a short while later, she would barely look at him. He felt like he was ripping apart. He'd come home to make things better and had only made them worse. And he feared that time and separation were cleaving a distance between them that he would never be able to bridge.

Not wanting to make it worse, he didn't tell her about Fin.

∞

What am I doing here?

Margaret stood on the ramparts staring forlornly out to sea, wondering how her life could have changed so much in one year. She wasn't the "fair maid" of Galloway anymore, she was the abandoned wife of an outlaw. She wasn't living with a father and eight brothers who loved her, she was a pariah among strangers—most of them hostile. She wasn't the laughing, lighthearted hostess who'd presided over her father's table with confidence, she was the "unfortunate" mistake who sat below the salt and rarely spoke to anyone other than Tilda. And she wasn't the lady of the castle who was busy helping to run a fiefdom for her father, she was the formerly irreverent girl who's work at a convent was the only thing that kept her from going mad with boredom.

And what was it all for? Was she waiting here for nothing? Where was Eoin? When would he come back? *Would* he come back?

After the way they'd parted the last time, she wasn't sure he'd want to. It had been nearly a month since that horrible night when her husband had appeared like a phantom in the dark to tell her of his plans. She deeply regretted some of the things she'd said, and the way she'd responded to his news with demands. But she'd been upset, frustrated, and desperate for him not to abandon her once more in this miserable place where she was cut off from everyone and everything that she loved—even the husband who'd brought her here.

But it had been his words that haunted her. How could he suggest—even in anger—that she would wish for his death to escape this marriage? She *loved* him. She only wanted to be with him.

But he was right. What choice did she have? She turned away from the sea to return to the tower. No matter how much it beckoned, she could not leave.

She didn't understand how everything could have gone so wrong. How could the marriage that had seemed so romantic and perfect feel like such a mistake? It seemed as if nothing had gone right since the moment they'd spoken their vows in the cottage. The world had turned against them. And there was nothing romantic about being married to a man whose misplaced loyalty had taken him away from her side for a year.

All for a lost cause. She still couldn't believe that he'd chosen to stay with Bruce. Even Eoin's foster brother had surrendered to the Lord of Lorn. Fin, John MacDougall's newest toady, had arrived at Gylen Castle as its keeper a week ago. With the MacLean laird and his son being declared outlaw rebels, the clan's lands had been forfeit to the crown—the *English* crown. As sheriff of Argyll—the English king's authority in the area—Lorn had given Fin command of the castle.

At first Margaret had been horrified by the news of Fin's return, until she'd learned the reason why. Fin had been given Marjory as a bride. The marriage that Eoin's sister had always wanted would be hers as soon as the banns could be read.

Margaret tried to be happy for her. She desperately hoped that she was wrong about Fin. He seemed to be doing his best to avoid her, for which she was grateful—and relieved.

It wasn't until the night of the betrothal celebration that Margaret learned he'd only been biding his time. Despite the happiness of the bride-to-be, there was a pall cast over the occasion by the absence of the laird and his sons—none of whom had been heard from since Eoin had left. Though the clansmen had been forced to swear to their new overlord, their loyalty was still with their laird, and they looked on Fin as something between an opportunist and a traitor.

Fin had assured them that he'd only done it to protect them—and that Eoin understood—but Margaret didn't fully believe him. She sensed that Lady Rignach didn't either but had chosen to make the best of the situation by pretending to do so.

The celebration was a stilted, awkward affair that was continuing late into the evening out of duty, not desire. Feeling the absence of her husband and finding it hard to hide her misery, Margaret slipped out of the stifling Hall into the stables to bring Dubh a special treat—an apple pilfered from the feast.

She didn't realize she'd been followed.

"What are you doing out here?"

She startled at the sound of the voice behind her, and recognizing it as Fin's, her heart immediately started to race. Racing that spurred when she glanced around and realized he'd cornered her in the small stall and gotten rid of the stable lad who'd been sitting near the door. The door that was now closed.

Straightening her spine, she squared her shoulders to face him. "Giving Dubh a treat. Now, if you'll excuse me," she said, trying to brush by him, "I told Tilda I'd be back in a moment."

He caught her arm. "Not so fast. We have a few things to discuss, you and I."

The pounding of her heart echoed in the growing pit in her stomach. She could smell the heavy scent of whisky on his breath, and his eyes were wild with a drunken haze. Every instinct in her body seemed to ring in alarm.

Being alone with Fin always made her nervous, but being alone with a drunken Fin made her terrified.

"How did you do it?" His eyes scanned her face, and then dropped to her breasts, where they lingered with an unmistakable glint of lust before returning to her mouth. "How did you beguile him into marrying you so quickly? You're beautiful, but he's never been distracted by a pretty face. It must be something else. Did you get on your knees? He's always had a weakness for a lass who sucked his cock. But then what man doesn't?" He laughed crudely.

Margaret gasped, so shocked and outraged she didn't know what to say. Did women . . . ?

She wrenched her arm away. "How dare you! When Eoin comes back—"

"Comes back?" He laughed harder—crueler. "Eoin's not coming back. Haven't you realized that yet? If he comes here, he's a dead man. Hell, he's probably a dead man already."

Anger dulled some of her fear. She hated hearing her own fears echoed by this brute. "How can you say that? He's your friend."

Fin sobered just a little. "Aye, but he made his choice. I made mine. We'll both have to live with them. I'm surprised you are still defending him, considering."

"Considering w-what?" Margaret hoped her voice wasn't shaking, but her heart was in her throat. He'd blocked the only exit to the stall with his body and was now backing her against the back wall.

He smiled, but it never reached his drink-crazed eyes. "Considering that he left you here unprotected." He leaned down, and she shuddered as his whisky-laden breath crawled over her skin. "You are a beautiful woman. Many men would be tempted—"

"Then they would be fools," she said, standing up straight, refusing to be cowed. "If my husband does not return to avenge my honor, I assure you my father and brothers will."

That gave him pause. But then his eyes narrowed on her once more, like a hawk with its prey in sight. It seemed he was no longer biding his time. "Your father and brothers are a long way away, but perhaps if you look around there is someone closer to home whom you can rely on."

"Who?"

"I might be persuaded. With the proper enticements." If the look he swept over her body left her any doubt of what he meant, his next move did not. He reached for her, drawing her up so quickly she didn't have time to react before his mouth was crushing hers.

He tasted of whisky and lust, and she would have gagged had she been able to breathe. He was just as big and muscular as her husband, and the assault of such a powerfully built man filled her with terror, but she was prepared. Vowing that she would repay her brothers if she had the chance for insisting she learn how to defend herself, Margaret lifted her knee between his legs. Hard.

He crumpled like a poppet of rags, crying out in pain. She didn't waste time, but drew her eating knife from the scabbard at her waist and held it to his neck.

"If you ever touch me like that again, I'll kill you."

The lust was gone. It was pure hatred that glared in his eyes now. "You'll regret that, bitch."

She did not doubt he meant it. Not wanting to give him a chance to recover, she ran past him out of the stall. There was nothing to do: she had to go to Lady Rignach.

She would have—had she not run right into a stunned Marjory who was standing just outside the stall. From the stricken look on the girl's face, if she hadn't seen everything, she'd seen enough.

When she turned and ran, Margaret chased after her. "Wait," she said, catching her at the bottom of the tower stairs. "Oh God, Marjory, I'm so sorry you had to see that. But maybe it's better if you learn the truth now."

"Learn what truth?" she repeated angrily. "That you've

betrayed my brother and tried to seduce my betrothed? I saw you kiss him." The facade of anger crumbled like a dry wall. "How could you?"

Seeing the devastation in the other woman's eyes, Margaret fought for patience as she tried to calmly explain. Marjory was hurt, but there was no interpretation that could have construed the events that had just occurred as Margaret's fault. "Fin attacked *me*, Marjory. He was drunk. When he tried to kiss me, I was forced to defend myself. You must have seen the knife?"

"Attacked? You mean provoked. What do you expect when you've been taunting him, seducing him for weeks—months? Then when he finally decides to take you up on your offer, you play the innocent and pull out your knife." The tears had started to fall, and Marjory was sobbing uncontrollably. "God knows, you've done your best to confuse him. But Fin loves me, and everyone knows you're a whore."

The sound of a slap shattered the cool night air. Margaret didn't know which one of them was more shocked. But she wasn't going to let anyone say something like that—even a woman who was supposed to be her sister.

They stared at each other in the torchlight. "I hate you," Marjory said, holding her cheek in her palm. "Everyone hates you. No one wants you here. I wish my brother had never married you, so you could just leave."

This time when she ran away, Margaret didn't chase after her.

Stonily, she climbed the steps to her chamber, donned a dark cloak, packed a few belongings in a bag—including the chess set she'd worked so hard on—and slipped out of the postern gate in the crowd of revelers without anyone noticing.

She left behind a broken heart, her cherished horse that she could not sneak away without being seen, and a note for her husband should he ever return. He'd done what he had to do, and now so was she.

Margaret MacDowell had had enough: she was going home.

14

Near Garthland Castle, Galloway, Scotland,
St. Valentine's Day, 1307

THE WIND TORE the bindings from her plaits, sending her hair streaming out behind her, as Margaret lowered her head to the palfrey's neck and raced through the shadowed trees.

She could hear the shouting of her companion behind her, but he didn't catch her until she drew up at the loch. "God's bones, Maggie Beag, what the hell do you think you are doing?" He reached over and grabbed the reins from her, forcing her mount to come to a complete stop. "Are you trying to kill yourself, riding through the trees like that? I should take you over my knee."

Margaret stared at the familiar handsome face, although it wasn't often turned toward her with such fury. Lord, she almost believed all those stories she heard of his fierceness on the battlefield when he looked like this. But Tristan MacCan had been her friend for as long as she could remember; it would take more than a dark look to send her cowering.

She narrowed her eyes right back at him. "I was racing— and winning I'll point out. And last time I looked you are not my father or my husband, Tristan MacCan, so don't try to order me about."

With a toss of her head, she dismounted—hopping down with a loud exclamation. She strode to the water's edge.

But he was right behind her. Catching her by the arm, Tristan swung her around to face him. "Not yet, maybe. But when I am, I *will* take you over my knee, if you ever do anything like that again. You could have ridden into a limb in the darkness going that fast. You scared my heart right out of my chest."

He always did this, blast it. He took the anger right out of her when he said sweet things like that. She'd frightened him, and his reaction had been out of concern.

But it was more than that. Tristan cared for her—more than she'd realized. It wasn't until she'd returned home from Kerrera that she'd noticed the subtle changes. The way he stared at her with longing, and maybe a slight edge of possessiveness when he didn't think she was looking. The way he no longer followed every pretty lass who fluttered her lashes at him out the door. The way he'd tried to ease the transition of her return home with her father and brothers.

Tristan had always assumed—as she had—that her marriage would be a political one. Her marriage to Eoin had changed everything. Now that she was back, he thought he'd been given a second chance—thanks to her father. But she cared about him too much to give him hope where there was none. Her heart belonged to one man, and until she learned differently, she would wait for him.

Four months after returning home, Margaret wondered if she'd made a mistake. The episode with Fin and Marjory had shaken her to the core; her only thought had been to escape. Had she given up too easily? Would Lady Rignach have listened to her? Had Eoin come home for her only to find her gone?

She'd heard nothing from him directly, only rumors of Bruce and a handful of men fleeing to the Western Isles. It was as if they'd vanished into the mist five months ago. Recently, she'd heard rumblings of the "king's" return—and her father was certainly being secretive about something with messengers coming and going at all hours—but the soldiers who'd garrisoned the nearby castles had been idle for months. For which she was relieved. God knew she had no love of King Edward, but neither did she want the war to resume. She just wanted Eoin to come home safely. No matter what her father said, she refused to believe he was dead.

She turned to Tristan, who'd relaxed his hold on her arm but still was standing close to her. "I know what my father wants, Tristan. But I will not go along with his plans to dissolve my marriage with the claim of a precontract. You and I were not secretly betrothed, and I will not say we were."

It wasn't yet dark enough to mask Tristan's expression, and she could see the glint of annoyance in his ridiculously green eyes—Lud, they would put emeralds to shame! "I can't believe you are still holding on to a man whom you barely know, who deserted you among strangers, and then expected you to sit by the hearth waiting for him. If you were my wife, I would have taken you with me. Nothing would have kept me from having you by my side."

Margaret felt a pang in her chest, knowing that Tristan spoke true. He would have taken her with him, and she couldn't escape the thought that if Eoin had really loved her, he would have done so, too.

He held her gaze. "He's probably dead, you know."

She didn't say anything, but looked away. She would know if he was . . . wouldn't she?

He forced her face back to his with a hand on her chin. "But even if he's somehow survived the past few months, you don't think he'll come for you here, do you? You *left* him, Maggie."

The pang intensified, Tristan's words an echo of her fears. "I told you why," she said, her voice breaking.

"Aye, but I doubt he'll bother to come around and ask questions. You made your choice clear when you came back to your family—where you belong."

But that was just it. She wasn't sure she belonged anywhere anymore. Garthland was the same, but it was also different. Or maybe she was the one who was different. She laughed and jested, she spoke her mind, and did what she wanted without asking permission. Her days were busy and filled with purpose. She'd slipped right back into her role as chatelaine and had hosted countless feasts since she'd returned. She was no longer miserable.

But neither was she happy. How could she be when Eoin was somewhere out there in danger? And just like at Gylen, there was no one she could talk to at Garthland about her fears for her husband. Not even Brigid. The distance she'd felt from her friend before leaving Stirling had widened since Margaret's return. Normally Brigid would have accompanied Margaret and Tristan on the ride to the loch, but all Brigid seemed to want to do since she and her brother had arrived was to sit by the window and watch the men in the yard as she sewed. Margaret was even more convinced that Brigid had fallen in love, but every time she asked her friend about it, she got a pained look on her face and refused to talk about it.

Just like at Gylen Castle, Margaret was caught between two loyalties. She didn't fit in anywhere anymore, belonging to neither clan completely and distrusted by both.

"Eoin loves me," Margaret said to Brigid's brother, trying to twist out of his hold. "He'll come for me when he can."

She must have sounded more certain than she felt, because Tristan's expression hardened. "And how long will that be?" He drew her closer, so their eyes were only inches apart in the darkness. "You are a beautiful, young woman, Maggie. Are you prepared to wait *years* for it to be safe enough for MacLean to try to sneak back here to fetch you? For sneak is what he will have to do. As long as your father lives—as long as any of the Lord of Badenoch's kin live—it will never be safe for Bruce and his men in Scotland. He killed him before an *altar*, for God's sake." Ignoring his own blasphemy, he lowered his voice huskily. "And you forget, I've had you in my arms before. I know how passionate you are. Do you want to go months—years—without this?"

He'd always been good at surprising her, and he did so again when he bent his head and kissed her. His lips were warm and soft, and his mouth tasted of cloves. It was instantly familiar, but it was also instantly wrong.

He tried to cradle her head in his hand and bring her mouth closer to his to slide in his tongue as he used to do, but she pushed him forcefully away. He stumbled backward, swearing.

"Blast it, Tristan, stop!" She put her hands on her hips and glared at him furiously. "What do you think you are doing?"

His eyes blazed just as hotly—but with something else. "Showing you what you are missing. Proving to you that you'd be a fool to wait for a man who will never come back, when you have one right here who wants you."

He took a step closer to her, but she held him back. "Stop it, Tristan! I don't want this."

His eyes grew fierce, he leaned toward her, as if he might draw her into his arms. "I can make you want it."

There was a powerful edge to his voice that she didn't recognize. It sent a shiver of trepidation running down her spine. But Tristan wasn't Fin MacFinnon. He would never hurt her. "No, you can't," she said firmly. "We have been friends for a long time, but if you persist in this, we won't be any longer."

For a moment he looked as if he might press his case, but then her words seemed to penetrate. She could see the anger and frustration warring on his expertly crafted features.

"You're making a mistake, Maggie. I hope by the time you've figured it out, I haven't grown tired of waiting. I'll not sleep alone forever. But continue this stubbornness, and you very well might."

Taking his horse by the lead, he stomped off into the darkness. She wanted to call after him, but she knew it was probably best to give him time to cool his temper. The castle was only a shout away.

A moment later she reconsidered. It had gotten dark all of the sudden, and the shadows of the forest had taken on a sinister cast. Something felt wrong.

The sound of leaves rustling sent a shiver racing down her spine. She looked around, peering into the darkness.

It's only the wind, she told herself.

But it wasn't. The hair at the back of her neck prickled. She could feel something. Someone was out there.

She started to scream for Tristan, when a hand slipped over her mouth, and a man grabbed her roughly from behind.

He shouldn't be here. Eoin had promised Lamont that he'd take a quick look at the castle and meet back at the rendezvous in an hour. He wasn't supposed to let *anyone* know he was here—even his runaway wife. Too much was riding on it.

After five months of biding their time in the Western Isles while Bruce gathered the support necessary to retake his kingdom, they were ready. Tomorrow night the king and about three hundred men would lead an attack at Turnberry farther up the coast, and the larger part of their forces—about nine hundred men—under the command of Bruce's two brothers Alexander and Thomas, would lead an attack on Galloway on the south coast.

Everything was ready, and the warriors of the Highland Guard had been given the dangerous task of scouting the landing areas the night before. In Galloway that meant Eoin and Lamont. In Ayrshire that meant MacSorley, MacLeod, and MacGregor. The other half of the Guard were somewhere in northwest Scotland, leading Bruce's womenfolk to safety.

Eoin and Lamont's mission was simple: reconnaissance of the enemy strength and position, and to make sure no one was expecting them. The site chosen for their landing was less than ideal. Indeed, Eoin had argued against it. The deep narrow cove at Loch Ryan could enable the enemy to pick them off from the shore like fish speared in a barrel. But with the currents, it was the only place to land so many men safely, and he'd lost the argument. Their success would hinge on surprise.

Yet here he was, on the most important mission of his

life, risking everything because he was too furious—too consumed by jealousy—to heed caution.

He'd been high in a tree just outside the castle walls, trying to see into the yard to get an idea of the number of men inside—and hoping for a glimpse of his wife—when the woman and man rode out of the gate. The light was low, and she was wearing a cloak over her head, but he'd recognized her instantly. The laugh over her shoulder and the way she'd shot out through the trees on her horse had only confirmed it. He'd scrambled down and followed after them.

He couldn't believe it. He'd been berating himself for months about how he'd left her, to find out that not only has his wife left him with barely an explanation (he didn't need to look at the note—how had she learned to write?—in his sporran to recall the words, misspelled and all: "*I love you, but I canot stay here withowt you any longer. I will be wating for you at Garthland. Forgive me.*"), but when he finds her, she's gallivanting across the countryside with another man.

A man whom it doesn't take him long to realize must be Tristan MacCan. The bastard who had probably given her her first kiss. And her second. And how many more? And how *much* more?

The pernicious thoughts assailed him in the darkness. Jealousy coiled inside him like a snake, waiting to strike. It wasn't helped by the fact that MacCan could hold his own on the battlefield and give MacGregor a contest in visage. When the bastard kissed her, Eoin went mad with rage. It had taken everything he had not to rip MacCan off her and tear him apart limb by limb.

If she hadn't pushed MacCan away herself, Eoin might have. But sanity intervened.

For a moment at least. Until she sensed his presence and opened her mouth to scream. Knowing he couldn't let her alert the castle to their presence—men swarming all over the area was a chance he could not take—he was forced to reveal himself.

"Shhh," he whispered in her ear. He felt the sharp intake of air under his hand, as her body stiffened with shock and recognition. "Unless you want to bring your father's men down on me, *wife*."

Even in his anger he was aware of the press of her body against his. All those soft curves that he loved fit perfectly against him, and he reacted like a starved beast, hardening, as blood rushed to all parts of his body in contact with her.

As soon as he released his hold, she turned and threw her arms around him. "Eoin!" she sobbed. "You came."

He held her away from him. "Aye, and just in time, from what I just saw."

Something in his voice must have alerted her. She eyed him anxiously, although it might have had something to do with his appearance. All those months on the run had taken their toll; he not only fit but looked the part of the outlaw. Remembering that he was wearing the blackened nasal helm favored by the Highland Guard, he let her go to remove it. Tossing it on the ground, he waited.

She bit her lip, clearly embarrassed. "It was nothing, Eoin."

"Nothing?" he exploded, his mind racing back to that day at Stirling Castle, and how easily she'd dismissed young John Comyn's kiss. "He had his mouth on you, Margaret, and that is sure as hell *something* as long as you are my wife—a fact you seem to have forgotten."

"Of course I haven't forgotten."

"Haven't you?" He hauled her up against him. His

senses exploded, but anger held him back from crushing his mouth to hers. "Then what the hell are you doing out here alone with him? Or maybe I don't need to ask? You and I went riding once alone."

She gasped with outrage, her eyes narrowing to angry slits. "Just what are you insinuating?"

"I'm not insinuating anything, I'm asking. Just what in the hell is your relationship with Tristan MacCan?"

"I don't have a relationship with him. You should know that." She must have seen something in his expression. "What?"

"You didn't bleed."

It took her a moment to realize what he meant. She gave him a look that made him want to crawl under a rock.

"And so I must not have been a virgin?" She gave a harsh laugh. "Jealousy has made you a fool as well as an arse. Not all women bleed their first time, Eoin. Even I know that. I was a virgin when I met you, and I've been faithful to you every day since, though right now I'm asking myself why." She paused, as if fighting to calm her temper. "Tristan was wrong to kiss me, and I'm sorry you had to see that, but I am not a whore. And just because I fell into bed with you doesn't mean I will with any other man."

Bloody hell, she was making *him* feel in the wrong. But it wasn't he who was kissing another woman in the forest. It wasn't he who was discussing how to end their marriage. "Why the hell do I find you here at all? My *wife* should be at Gylen. Is MacCan the reason you left me? Did you grow tired of waiting for one husband and decide to take another?"

"Maybe I should have! I'm not the one who left you alone and unprotected. I'm not the one who disappeared for months without telling you anything. I'm not the one keeping you in the dark. I'm not the one who leapt out of the darkness, scaring me half to death, hurling accusations like a wild man, when I haven't seen you for months. Months when I didn't know if you lived or died. That is not a marriage, Eoin—or at least not one I will be a part of."

Unprotected? What did she mean? He would have asked, but she tried to draw away and he knew he couldn't let her go. Part of him feared he'd already lost her.

He leaned his face toward hers, so that only a few inches separated their eyes. "As long as there is breath left in my body you belong to me. If MacCan or your father thinks they are going to change that with some false claim of precontract, they can go to Hades. I'll put them there myself."

Her eyes flashed. "I don't belong to anyone. I'm not a possession to be fought over, I'm supposed to be your wife. But if this is your idea of how to treat someone you are supposed to love, then I've had enough, and it is you who can go to Hades—or back to the war that is so important to you."

But God, he did love her. That was the problem. He couldn't let her go, even though she deserved more than he could give her right now. He had to hold on to her. Had to find some way to put the broken connection back together.

So he did the only thing he could think of. The only thing that she couldn't deny. The only thing that he knew could quiet the storm raging inside them both.

He covered her mouth with his and kissed her with all the pent-up passion, all the unfettered anger, all the fear lashing around inside him. His need for her was raw and powerful, fierce in its intensity. Like a lightning storm it clattered and thundered, whipping the elements around them both in a violent frenzy of lust and desire.

Her mouth was open, her tongue was thrusting against his with the same hunger, the same need, the same frantic desperation. She was grasping his shoulders, squeezing his arms, moving her hands over his body with the same fervor. He loved when she touched him, loved the feel of her greedy hands all over him.

His mouth was on her throat, his hands on her breasts, on her bottom, lifting.

She reached for him, molding her hand around his cock. It felt so damned good, he thought he was going to explode.

They were pulling at each other's clothes. His chausses were unlaced, his braies untied, and his erection bobbed free.

The cold night air didn't give any relief against the heat hammering through his veins. He was on fire. They were on fire.

He pressed her back against a tree, lifted her skirts, and slid his hand between her legs.

Jesus. She was already ready for him, and he couldn't wait another second to be inside her. It had been so long . . .

He slammed into her with a thrust that surprised them both. A thrust of possession. A thrust of exclamation. And a thrust that couldn't be denied.

They belonged together.

Over and over he proved it to her, as his hips rocked back and forth, first slowly, and then as her cries grew more insistent, faster. Pumping harder. Circling deeper in a fierce, primitive drum of need and desire.

Yes. Oh God, yes. It felt so good.

It was building. Surrounding them. Clamoring for release.

He could feel the pressure spiking at the base of his spine. Unrelenting, all-consuming, and irrepressible.

The sound of her cries sent him over. "Oh God, Maggie . . . I love you so much."

The words echoed over and over in his head as his body seized and the powerful emotions tore him apart. He filled her with the proof of that love, exploding deep inside her.

Only when the roar of the flames had dimmed did he notice the quiet.

∞

Something *had* been different.

Since that first time in the cottage, Margaret had known that there was something different in her husband's lovemaking. She sensed he'd been holding back. But it wasn't until now that she realized what that was.

He pushed back, his manhood coming out of her—*out* of her—from where he'd found his release. She felt the coldness and wondered how she could have missed something so significant. Except for that first time, every time he'd made love to her, he'd pulled out of her.

"Oh God, Maggie, I'm sorry." He drew his hand back through his disheveled hair—hair that was much shorter than she remembered it. He looked so different. All vestiges of youth were gone. He was a man, and a dangerous-looking one at that. This man belonged to the shadows—lived in the shadows. He wasn't the man she'd married. "I didn't mean for that to happen like that."

She didn't move from her place against the tree while he re-did his clothing.

Why? Why? The question rang in her ear. She feared she didn't want the answer, but she asked anyway. "Didn't mean for what to happen like that? Why, did you forget to do something?" He stared at her, obviously confused. "Is there a reason you have chosen to take your pleasure *outside* of me until now?"

He didn't flinch from the accusation in her eyes. "I thought it was best."

Her fists squeezed at her side, her voice shrill. "What was best?"

"There is less chance of a child."

She stared at him in the darkness, unable to breathe, feeling as if he'd just kicked her in the chest. "You don't want a child with me," she whispered. His wild, backward mistake of a wife.

He took her icy hand in his, but she feared she would never feel warm again. "Of course I do—just not right now. I haven't known whether I was going to be alive from one day to the next for almost the past year, Maggie. I thought it would be easier on you."

"How thoughtful of you." Her voice sounded as dull and far away as she felt.

He'd been holding himself back from her in so many ways, why should she be surprised? He told her nothing about his plans to fight for Bruce, where he'd disappeared to for months, where he was going, and what he was doing. He'd refused to take her with him, and left a man who hated her—who might have hurt her—to "protect" her. And only now did he come for her?

"Why are you here, Eoin? Why have you come to fetch me now?"

The grim angle of his jaw was her answer.

She sucked in her breath, the tightening in her chest a cruel, burning pain. "I see," she said softly. "You didn't come to fetch me at all, did you?"

He reached for her, but she flinched away. "I hoped for a glimpse of you, but I can't take you with me. Not yet."

"Why not?"

She didn't expect an answer, and he didn't give her one. "It wouldn't be safe. I shouldn't even be here right now. You can tell no one of my presence."

"You are planning something, aren't you? That's why you are here."

He betrayed nothing by his expression, but his voice intensified. "I mean it, Maggie, *no one*. Under any circumstances. I'm trusting you with this. My life and the lives of others depend on it. As soon as it is safe, I will have Fin send his men to bring you back to Gylen."

"No."

The flatness of her voice seemed to take him aback. "What do you mean no?"

"I will not go back to Gylen—especially with Fin. Aren't you curious about why I left? Your foster brother attacked me, Eoin. He kissed me, and I believe he would have tried to force me, if I hadn't managed to get away."

Eoin looked absolutely stunned. "Jesus, Maggie. Are you sure? Maybe there was some kind of misunderstanding? He's married to Marjory now."

"Of course I am sure, and there is no misunderstanding. Your sister saw everything, although she convinced herself that I kissed him."

He didn't say anything, but for one moment—one fraction of an instant—she saw the question in his eyes, and it felt as if he'd stabbed her with a dagger, so sharp and piercing was the blow.

She stared at him in disbelief. How could he claim to love her and believe that of her—even for an instant?

It seemed the final blow. She was tired of jealousy, tired of suspicion, tired of the distrust, but most of all she was tired of being alone. He had never really committed to her or to their marriage.

"Go to hell, Eoin. And don't bother coming back."

His frown turned fierce and angry. "What is that supposed to mean?"

"It means I'm done waiting for you to trust me. I'm done trying to prove myself to you. How could you think for one moment . . . ?" She stopped, taking a deep breath through the ball of hurt burning in her chest. "I will no longer defend myself to you or anyone else. I won't be half a wife. I won't be a dirty little secret to hide away in some castle for you to swive whenever the urge strikes. This was a mistake."

There was a note of finality in her voice that must have alerted him. "That isn't how it is, Margaret. If you would just try to see things from my perspective. I've made vows. I have a duty."

"What about your vows and duty to me? You say you love me, but this isn't love, Eoin. This is loneliness, secrets, and suspicion interspersed with moments of physical pleasure."

He stared at her. The helplessness in his eyes tore at her, but she held firm.

"I'm doing the best I can, Maggie. I know this has been difficult, but please try to be a little more patient."

"No," she said, and then repeated more firmly, "No. I'm done being patient. I want all of you. If you leave now without me, don't bother coming back."

She knew he didn't like ultimatums, but she would not back down. Not this time. They couldn't go on like this. There would be nothing left.

Maybe there was already nothing left. His expression had turned to ice, cold and hard. "Is that what you really want?"

Her insides knotted. "Aye."

She wanted to call the word back as soon as she said it, but she knew it had to be said. He had to choose.

She just didn't think he'd choose to leave her.

15

MARGARET LOST sense of time. She didn't know how long she sat at the base of the tree sobbing. A minute? Two? Ten? But suddenly Brigid was there.

"Maggie! Thank goodness, here you are! Didn't you hear me calling you?"

Margaret lifted her head and met her friend's gaze in the moonlight.

Brigid paled, her eyes widening in horror. She raced forward to kneel beside her. "Dear God in heaven, what has happened?"

Margaret blinked through the tears of her swollen eyes and shook her head, her throat too tight to respond.

"Did Tristan do this to you?" Brigid said. "I was worried when I saw him come back to the castle without you in such a temper. Oh God, please tell me my brother didn't force you?"

Only then did Margaret realize the state of her clothes. She hadn't tied the laces of her gown where Eoin had loosened them, and she probably bore his mark where he'd ravaged her mouth and throat with his kiss. Following the direction of Brigid's gaze, she looked down and saw the scratch low on her bodice that must have been from his beard.

She shook her head. "N-not T-Tristan."

Margaret could see the relief on her friend's face, before it hardened into steel. "Then who? Who did this to you? We must get back to the castle to tell your father."

Margaret grasped at her to prevent her from standing. "No," she said. "No, you mustn't."

"Of course we must. The fiend might still be in the area."

"No, Brigid. I mean it. You can't," she said frantically. "It isn't what you think. They can't know . . ."

Margaret stopped, not wanting to say too much. Eoin might have broken her heart, but that didn't mean she wanted him to die for it.

She forced herself to stand, though her legs wobbled, and tried to compose herself. Her friend watched her every move, as Margaret did what she could with her appearance.

"It was him, wasn't it?" Brigid asked. "Your husband. He's the one who did this to you. He's the one you are trying to protect."

Margaret tried to deny it, but she was a horrible liar, and Brigid knew her too well. In the end she was forced to admit it, or Brigid swore she would go right to Margaret's father. "But you must swear to say nothing, Brigid—not to anyone. It might be over, but I still love him." Hot tears filled her eyes again. "It's over, Brige. It's really over."

Her friend enfolded her in her embrace and did her best to console her. But Brigid could not put back together what had been shattered.

"Are you sure?" Brigid asked.

There was something in her friend's gaze that Margaret didn't understand. An intensity—a vehemence—with which she asked her question.

Margaret nodded. "Aye. I'm sure." Her voice caught with a sob. "He doesn't want me."

Once again she was enfolded in her friend's arms. Brigid squeezed and rocked her back and forth. "Then he's a fool, Maggie Beag, and he doesn't deserve you. Maybe . . . maybe a definitive end will be best."

It almost sounded like a question, but Margaret was too devastated to heed the warning.

❦

Margaret didn't realize her mistake until the following morning, when she rose after a sleepless night and tried to open her bedchamber door. Perhaps the only benefit of being the sole female in the family was that she'd been given a small, private solar on the second floor of the tower house.

She pulled a few times on the handle, but it had been barred from the outside. At first she thought it was a mistake and knocked loudly, calling for someone's attention. But when one of her father's soldiers brought her food to break her fast, she realized it wasn't a mistake.

She barraged him with questions, which went unanswered, and demanded to be released, which he uncomfortably refused. When it was clear she would get nowhere with him, she asked to see her father.

Over the long hours that her father kept her waiting, she was forced to consider the possibility that her best friend had betrayed her.

A fact that was confirmed for her a few minutes after

Dugald MacDowell strode into the room. He looked like a cat who'd just eaten a big fat mouse as he took off his helm, slammed it on the table, and collapsed in her favorite chair before the brazier.

She stood in front of him practically shaking in frustration. "What is the meaning of this, Father? Why have I been locked in my chamber all day?"

His eyes narrowed just a little at her tone, and maybe on another day he would have chastised her, but today he was too pleased with himself. "It's for your own protection."

"For my *what*?"

His smile turned just a tad cold. "I wouldn't want your duty to become confused."

Then he told her just how horribly she'd been betrayed. Brigid had told him—actually she'd told Dougal—everything. She stared at her father in numb disbelief. "But why? Why would Brigid do this?"

He shrugged indifferently. "Why should I care? But I suspect it's some silly lass's infatuation with your brother. She has always mooned after him."

She had? How could Margaret not have noticed? But it still didn't make any sense.

"Would that it had been my own daughter who brought me news of the rebel's presence instead."

She didn't miss the none-too-subtle reproach. But even her father could not deny that she owed Eoin her loyalty. "He's my husband, Father."

"Not for much longer."

His certainty sent a chill into her heart. "Please, Father, you must believe that I have no idea where he is. I'm sure Eoin is long gone by now."

"I'm sure he's nothing of the sort. We've been expecting an attack, and your husband's presence in the area has all but confirmed it. Loch Ryan is the perfect place to safely land a significant number of ships. Have you not noticed all the men I've been mobilizing in the area for the past month? I've spread them out among the nearby castles trying to prevent the rebels from knowing our strength. We'll have a wonderful surprise waiting for them. Tonight, I'd wager."

Oh God . . . no. Margaret dropped to the bed, no longer able to stand. The room seemed to be spinning. Her head was pounding with his words: "*Tell no one of my presence.*"

She hadn't meant to. But Brigid had guessed, and she'd thought she was protecting him by confirming it. She'd thought she could trust her. She'd never imagined her friend would do something like this.

But it didn't matter. Unwittingly or not, Margaret had revealed his presence here, and in doing so, betrayed him. But she couldn't let her mistake cost him his life.

"Please, Father, you misunderstand. He came to see me, that is all. W-we argued. He saw me with Tristan and misunderstood."

Her father stood, his gaze hardened. "I wondered why he'd be fool enough to chance a meeting with you. Undone by jealousy." He laughed, shaking his head. "If you are telling the truth, you have nothing to worry about. But if you are lying . . ." His mouth fell in a flat line. "If you are lying, nothing will save him anyway, because nothing will stop me from exacting vengeance on the men who killed my kinsman. And if this is Bruce's 'glorious' return to retake his kingdom, we will finally get the recognition our clan deserves. Can you imagine how Edward will reward the man who brings him the head of the murderous traitor King Hood?"

Margaret pleaded her case, but she knew it was to no

avail. Her father had set his course, and her happiness was a small price to pay for vengeance and ambition.

Her mistaken attempt to protect her husband could well end up costing him his life. He'd warned her. *"Tell no one . . . Under any circumstances."* Oh God, how could she not have listened to him?

She had to do something.

❦

It was a slaughter. Eoin's stomach lurched as he fought off the MacDowell warriors while knee deep in the blood and gore of his compatriots. Hundreds of bodies, most of them Bruce's men, were strewn across the beach and floating facedown in the loch that in dawn's light would be a grisly red.

They'd realized they were trapped too late. The fleet of ships and army that had taken Robert the Bruce five months to put together—over two-thirds of them Gallowglass mercenaries from Ireland—had sailed into the loch under the moonless sky without the vital element of surprise. The enemy was waiting for them. Far more than their intelligence had led them to believe.

Eoin grimaced as a fountain of blood splattered on his face from the slash of his sword across his opponent's neck. He didn't have time to wipe the grime from his face—or think about how MacDowell might have come upon his intelligence—before the next Gallovidian swarm of warriors was upon him. Two, three, sometimes four men at a time. MacDowell's men poured out of the trees where they'd hidden like plaid-covered locusts.

MacDowell was a wily bastard, Eoin would give him that. The Galwegian chief and his men had lain in wait until a large part of Bruce's army had dragged their *birlinns* up the beach before attacking—and then with only a small force meant to entice more of Bruce's army to come to their aid.

It had worked. Thinking they were sailing to the rescue, the crews in the second wave of ships had been surprised, and then overwhelmed as a much larger force of MacDowell's men suddenly appeared.

As part of the vanguard, Eoin and Lamont had been among the first men on the beach. Realizing what was happening, Eoin tried to warn the ships behind them to turn back, but his shouts could not be heard from above the clatter of the battle, and he couldn't break away from his attackers for long enough to do anything else. In between swings of his two-handed great sword, Eoin watched as men he'd fought alongside for months were cut down under the vicious onslaught.

Their only stroke of luck came when someone had lit a beacon meant to guide the seafarers into the mouth of the loch. It had alerted the last ships to the danger, and two had managed to escape before they sailed into the trap. Of the eighteen ships and nine hundred men who sailed into Loch Ryan to launch Bruce's rebid for the crown, all but a little over a hundred men had been caught in MacDowell's web.

The rest of them were left to fight their way out or die. Eoin fought like a man possessed, but it wasn't enough. Outnumbered and outmaneuvered, Thomas Bruce, one of the commanders, gave the order to retreat, which in effect was a call to flee by whatever means possible. A moment later, Eoin watched in horror as Thomas, along with his younger brother, Alexander, were surrounded by MacDowells and forced to surrender.

With their commanders taken, it became a free-for-all—every man for himself—as what remained of Bruce's army ran for the trees, their only hope to evade capture in the forest.

Above the din of the mayhem, Lamont shouted to get Eoin's attention and motioned for him to head his way. Eoin nodded with understanding and dispatched one of the two swordsmen attacking him with a disabling swing of his sword across his legs, followed by a deadly one across his neck. He slashed his way through a few more enemy warriors, slowly forging his way up the beach toward his partner.

He was only a few feet away from Lamont when a large warrior stepped in his path. From the quality of his armor and weaponry, Eoin knew he wasn't a regular man at arms, but it wasn't until their swords met in the first clash of steel that Eoin recognized the face beneath the helm and grime: Dougal MacDowell, his wife's eldest brother.

Eoin cursed and stepped back. He was furious with Margaret, but there was no way in hell he'd go back to her as the man who killed her brother. For despite her ultimatum, he had every intention of claiming his wife at the first opportunity. She wouldn't be rid of him that easily, but he wasn't going to stand there arguing with her when she was being so irrational. "Let me pass, Dougal."

"Surrender," the MacDowell heir responded, "and my father may be persuaded to spare your life. You deserve some credit for this, after all."

Eoin's stomach dropped; his bones turned to ice. *No.*

Dougal smirked, reading his shock. "Your devotion to my sister has turned out to be surprisingly useful—for us."

He laughed, and Eoin felt as if he'd just taken a dirk in the gut. Nay, in the back. He couldn't believe it. She'd told someone about his presence. He'd known he'd made a mistake when he followed her and had been forced to reveal himself, but not once had he ever really thought she would betray him.

She'd betrayed him. The words echoed over and over in his head, but still they couldn't quite penetrate.

"MacLean, watch your back!"

He heard his partner's warning an instant too late. His inattention—his shock from his wife's treachery—had cost him in more ways than one. While he'd backed away from Dougal, another MacDowell warrior had come up on his flank. He turned in time to see the flash of silvery steel right before the blade struck the back of his head with a felling blow.

As Eoin fell to the ground, he was almost glad he wasn't going to have to live with the knowledge of what his weakness for his wife had done.

∞

Margaret was still miles away from Stranraer and the beach at Loch Ryan when she began to hear the sounds. Horrific sounds. The violent clash and clatter of metal, the shouts of angry voices, and the hideous cries of the dying.

She was too late. It had taken her too long to escape and reach the old beacon at Kirkcolm. Her warning hadn't worked. The ships must have been ahead of her.

Oh God, please don't let anything happen to him!

If only it hadn't taken her so long to light the beacon. She'd brought a tinderbox and was able to get a small fire going, but the last keeper hadn't left the basket ready, and it took her some time to gather the wood and twigs, and then climb up and down the rungs on the pole to place them in the iron fire basket.

Her heart seemed to have stopped beating as she rode

as fast as she dared through the dark forested path—praying, begging, bargaining every step of the way.

But the sounds from the beach only grew worse as she drew nearer. The fierce clatter of swords that had reverberated in the air dulled as the battle lost its intensity, and the cries took over. They were cries unlike any she'd ever heard, and would haunt her dreams for years to come, but instinctively she knew what it meant: it was the sound of a massacre.

The world seemed a blur, whether from the tears pouring from her eyes or the horrible images spinning through her mind. But by time she reached Stranraer, jumped off her horse, and pushed her way through the hundreds of celebrating clansmen, Margaret seemed to have lost all sense of reality. She felt like she was in a hideous nightmare, a slow-moving world of disbelief and horror, as she raced toward the beach, her path lit by the torches that seemed to have sprung up all around her.

Some of the men recognized her—she heard more than one surprised "my lady"—but no one tried to stop her. She knew why the moment she broke through the trees and the crescent-shaped beach spread out before her: the battle was over.

Her stomach heaved at the sight that met her eyes. Bodies—or parts of bodies—were everywhere. A few patches of light sand were all that remained in the sea of blood and gore. She retched, the sickly, coppery smell overwhelming.

When she lifted her head, she gazed around blindly, not knowing where to look—not knowing how to look—so scared of what she might find.

Eoin. Please, not Eoin.

Her father's men were dragging bodies into piles. The

sudden roar of fire and the first throat-searing, acrid wafts of burning flesh that hit her nose explained why.

With a sharp cry of desperation, she began to frantically search among the bodies. Bile rose to the back of her throat more than once at the grisly images, the faces mutilated beyond recognition, the blood, the unstaring eyes, swirled in front of her, as she picked her way through the dead.

Many were young, and few wore mail. From the saffron-dyed *leines* and quilted *cotuns*, she realized most were Irishmen. But no blackened nasal helms and black leather *cotuns* studded with mail.

"Margaret, what the hell are you doing here?" Duncan had come up behind her, and spun her around by the elbow to face him. "Satan's stones, as if I need to ask! I couldn't believe it when one of the men said he saw you. You must be mad coming here like this. It could still be dangerous. Father would be furious to see you."

"Where is he, Duncan? Where is Father?" she pleaded desperately. "I must see if he knows anything about Eoin."

Her breath caught as something flickered in his expression—sympathy?

"MacLean is dead, Maggie. Dougal saw him fall."

"No!" She staggered. "No!" She clutched at Duncan's arm to steady herself. Eoin couldn't be dead. "Where is he? If he is dead than show me his body."

"It's probably too late."

"What do you mean, too late?"

His eyes flickered to the far edge of the beach where she could see the flames of a fire beyond a large crowd of men. Her heart froze. Panic raced wildly through ice-cold veins.

She started to run. Duncan yelled after her to stop, but his words were droned out by the hammering of her heart in her ears.

He caught her when she was still a few dozen yards away. "You can't go over there," he said furiously, lifting her off the ground from behind by her waist. "Jesus, Maggie, trust me, you don't want to see that."

"Why not? What are they—"

A flash of silver above the heads of the men followed by a roar of cheering cut off the question in her throat. She stopped thrashing in her brother's arms and he turned her around to face him.

"Some of the rebels are being executed," he explained.

Her eyes widened with horror. Her father was exacting his vengeance with mercilessness and brutality that would be remembered for ages.

"Not your husband," he assured her. "He was killed on the battlefield."

Her mind screamed, refusing to believe it. She had to see for herself. "If he is in that pyre, I need to see it, Duncan."

He must have heard the desperation in her voice. After a moment he let her go. "Don't say I didn't warn you."

She should have listened to him. She reached the edge of the crowd just in time to see the executioner's sword take its deadly arc across the neck of a man she recognized: Duncan of Mar, the former Earl of Mar's younger brother, and Robert Bruce's brother-in-law twice over. Bruce had been married to Duncan's sister, Isabella, and Bruce's sister, Christina, had been married to Duncan's brother Gartnait, the former earl. She looked away, but it wasn't soon enough.

Margaret had seen men die, but this was different. This time she'd played a part in it. Nausea rose anew. Dear God, had these men died because of her?

She pushed through the crowd until she saw her father. He was watching from the side as Duncan of Mar's body was tossed onto the pyre and another man was brought forward. This one looked to be an Irish chieftain.

Her father didn't look surprised to see her, but she could tell he wasn't pleased by the interruption. "Daughter," he said sharply as she drew near. "Next time I will lock you in the garret."

She ignored the threat. She would have escaped that as well, although admittedly using the iron poker for the brazier as a bar across her window, tying one of the bedsheets to it, and only having to drop fifteen feet had been much easier. "Where is he, Father? Where is my husband?"

The reddish orange of the flames was reflected in his dark eyes as his gaze turned to the fire. "Halfway to hell, if the fire has done its job."

He pointed to a body consumed in flames near the top of the pile. Near it she saw the helm that must have fallen off. A blackened nasal helm just like Eoin had been wearing.

Margaret stared into the flames and felt the light inside her go out. The world turned dark. She sank to her knees, a soft, broken cry the only sound of the searing pain that her father's words had unleashed.

Eoin was dead. Because of her.

God forgive me.

16

St. Mary's Church near Barnard Castle,
Durham, England, January 17, 1313

EOIN HADN'T expected her to faint. And he sure as hell
hadn't expected to be the only one with the presence of
mind to catch her before she hit the ground.

But there he was holding his wife in his arms again,
wondering why he hadn't let her fall. It was no more than
she deserved. And he wouldn't be stuck with the scent
of her in his nose, the weight of her breasts on the arm
that had snaked around her waist, and the soft, erotically-
curved body that had haunted his dreams for almost six
years pressed snugly against him.

Nor would he be forced to gaze up close at the face he'd
never quite been able to forget, though God knew he'd
tried.

He was sorry to see that she was still beautiful, her
features seemingly unmarred by the passage of time. Her
lips were still the same vibrant crimson, her siren's slanted
eyes still framed with the long, dark lashes, her skin still a
youthful powdery cream, and the hair peeking out from the
sides of the veil still a bold and fiery red.

She didn't look much older than the last time he'd seen
her, almost six years ago, when he'd watched from the

safety of the forest where Lamont had dragged him, after the blow to the back of the head that should have killed him, as she'd sunk to her knees in apparent regret before the fire that could have well been his funeral pyre.

Even from afar he could see her devastation, but it was too late. His heart had already hardened. He'd been glad she thought he was dead, for she was dead to him. He'd turned and never looked back.

Or tried not to. Sometimes late at night, in moments of weakness, he wondered what had become of the wife who'd nearly cost him everything. Where she was. *Whom* she was with.

Married, he thought bitterly. He was surprised she'd waited this long.

But maybe it was partly his fault. He should have dealt with his ill-advised marriage a long time ago. It was well past time to put Margaret MacDowell behind him for good.

But as his gaze lingered one more moment on the face he'd once thought to look at for the rest of his life, his jaw hardened at the injustice. Surely her countenance should show some of the blackness of her soul? She looked more like an angel than a treacherous bitch who'd betrayed him and sent so many men to their deaths.

Sure, Eoin knew what Lamont and the rest of his Highland Guard brethren said. That MacDowell had been prepared for them. That rumors of Bruce's planned attack had already reached him. That the Galwegian chief's garrisons had been packed and his men had been at the ready. That their own intelligence had been faulty. That Eoin's mistake was not to blame for what had happened. That it wasn't his fault.

When he could think rationally about it—which was

rare—he probably even agreed with them, but it didn't change what she'd done.

Or what he'd done. His weakness for his wife had cost him. *She'll hold you back.* Fin and his father had been right. He'd lost his kinsman's trust, and his place in the Guard for a short time—although Chief had made Bruce reconsider quickly.

Eoin would never have a place in Bruce's government. No matter how many successful plans Eoin came up with, none could make up for the disaster at Loch Ryan. Eoin knew the king laid part of the blame for the deaths of his brothers at Eoin's feet. He accepted that, but Dugald Mac-Dowell would finally account for the rest.

Reminded of his purpose, Eoin turned his gaze from the woman in his arms to the men standing before the church door, who were still reeling from the shock of his announcement and had yet to move.

Which was exactly what Eoin had counted on. A quick scan around the yard told him his men were almost in position. A few more moments, and the churchyard would be surrounded.

He pictured how it would play out in his head, anticipating how MacDowell and the English would react and accounting for every possible move. He could have attempted the straightforward surprise "pirate" raid for which Bruce and his men had become known—riding in with swords drawn for the fierce attack—but that would have left too much to chance. MacDowell had proved as slippery as a snake. Relying on the disguises might be more risky if someone noticed them too early, but by surrounding the churchyard, MacDowell would have nowhere to go. A quick snatch and grab, and Eoin and his men would be on the way back to Scotland before the English—and the garrison at the castle—knew what had hit them.

Conyers and his men would have to be neutralized, but Eoin's target was the MacDowell chief and his sons—as many of them as could be taken. Eoin recognized the eldest two standing beside Conyers and their father with a young lad. His gaze skimmed over the boy standing with his back to him, who was too young to be one of Margaret's other brothers. The boy must be Dougal's.

Margaret's eldest brother had married an English heiress not long after Loch Ryan—one of the MacDowells' rewards from Edward of England for the service they'd done that day in capturing Bruce's brothers and crushing the southern attack. Fortunately for Bruce, the northern prong of the attack at Turnberry had proved more successful, and despite the loss of nearly two-thirds of his army at Loch Ryan, Bruce had defied the odds against him and risen from the ashes of defeat to establish a foothold in his kingdom. A foothold that in the last few years had become entrenched. MacDowell and his Gallovidians were the last of the significant Scottish resistance.

And Eoin would be the one to put an end to it by capturing him—as soon as he could unload the burden (literally and figuratively) in his arms. He started to push Margaret toward Conyers, who as the groom in this farce of a wedding was standing closest to him, when her eyes fluttered open.

Their gazes locked, and not even six years of bitterness and hatred could make him look away.

He hadn't expected to be affected. He hadn't expected to feel anything. He hadn't expected the air to squeeze out of his lungs and his heart to feel as if it were burning a hole in his chest.

But it was as if he was on that battlefield all over again, listening to her brother taunt him with her betrayal, and it all came rushing back. All the anger, all the rage, all the heartbreak, and most of all, all the questions.

Why shouldn't matter. *Why* was irrelevant. He'd trusted her, and she'd betrayed him. That should be enough. But damn it, how could she have told someone, when she must have known what it would mean? Did she wish to be rid of him so badly? Had the marriage that had started with such happiness become so unbearable? Had her love once tested proved no deeper than a young girl's feckless fancy?

A wave of fury and rage rose up hot and heavy inside him. His blood boiled. His body shook. He wanted to lash out at the injustice. How could she have done this to them? Why couldn't she have been more patient? Why couldn't she have done her duty and tried to understand? Why couldn't she have been like the other wives? Since Loch Ryan, seven of his brethren had married, and not one of their wives complained about what they did or how long they were gone.

Margaret read none of the storm of emotion taking place inside him. Her eyes softened. The lips that he could still taste in his dreams curved into a dreamy, delectable smile.

She reached up, the hand she placed on his face stopping his heart. "You came back! It wasn't a dream. You're alive. Thank God in heaven, you're alive."

Not even the most accomplished liar could have feigned that reaction. He could not doubt that she was happy to see him. It gave him pause, but a movement out of the corner of his eye stopped him cold.

The precious few seconds of inattention—the previous few seconds he'd spent locked in a fool's trance with his wife—had cost him. Where in Hades was MacDowell?

Not again, damn it.

∞

Margaret couldn't believe it. It was really him. Eoin was standing before her alive, and by the looks of it, perfectly hale.

Perhaps more than hale. From the breadth of his shoulders and the size of the rock-hard arms around her, he was in fine form. A shudder of awareness ran through her as her swooning senses began to focus and sharpen. In *very* fine form indeed. Good gracious, he was built like a . . . *built*.

Six years of war had hardened him. He was bigger, fiercer, and scarier. He not only looked strong enough to take out an entire army, his eyes possessed the cold ruthlessness to do so. There was a hard glint to the midnight blue that had not been there before, and the lines etched in his face were deeper and angrier, and punctuated by a few more scars. No smile would erase the furrow between his brow now.

The serious young warrior she remembered had needed to be reminded to laugh; the grim, imposing, mail-clad brigand before her looked incapable of doing so.

But no matter how changed, she was so happy to see him, she couldn't resist touching him. His jaw hardened under her hand, but the roughness of the stubble under her palm sent a shiver of remembrance shooting down her spine. She'd loved to feel the scrape of his beard on her skin when he'd kissed her.

But if the way he suddenly pushed her out of his arms toward Sir John was any indication, her husband did not share the same fond memories of her touch.

"Take her," he said with a sneer of disgust.

Then she remembered what she'd done, and how he must despise her. Her chest stabbed with a knife wielded by her own hand.

"Are you all right?" Sir John asked, wiping her brow with a tender caress of his thumb.

It was a thoughtless gesture that she would not have noticed an hour ago, but that in the presence of her suddenly-risen-from-the-dead husband felt wrong.

She need not have worried though. A sidelong glance at Eoin told her that he'd forgotten all about her.

Mumbling assurances to Sir John, she quickly extracted herself from his arms where she'd been so unceremoniously tossed like an unwelcome sack of grain.

It wasn't until Sir John drew his sword and pushed her behind him that she realized what was happening. The movement she'd sensed earlier was Eoin's men—wearing the armor and surcoats of English knights—surrounding the churchyard.

How did he still have the power to hurt her after all these years? This wasn't about her wedding, she realized. Eoin hadn't come for her. It wasn't about her at all. It was about her father and brothers. He must have discovered that they would be here and hoped to use her wedding as a trap by creating a diversion.

He'd done that all right. While everyone had been gaping at Eoin, stunned by his pronouncement, his men had quietly moved into position.

But the diversion was over, and all hell had broken loose. Perhaps he'd counted on that as well? Perhaps he'd hoped to nab her father and brothers quickly in the ensuing chaos?

If that had been the plan, it hadn't worked. It was certainly chaotic—the wedding guests had slowly realized something wasn't right and were fleeing in all directions—but like Sir John, her brothers had drawn their swords and were preparing to put up a fight.

This was madness. With all these people in this confined space innocent people would be . . .

Her heart dropped. Oh God, Eachann. Where was her son?

Her gaze shot to the last place she'd seen him. He'd been standing between her father and Dougal on the other side of the priest near the church door as she started to say her vows. She could see Dougal and Duncan with their swords drawn standing before the door, but neither the boy, the priest, nor her father were with them.

Eoin must have realized her father wasn't there as well; she heard him shout an order to one of his men to find MacDowell. He likely would have done so himself, except that he was fending off a threat from Sir John.

"You should have stayed dead, MacLean," Sir John said in a menacing voice she'd never heard before.

"And you should have found a bride who was not already married," Eoin replied. "But I did not come here for you—or her," he added with a scornful look in her direction. "None of your guests needs to be hurt. I want Mac-Dowell. Do not interfere, and I'll write to the pope myself. I'm sure my wife can think of dozens of reasons why our marriage could be dissolved."

Margaret didn't miss the dig about the conversation with Tristan that Eoin had overheard all those years ago, nor was his obvious eagerness to be rid of her not without a painful pinch or two (or handful) in her chest, but her focus was on her son.

Where was he?

She tried to peer over the crowd, but there were too

many people in the way—including Sir John and Eoin. She had to get around them. Sir John had pushed her behind him against the church, thinking he was protecting her, but now she was stuck.

"Writing to the pope won't be necessary," Sir John said meaningfully. "Not when I'm done."

He punctuated his words with a crushing swing of his sword, which Eoin deflected with his own. The clash of battle sent a wave of panic shooting through the crowd, and a woman screamed.

Sir John's act had snapped the unspoken standoff and the clash of more swords followed.

Margaret cursed, knowing that spilling of blood was inevitable. But damned if she would allow her son to be caught up in the mess. This was everything she'd hoped to avoid. But her husband had brought the war to their doorstep. She would curse him—after she found Eachann.

Assuming Sir John didn't kill Eoin first. Her erstwhile bridegroom was one of King Edward's best swordsmen. But a quick glance at the men exchanging blows of the sword told her that Sir John was the one she should be worrying about.

She'd never seen Eoin fight before, and the primitive fierceness of it both shocked and unsettled her. She hadn't expected him to be so skilled with a blade. He deflected the blows effortlessly—almost as if he were toying with the powerful knight. When Sir John grew impatient and moved in too close, Eoin didn't just use his sword, he used his elbow to smash into Sir John's nose and his foot to twist around behind the other man's ankle and drop him to the ground.

He lay there so still Margaret prayed he was just knocked out.

She would have gone to him to make sure he was all right, but Eoin had given her an opening. She darted forward toward the church where her two eldest brothers had just defeated a few of Eoin's men and were in the process of urging her younger brothers inside. Did they hope to take refuge in the church? For some reason, she doubted Eoin and his men would heed the laws of sanctuary.

Duncan had caught sight of her and motioned her forward. "Hurry, Maggie, there isn't much time."

"Where's Eachann?"

"Safe," Duncan said. "Father has him."

Margaret let out a huge sigh of relief and muttered a prayer of thanks. Following her brother inside, she immediately realized it wasn't sanctuary they were seeking. The church had a back door.

Always be prepared, Maggie. Always have a means of escape.

How many times had her father told her that over the years? He had avoided capture all these years by following those rules. Today was no different. The rear of the church was where they'd put the horses.

Her father had just mounted a horse and pulled Eachann up behind him when she and the rest of her brothers poured outside. There were only a handful of horses so a few of them would have to ride tandem.

"Father, wait!" she cried. She wanted her son with her.

He turned and met her gaze. "I have him. Go with Duncan. Hurry."

He assumed she would leave with him. Is that what she would do? What about Eoin?

She didn't have time to think about it. Her father's gaze shifted behind her, and when his face darkened with anger, she knew it was too late for her.

In a panic she started to cry for her father to wait—to leave her son with her—but he'd already turned away. Gathering Eachann closer around his waist, her father snapped the reins, and clicked his heels. The horse shot off like an arrow, tearing across the yard toward the trees.

She heard Eoin's voice shout from behind her. "Shoot him, now, damn it. He's getting away."

Margaret's face drained in horror. She turned around and saw Eoin and another man a few feet away.

The other man was holding a bow, with an arrow pointed at . . .

She didn't think before she reacted. "No!" she screamed and lurched forward, putting herself between the arrow and her father's fleeing form.

The archer couldn't have stopped the shot if he wanted to. Her movement had been well timed. He was already releasing his fingers as she lurched.

By all rights the arrow should have slammed into her chest an instant later. But with a vile curse, Eoin knocked the bow to the side, causing the arrow to skid off harmlessly to the ground.

He was on her a moment later, lifting her up by her arm to shout at her furiously. "You little fool! I should have let him kill you. What the hell did you think you were doing?" He turned back to the archer before she could respond. "Fire again. Don't worry about the others, get MacDowell before he disappears."

"No!" She'd never seen Eoin so angry—and given the circumstances she probably should have shown more sensitivity. But her heart was still hammering with panic, and she felt her own temper rise. Her gaze blared right back at him. "What was I doing? I was stopping you from possibly shooting your son, that's what I was doing!"

∞

As a member of the most elite group of warriors ever assembled in Christendom, handpicked by the Bruce for the most dangerous and difficult missions, Eoin had suffered his share of devastating blows that had left him stunned and reeling—most of them on the practice yard at the hands of Chief and Raider. But no knock in the head or slam across the chest had ever left him so completely poleaxed.

He felt as if the mucky ground had just been pulled out from under his feet, as if the world had tilted, as if everything he knew—or what he thought he knew—had changed in an instant.

Your son.

The boy was his? He tried to recall what he'd looked like, but the memory was a blur. Eoin hadn't paid much attention, never considering . . .

He stared down into those flashing, golden eyes, saw the challenging tilt of her chin and furious purse of her mouth, and felt such a wave of fury rise inside him he had to fight to keep his fingers from clenching harder around her arm. "Say it again," he gritted out slowly.

If he'd thought to intimidate her, he'd forgotten to whom he was talking. Margaret MacDowell didn't get intimidated—even when she should. She thrust that chin up higher and narrowed her gaze right back at his. "The boy your archer could have killed is our son, Eachann."

Eachann. The boy was named after one of the greatest warriors of all time, Hector of Troy, who was also known as a tamer of horses. The perfect ode to . . . them?

He hauled her up to him, their faces only inches apart. "If you are lying to me, Maggie, I swear by all that is holy, I'll make you regret it."

She pushed away from him with a hard shove. "Of course I'm not lying to you. Eachann turned five last November. I assume that brilliant mind of yours can count back easily enough, but your visit that night left me with more than a broken heart. Ironic, isn't it? All that trouble to avoid a child and one lapse was all it took." She made a sharp scoffing sound. "It's no secret who his father is. Ask anyone."

She looked around, obviously realizing what he already knew: her brothers were gone. They'd left without her.

A son? Devil take it, a son who was five years old? How could she have done this to him?

If he could think rationally, he might realize that this was not a sin he could lay at her feet, but he was too angry to be rational. "Your father used *my* son as a shield so that he could get away? I'm going to tear the bastard apart with my own hands."

Margaret looked outraged. "He wasn't using him as a shield, he just wanted him with him to keep him safe."

Eoin was so furious he didn't realize he was bellowing at her. "Safe? By putting him in the way of my archer? He was counting on the fact that I would not shoot with the boy behind him."

She shook her head. "He wouldn't do that. He loves Eachann. He is his only grandchild. He would never hurt him. I know you have cause to hate my father, but whatever else you may say of him, he is no coward, and he would die before letting anything happen to that boy. I was there, I saw what happened. He wanted him with him, nothing more."

Eoin heard the conviction in her voice and gritted his

teeth. Even if she was correct in the estimation of her father's actions this time, they would never see eye to eye on the subject. There was little of which Dugald MacDowell wasn't capable, and Eoin wouldn't put anything past him.

But he was done arguing with her. He needed to focus on salvaging the mission. Not only had he let MacDowell slip through his net—how the hell had they missed the back door to the church when they'd scouted the area last night?—he had a son who'd been stolen from him for five years.

Failure wasn't an option. He'd get them both back, damn it.

Forgetting about Margaret, he told Douglas's archer to follow him, and they returned to the churchyard, where Hunter and the rest of the men had just finished subduing the English.

They'd already overstayed their welcome. Eoin kept one eye on the castle that he knew at any moment could open to release a flood of more soldiers.

"What happened?" Hunter said.

"I'll explain later," Eoin said. "We need to get to the horses. MacDowell and his sons"—*and my son*—"rode into the forest."

"They're headed for the castle?"

Eoin shook his head. He'd prepared for that, posting a few men on the road in case MacDowell had managed to slip away from the churchyard. But he hadn't planned on that back door. Eoin didn't make mistakes like that. At least he hadn't in about six years. "I suspect he's heading for the coast."

Lamont swore, knowing as well as Eoin did that if MacDowell made it to a ship they wouldn't be able to catch him. If they were in Scotland with Hawk, they might have a chance of slipping through the heart of the English naval forces, but without the famed seafarer it would be suicide.

"Don't worry," Lamont said. "We'll get him."

Eoin didn't need to nod, his grim look said it all. Damn right, they would get him.

Lamont whistled and motioned for the men to follow.

He would have gone after them, but Margaret stopped him.

"Wait," she said, grabbing his arm.

He looked down at it and told himself the coiling and twisting in his chest, the feeling that he was coming out of his own skin, was because he was angry. Her touch had lost the power to affect him years ago. But there was no denying the heavy drum of his heart.

Perhaps sensing the dangerous emotions boiling inside him, she dropped her hand. "I'm going with you."

He almost laughed. Glancing over, he noticed Sir John starting to stir. "I don't think your fiancé will like that very much. Besides, I lost the taste for treacherous redheads six years ago."

She flushed angrily but refused to be baited. "This has nothing to do with you. My son needs me."

His gaze turned as wintry as his blood. "*My* son will have his father."

"He doesn't know you, Eoin. He'll be scared. I know you hate me, but don't take your feelings for me out on our son. He's only little boy. Please, he needs me. I swear I won't get in the way."

He gave a harsh laugh. As if that were possible. She'd been in his way since the first day he'd met her.

"You need not worry that I won't be able to keep up," she persisted. "I know how to ride."

He gave her a long look. "I remember."

And bloody hell, it infuriated him.

She flushed again, realizing to what he was alluding.

His jaw hardened, refusing to let her sway him. "The boy will be fine. Though the same cannot be said of your father when I catch up with him."

"I can help you find him."

Now *that* caught his attention. His eyes narrowed on her, assessing. If she was lying to him . . . "You know where he is going?"

"Not exactly, but—"

He cut her off with a harsh sound. "I didn't think so. I don't need your kind of help. I'll find him on my own."

Lamont was the best tracker in Scotland.

"And what if you don't? Think about it, Eoin. If you want to catch my father, are you better off taking me with you or leaving me here? I have knowledge you may need."

She was right. But that didn't mean he thought she'd give it to him . . . *willingly.* Torture, now *that* was tempting. His mouth curled. "You offer to betray your father so easily? Why am I not surprised?"

Her cheeks went hot with anger, but she didn't attempt to defend herself. How could she? They both knew what she'd done. She lifted her chin. "There is nothing I wouldn't do to see my son safe—nothing."

She might be a liar, but she wasn't lying about that.

He might be able to use her. To hold over her father's head if nothing else. Would MacDowell trade his foul life for that of his daughter's? He should be so damned lucky.

He turned to one of his men. "Find the *lady* a horse. She may be of some use to us." He turned back to his deceitful wife, making sure she understood the stakes. "But lie or do anything to make me regret this, Margaret, and I swear I'll do everything in my power to ensure that you never see the boy again."

17

THE CHILL OF his words followed her hours later. He hadn't meant it, Margaret told herself. Eoin was angry. He wouldn't try to take her son away from her . . . would he?

Years ago, she would have said it was impossible. The man she'd married would not be so cruel—no matter how angry he was with her. But Eoin was no longer the man she married, and guessing what this cold, imposing stranger might do seemed a fool's gambit. The serious young man she'd fallen in love with had become a grim, caustic stranger.

But maybe that had been the problem all along. She had never really known him—not really. It had all happened too quickly. Love, marriage, passion—and not even in that order. The physical closeness they'd shared had given an illusion of more. They hadn't had time to learn to trust one another before war had separated them.

Looking back with the perspective of time and maturity, she could see that they'd never really had a chance. They'd been too young. Too passionate. Too unsure of one another. It had been all fiery emotion and attraction, with a few precious moments of something deeper. Something that might have blossomed if given the chance to grow. Maybe if the war hadn't come, it would have been different. But the war had come, and the fragile bonds between them had been strained to the breaking point. Love like everything else needed nourishment. Without it, it had died.

In so many ways, their marriage had been a mistake. They'd been too different. He'd wanted her to be something she was not. But it had also been right. She'd never felt about another man the way she did about Eoin. She'd tried—God knows, she'd tried—but he'd made her feel things she'd never felt before. Passion she'd never felt before. When they'd been together, she'd been unbearably happy. Which made their separation almost harder to take.

Mistake or not, she regretted the way they'd parted the last time. She never should have sent him away like that— with ultimatums and demands—but he should have given her *something*.

Words and promises had not been enough. The fierce lovemaking had not been enough. She'd needed tenderness and love, not lust. She'd needed trust and faith, not doubt and suspicion. She'd needed to know that she was important to him. That she mattered. That she wasn't merely a bedtime distraction for the war that had always defined him.

She couldn't believe he was alive. But the initial jump of hope in her heart for what this might mean had been swiftly crushed by the knowledge that he'd returned for her father, not her. Of course, he wanted nothing to do with her. And she . . . she didn't know what to think. She'd accepted Eoin's death, and put her love for him behind her. But seeing him again had brought it all back.

They'd been riding hard for about three hours, slowing

only when they were forced to veer from the road near one of the larger castles, or, like now, when they had to pause to determine which fork in the road her father had taken. Although it was clear her father was heading for the Cumbrian coast, there were many different roads to get him there.

Out of the corner of her eye, she took advantage of the rare pause in their chase to observe her husband, who'd ridden up ahead of her to speak with the handsome, if stoic-looking, warrior who appeared to be leading the tracking of her father.

Her husband might have changed—the overly muscled scary-looking brigand was not the young warrior she remembered—but he was still undeniably handsome. Maybe even more so, time and battle having put a few more hard edges on his fiercely wrought features.

But that had never been what had attracted her. It had been something deeper—something far more elemental. It was the razor-sharpness of his mind, the aura of strength around him, and the way he looked at her. All that brooding intensity that had been impossible to resist. She'd wanted it for herself. She'd wanted to know what he was thinking. She'd wanted to *be* what he was thinking. And like a moth to the flame she'd been drawn in until they'd both gone up in flames.

Him in that pyre, and her in the pits of hell that she'd trudged through in the days after. She'd cried for days, unable to sleep or eat. She'd blamed herself and wanted to die—thought she deserved to die. If it hadn't been for the discovery of her pregnancy, she might have done just that.

Eachann had given her a reason to live, and she'd be damned if she'd let the husband that had let her think he was dead for six years take him from her.

No matter what she'd done.

She'd made a mistake—a horrible one—but it hadn't been intentional. She hadn't thought she'd had a choice. But he had. Eoin had chosen to let her think he was dead, and in doing so, had cost her son a father for five years. If Eoin did not know his son, it wasn't because of her.

Almost as if he knew what she was thinking, his eyes shifted to hers. Their gazes held for a long heartbeat, before his expression darkened and he resumed the conversation—if the brusque exchange of words could be considered a conversation—with the other warrior at what seemed a harsher clip.

Eoin hadn't spoken to her since they left the church, and it appeared he was doing his best to pretend she didn't exist. He should be good at it, with six years of practice. Now that the shock of his survival had waned, Margaret felt herself growing angry. How could he have done this?

Her anger only grew worse as the chase resumed. Despite the grueling pace, her father was eluding them. Margaret didn't know whether to be sad or glad. Even with her father's increased bitterness over the past few years, she still loved him and didn't want to see him captured. After the slaughter at Loch Ryan and the execution of Bruce's two brothers in the aftermath, she didn't want to think about what kind of vengeance the king would take from the man responsible. Although "the Bruce," as the people called him, had been remarkably conciliatory toward some of the men who'd stood against him—including the Earl of Ross, who'd violated sanctuary to capture his wife, daughter, sister, and the formidable Countess of Buchan—would he do the same for the man who'd turned over his two brothers to King Edward for certain execution?

He might. Which was one more sin her husband could

lay at her feet. The Bruce had lived up to Eoin's faith in him; the king and his "lost cause" had been good for Scotland. Margaret should have had more faith in her husband. But it had seemed so hopeless, and she'd been terrified of what would happen to him if King Edward caught up with them.

It wasn't unlike the fear she felt now. Her fear for her father warred with her fear for her son. The boy must be terrified and exhausted—her father must be holding him up in the saddle by now.

As the sky grew dark, her fear worsened. Where were they? Surely they should have caught up to them by now? If they continued like this through the darkness someone would get hurt.

The next time they paused for one of their painfully short breaks to water the horses, Margaret could hold her tongue no longer. She found Eoin, talking to that same warrior again. Both men fell silent as she drew near. She looked back and forth between them, thinking that there was something similar about them. They were both tall, broad-shouldered, and built like a couple of King Edward's siege engines, but it was something more than that. It was the way they held themselves, the aura of invincibility, and the granite stillness of their expressions.

If she'd hoped to find sympathy from one of these men, however, it would not be from the tracker. The hostility in Eoin's dark-blue eyes was only marginally less in the tracker's.

From their continued silence, it seemed the other man also shared her husband's gruffness of manners and propensity for silence. They must be grand friends.

She pursed her lips and tipped her head to the unknown warrior. "My lord. I assume you know who I am. But as

'Lazarus' here has decided to dispense with the pleasantries, I'm afraid I don't know whom I am addressing."

He arched a brow and shot a look to Eoin before turning back to her. "Ewen Lamont, my lady."

She smiled as if to say, *Now that wasn't too hard, was it?*

Eoin must have objected to the smile because he bit out, "What do you want, Margaret?"

Aside from this scintillating conversation? Aside from an explanation of where in Hades he'd been for almost six years? She gritted her teeth so the bitter words wouldn't fly out and forced moderation to her tone. "We have to stop."

"There are plenty of castles in the area. If you are too tired to go on, I'm sure they will open their gates to Dugald MacDowell's daughter."

She was tempted to point out they might not welcome Eoin MacLean's wife. "I'm not too tired. But it's getting dark. If you keep pushing like this someone will get hurt— *Eachann* could get hurt."

He stiffened, and the other man—Ewen Lamont— turned to look at him. "Eachann?"

"My son," she explained. "*Our* son."

Lamont muttered what she thought was a rather strong curse, and his gaze went to Eoin's for confirmation.

Eoin's mouth tightened. "She claims the lad with MacDowell is my son."

Lamont gave a long, low whistle and shook his head, his expression seemingly one of sympathy for Eoin.

Margaret had to bite her tongue to keep from arguing about "claims." "I know you want to catch my father, but if you keep pushing like this, my father will keep pushing, and Eachann is the one who will suffer. Have you thought of what this pace must be like for him?"

Eoin answered with a flex of his jaw that made a muscle

start to tic. "What do you suggest we do? Let your father escape? If he makes it to the coast and a ship, we won't have a chance of catching them before he reaches whatever heavily fortified castle he decides to hole up in. They can't be more than mile or two ahead of us. We would have caught them by now had we not needed to avoid the parties of English soldiers your father sent after us. But there is no bloody way in hell I'll stop now."

Margaret couldn't believe this brutal, uncompromising man was her husband. He was more like . . .

She grimaced. He was more like her father. "So you would put your son's life at risk to prevent my father slipping through your fingers?"

Eoin kept a tight rein on his temper. He didn't need to defend himself to her. "It isn't me who has put his life at risk. It's your father." He looked to Lamont. "Come on. We've rested long enough."

Eoin walked away. But just before Ewen Lamont went after him, she thought he glanced at her with a glimmer of sympathy.

∞

"Your *son*, Striker? Christ, why didn't you tell me? I thought you took her with us for information."

Eoin mounted his horse. "I did, and there wasn't time."

Lamont shot him a look as if he knew the explanation was shite—which it was. But finding out that he had a son—a *five*-year-old son—had thrown him in such a state of shock and confusion the only thing he'd been able to concentrate on had been the mission. Find MacDowell and then he'd try to come to terms with the knowledge of a son. He sure as hell hadn't been ready to talk about it. He still wasn't.

"The lass is right," his partner said. "This could be dangerous for the lad. *If* he is yours—"

"He's mine," Eoin said, cutting him off angrily.

Lamont lifted a brow. "You didn't sound so certain a few minutes ago."

Eoin grunted a nonanswer.

"More than one way to exact retribution, is that it?"

Eoin glared at him. "Do you blame me? You know as well as I what she did."

His partner acknowledged the truth with a grim nod. "Aye. Although . . ."

Eoin's gaze narrowed. "Although what?"

Lamont shrugged. "I don't know. She's just not what I expected."

"She hides the snakes beneath the veil."

Lamont ignored the sarcasm. "She can't be much older than three and twenty."

"She turned five and twenty last June."

"She appears to genuinely care about the lad. And I saw her face when she saw you at the church. She didn't look like someone who had sent you happily to your death."

Eoin's mouth drew in a hard line. "Yet that is exactly what she did."

Lamont eyed him carefully. "You also didn't mention that she is rather . . . attractive."

Eoin felt his muscles tense in a way they hadn't in a long time. His wife had always drawn attention—masculine attention. Maybe more so now than she did at eighteen. How had Fin put it? Ripe as a peach? She was even riper. "I didn't think it mattered."

"It doesn't. But it was still a surprise. I didn't think anyone could rival MacLeod's wife."

Eoin shot him a glare. "How about your own?"

Lamont lifted a sly brow, and Eoin swore, realizing his partner had tricked him into admitting more than he wanted. Eoin didn't care about her anymore, how the hell could he still be jealous?

"If you're finished, I want to get back on the trail before we lose it again," Eoin said sharply.

MacDowell was a tricky bastard. He was also good at minimizing his tracks. But Lamont was the best tracker in Scotland. If there was a trail, Hunter would find it. Even in the dark.

But as they raced across the countryside, plunging deeper into the moonlight-shrouded forest, Eoin couldn't help but think how easy it would be for a horse to miss its footing. For a fall that could send a rider and the young boy with him sailing through the air to the hard ground. How easy it would be to snap a slim neck. Why were there so many branches sticking out? This was a damned "road." One of those branches could pluck out an eye or . . .

He stopped. Bloody hell, she'd gotten to him. She'd filled his head with a parade of horribles to make him do her bidding. They couldn't stop, damn it. MacDowell would get away—*with* his son. A siege could take months. Besides, there was no guarantee even if they did stop that MacDowell would follow suit. His son could still be in danger even if Eoin did call a halt to the chase.

But the decision was taken from his hands a short while later. They'd slowed for Lamont to check the prints, when he swore and called for a torch.

"What's the matter?" Eoin asked.

Lamont shook his head. "I think they split up."

Eoin felt the fury rise inside him. "Why?"

"There don't seem to be as many prints." He dismounted to walk up and down the path, counting off the horses in what seemed to be a jumbled mass of hoof marks. After seven and a half years as partners, Eoin had picked up enough tracking to know that Lamont could identify each horse by some defining mark—no matter how seemingly trivial—in its hoofprint. He counted off four. MacDowell and his sons had set off on five horses.

"There's one missing," Eoin filled in, swearing when Lamont nodded.

"Where?"

Lamont shook his head. "Probably at the last crossing. Damn it, I can't believe I missed it."

"It isn't your fault." It was Eoin's. With his quarry in sight, he'd pushed them too hard. He'd been the one to hurry Lamont at the last crossing near Cockermouth. "It doesn't matter. We'll catch them."

But they didn't. They backtracked to the previous crossing and rode for only a mile or two before coming to a large village where MacDowell had switched horses. By the time they tracked the new horse it was too late. The Cumbrian coast at Wyrkinton was only a handful of miles away—as was the heavily garrisoned peel tower of Sir Gilbert de Curwen. They wouldn't be able to evade the English soldiers and catch up to MacDowell in time. They'd lost them.

"What now?" Lamont asked.

"We'll find them in Galloway."

"I can think of at least six castles he might take refuge in. It could take weeks to find him."

Eoin didn't realize Margaret had come up beside them. "He'll go to Dumfries," she said. "It's the strongest, and easiest to access from the river."

"You sound so certain," Eoin said.

"As certain as I can be. It's where I think he was

planning to go after the—" She stopped. "When he returned from England."

After the *wedding*. Eoin felt his teeth gritting again. "And I'm just supposed to take your word for it? He could just as easily go to Buittle. It is also easily accessed by the river and heavily defended."

"Aye, he could, but I think he'll go to Dumfries. It's his favorite castle, and the keeper is one of his most trusted men."

"Who?"

Even in the mist-shrouded moonlight he could see the pink flush rise to her cheeks. "Tristan MacCan." Eoin felt every muscle in his body tighten, but he didn't say anything, and she continued. "I don't expect you to trust me—you never have before—but I thought you wanted my advice."

"I do. And I did trust you once."

Their eyes held, and he could see the guilt the darkness couldn't quite hide. She looked like she wanted to say something, but after a glance at Lamont and the other men who were pretending not to listen, she took a deep breath instead. "I have no reason to lie, Eoin. I told you I would do whatever it takes to get my son back. I want him as badly as you want my father. This is why you brought me, isn't it? But if you think you know my father better than I, by all means, do what you want. But I'm going to Dumfries."

Some things hadn't changed. Outwardly she might look like the proper lady—he'd been surprised by the difference in her appearance and reserved manner—but the lass who'd strolled into the Great Hall of Stirling Castle like a pirate taking over a ship and had been too confident and bold for her own good was still there. She'd never shied from a challenge before, and she certainly wasn't doing so now.

He'd known she would be trouble from the first; he'd just never guessed how much.

He turned to Lamont. "Tell the men to get a few hours of rest. We'll ride for the border at dawn."

"We're sleeping here?" Margaret asked him as his partner walked away.

"Rustic sleeping arrangements didn't used to bother you."

She didn't miss the pointed reminder of those nights they'd shared by the campfire all those years ago—why the hell was he acting like he remembered?—and lifted her chin. "I was referring to the fact that we are a few miles away from Wyrkinton."

He gave a sharp laugh. "The English lack the courage to attack Bruce's men at night in the forest. They'll not stray from the safety of the castle walls until dawn. You need not fear for your safety." He paused. "Although you might be cold in that fine gown, so I'd stay close to the fire."

She flushed angrily at the sarcasm he couldn't quite hide. She'd been about to get married, damn it. It shouldn't bother him.

"I wouldn't be wearing a wedding gown if I'd known I still had a husband. How could you, Eoin? You *promised* you would come back to me, if it was in your power. How could you let me think you were dead all these years? Did you not think I had a right to know that my husband lived?"

"Right?" Six years of pent-up anger, six years of festering on a wound that hadn't healed, six years of pretending it didn't matter that his wife had betrayed him, couldn't stay buried another moment. He'd promised, aye, but that was before she tried to put him in the grave.

He took a threatening step toward her, practically

baring his teeth. "After what you did, you lost the 'right' to know anything. As I recall you made a number of promises as well. I don't owe you a damned thing, Maggie."

"What about Eachann? What did you owe him?"

He stilled. "I didn't know about him."

"Whose fault is that?" She spoke softly but the challenge hit hard.

He fisted his hands at his side so he wouldn't touch her. What the hell was it about this woman that made him want to drag her into his arms and kiss that defiance right from her mouth?

But her anger fell as quickly as it had risen. She looked sad and defeated, and somehow that unsettled him even more. "Maybe you don't owe me anything, but don't think that I haven't blamed myself for what happened to you—or what I thought happened to you—every day since. I never meant to betray you, Eoin. I *loved* you."

Loved him so much she'd left him. Loved him so much she'd been discussing dissolving their marriage with her girlhood sweetheart right before he'd kissed her. Loved him so much she'd sent him away and told him to never come back. "So it was all a big mistake, is that it? Did your brother lie then? Did you not tell someone of my presence that night?"

She shook her head, her eyes stark. "No, it wasn't a mistake. I did tell someone, but I was trying to protect you."

"By betraying me?"

She ignored his sarcasm. "Brigid found me in the forest after you left and threatened to tell my father I'd been raped if I didn't tell her what happened. I made a mistake in trusting someone who'd been like a sister to me, but I didn't feel like I had a choice."

"How about the *choice* to keep your mouth shut?" He

stepped toward her, anger pounding through him. "How much more clear did I need to be? Was 'no one,' 'under any circumstances,' and 'my life' subject to interpretation? I *trusted* you, damn it. I told you how important it was that you not tell anyone I was there. I let down every one of those men on that beach because I believed my wife—the girl I loved more than anyone else in the world—would know to keep her *damned mouth shut*. Your intentions don't make a damned bit of difference to all those men on that beach."

She looked stricken. Her eyes filled with tears as she tried to explain. "I'm sorry. I had no idea what you planned. I didn't want to risk having my father's men chasing after you. I thought by telling her that I was protecting you. I never imagined she would go to my brother with the information."

His mouth fell in a hard line. He supposed he should be glad she hadn't gone to her father herself. Glad it hadn't been some petty form of revenge for all his perceived wrongs. But six years of hatred had formed a thick layer of steel around his thinking where his wife was concerned that was not easily penetrated. She'd told someone. Did it matter why?

And the result hadn't changed.

Still, he was surprised to learn of her friend's part in it. "Why did she?" he asked.

"She was in love with Dougal and thought it would ingratiate her enough to my father to permit a marriage between them. Ironically, Dougal did receive a bride for what happened, it just wasn't Brigid."

A flicker of pain crossed her face, and he found himself asking, "What happened?"

Margaret gazed at him unflinchingly. "Brigid threw

herself off the cliffs at Dunskey Castle, not long after Dougal's marriage. She never forgave herself for what happened that night. All those men . . ." She shuddered, and then looked up at him. "She didn't realize what would happen, and neither did I." When he didn't say anything, she added, "I don't expect you to forgive me. You trusted me to keep your secret, and I didn't. I should have let Brigid tell them I'd been attacked and maybe . . ." She stopped and straightened. "I made a mistake, but it was in trusting a friend when I shouldn't have. I tried to help when I realized what Brigid had done, but I was too late."

"What do you mean, you tried to help?"

"My father locked me in my chamber, but I climbed out of the tower and lit the old beacon near Kirkcolm. But your ships had already reached the beach."

He was silent, taken aback by what she'd revealed. *She'd* lit the beacon? He'd always wondered about their mysterious helper. "It wasn't too late for all the ships," he admitted. "Two were able to escape in time."

He'd give her that, but his steely expression told her that was all he would concede. Whatever her intentions, she *had* betrayed his trust by telling her friend.

"I'm glad," she said softly.

He believed her. Not that it changed anything. Too much had happened between them. Too many years had passed.

For a man known for seeing everything on a battlefield, ironically he'd never seen her coming.

Margaret had made him feel something he hadn't felt before or since. The passion had been incomparable. But it was more than physical. Far more. For so long his life had revolved around war—being the best warrior not just physically but also mentally. He loved the challenge of outthinking and outwitting the enemy ever since he was a lad. It was all he'd ever thought about—cared about—until he'd met her. For a short while, she'd made the world a little bigger than the battlefield. He'd cared about something else.

And it had cost him. He'd done stupid things to see her. Taken chances where he shouldn't have.

Maybe that was the real problem. As much as he blamed her for what happened, he blamed himself even more. He should never have confronted her that night. Maybe it wouldn't have changed anything, but it had still been a mistake. He shouldn't have trusted her with something so important. Bruce knew that, and he knew that. He couldn't fault his kinsman for questioning his judgment. When it came to Margaret MacDowell, Eoin had never seemed to have any.

Even now just looking at her was enough to get him hard. The memories flooded him. He could recall every inch of creamy skin beneath that blasted gown that he wanted to rip to shreds. He remembered burying his face between the generous breasts displayed to such tempting perfection in the layers of formfitting silk. He remembered the scent of her skin, the silken honey of her pleasure, and the sound of her moans as he'd made her shatter. He remembered the way her hips would lift up to meet him as he'd thrust, taking him deeper, harder, faster.

Christ.

He stepped back. The sooner this was over the better. The quick dissolution of their marriage had been complicated by the discovery of a son, but it hadn't changed his desire to put an end to it. The end of the war was drawing near, and Bruce had already hinted at the lands, which would be his reward. Lands *and* a bride, if Eoin wanted one. Surprisingly, he did. Seeing his brethren with their wives made him realize what he was missing. He'd been alone for too long.

Hell, even Lachlan MacRuairi was bloody happy. Like Eoin, the Guardsman with the disposition of the viper that had given him his war name made a disastrous first marriage to a woman who had betrayed him. But he'd found happiness in his second, and Eoin took some hope from that.

Almost as if she knew what he was thinking, she asked, "What happens now, Eoin?"

He gave her a hard stare. "What do you think? We sure as hell can't go back."

"We could try to go forward."

Angered by the unmistakable hitch in his chest, his response came out harsher than he intended. "What would be the point of that? You seem to have found England much more to your liking than you ever did Kerrera."

The slight flush to her cheeks and pursing of her mouth were the only signs that she'd heard the none-too-subtle criticism. But she'd always known how to strike back. "Aye, Sir John ensured I always felt welcome and did everything to see to my happiness. He wanted to share his life with me—*all* of it."

The dagger slid right between his ribs and twisted. The sharpness of the pain almost made him flinch. Damn it, it shouldn't hurt so much. After all these years, nothing she could say or do should be able to get to him. "I'm sure he did."

He tried to walk away, but she caught his arm. The shock of her touch did make him flinch this time. "I know I wasn't the kind of wife you wanted, Eoin. But if you wanted someone like Lady Barbara, why didn't you just marry her? It would have been much easier on us both."

"Aye, it would have."

It was the truth, although he hadn't intended to strike so hard. From the look in her eyes, there was no doubt he'd done just that.

He didn't want to do this anymore—any of it. The more they were together, the more they would hurt each other.

He looked down into the beautiful features bathed in moonlight of the woman who'd haunted his dreams for too long. "I think it will be best for us both if you and I part ways permanently when this is over."

She drew herself up stiffly with a sharp intake of breath. Her eyes scanned his face, as if looking for an opening. "If that is what you want."

Right now what he wanted was to pull her up against him and kiss her until he could no longer feel her pounding through his blood, invading his bones, and haunting his dreams. Instead he answered with a nod and walked away.

18

*P*ART WAYS PERMANENTLY . . .

After all this time, it shouldn't hurt so horribly. Of course he wanted nothing to do with her. But hearing him speak so unequivocally of ending their marriage—God knows how he intended to do so without making their son a bastard—hurt very horribly indeed.

Through the long, sleepless night in the cold (sleeping outside wasn't nearly as comfortable without Eoin beside her), and the even longer ride north to Scotland, Margaret asked herself how she could have thought even for a moment that Eoin would want anything more to do with her. He hated her—as she'd known he would if he lived. What had she expected? Forgiveness?

Some mistakes were unforgivable. She'd left him, told him never to come back, and betrayed his trust, leading to the deaths of so many men. Even if she'd thought she hadn't had choices, she had. Looking back, given the consequences, it might not seem as if she'd made the right decisions, but she'd done what she thought best at the time. Obviously, Eoin didn't agree, and given the consequences how could she blame him?

But as she tossed and turned on the hard ground shivering and miserable, on what was to have been her wedding night to a man she'd come to care for—a good man who'd been nothing but kind to her and her son—she found her bitterness toward Eoin growing. She might have deserved this, but Sir John didn't—and neither did Eachann. For Eoin to let her think he was dead for *six* years, mourning for him, suffering, blaming herself, raising *their* child alone, only to suddenly appear on her wedding day when she'd finally let herself try to be happy was just as unforgivable.

She could have been happy, too—or at least she would have tried, blast it. Poor Sir John. She felt horrible about how quickly she'd had to leave him. She'd barely had a chance to mumble a hasty apology before she'd hopped on the horse to try to catch up to Eoin, who was already riding away.

She would write Sir John at the earliest opportunity and tell him . . . what? That she was sorry she couldn't marry him now because the husband she'd mourned for six years, the husband who despised her, had decided to return and throw her life in disarray? Make her miserable? Divorce her?

Her chest squeezed. But even if he did dissolve their marriage, Margaret knew there was no going back to Sir John. It wouldn't be fair to him. If Eoin had truly died that horrible day, they would have had a chance. But while her husband lived . . . how could she contemplate a life with someone else?

Blast him!

Aye, it was a miserable night filled with anger, frustration, disappointment, and heartache.

She would have liked to say she found some solace when she woke and learned they were heading to

Dumfries. But she suspected it wasn't Eoin trusting her as much as him reaching the same conclusion on his own.

By time they arrived late the following evening, Margaret was exhausted. She barely raised an objection when Eoin left her with the Benedictine nuns at the Abbey of Lincluden for the night, while he and the other men rode to a location he would not share with her to rendezvous with more of Bruce's men.

At the first opportunity she'd written her note to Sir John. It had been more difficult than she'd anticipated, and she'd been grateful for the solitude to try to find the words to express her regret and disappointment, yet still make it clear that their relationship must end.

But with her task complete, she'd begun to fear the solitude would be permanent, and Eoin would not return. Finally on the third morning, the prioress came to the small chamber she'd been given to announce that she had a visitor.

Eoin was waiting for her in the cloister garden. She tried to quell the sudden quickening of her pulse. Like her, he'd bathed and changed his clothes. He no longer wore the mail shirt of an English soldier, but a black leather *cotun* studded with bits of mail. His chausses were also made of the darkened leather. Illogically, he seemed even more imposing without the heavy armor.

Dear God, who was this man? Was this grim, fierce-looking fortress of war really the serious but still capable of smiling young warrior she'd married? Her husband might be alive, but he was not the man she remembered. He was a stranger, and the pain of that burned in her chest.

His gaze slid over her as she approached, and she didn't miss the slight lift of his brow at her attire. "I see you are being well tended."

How easy it was for him to poke old wounds. "The nuns were kind enough to lend me another gown. I know you think a harlot's yellow hood is more appropriate, but I'm afraid a black habit was all they had."

He frowned, clearly taken aback. "I never thought that."

"Didn't you?" She laughed harshly, remembering the accusations of that night, even if he didn't want to. "I didn't bleed, don't you remember questioning whether I was a virgin? What about all those trips I took to Oban? And I tried to seduce your friend—I'm sure your sister told you all about it."

For the first time since he'd reappeared in her life, the impenetrable facade of hatred dropped. He appeared genuinely discomfited. "I was out of my mind with jealousy that night, Margaret. I wasn't thinking rationally. All I could see was the woman who'd left me in another man's arms. I never doubted your innocence—not really. Nor did I think you were unfaithful to me. I owe you an apology. I should have believed you about Fin, I just didn't want to think my oldest friend could . . ." He drew himself up and looked her in the eye. "He admitted to kissing you in the barn. He said he was drunk and never meant to scare you. I'm sorry that happened to you. You were my wife, and I should have protected you."

Margaret felt the heat in her throat burning in her eyes. They were the words she'd desperately wanted to hear, six years too late. She looked away. "You were gone. There was nothing you could have done."

He took her arm and forced her to look at him. His fingers seemed to burn through the cloth to imprint on her skin. Even now, after all these years, her heart still did a tiny flip when he touched her and her skin flushed with a blast of heat.

"I could have listened to you when you first voiced your problems with Fin. I could have made sure my mother was aware of the situation. I could have tried to stop him from marrying my sister."

She saw the rage and self-recrimination in his eyes and instinctively wanted to soothe it. She of all people could understand. Like her, he'd trusted a friend. "It was a long time ago, Eoin. I'm sure there are things we would have both done differently had we known what would happen. You were right: there is no use trying to go back."

He looked like he wanted to say something else, but he let go of her arm and stepped back. "Aye, well, you defended yourself well. Your knee did some damage. From what I hear he was in bed for days." He gave a slight shudder as if the thought of it caused him pain. "Remind me to not make you angry."

Though she didn't like to think of anyone suffering, in the case of Fin she would make an exception. Her mouth twisted in a smile. "I will."

He smiled back at her for a moment, and then seemed to remember himself and shook off the moment of connection. "I came to tell you that you were right. Your father has taken refuge in Dumfries Castle."

"And Eachann?" she asked anxiously. "He is all right?"

"A boy was with your father. That is all we know. Your brothers have taken refuge at Buittle."

She nodded, not surprised that they'd separated. "Have you attempted to communicate with my father?"

Eoin nodded. "He has refused to release the boy."

Though she suspected the answer, Margaret's heart squeezed. "He won't hurt him, Eoin."

He didn't respond. Clearly, he was not inclined to trust her judgment. She didn't blame him, but she meant it. Her father loved Eachann. He would not hurt him . . . intentionally.

Her heart squeezed with fear. "What happens next?" she asked.

His mouth fell in a grim line. "Edward Bruce is laying siege on the castle."

The blood slid from her face as panic jumped in her pulse. "No! You can't let them do that. Our son will suffer along with them."

She could see the fear in his eyes that matched her own—and something else: anger. "There is nothing I can do." He'd obviously tried. "Now that we've cornered your father, he will not be allowed to escape. The siege at Perth is over, the castle has fallen, and the king is on his way here."

She would have blanched if there was any blood left in her face. "Bruce is coming here?"

He nodded. "Galloway's castles are next." The former Balliol and MacDowell strongholds of Dumfries, Buittle, Dalswinton, and Caerlaverock.

One by one Robert the Bruce was taking back Scotland's castles from English control and destroying them so that they might not be used against him again.

"But Eachann . . ." She shuddered, thinking what a long siege could do to him. "Let me talk to my father. He will listen to me."

Eoin shook his head. "Carrick won't allow it," he said, using the title (along with Lord of Galloway) that Robert Bruce had given his younger brother, Edward. He tried to console her. "Try not to worry. It won't last long. The castle hasn't been properly provisioned in months. Your father will agree to parley soon."

She shook her head. "You don't know my father. He will never surrender to Bruce. He'll starve first."

He didn't say anything, and from the grim look on his face she suspected he did know her father and agreed. "I should go," he said. "I just wanted to keep you informed. I will try to send word every few days or so."

"You can't expect me to stay here!"

∞

That was exactly what he expected her to do. Eoin stared down at the outraged woman who could be wearing a sackcloth and still manage to stir his blood. The proof was pounding against his stomach. What the hell was wrong with him?

"Where do you expect to go?" he asked impatiently.

"With you."

In his tent? *God's blood!* He almost shuddered. "That's impossible."

"Why?"

Because apparently six years hadn't made his cock any smarter. "Camp is no place for a lady."

"Perhaps not, but there must be some women?" She continued before he could object to the sort of women who were about camp, stepping close to him to make her case. Probably closer than she realized. Their bodies were practically touching, and every muscle in his body tightened. "Please, Eoin. I won't be in the way. I swear I won't embarrass you. I've changed."

He frowned. "What are you talking about?"

Her eyes dropped from his as a delicate shade of pink rose to her cheeks. "I'm not the ignorant girl I was when we married. I'll not say the wrong thing or do something foolish like move the pieces of a chess game around. I can read and write now. I'll not challenge your friend to a race or see who can drink a mug of ale the quickest. I haven't worn breeches in a long time. I am no longer the backward, irreverent creature you need to try to turn into a proper wife."

Eoin stared at her in shock. Was that what she thought? "That isn't what I . . ." *Ah hell*. It was what he'd wanted. But he'd never meant her to think he was ashamed of her. He'd just wanted her not to stand out so much. Not to be so outrageous. To not look at him as if she couldn't wait to get to the bedchamber. He'd wanted her to show a little restraint and decorum. To be more like the other ladies.

But if he'd wanted someone like Lady Barbara, why had he married Margaret?

Because she'd been different. Because she'd been fresh and sweet, and yes, outrageous. Because she'd made him laugh. Because she'd teased and challenged him, and driven him crazy with lust. Because she'd breezed into a room like she owned it, with her unbound hair flowing wildly around her shoulders, and he knew there would never be another woman for him.

It was *her* he'd wanted. Why had he tried to turn her into someone else?

Guilt twisted in his gut. "You never embarrassed me," he said gruffly.

She gave him a wry smile that said she didn't believe him. "It was a long time ago, Eoin. It doesn't matter anymore."

She tried to turn her face, but without realizing what he was doing, he reached out and cupped her chin in his hand to force her gaze back to his.

It was a mistake. Her skin was every bit as warm and baby soft as he remembered. He wanted to run his thumb over the smooth curve of her cheek and the delicate point of her chin.

"It does matter. I'm sorry if I made you feel that way. I thought it would be easier for you to fit in if you were—"

"Like everyone else?" she finished for him.

He nodded, embarrassed.

"You don't need to apologize. Just please, take me with you. I can't stay here not knowing what is happening. I need to be there, Eoin. I promise you won't even know I'm there."

As if that were bloody possible. He'd always been too damned aware of her. Even now when by all rights he should want nothing to do with her. But he understood her urgency. She was worried about the boy.

She must have sensed his hesitation. "I can be of help. I know the castle, and I know how my father thinks. I can help get Eachann back, I know I can."

He shook his head. "You aren't wanted, Margaret. Your presence would make things difficult."

She misunderstood, her breath catching as if his words had stabbed. "You have made your feelings for me clear, Eoin. I know you don't want me. I won't interfere if . . ." She looked down, her cheeks pale. "If you already have a woman in your tent. I will sleep outside if you desire privacy."

He knew he didn't owe her any explanations. She was the one who'd been about to marry another man. He shouldn't care what she thought. Hell, maybe it would even make it easier if he did have a woman in his tent.

But it hadn't been himself he'd been talking about but the others in the Bruce camp. Too many people knew what she'd done. His brethren, the king, some of his men. She was Dugald MacDowell's daughter and the enemy. He of all people shouldn't need a reminder.

He hardened his jaw, refusing to let her sway him. "You will stay here for now. I will send word as soon as I have anything to report."

"But—"

"It's not a request, Margaret," he said, cutting her off.

Her eyes blazed golden fire. She straightened her spine and lifted her chin in that defiant way he remembered. "Apparently all that extra muscle has turned you into a bully. You have no right to order me to do anything."

"Don't I?" he challenged. "I'm still your husband." He paused significantly. "At least for now."

She flushed angrily. "A fact you seem to have conveniently forgotten for six years."

He hadn't forgotten. That was the problem. And being around her was making him weak. He couldn't soften toward her, damn it. He hated her, didn't he?

He'd thought so, but maybe "the why" had mattered more than he wanted it to. He'd thought of her as a traitorous bitch for six years, but he couldn't think of her that way now—not after hearing her explanation. It wasn't as black and white as he'd thought. She hadn't intentionally betrayed him. She hadn't been trying to get back at him by revealing his presence in the area to her father. She hadn't purposefully sought to see him captured or killed. And that knowledge had taken the bite out of his anger and hatred.

Aye, what he was feeling right now was definitely not hate. It was hot and fiery, surged through his blood, set his nerves on edge, and made him want to lash out, not with anger but with something else. Six years or sixty years, he didn't think it would make a difference: he would still want her.

Fuck. The oath was painfully appropriate.

He gave her a hard look to hide the emotions teeming

inside him. "Aye, well I wasn't the first one to forget. Perhaps this time you can remember that you are married and stay where I leave you."

Not wanting to hear what he was sure would be her furious response, he turned on his heel and left.

❀

Maybe this wasn't such a good idea. Aware of the number of eyes following her, Margaret drew the cloak more firmly around her. She wished she had a hood. The long unbound waves of red streaming down her back beneath the gossamer-thin, silky golden veil suddenly felt conspicuous.

Perhaps she shouldn't have changed gowns and veils? The nun's habit would have certainly discouraged the blatant staring. But when the package arrived yesterday at the convent, Margaret assumed the gown and veil were a gift from her husband—an apology for his high-handed attitude at the convent a few days ago.

All right, she didn't *really* believe the gown was an apology (Eoin had been far too assured in his "lord and master" role), but it was as good as an excuse as any to come find him.

Goodness knows how he'd been able to procure something so fine in such a short time. She would have thought the mossy green velvet gown trimmed in gold embroidery and matching gold silk veil had been made for her, were it not a smidgen too small in the bodice and hips.

In any event, she thought it the least she could do to wear the gift, given that he wasn't going to be pleased to find her here. But if he thought she would meekly stand aside and do his bidding . . .

She fisted her hands at her sides and tightened her

mouth, recalling his imperious order to stay put. She hadn't changed *that* much.

Still, she hadn't thought it would be so difficult to find him—the camp was much larger than she'd realized. Hundreds of men had gathered for the siege, turning the grassy moorlands of the countryside around Dumfries Castle into a makeshift village of tents, carts, stalls, kitchens, and pens for the livestock and horses.

She was forced to walk a gauntlet of men—rather *big* men, she couldn't help noticing—as she wound her way through the bustling camp.

Though her impulse was to bite her lip, look down, and try not to make eye contact with the rough-looking bunch of warriors sitting outside the tents, Margaret knew better than to show weakness. Instead, she met the bold stares and tried to pretend she didn't hear the suggestive comments that followed her. As Eoin had warned her, it was clear from the "invitations" being hurled in her direction what type of woman typically frequented an army's camp.

Bruce's men had a reputation for being brigands, and she must admit they looked the part. Most of them appeared not to have seen a razor or a bath in months and looked far more familiar with a barber's cauterizing iron than his scissors. Fierce, scarred visages, and hard, unsmiling mouths were half-hidden behind scruffy beards and long, unkempt hair. They were big, imposing men made even bigger and more imposing by the abundance of armor and weaponry surrounding them. Most wore leather *cotuns*, some of which were studded with mail, and she seemed to have arrived at weapon preparing time, as many men were sitting outside their tents sharpening or otherwise tending to their various swords, axes, pikes, and hammers.

Too bad she couldn't have arrived at nap time instead.

Truth be told, they didn't look all that different from her father's Gallovidian warriors; the difference being that her father's men all knew who she was and wouldn't look at her so rudely—or crudely for that matter.

Licentious stares were nothing she hadn't had to deal with before—if on a smaller, less intimidating scale. Still, she was looking rather anxiously for the leaders' tents. Eoin might have been a regular man-at-arms for his father when she'd met him all those years ago, but it was clear he'd made his way up through the ranks in the intervening years. She couldn't say she was surprised. Even her father had been aware of his promise. This was always what had been important to him—maybe it was all that had been important to him.

Catching sight of larger tents on the ridge, she started to walk in that direction when an arm snaked around her waist from behind, and her breath jammed as she was jerked against a hard, mail-clad body. She got a quick glance of the grizzled face of a thickset, dark-haired warrior, and a not so quick whiff of pungent days' old male sweat. The stench was overwhelming, and instinctively she tried to break free.

His hot, ale-laden breath rang in her ear. "Not so fast, lass. Damn, you're a fine-looking piece." Good lord, he was drunk. She could feel his hand moving toward her breast and tried to twist to evade the touch, but he managed to get in a good squeeze anyway. "Malcolm and I could use a little company. Isn't that right, Malcolm?"

A taller, leaner soldier stepped in front of her. He was no less grizzled in appearance, and was missing a few teeth, but he seemed to smell marginally better. Or maybe it was that the first warrior smelled so terribly, he drowned out everything else. Her stomach was rolling, and she was in danger of losing its contents if she didn't breathe fresh air soon.

"Aye," Malcolm said appraisingly. "Been a long time since I've had company like you. Christ," he said with a glance down her chest, which was no longer hidden behind her cloak thanks to the first warrior's groping. The new gown with its too-tight bodice displayed her breasts rather . . . prominently. "Would you look at the size of those tits!" He frowned. "That's a fine gown for a whore."

"That's because I'm not a whore," Margaret said angrily, trying to use her elbow to wrench away from the brute. But it was like trying to dent steel. "Let go of me," she said.

"What's going on here?" a deep voice said. "I think the lass isn't interested, Captain."

"Stay out of this, MacGowan. It's none of your business."

"I'm making it my business." The man came into view, stepping between Malcolm and the man he'd identified as a captain. Margaret had seen her fair share of handsome men, but her breath still sputtered a little. If she weren't partial to dark-blond hair, midnight-blue eyes, and mysterious, this man might have persuaded her to consider dark—almost black—hair, steely-blue eyes, and dangerous. Good lord, he was a handsome devil, possessing the dark good looks that conjured up all kinds of wickedness. Perhaps a couple of inches taller than Eoin with a heavily muscled build, this man could no doubt hold his own on the battlefield. "Let her go, Captain."

"You forget who you are talking to, MacGowan. I give you the orders, not the other way around. Get out of here, before I see you tossed in the stocks or flogged for insubordination."

The man's eyes met hers. "Are you willing, lass?"

"Most assuredly not," she said.

No doubt hearing the refined tones of her speech, which in their drunken lust the other two had apparently missed, MacGowan frowned. "What is your name, my lady?"

She almost proudly belted out that she was Margaret MacDowell, daughter to the MacDowell chief. Realizing this might not be the best audience for that information, she quickly changed her response. "The wife of Eoin MacLean."

The captain let her go so quickly she almost stumbled.

"MacLean isn't married."

MacGowan must have heard the same uncertainty in his voice that she had and responded to the captain, "You better hope he isn't."

Malcolm's face had taken on a decidedly ashen hue. "We meant no offense, my lady. It was a misunderstanding."

Margaret would have been inclined to let it go, if the captain hadn't decided to take his foiled plans out on her rescuer. Without warning, the captain's fist plowed into MacGowan's jaw. A second landed in his ribs. And then a third. In between shots, the captain was mumbling about "knowing his place," and "peasant get."

As it was clear, MacGowan wasn't going to fight back, Margaret tried to put a stop to it herself. Unfortunately, the captain was too angry, too belligerent, and perhaps too drunk to notice that his next punch was headed toward her face and not the young warrior's shoulder.

She cried out as her head was slammed back with the force of the punch and pain exploded in her head. The last thing she heard before she fell back was a great roar.

19

THE SOUNDS OF a disturbance outside interrupted their meeting. "What in Hades is going on out there?" Edward Bruce asked his squire. "Find out."

The lad ran out and Eoin tried to get the king's brother back on track. Of Bruce's four brothers, Edward was the only who still lived and the only one whom Eoin had never liked. His dislike had only grown after fighting beside him for the better part of five years.

When the king had sent his brother as his lieutenant to try to wrestle the troublesome south and Borders into submission, in addition to Sir James Douglas and Sir Thomas Randolph, four members of the Highland Guard had gone with him: Eoin, Lamont, Boyd, and—until he'd defected to the enemy—Seton. Though they were sometimes called elsewhere for various missions, and at times the rest of the Guard would join them, Eoin had spent most of his time since their return to Scotland in the south with Edward.

At his best, Edward Bruce was an arrogant prig, impetuous, and mercurial. He was both fiercely loyal to his brother and deeply jealous of him. The love that "the

Bruce" inspired in his men was conspicuously missing toward his brother. It wasn't hard to see why. Edward was not half the leader his brother was. He didn't like taking advice or letting anyone else get the credit, which often put him at direct odds with the members of the Highland Guard—like now.

"We can get in there," Eoin said with forced evenness. "What harm is there in at least letting us try?"

"The harm is having you killed. What do you think my brother would say if I ordered a mission that had some of his prized warriors killed? Nay. We'll proceed with the siege. MacDowell won't be able to hold out for long. You and your brethren have seen to that. There hasn't been a shipment of provisions that has made its way through in months."

Eoin's patience was running out fast. This wasn't about them getting killed, it was about Edward getting credit for bringing down MacDowell. He'd barely been able to hide his glee when Eoin had returned from England without him.

But there was more to this than getting MacDowell now. "My son is in there," Eoin said.

Edward's gaze sharpened, hearing the warning—or threat—in Eoin's voice. "That is unfortunate. But I'm sure the boy will not be harmed. He's MacDowell's grandson, after all."

The sneer was unmistakable. Edward would never let Eoin forget that it was his wife and her family who'd been responsible for the death of two of his brothers. Eoin had never blamed him for the sentiment, but something pricked now. He was saved from what would probably have been an ugly exchange of words with his kinsman by the return of the squire. "It's a fight, my lord," the lad said.

"Between the captain and one of your men-at-arms over a lass."

"A lass?" Edward asked.

The boy nodded. "Aye, a beautiful one with red hair."

Eoin's blood went cold. It couldn't be. There were a lot of beautiful lasses with red hair. But he couldn't convince himself that it wasn't her. He'd half-expected Margaret to defy him. Hell, he was more surprised it had taken her three days to do so.

Trouble.

He left the tent without a word. As soon as he stopped outside he could hear them. But it was what he saw that made his heart drop like a rock at his feet. It was Margaret all right, smack dab in the middle of a brawl. Fury rose inside him. What the hell was she doing? She was going to get herself killed!

Eoin saw the man's fist fly back, but he was too far away to stop it. All he could do was roar as a primal rage tore through him. He watched in agonizing helplessness as Margaret's head snapped back, and she flew to the ground with the force of the fist that pummeled into her jaw.

She didn't move.

Eoin crossed the distance of fifty or so yards in seconds flat. He couldn't think. A red cloud swarmed in front of his eyes. Like his Viking ancestors before him, he went berserk. He slammed his fist into the captain again and again. He would have killed him had Boyd, Lamont, and Douglas not pulled him off.

It took all three of them.

"What the hell is going on here, MacGowan?" Douglas addressed the tall, dark-haired warrior a few moments later. From his biting tone, it was clear Douglas didn't like the man.

Slowly the red haze started to dissipate; Eoin's head cleared. Vaguely he realized that MacGowan had been fighting the captain until Eoin had intervened. Now, however, Eoin was patently aware that this MacGowan had gone over to help Margaret and was carefully easing her up. Suddenly, he could sympathize with Douglas's animosity.

But Margaret wasn't looking at the young warrior. She was looking at Eoin. Their eyes met and he could see her fear, her worry, and her concern. For him. "I'm fine," she whispered.

Eoin's mouth clamped shut. She wasn't fine, damn it. She was hurt. Even now he could see the bruise forming on her jaw. God, she could have been killed.

His fists clenched. He must have looked like he was going to finish the job because she added insistently, "It was a misunderstanding, Eoin."

"Someone better tell me what is going on here," Edward Bruce demanded. "Who is this woman?"

"My wife," Eoin said without hesitation, although he knew what the response would provoke.

Edward Bruce's face turned livid. His gaze slid over Margaret with unrepressed hatred before turning back to Eoin. "What is she doing here? How the hell could you bring a spy into camp?"

Margaret wobbled as she stood, and Eoin would have lurched for her, but MacGowan steadied her. "I'm not a spy," she said. "I'm here to help free my son."

Edward ignored her. He turned on Eoin with fury raging in his eyes. "Get the bitch out of here. She is responsible for the deaths of my brothers. She's a fucking *MacDowell.*"

Edward Bruce wasn't saying anything that Eoin hadn't thought a hundred times in the past six years. But hearing the words from someone else—especially from Edward—grated on every nerve ending in his body. It was wrong, and Eoin couldn't let it stand.

He took a threatening step toward Bruce's second-in-command. "She is also my wife, *cousin*, and as long as she remains so, you will give her the respect that position deserves. What happened was not Margaret's fault. She made a mistake but didn't intend to betray us. If you want someone to blame, blame me."

It was clear from the look on his face that Edward did. But he'd seen Eoin fight and was wise enough to hold his tongue—or Douglas held it for him by steering the conversation away from Margaret.

"So what happened?" Douglas was looking at MacGowan again with barely contained animosity. "You do know that you can be punished for hitting a superior? Perhaps Carrick should send you home?"

"Stay out of it, Jamie," MacGowan clipped back at him. Eoin had never heard anyone call Douglas Jamie before. "Besides, I thought you were happy to see me gone from Douglas."

Douglas clenched his fists and looked like he might strike the other man when Edward intervened. "I've told you before to stop interfering, Douglas. MacGowan is my man, and a good soldier. I don't care about your past—leave it there." He turned to MacGowan. "But in this case, I'm going to have to agree with him. You better have a damned good excuse."

"He does," Margaret said. "He was protecting me."

Eoin didn't like the sound of that at all. Douglas wasn't the only one clenching his fists. "From what?" he demanded.

Margaret bit her lip and a soft blush rose to her cheeks.

A different kind of swelling rose inside him. "These men mistook me for someone else. MacGowan corrected them, and the captain took offense. When MacGowan wouldn't defend himself," she turned to Edward, "I assume because he was following protocol not to fight with a commander, I tried to stop it and got in the way. It wasn't until after I was struck that he fought back. I hope he will not be punished for my mistake."

They all understood for whom she'd been mistaken. Eoin would have been furious, if he wasn't too busy being proud. After the way Edward had verbally attacked her minutes before—not to mention having to admit to being mistaken for a camp follower—Eoin couldn't help but admire how confidently and matter-of-factly she faced her detractor. It was a glimpse of the girl he'd fallen in love with. The devil-may-care girl who knew her own worth and didn't care whether those around her agreed.

Even Edward appeared taken aback. He wasn't wholly unlike his brother, and he, too, had been steeped in chivalry for most of his life. It reappeared now. "I would not punish a man for defending a woman's honor—any woman's," he added.

Margaret didn't seem to mind, even if Eoin did. She brightened. "Then I think it's best if we forget all about this."

She must have sensed Eoin's gaze on her. She turned and their eyes met. When she bit her lip again, he knew she'd gotten the message: there was no way in hell he was going to forget about this.

∞

Margaret tried to tell herself it didn't mean anything. But how could she ignore what Eoin had done? He'd come to her defense. Not only had he practically killed that vile captain for striking her (she decided it prudent not to mention how the captain had groped her—the brute had paid enough in broken bones and bruises), Eoin had also told Edward Bruce that it wasn't her fault.

Had he meant it?

Unfortunately, she knew there was going to be hell to pay before she could find out. She did not mistake the calmness with which he led her to his tent. A storm was brewing inside him, and she was right in the center of it. Why that gave her a thrill, she didn't know.

By all rights she should be terrified. But big and scary, or brooding and serious, it didn't matter. She knew he would never hurt her.

Barely had the flap fallen behind them when he turned on her. "What the hell did you think you were doing coming here alone?"

"I assumed you had changed your mind."

"You assumed *what*?"

She winced at the sound of his raised voice. "You didn't used to bellow so much."

From the white lines forming around his mouth she sensed he was quickly running out of patience. "I'd say you didn't used to be so much trouble, but that wouldn't be true, would it?"

She couldn't help smiling. "Probably not. Although I will state—just to be clear—that I am not usually trouble anymore."

He made a sharp sound of disbelief. "What in Hades made you think I changed my mind?"

She pushed back the edges of the cloak to hold out the dress and beamed. "Why this beautiful dress, of course. I assumed it was your way of apologizing for being such an ars—" She stopped, as if the word had been a slip, which they both knew it wasn't. She smiled. "Such a bully."

He didn't seem to appreciate the amended word any better than the first. "You know very well it wasn't an apology."

"It wasn't?" She quirked a brow in mock surprise. "Well, it should have been." She gave him a long look. "Is everything all right? You seem to be a little tense."

His eyes flared, and she almost regretted baiting him. But she hadn't had this much fun in . . .

Her heart squeezed. Almost seven and a half years. Since those first days of their marriage.

"I should have let you stay dressed as a nun. Maybe you wouldn't have every man within a hundred yards panting after you."

She shrugged indifferently. "Maybe." There was only one man she'd ever wanted that kind of attention from. But he no longer wanted her.

Or did he?

Glancing over his hard-wrought control and tautly held body, she wondered.

"I'm taking you back to the convent."

She shook her head. "I'll just keep coming back. You'll have to have them lock me in."

"Don't tempt me," he snapped.

Margaret had taken a quick glance around the wood-framed canvas tent, scared of what she might see. She drew a deep breath and forced herself to take closer inspection and was more relieved than she wanted to admit to see no signs of a female presence.

Simple was an understatement. On opposite sides of the room there were two basic wood-framed beds, she assumed tied with ropes for a mattress, with a few wool plaids and animal skins on top for warmth and comfort. In one corner, which she assumed belonged to Eoin, was a desk laden with rolls of parchment. Aside from two trunks, another table, a couple of stools, a handful of stone cresset oil lamps, and a brazier, there was little else in terms of comfort or decoration.

His mother would be appalled.

"You aren't sharing your tent with a woman, are you?"

She didn't think he was going to answer, but eventually his mouth fell in a hard line, and he shook his head. "With Lamont."

She brightened. "Please let me stay, Eoin. I promise I won't be in the way. I can help, if you let me."

She didn't realize she was touching him, until his eyes looked down at the hand that had fallen on his arm. "How?"

Did she imagine the huskiness in his voice? *Something* had made her skin prickle. "Let me talk to my father. I know I can convince him to let Eachann go."

"Absolutely not. It's too dangerous."

She drew back. "My father wouldn't hurt me."

"Your father is desperate. There is nothing I would put past him."

Maybe it was too soon to press him, but the opportunity was too tempting. "I wouldn't think you would care if something happened to me. It would make it easier for you to be rid of me."

The tic jumped in his jaw, his reaction visceral, even if a moment later he hid it. "It's the added danger to the boy that I'm worried about."

She held his gaze for a moment and nodded. "Of course." But she didn't believe him. He did care about her—at least a little—even if he didn't want to.

For more reasons than one, she had to stay. "Please, Eoin, you can't send me back to the convent."

He didn't say anything for a long moment, but just studied her carefully. "If I were smart that's exactly what I would do."

Her hope soared. "But . . ."

He finished for her as she hoped he would. "But God knows what kind of trouble you will get in if I don't keep an eye on you."

Without thinking what she was doing, Margaret threw her arms around him. "Oh Eoin, thank you!"

∽

The moment her body pressed against his, Eoin knew he'd made a mistake. How the hell was he going to share a tent with her for God knows how many days without touching her, without kissing her, without making love to her, when every bone in his body was clamoring to do exactly that?

God, she felt good. He'd forgotten how good. Warm and soft, her body molded against his like a tight glove.

He cursed inwardly. It was the wrong thing to be thinking about when his cock was pressed up against another tight glove.

But he'd been down this path before. His desire for her had clouded his reason. He wouldn't let it happen again. No matter how much he wanted her.

Very purposefully, he set her away. "There are going to be a few rules."

She blinked up at him, apparently still suffering from the delusion that he'd been moments away from kissing her. "Rules?"

"Aye. You won't interfere, you won't snoop, you'll do

everything that I ask you, and you won't throw yourself at me. I told you I wasn't interested in redheads anymore."

Her eyes flared. "I wasn't throwing myself at you!" Her gaze narrowed and moved down his body with familiarity that belied a six-year separation, lingering for a moment on the place that proved him a liar. "And you didn't seem all that *un*interested."

His mouth flattened. "I hear the nuns calling, Margaret."

She looked like she wanted to hurl something at him. But for once, discretion prevailed. Her smile was far too pleasant for his liking. "I promise I won't 'throw' myself at you, interfere, or snoop. I'll be the perfectly biddable wife and do whatever you ask."

He didn't believe her for an instant, but smiled, knowing how much that must have cost her. He *smiled*. Hell, how long had it been since he'd done that? "Then welcome to your new lodging. I shall send for your things from the convent."

"Don't bother. I will not wear that dress again, and I had nothing else that belonged to me."

He didn't comment on the dress, but just thinking about it made his back teeth grind. "Make a list of anything you need, and I'll send a lad to town and see what can be procured."

"I don't have much coin with me. Only what I was carrying in my purse for the church offerings."

He waved her off. "I will see to it."

"Thank you. I will pay you back."

Like hell she would.

She looked around the tent. "Where shall I sleep?"

He pointed to his bed on the right. He would sleep in Lamont's. He wasn't going to analyze why he didn't want her in his partner's bed.

She frowned. "What about your friend?"

"He will bed down in one of the other tents."

She bit her lip contritely. "I didn't mean to force him from his bed."

"Lamont won't mind," he assured her. "I do the same when his wife is with him."

"He is married?"

"You sound surprised."

She shrugged. "He doesn't say much."

Eoin couldn't help smiling, thinking of Lamont's wife, Janet of Mar. The lass hadn't met a word she didn't like. "His wife makes up for it. When you meet her—"

He stopped, suddenly realizing that was very unlikely. *Part ways permanently.* That's exactly what he wanted.

An awkward pause followed. Eoin didn't miss the flash of hurt in Margaret's eyes, before she broke the silence by asking, "Is there any word on Eachann?"

Grateful for the change of subject, Eoin shook his head. "Nay."

"How do you plan to get him back?"

He was surprised by the question. "Why do you think I have a plan?"

She rolled her eyes. "I might not be able to keep up with it all the time, but I know the way your mind works. You always have a plan."

"Aye, well little good it will do me this time." He couldn't hide his bitterness. "Carrick has refused to consider it."

"What did it involve?"

He didn't say anything. He wasn't going to tell her the details. Not just because he didn't trust her—which he didn't—but also because the less he said about the Highland Guard the better. MacGregor's recent unmasking and the abduction of his betrothed by the English was a reminder to them all about the importance of keeping their identities secret.

He didn't want her asking too many questions, which she was bound to do if he spoke of a small highly-trained group of warriors who would attempt a sneak attack on an entire garrison. Word of their exploits had spread too wide.

It would be even more difficult when Bruce and the rest of the Guard arrived. The rest, that is, with the exception of MacGregor. The expert marksman—and the man known as the most handsome in Scotland—was apparently having some difficulty with his betrothed. Used to seeing women throw themselves at the famed archer, Eoin was looking forward to meeting the lass who had trapped the untrappable.

But the imminent arrival of his brethren was the one thing Eoin hadn't considered when he'd agreed to let her stay here. Margaret was too observant. This was bound to get complicated—as if it wasn't already.

"I'd rather not say," he answered finally. "But I will have a better chance when the king arrives."

She blinked. He hoped to hell that wasn't dampness in her eyes, but he found his chest growing a little heavier.

"I understand," she said softly. "When do you expect him?"

"Soon."

She nodded and turned away. She looked so dejected that he reached for her before he caught himself and had to pull his hand back sharply to his side.

Bloody hell. What was it about her that made him act like an idiot even when he knew better? Where the hell was all that hate and bitterness when he needed it? Without it he was weak.

He could never forget what had happened. Loch Ryan would always be between them. She might not be the treacherous bitch that he'd thought for years, but her mistake—his mistake—had cost too much.

But he had better find some damned self-control or the next few days—weeks—were going to be torture.

20

TORTURE WAS putting it mildly. Even though Eoin found every possible excuse to stay away, every time he walked into that tent and saw her—or caught the faint whiff of whatever floral concoction she'd decided to wallow in that day—it was as if someone was punching a hole through his resolve. Pretty soon, there wasn't going to be anything left *but* holes.

Two days ago, he'd made the mistake of returning to the tent after breaking his fast only to find her in the bath. Somehow she'd talked the lad who was serving as his squire of sorts into "borrowing" someone's wooden tub. Unfortunately, it didn't hide much of her, and the pink expanse of creamy skin that he'd glimpsed before turning on his heel and walking—all right, bolting—out had been haunting him ever since. Night *and* day.

He was having a hard time remembering why touching her was a bad idea. The little voice that kept telling him he could have her and still walk away was getting louder.

It was just lust. It didn't need to be anything more. Emotion didn't need to get in the way—not if he didn't let it. After six years he'd earned it, hadn't he?

But even if she'd welcome him into her—his—bed, which he wasn't all that sure she would (she no longer looked at him as if he were a treat she couldn't wait to devour, which he was sure he was grateful for, damn it!), he knew it would only complicate matters between them.

An annulment was no longer an option. He would not make his son a bastard. But that left him with the difficult prospect of seeking a divorce. It wouldn't be easy to obtain—and might take years—but he didn't have any other choice. Not if he wanted to be rid of her. Which he did, didn't he? He'd thought of nothing else for six years.

But seeing her again . . .

It was harder than he thought it would be. Harder than it should be, damn it. And Eachann made it doubly so. He wanted to know his son. He couldn't just walk away from him, but neither could he take him away from his mother.

Bloody hell.

By the time Bruce and the rest of the Guard arrived an excruciating three days after she'd moved into his tent, Eoin was at the end of his rope. His temper—which admittedly had veered toward "on edge" since Loch Ryan—was decidedly black. Foul might be a better description. Even Lamont had avoided him for the past few days.

Eoin was chomping at the bit to put his plan in motion. The sooner the siege was over, the sooner his son would be safe, and the sooner he could be rid of the woman who was driving him mad with temptation.

Despite Edward Bruce getting to his brother first, and the king's fury upon learning that Margaret was in camp, Eoin was able to convince Bruce to let the Guard attempt to take the castle by subterfuge. After similar successes at Douglas, Linlithgow, and Perth castles, the king trusted the judgment of his elite warriors. Bruce had no love of investing castles, and he was almost as anxious as Eoin to see an end to the siege. Once Dumfries fell, the other castles in Galloway would follow, and the king was eager to turn his eye toward the biggest prizes: Stirling, Edinburgh, and Roxburgh castles. With those lost, the English grip on Scotland would be broken and the kingdom would be his.

But first was putting an end to the MacDowell hold on Galloway. Eoin's plan was straightforward, and it didn't take long for all the details to be worked out. Margaret had provided some additional information about the castle, but it was pretty much as he remembered it.

A short while later, the warriors left the king's tent to get some food and rest before making their attempt later that night. In addition to nine of the ten remaining Guardsmen—MacLeod, MacSorley, Campbell, MacRuairi, MacKay, Sutherland, Lamont, Boyd, and Eoin—Douglas and Randolph would also take part in the raid.

Eoin was walking beside Douglas when he heard Mac-Sorley let out a low whistle. "Damn, Striker, is that her?"

Eoin looked up and followed the direction of MacSorley's gaze. He stiffened, seeing the familiar deep red tresses shimmering like gold and copper in the falling sunlight. But it wasn't the absence of the veil that chilled his blood, it was the closeness of that head to another. His eyes narrowed on the dark-haired warrior beside her.

"Aye," he snapped. "That's her."

For once the always-ready-with-a-quip seafarer wasn't jesting. Actually, the glance MacSorley gave him was full of sympathy. "Looks can sure as hell be deceiving. Hard to believe she sent so many men to their death."

Eoin had to quash the impulse to defend her. He knew his friends wouldn't understand. Hell, he wasn't sure he understood.

"Who's she with?" Boyd asked. "He looks familiar."

Douglas drew tense beside him and answered, "Thom MacGowan."

Boyd's brow shot up. "The childhood companion your sister mentioned to my wife?"

There weren't many men who would dare to shoot a withering glare toward the strongest man in Scotland, but James "the Black" Douglas did just that. "Aye, he's the blacksmith's son from our village. We were friends before I left to squire for Lamberton, but he is no 'companion' to me or my sister now."

Douglas's vehemence spoke more than he intended. Eoin suspected Douglas's sister, Elizabeth, had something to do with his animosity toward the other man.

"A smith's son?" Randolph asked. "How did he come to be a man-at-arms for Edward?"

"Thom has never known his damned place," Douglas replied angrily. But after a pause, he answered the question. "His mother was the daughter of a knight. I believe she left him some silver when she died."

Eoin didn't care who the hell he was, he just wanted to know why MacGowan was with his wife again. And what was Margaret doing out of the tent? So much for her adherence to his rules. He'd warned her about moving about camp on her own. She was supposed to not be drawing attention to herself—as if that were bloody possible. His wife was always the center of attention, good or bad.

She must have sensed that black glare he was giving her. She glanced up. Their eyes met and held. Something passed between them. Something hot and penetrating, and dangerous.

She seemed to get the message. She winced—guiltily—said something to MacGowan, and dashed off in the direction of the tent that she wasn't supposed to have vacated.

Eoin had been so caught up in his wife he hadn't noticed that the king had moved up behind him. Bruce's narrowed gaze expressed his anger. "What is she really doing here, Striker?"

Eoin heard the underlying question. But a reconciliation wasn't what he wanted. "As I told you, she is concerned for the boy and wants to help if she can."

Rarely did his kinsman vent his rage at the personal toll exacted on him by this war, but he did so now. Bruce's eyes flashed hard as steel. "Just like she 'helped' kill my brothers?"

Eoin looked him right in the eye. "That was as much my fault as it was hers."

Bruce didn't disagree. At least right away. But after a moment, he seemed to collect himself. He was the king again and not the man who'd lost three brothers and countless friends to the executioner's blade, and his wife, sister, and daughter to English captivity. "MacDowell was prepared and knew we were coming. Your wife's information only confirmed it." He paused for a moment, considering. "I'm willing to accept what you have told me that she did not intentionally betray us, but that doesn't mean I trust her. Remember your vow and make sure she doesn't learn anything that could jeopardize our mission here. She's your responsibility, cousin."

The reminder of their kinship Eoin took to be the king's apology for showing the anger and resentment that Eoin knew lingered, in spite of everything Eoin had done in the years since. He would never atone for what he'd done.

He nodded, but wondered whether in Margaret he'd taken on more than he could handle.

Margaret had expected Eoin to come storming through the flap of the tent at any moment, so she was surprised when darkness fell and he had yet to return.

It had been obvious that he'd been furious to find her outside with Thom MacGowan, and she was ready with an explanation, but he hadn't appeared for her to give it to him.

Not appearing seemed to be a common occurrence since she'd moved into the tent. Eoin darted in and out infrequently during the day, barely giving her time to question him about the progress of the siege. He'd moved his trunk out with his friend's, so she assumed he dressed and washed elsewhere.

She would have thought that he slept elsewhere as well, but last night she'd feigned sleep and waited to see whether he would come in. He finally did at what must have been hours past midnight. He'd stood close enough to her bed for her to feel the brace of cold night air on his skin, and it had taken everything she had not to open her eyes, knowing that he was watching her. He'd stood there for a few minutes until she feared the stillness of her breath had given her away.

Muttering a curse, he'd left.

She'd wanted to call him back, but for once she didn't want to press him. Her husband was struggling with his feelings toward her, and she knew one wrong move could push him over the edge. Which edge was the problem. Would he send her away or give in to the desire that she knew he was fighting?

Which did she want? Truth be told, Margaret didn't know. She was struggling with her own feelings. Not two weeks ago she'd been getting ready to marry another man. A man whom even if she didn't love, she'd cared for.

She was no longer certain that love was all that mattered. Years ago she'd loved Eoin with everything in her young girl's heart and it hadn't been enough. He'd never made her a part of his life. He'd never truly committed to her or to their marriage. He'd kept her in the dark and showed her in every way that mattered he did not trust her.

If he had, maybe what had happened would not have occurred. Had he taken her into his confidence and told her what was at stake, she would never have told Brigid. She would have let her friend think she'd been attacked rather than give any hint that Eoin was in the area.

She'd betrayed his confidence, and there was no doubt the consequences had been horrific, but she'd made the best decision she could with the information she had at the time.

It was an epiphany. Some of the blame and guilt that had haunted her for years lifted. It wasn't all her fault. She'd betrayed him that day, but he'd betrayed her and their marriage every time he'd left without telling her anything. He'd betrayed her again by letting her think he was dead for six years.

She still loved him—she suspected she always would—but it wasn't enough. At eighteen she hadn't known any different, but now she did. Sir John had shown her what it could be like. He'd trusted her and shared his life with her. She wouldn't settle for anything else.

But now that Eoin had even less cause to trust her was that even possible?

She didn't know, but she intended to find out as soon as their son was free.

It was the thought of what was going on in that castle,

and the boy's possible suffering, that dominated her thoughts. Until Eachann was safe, her feelings for her husband would have to remain unsorted.

She hoped that Robert the Bruce's arrival would bring them one step closer to seeing her son returned to her. Although she'd been focused on her husband earlier, she hadn't missed the man who'd come up behind him. The former Earl of Carrick had aged in the years since he'd declared himself king, but she would know him anywhere.

It was hard to believe all this man had accomplished, but it hadn't been without suffering. He'd lost three brothers and his wife, sisters, and daughter were in English hands—one of his sisters had even been hung in a cage.

Learning of Bruce's arrival was worth the tongue lashing she was sure to receive for breaking one of his so-called "rules." Anxious to learn what was happening, she was about to break it again and go search for him, when her husband finally deigned to gift her with his presence.

He stood just inside the flap staring at her, clearly trying to intimidate her with that brooding, heavy glare he'd perfected. He'd always been intense, but that intensity had taken on a harsh edge in the intervening years. She shivered. A *scary* edge.

As he was dressed head to toe in black leather and steel, and had what must be every deadly looking weapon known to man strapped to him, the glare wasn't altogether ineffective. But suspecting that he'd taken so long to come to her because he knew how anxious she would be—exacting a punishment of sorts—she lifted her chin and glared right back at him.

His mouth tightened, and most of the impressive number of muscles in his body tightened. Good gracious! What must his chest and arms look like now?

She felt a flutter low in her belly and the familiar flood of heat. It was probably best not to think about that.

He took a few steps toward her. He was obviously ready for battle, and she had no intention of disappointing him.

"Whatever it is you feel you have to say, say it," she said with an indifferent wave of her hand.

His eyes turned positively predatory. "Now what makes you say that, Margaret? Could it be that I specifically told you not to leave the tent, and yet I find you gallivanting around camp with MacGowan?"

The way he practically spat the other man's name gave her an inkling of why he was so furious.

"I wasn't gallivanting," she clarified. "I was merely ensuring that Thom had recovered from his injuries after coming to my aid the other day. I hope you don't mind, but I used some of the coin you left me to purchase a new blade for him."

"You did *what?*"

She winced at the reverberation in her ears. "I will pay you back."

"I don't want your damned money! And from what I hear, he can bloody well make his own blades. You shouldn't be buying things for *Thom* or any other man."

She lifted her brow, fighting the smile at the way he'd said Thom. "Why not?"

"It isn't right, damn it."

She couldn't resist tweaking him just a little. He *had* made her wait for hours. "You have no cause to be jealous of him."

She didn't think it possible that blue eyes could turn so black. "I'm not jealous of him!" he snarled.

"You aren't? Oh that's good. Although it would be understandable it you were. He really is quite handsome. That dark hair with those blue eyes really is a stunning combination." She appeared to ponder that while he struggled not to explode. "I've always liked tall men." She raised her hand an inch or two over his head as if gauging. "He must be at least four inches over six feet, don't you think?"

When he made a low growl in his throat and took another step toward her, Margaret decided she'd pressed him far enough. He looked like he was contemplating strangling her or tossing her back onto that bed. No matter how much she wanted the latter—and the thrill racing along her skin told her she wanted it very much—she wasn't ready for it. Passion had a way of confusing things. She'd learned that the first time around.

"Did Bruce agree to your plan?" she asked, clearly surprising him by the swift change of subject. "Is that why you are dressed for battle?"

The suddenly blank look on his face answered her question even if he did not. Though she could not expect him to trust her, her heart still twisted.

She scanned his hardened features for any sign of an opening. "Just tell me, is it dangerous?"

Still he didn't say anything, and her heart twisted again.

"Of course it's dangerous," she said, answering her own question. "How can it not be?" She was torn: wanting her son free but not wanting Eoin to be hurt in the process. She renewed her plea. "Won't you let me at least try first—"

"Nay. We've been through this before. I'll not risk you and the lad. This is what I do, Margaret. Let me do my job."

She looked up at him and felt a yearning so strong it stole her breath. Tears welled in her eyes. She wasn't sure what they were for. Fear? Longing? The life they'd lost or the love that they'd once shared?

He seemed to want to say something, but instead bowed his head and turned to leave.

"Wait," she said, running after him. She reached him as he pulled aside the flap.

"What is it?"

"This." And without hesitating, she stood on her toes and pressed a kiss to his lips. It was chaste and brief, but long enough to stir memories. She'd forgotten the surprising softness, the subtle taste of spice, and the way her heart jumped at the contact. The way her whole *body* jumped.

It took everything she had to draw back. But when she did, she could see that she'd surprised him.

"Stay alive this time," she said, breaking the silence. "And by the way, that was not me throwing myself at you."

One corner of his mouth lifted. He shook his head. "Thanks for the clarification, and I'll do my best."

"See that you do."

He nodded, and a moment later he disappeared into the blackness of the night. She didn't know how long she stood staring after him.

Best if we go our separate ways . . .

How was she going to let him go again?

∞

Robert the Bruce didn't have trebuchets with intimidating names like Warwolf—he had something better. The warriors of the Highland Guard were every bit as destructive as England's powerful siege engines, but they were far more nimble, and they didn't require dozens of carts to move them or months of digging in and waiting.

After seven and a half years of fighting side by side in the worst trenches of this cesspit of a war, the Guard operated like a finely tuned instrument of war. They communicated silently and anticipated each other's movements. But they were always prepared for the unexpected. Unlike the legends that proclaimed them supermen or phantoms, they were not indestructible (the death of William "Templar" Gordon had reminded them of that), nor were they infallible (the failure to take Berwick Castle last year still grated).

But this night everything was proceeding according to Eoin's plan.

The stone keep of Dumfries Castle sat upon a high motte. The steep sides of the hill itself were a form of defense, preventing attackers from being able to approach quickly. The wooden palisade that surrounded the keep and bailey had been replaced and fortified by the English with a stone wall, after the Highland Guard rescued Mac-Leod's wife seven years ago, starting the chain of events that would lead to Bruce's bid for the throne. Additional defense was provided by the deep wet ditch that abutted the wall.

The castle had two gates: an inner gate over the wet ditch surrounding the motte that guarded the stairs leading up to the castle, and a much stronger gate with bridge and portcullis that protected the main entrance into the bailey. To take the keep, attackers would need to go through both the outer gate and the inner gate.

The Highland Guard bypassed both. Under the cover of night, Eoin and his brethren approached the keep from the back side of the motte. With the wet ditch, the steep hill, and the imposing wall that surrounded the keep, this side of the castle was the most impenetrable and unlikely point of access—which is exactly why they were there. Impenetrable meant lightly guarded.

An army would never be able to launch a surprise attack on the castle from here. But a small force of men could. As they'd done when rescuing Christina MacLeod, the Guards-men swam across the filth-laden wet ditch and slithered up the hill on their bellies. The high stone wall, however, required something more than ropes. Fortunately, Douglas had recently developed an ingenious contraption that en-abled them to scale walls even higher than the twenty-foot barricade around Dumfries. The rope ladders fitted with footboards and grappling hooks had been put to good use at both Berwick and Perth castles. A barking dog had foiled the attack at Berwick, but the ladders had been used success-fully a few weeks ago at Perth.

Once all the men were safely over the wall, they broke off into groups. Eoin and MacRuairi would go in search of the boy, Lamont, MacSorley, MacGregor's brother John, Boyd, MacLeod, and Douglas would keep watch and provide defense if needed, and the others would open the inner and outer gates to let in the rest of Bruce's army, which was hiding in the forest to take the castle.

Eoin's mission was to get his son out of harm's way before the cry was raised and the chaos of battle ensued. Stealth and surprise were paramount—which is why Mac-Ruairi was with him. The coldhearted bastard hadn't just earned his war name of Viper from his disposition: like a snake he could get in an out of anywhere without a trace.

Having neutralized the soldiers guarding the keep with relative ease, Eoin persuaded one—at the end of his dirk—to show them where the boy was being held. Having experience with MacDowells, Eoin wasn't surprised when the man tried to lead them into a room full of sleeping warriors. After a few encouraging pokes, however, the man headed up the stairs.

Eoin could feel his chest pounding with anticipation. His son was near, and soon he would be safe.

Exiting the stairwell on the third floor, they passed through a small antechamber before their reluctant guide stopped before a door and nodded, indicating this was it. Eoin knocked him out with a swift blow to the back of the head. With a look to MacRuairi to be ready in case this was another surprise, he took a deep breath and opened the door.

The room was pitch-black, and it took a moment for his eyes to adjust. A flicker of torchlight from the corridor spilled into the room, enabling him to make out a small form huddled on a bed beneath a thick fur coverlet. The shape shifted, and a small head popped up.

Eoin reacted like lightning, lurching forward and putting his hand over the boy's mouth to muffle the scream that had been about to tear from his lungs.

Their eyes met in the semidarkness, and he saw the recognition in the boy's gaze that was no doubt mirrored in his own.

Christ, he looks just like me.

There could be no doubt that this was his son.

Eoin felt stunned—rocked—as if someone had just hit him with a taber across the chest. Being told that he had a son was a hell of a lot different from being confronted with the living proof. The *five-year-old* living proof.

Regret and about a hundred other complicated emotions squeezed his throat.

"Do you know who I am?" he asked in a low voice.

The boy nodded, but then opened his eyes wider and tried to scream again.

Eoin looked over his shoulder angrily. "Christ, Viper, you scared him," he said in a harsh whisper.

MacRuairi looked like the bogeyman with his eerie

green eyes glowing beneath the darkened metal of the nasal helm. His face seemed to disappear in the blackness.

"Your reunion will have to wait," MacRuairi said. "We need to get out of here. Make sure he stays quiet."

Eoin didn't waste time arguing. MacRuairi was right. Still holding his hand around his mouth, Eoin pulled the little boy from bed as if he weighed nothing—which wasn't that far off the mark—and carried him from the chamber. Although Eachann wasn't resisting, Eoin didn't want to take any chances until they were outside of the keep. Only then did he put him down and look him right in the eye. "I'm going to take my hand off your mouth, but if you make a sound, I'll have to put a gag on you. Do you understand?"

The lad—*his* lad—nodded.

Eoin studied him intently, seeing something in the little boy's eyes. "Do I have your promise?"

His son nodded again, this time with far less enthusiasm, and Eoin tried not to smile. It wasn't hard to imagine what he was thinking. But the fact that Eachann didn't like being forced to promise gave Eoin enough reason to think he would keep it, and he released his hold over his mouth.

The lad took a few deep breaths of air as he eyed Eoin—who'd bent down on one knee—warily.

Eoin took a skin from around his shoulder and handed it to him. "Would you like some water?"

Eachann didn't hesitate, taking the offering with an eager nod.

Eoin swore as the little boy gulped down the water as if he hadn't had a drink in God knows how long. The situation was obviously more dire in here than they'd thought, and the thought of his son suffering . . .

Dugald MacDowell was glad he wasn't standing here right now.

MacRuairi nudged him to hurry, but Eoin waved him off. "He's thirsty, damn it." And probably hungry. He dug in his sporran and pulled out a piece of dried beef. "Take this. I should have brought more, but as soon as we are back at camp you can have whatever you want."

The boy's eyes widened at his words, and Eoin felt as if he'd just offered him a kingdom. The lad chewed on the beef with relish, each bite making Eoin feel angrier and angrier.

He looked sharply at Lamont and MacSorley as they came up beside them.

"Any problems?" he asked his partner.

Lamont shook his head. "It's quiet. About fifty men in the keep."

"Good, less than we thought. Let's go."

They were about to continue down the motte when the others came rushing up the stairs toward them. Eachann recoiled instinctively in terror at his side, and Eoin put a hand on his shoulder to comfort him. "It's all right, they're friends."

The boy seemed to take offense and stiffened. "I'm not scared," he said proudly. "MacDowells don't get scared."

Eoin's jaw clenched, and he would have corrected him—the boy was a MacLean—but he saw Douglas's expression.

"There's a problem," the big warrior said. Aside from Eoin, who hadn't wanted to scare the boy, Douglas was the only one not wearing a nasal helm. Douglas didn't care if everyone knew the "Black Douglas" was about. "We can't open the gate."

"Why not?" MacRuairi demanded impatiently.

To Eoin's surprise, his son answered. "The guard doesn't have the keys. My grandfather has them."

MacLeod looked at the boy, and then turned back to Eoin. "It doesn't matter. We can swim across the ditch for now to open the main gate. Ice can get one of his bags of powder ready for this gate."

Everyone started to move toward the stairs except for Eoin. He was still staring at his son. There was something . . .

Damn.

"The outer gate won't work either, will it?" he said.

Eachann didn't say anything, but one corner of his mouth lifted.

"Are those keys missing, too?"

Eachann nodded. "And the ropes for the portcullis."

The others had stopped, too, and like Eoin were staring at his son.

"Who told your grandfather to do that?" Eoin asked, already guessing the answer.

Eachann didn't say anything, but the quirk of his mouth gave him away.

Lamont gave a sharp laugh and said to Eoin, "He's your son, all right."

I'll be damned. Eoin couldn't take his eyes from the boy. The swell of pride that rose inside him threatened to burst his chest.

For a moment, Eachann seemed to swell up, too, and he started to give him a tentative smile. But then he seemed to remember something and jerked away from him as if scalded. His little face contorted in rage. "I'm not your son," he said angrily. "I'm a MacDowell, and you're a traitorous baserd! I hate you and wish you'd never come back!"

Eoin jerked back as if the boy had just struck him.

The shock gave Eachann his opening. Before anyone could stop him, he darted toward the keep. And obviously thinking better of his promise, he did so yelling.

21

KNOWING SHE wouldn't sleep, Margaret didn't bother trying. How long had it been since Eoin had left? An hour? Two?

She paced the small tent, the flame from the oil lamps flickering, and occasionally paused to open the flap and peek outside.

From the position of the tent on the small rise, she could easily make out the castle in the not-so-far distance. The dark castle that . . .

Her heart jumped to her throat as the castle suddenly sprang to life. Torches went up everywhere and the sounds of shouting and clamor of men roused for battle shattered the night air.

Had Eoin been discovered or was this part of his plan? Oh God, what was happening? Why hadn't she forced him to confide in her?

She watched in horror as her father's men started to line the ramparts. Not just his men, she realized a moment later, but his archers.

Arrows unfurled into the darkness, apparently aimed at targets below.

Not Eachann. Not Eoin. Please!

A few moments later the camp around her responded, roaring to life as well. Men rushed about everywhere. Men in full armor ready to attack. But they weren't attacking. *Something is wrong.* Her chest pounded high in her throat. She tried to question the men running by her, but they ignored her.

Bruce's archers started to return fire, slowing the hail of arrows on the targets below. *Please . . .*

It took at least another five minutes for her prayers to be answered, when down at the far edge of camp she saw at least a dozen warriors plunge out of the darkness. Eoin! It had to be. She scanned the unusually imposing figures. Her heart stopped on the man being carried between two others. Even from a distance, she recognized him.

Heedless of Eoin's warnings about leaving the tent, Margaret ran. She didn't stop until she reached the gathering of men, and then she had to push her way forward through the crowd to see him.

When she did, a cry escaped from where she'd held it tightly in her chest. She would have launched herself toward him, if he wasn't being held up by two men.

"You're hurt," she said, taking a more tentative step toward him.

"I'm fine," he said, but winced as he tried to stand on his own legs to prove it to her. "I just jammed my knee."

Only then did she notice that the two warriors holding him were wearing blackened nasal helms like the one Eoin had been wearing six years earlier. Of the dozen or so warriors who were with Eoin, only a few wore regular helms like he did, but all of the men wore black from head to toe. Black leather war coats, blackened mail shirts, blackened helms, black leather boots, even some of the faces beneath the masks seemed to be blackened. They seemed to blend into the night.

There was something about them that made the hair on her neck stand up. Who—*what*—were they?

But her attention was drawn off by one of the nasal-helmed monoliths holding Eoin. He sounded irritated. "Might be jammed or might be torn or broken, so don't try to stand again until Helen has a chance to look at it."

Suddenly what—or who—was missing penetrated. Her eyes met Eoin's.

When he gave her a grim shake of his head, she knew he'd understood her question. It hadn't worked. He hadn't been able to free Eachann.

"What happened?"

Margaret recognized the voice as Robert Bruce's, even if the mail-clad warrior who stood in the crowd of men surrounding them was otherwise indistinguishable. None of the men wore arms or colors, she realized. Bruce's secret warfare, an army of pirates and brigands, they said. It wasn't hard to understand why.

"We were outsmarted by a lad," one of the men quipped dryly.

Margaret's heart jumped as her gaze found Eoin's. "Eachann?"

He nodded and explained to the obviously impatient king. "We couldn't open either of the gates. The keys had been removed, as were the ropes to raise the portcullis. MacDowell anticipated a sneak attack and knew that even if we managed to get a few men inside, we wouldn't be able to get the rest of the army in fast enough to take the castle. It was a simple but effective defense." The note of pride in Eoin's voice warmed some of the chill from her bones. "It was my son's idea," he added.

Bruce was incredulous. "You must be jesting? You said the lad is only five."

"He's not jesting," one of the men holding Eoin said. She recognized the voice as Lamont's. "We all heard the boy."

Margaret felt the king's gaze on her; he was looking at her as if it were her fault.

She smiled sweetly back at him. "My son knows how to play chess as well, my lord."

For a moment no one said anything, and then all of a sudden Bruce let out a sharp bark of laughter. "I'll remember that."

Margaret turned back to Eoin, whose mouth was twitching suspiciously. It was the first glimpse of light-heartedness she'd seen in him since he'd returned from the dead. Those hard-wrought smiles had always been her weakness. Turned out they still were.

Unfurling the fist that had wound its way around her heart, she forced the emotions away and asked, "But why is Eachann not with you, if you spoke to him?"

A shadow of pain crossed his face. "He ran away from me."

One of the other men hastened to cover the awkward pause. "We had to get out of there the same way we went in. MacLean hurt his leg having to drop from the wall, and Randolph was grazed in the shoulder with an arrow, but we were lucky."

The man who'd mentioned the healer grunted and read-justed his hold on Eoin. "We need to put him down, sire. Chief can fill you in on the rest."

"Helen is nearby?" the king asked.

"Near enough. I will fetch her tonight."

Bruce looked to Margaret. "I assume you can tend to him until the healer arrives?"

"I'm fine, damn it," Eoin complained.

Both she and the king ignored him. She nodded. "Aye."

"Good." To Lamont, the king added, "See that she has what she needs."

Bruce turned his attention to one of the most imposing of the warriors standing next to them, as the two men carried Eoin toward his tent.

They were all drenched, she realized, and smelled faintly of a bog. She wrinkled her nose. They must have swum the ditch.

They were about to put him down on the bed when she stopped them. "Wait!" She grabbed an old plaid and spread it over the bed to protect the bed coverings. Realizing they were all staring at her with amusement—they weren't exactly fine linens—she thrust up her chin. "He'll catch a chill."

Peter, the lad who helped Eoin, had rushed into the tent, and Lamont sent him out for fresh clothes and water.

It quickly became clear that her husband was not going to be an easy patient. The complaining started as soon as they had him down on the bed. He didn't need a healer, Eoin cursed, but the unnamed warrior left anyway to fetch her. When Lamont asked him if he wanted help with his armor, Eoin's blistering reply made her ears burn. And she was used to foul language from her brothers!

After a few minutes trying to make him comfortable, Lamont gave up. "Have fun, my lady. I'll have the lad bring you some whisky for the pain."

"I don't need any blasted whisky," Eoin said.

"It's not for you, it's for her," Lamont responded.

Margaret laughed. "Thank you, but that won't be necessary. I'll manage just fine."

Lamont looked at her as if he wasn't so sure, but left with a short bow a few moments later.

Peter must have been warned by Lamont about Eoin's foul temper, because the lad rushed in shortly afterward with a bucket of water and change of clothing, and then rushed back out.

Eoin had sat up a little to start jerking off his weapons and armor, and she silently moved over to help him. He stopped her when she tried to help him remove his tunic.

Their eyes met. "I'll do it," he said gruffly.

Heat rose to her cheeks, and she nodded. Helping him remove his shirt was probably not a good idea for either of them—the current situation was intimate enough. By the time she turned back around, he'd washed the worst of the muck away and donned a new tunic.

He didn't protest, however, when she helped him with his boots, no doubt realizing that he wouldn't be able to remove them on his own with his injured leg. Even with her help, it was obvious that pulling them off had caused him considerable pain.

"I'm sorry," she said. "Does it . . . is it . . . you aren't . . . ?" Her composure crumpled, her fear for him rushing out.

He tipped her face to him. Tears blurred her eyes. "I'm fine, Margaret, truly. It hurts a little." Her eyes narrowed through the tears. His mouth curved. "All right, it hurts a lot, but I'm sure it will feel much better in a few days."

"You're certain?" she whispered hoarsely.

He nodded.

And then as if it were the most natural thing to do, he lay back down on the bed and drew her against him so that her cheek was pressed against his linen-clad chest. How many times had she been curled up against him like this all those years ago? She'd never felt safer or more secure than when his arms were wrapped around her like this and the steady beat of his heart drummed in her ear.

Oh Eoin, why? Why had this happened to them? Emotion burned in her eyes and throat. They could have been so happy. All of them.

"You had him," she whispered.

He was silent a moment, and then said, "Aye."

She heard something in his voice and looked up. "He's yours, Eoin. Surely you could see it? Eachann looks just like you."

"He ran from me, Margaret. He knew who I was, and he ran from me."

He looked so destroyed her heart went out to him. "He was scared."

Eoin shook his head. "It wasn't that. He hates me. I could see it in his eyes. And how can I blame him? I let my anger take over, and it cost me my son." He looked at her, his eyes stark. "You were right, I have no one to blame but myself."

"He's a little boy, Eoin. He doesn't hate you, he doesn't know you. What he does know is mostly from my family. That's my fault. I should have spoken of you more, but it hurt too badly. This has been a shock for him. Once he gets to know you, it will be different. Just give him time. He doesn't hold grudges like my father."

"Or like his father?"

Their eyes held.

Surprised, Margaret didn't know what to think. Was it just Eachann or was Eoin admitting to something more? Did he regret the grudge that had kept them apart for so long?

❦

Eoin knew that regret served no purpose, but with the first glimpse of that small boyish face—the face that looked so much like his own—it so overwhelmed him he could have choked on it.

Five years. He'd lost five years of his son's life because he'd been too damned stubborn and too filled with hatred and anger to face the woman whose betrayal had cut so deeply and cost so much.

And now, in the ultimate cruel justice, his son hated him. *Hate begetting hate.*

It was his own damned fault. He should have come back years ago. But he'd been scared that anger and hatred weren't enough. Scared that he would see her again and be weak. Scared that what she'd done—what he thought she'd done—hadn't completely obliterated the love he'd had for her. So he'd stayed away like a bloody coward.

And what had it gotten him? All the confused emotions for his wife he'd sought to avoid, and a son who hated him so much he'd rather starve than come with him.

Eoin wanted to believe what Margaret said, but he'd looked into the boy's eyes. He'd seen the intensity of emotion and recognized it as his own. How could he expect forgiveness from his son, when he couldn't forgive himself?

She looked away first. "You had cause, Eoin."

He took her wrist and forced her to look back at him. "Did I? It no longer feels as black and white as it once did. I should have given you a chance to explain."

"Would it have made a difference?"

At the time, probably not. His emotions had been too raw. Her intentions wouldn't have mattered to him then. Without perspective, the consequences of her—his—mistake were too horrible for understanding. "I don't know. But I would have known that I had a son. And he wouldn't think I'd abandoned him."

"You didn't. He won't. Just give him a chance."

Neither of them said anything. Finally, he nodded. He would do his damnedest to make it up to the lad. As soon as he got him out of that castle.

The grim line of his mouth must have given his thoughts away.

She stiffened, as if bracing herself. "How did he seem, Eoin? Did he look"—her breath hitched—"well?"

His chest twisted, and he forced aside thoughts of the eager way the boy had taken the water and beef. "The lad is fine, Margaret," he said firmly. "Perfectly hale as far as I could tell."

She scanned his face intently, as if desperately wanting to believe him. "Then he is not suffering? He's so small, I fear . . ." She turned to meet his gaze. "He has enough to eat?"

He didn't answer her directly. "The castle has only been under siege for a short time. I'm sure whatever food there is is going to our son. He is not suffering."

Yet. But how much longer?

She nodded, as if satisfied, but he wondered whether she'd noticed his careful response.

He shifted a little on the bed, wincing when the pain shot through his leg. It didn't hurt that badly—until he moved. But he could feel the tight pounding of the swelling building in his leg. Despite all his protests to the contrary, he wasn't completely certain it wasn't broken or torn.

Margaret made a sharp gasp of horror that sounded a little bit like a squeak. "I forgot to bind your knee! The man who left to fetch the healer told me what to do. I'm afraid

I'm not giving you a very good impression of my nursing skills."

"Magnus MacKay," he said, before he could stop himself. But he supposed she would find out soon enough anyway, when the big Highlander returned with Helen. "Helen—the healer—is his wife."

She nodded, and then tilted her head to him contemplatively. "I should have guessed he was a Highlander from his size. Were the rest of the men you were with Highlanders as well?" She gave a mock shudder and laughed. "I felt as if a ghost had walked behind me the first time I saw them all."

Eoin cursed inwardly. Her jests were too damned close to the truth. Having her see his brethren in their helms and armor had been unfortunate. He'd wanted his son to recognize him so had dispensed with the nasal helm. But the blackened armor had become all too connected to Bruce's "Phantoms," as people called them.

Not wanting to risk any more questions, he shifted again—purposefully. The resulting wince he made because of the pain made her gasp again—this time with a muffled oath—and she hastened to fetch the cloth to bind his knee.

She returned quickly, but then stopped and paused, staring down at his leg. She bit her lip and looked at him uncertainly. "I need you to remove your chausses. Do you need help?"

He resisted the urge to shout, "Hell no." Instead, he shook his head. "I can manage."

The pain it caused him would be infinitely preferable to the pain of having her hands on him. Offering to help him remove his tunic had been bad enough—although he'd also wanted to prevent her from seeing his tattoo—but having her hands so close to . . .

He shuddered.

Clenching his teeth against the pain, he sat up and began to work the ties of the chausses. He had to move around quite a bit to get them off, but in a few minutes all that was between him and a whole heap of trouble was his tunic and a thin pair of linen braies.

He hadn't thought the injury looked that bad until she exclaimed, "It looks horrible. It's almost twice the size and already discolored with bruising. It must hurt terribly. Are you sure you don't want something for the pain?"

What he wanted right now would only cause more pain. He shook his head. "Just wrap it."

She did, but even that wasn't a good idea. She had to sit on the edge of the bed to lean over him, and every time she did her breasts grazed tantalizingly close to his cock, and her silky hair slid forward across his chest. He ached to bury his face in both of them. He was holding himself so tightly he forgot to breathe.

"Are you all right?" she asked, turning her face to meet his as she finished securing the bands of linen around his knee. "Am I hurting you?"

"Aye," he said with a grimace, "but not in the way you mean."

Clearly, she didn't understand.

"It's not my knee, Maggie."

It took her a moment, but then her eyes widened and fell on the place he meant—only causing him more pain. And a groan.

"Oh," she said softly. Their eyes met. He could see the questions looking back at him. Questions he couldn't answer. "Eoin, I . . ."

He heard her hesitation, and understood it because he felt it, too.

"It's probably not a good idea," she finished.

He shook his head in agreement, ignoring the disappointment in her voice. "Probably not."

"It would only confuse things, wouldn't it?" She looked at him as if she were hoping he would disagree with her.

But he couldn't. "Aye."

It would confuse things, and he was already confused enough. But that didn't mean that every nerve ending in his body wasn't clamoring to disagree. To pull her down on top of him and bury himself so deeply inside her nothing could ever tear them apart again.

Christ, she was too close. He could almost taste her on his tongue. Almost feel the softness of her skin under his hands. Almost smell the scent of her pleasure as he stroked her to release.

He remembered the way her eyes closed, her lips parted, and her breath quickened. He remembered the pink flush of her cheeks and the cry that always seemed tinged with surprise when she came.

He didn't know if he'd ever be able to forget. He wasn't all that sure anymore that he wanted to.

He didn't know what to say, so he didn't say anything. Instead, he pulled her down alongside him on the bed. She curled into his side as if she'd never left, resting her cheek and palm on his chest.

He stared at the ceiling, stroking her hair and thinking for a long time.

Margaret woke before Eoin and slipped out of the tent, needing to escape for a moment. She walked to the burn on the other side of the hill and scooped up some of the cool water to splash on her face. If she hoped for sudden clarity, it didn't help.

What had it meant?

Making love would have been confusing, but what had happened was even more so. The closeness from passion could be easily dismissed as lust—as a temporary moment of insanity. But the closeness—the tenderness—she'd felt from spending a night in her husband's arms could not.

It was hard not to let her emotions get carried away, but she forced herself to be realistic. One night of tenderness was no better than one night of passion to build a marriage upon.

Whether more was possible would need to wait until Eachann was free. Her heart squeezed, giving way to the disappointment in the failed attempt that she hadn't wanted Eoin to see. He was upset enough by what had happened.

Eachann is all right, she told herself. But she couldn't escape the feeling that Eoin hadn't been completely honest with her. He was holding something back, and she knew she had to do something.

She sat by the water, savoring the early morning quiet and watching the faint light of dawn brighten across the stark winter countryside. As soon as the men started to rise and the bustling sounds of camp interrupted her solitude, however, Margaret rose from the rock she'd been sitting on and walked slowly back to the tent.

Hearing raised voices as she drew near, she quickened her step. All three inhabitants stared as she ducked through the flap. Eoin was glaring angrily, but it was Magnus MacKay who spoke. "We caught him halfway out of bed."

Margaret hadn't known Eoin as a boy, but Eachann had

obviously inherited the mulish, disgruntled look when he got in trouble from him.

"Where were you?" he demanded. Perhaps realizing he'd given too much away, he tried to cover it up. "You left me alone with *them*."

Margaret glanced at the woman standing by the bed and was surprised she hadn't noticed her before. She was lovely. Soft, floaty red hair, fair skin, green eyes, and delicate features made her look like a pixie, even if her expression made her look like a battle commander.

The woman—the healer, Margaret assumed—gave her a decidedly cool look before turning to Eoin. She was pushing a cup toward his mouth. "Don't be such a bairn. Just drink it. It will make you feel better."

Eoin pulled back disgustedly. "It smells vile, and I told you, I feel fine. You said yourself I just wrenched it."

The healer put her hands on her hips, looking as if she were summoning patience from up high. "I told you it didn't *appear* to be torn, but I can't be sure. And I know it hurts, so you can stop that tough warrior routine with me." She rolled her eyes toward her husband. "Lord knows, I get it enough from him."

Eoin pushed it away. "Let him drink it then."

Magnus gave a shudder and stepped back. "Hell, no. It smells like animal dung. Every time I sniffle she tries to force one of those concoctions down my throat."

The healer—Helen, Margaret recalled her name—threw up her hands in exasperation. "Good lord, are you all born with some perverse predilection for suffering pain? Do you know how ridiculous this is?" She glared at Eoin. "I thought you were supposed to be the smart one."

Magnus cleared his throat, shooting a glance in Margaret's direction, and his wife pursed her lips.

Margaret frowned, wondering what she wasn't supposed to have said, but then turned her attention to Eoin. "Do you trust this woman?" she asked.

Eoin appeared completely taken aback. "With my life. She's one of the best healers that I've ever seen."

Margaret didn't say anything, she just approached the bed, took the cup from the healer, sat calmly on the edge of the mattress, and waited. Eoin was smart. He would put it together himself.

It didn't take him long. He cursed, grabbed the cup from her hand, and downed it in one long gulp. The face he made after was almost comical, but Margaret forced herself not to smile.

Helen looked at her questioningly, and Margaret shrugged. "He just realized that you were the one in position to know what was best for him, and that if you wanted him to drink the posset it was for his own good."

Eoin shot her a glare, as if he wasn't happy that she knew him so well.

"I wish all my patients were so reasonable," Helen said with a meaningful glance toward her imposing-looking husband.

The healer's gaze when it turned back to her was appraising, and perhaps marginally less cool. Margaret couldn't blame the other woman for her reserve, assuming she knew about her part in the battle at Loch Ryan. She should expect hostility from Bruce's followers and Eoin's friends (as it was obvious these two were), but it didn't make it any less uncomfortable.

Eoin must have picked up on it as well.

"Helen, Magnus," he said by way of introduction. "This is my *wife*, Margaret."

The pretty healer lifted a brow, obviously just as surprised as Margaret was at the way he'd stressed *wife*. "I've heard quite a bit about you," she said in a way that was definitely open to interpretation.

Magnus gave his wife a chastising frown, and Eoin looked as if he were about to intervene, but Margaret shook him off. She needed to fight her own battles. "I'm sure you have. And I'm sure most of it's true."

"Only most?" Helen asked.

"It's a matter of perspective. But I hope you will get all the facts before passing judgment."

Helen gave a twisted smile and turned to her husband. "I think I've just been very politely put in my place." When Margaret tried to object, she waved her off. "No, you were right. I will form my own opinion, and so far from what I've seen you can at least be reasonable, which is more than I can say for him."

Eoin scowled, but Helen ignored him and proceeded to give Margaret instructions on how to care for him—which mostly involved forcing the drink down him for a few days so he would rest and not letting him put weight on the leg.

"As for his grumpiness," the healer shrugged. "Well, I'm afraid there's nothing I can do about that. They're all that way when they're hurt."

"They?" Margaret asked.

Helen looked momentarily startled by the question, but recovered quickly. "Warriors. Highlanders. The whole blasted lot of them."

Margaret bit her lip to keep from smiling. "They do have their benefits though."

The two women shared a look, and Margaret knew she understood when the healer's gaze slid over her husband's broad chest. "Aye, you're right about that."

Magnus frowned, obviously confused. Margaret suspected Eoin would have been as well, but he was already fading.

"The medicine might make him a little sleepy," Helen said.

It did. And a few days later, with the siege dragging on and no end in sight, it also gave Margaret an idea.

Though Eoin was much improved and had even begun to hobble around with the help of a long stick fitted with a smaller stick crosswise to go under his arm to brace himself, she put a little extra of Helen's medicine in his cup that night. He protested, only relenting when she assured him it was the last time.

When he was out cold, she went in search of Bruce.

22

Eoin woke feeling more groggy than usual. He had to admit Helen's medicine helped with the pain, but he hated the fuzziness that came along with it. Now that he was feeling better, he wasn't going to let Margaret badger him into taking another drop. It didn't only smell like dung, it tasted like it as well.

Stretching, he looked around the room and wondered where she'd gone off to. He'd grown surprisingly used to having his wife around fussing over him. He'd also grown surprisingly used to having her ignore his rule not to leave the tent.

He knew she didn't go far, and the men knew who she was now, but he was still concerned when she didn't reappear by the time Peter arrived with the bread, cheese, and fruit to break their fast.

"Have you seen Lady Margaret?" Eoin asked.

The boy looked decidedly uncomfortable, and Eoin felt his first prickle of alarm. "Not since last night."

"Last night?"

He nodded. "She asked me to take her to the king."

Eoin's heart dropped. He swore and jumped out of bed,

forgetting his knee. Wincing, he grabbed the wooden brace MacKay had made him and ordered the lad to help him dress.

With considerable effort, a couple of near stumbles as he tried to navigate the uneven terrain, and quite a bit of swearing, Eoin stormed into the king's tent less than a quarter of an hour later.

"Where is she?" he demanded.

The men seated around the table—the largest piece of furniture in the king's tent—didn't look surprised to see him. They were the king's closest advisors: Tor MacLeod, Neil Campbell, Edward Bruce, Douglas, and Randolph.

"Have care, Striker," MacLeod warned, presumably for his tone.

But Eoin didn't bloody care whom he was talking to: he just wanted his wife. His wife who never did what she was supposed to do, damn it. What about his rule not to interfere?

"I assume you are referring to your wife?" Bruce asked.

"Aye."

"She's in the castle."

Hearing what he'd suspected confirmed didn't make it any easier to bear—or make him any less furious. Eoin forgot about his injury, about formality, and about royal deference. He leaned over the table and stared at the man who'd been his cousin far longer than he'd been king—even if Bruce didn't always like to be reminded of it. "Why the fuck is she in there?"

Bruce didn't flinch, putting his hand up to stop the others from objecting. "Leave us," he said. His guard dogs didn't look happy about it, but they complied with the king's order.

When they were gone, Bruce answered his question.

"Because she asked me to give her a chance to end the siege by negotiating her father's surrender."

Eoin's blood was boiling—literally. It felt like his head was about to blow off. "And you just let her walk in there without any protection?"

"I wasn't aware she needed protection. MacDowell is her father."

He seethed, the air moving tight and heavy through his lungs. "MacDowell is a cornered dog. You know as well as I do that there is nothing that bastard is not capable of, and that sure as hell includes using his daughter and my son if he thinks it will help his bloody cause."

The air of certainty in the king's demeanor lessened. "She was very insistent. She thought that her father would listen to her. She said she wanted to help—to atone for what had happened before."

"And will her being hurt or starving to death do that? Damn it, Rob." The old nickname slipped out. "She didn't know what would happen. She no more sought Thomas and Alexander's deaths than I did. You knew her. She was just a young girl—a little wild and a little reckless maybe, but not capable of intentionally sending all those men to their deaths."

The king held his gaze. "And yet that is what you thought."

Eoin took the shot—which was warranted. "I was wrong."

He'd been out of his mind with jealousy, hurt by her leaving, and afterward gutted by the slaughter at Loch Ryan. He hadn't been rational. He'd been angry and bitter, and so tied up in his own guilt he couldn't see beyond it.

His leg finally gave out. He collapsed in one of the chairs and put his head in his hands. God's blood, what the hell had he done?

"I'm sure she'll be fine," Bruce said after a minute.

Eoin lifted his head. "I hope to hell you're right." He gave his kinsman's words back to him. "I'll hold you responsible if anything happens to her."

"I thought you didn't care what happened to her."

"I didn't think so either."

It was a declaration of sorts, although of what Eoin didn't know. But the thought of what could be going on in that castle made him feel like he was crawling the walls.

Two days later he was half-crazed with the possibilities.

By the third evening, when the gate finally opened and he saw her walking out, he was completely unhinged.

∞

Margaret knew Eoin was going to be angry, but this . . . *this* went far beyond her expectations.

She felt her husband's gaze on her the moment she crossed the bridge beyond the portcullis. Hot, penetrating, practically radiating anger, his eyes took in every detail of her appearance.

Heat fired her cheeks. Blast her father and his temper! The bruise marring her jaw was going to make things much more . . . difficult.

She'd half-expected Eoin to be the first one of Bruce's men to meet her, as she made her way into camp. That he didn't come striding forward, but rather held his position on the periphery of the crowd of men waiting for her was mildly disconcerting.

Perhaps that was an understatement. The coiled snake approach was outright anxiety provoking—nerve-wracking in the extreme.

Refusing to be intimidated, she thrust up her chin and

met his glare defiantly. She'd done what she'd set out to do. Eachann would be safe.

Her defiance didn't last long. Barely had their eyes met for one pulse-pounding moment than she startled and quickly dropped her gaze.

Good lord! She knew what a mouse felt like. A fat, juicy mouse in the predatory sight of a hungry hawk.

Eek.

Margaret wasn't accustomed to backing down, but there was something in Eoin's eyes that told her now was probably not the time for challenges. Something that said he was of no mind to be rational about this. Something that made her pulse race, her skin prickle, and her breath quicken. Something that frankly made her want to run the other way.

Which is why she was relieved when she was led immediately into the king's tent to give her report.

She tried to ignore her husband, but suspected her hands weren't shaking and her palms weren't growing warm from having to face the king.

She felt Bruce's gaze sweep over her jaw. "You are all right, my lady?"

Margaret straightened. "It is nothing, sire. An unfortunate reaction to the messenger, I'm afraid, but I'm fine."

She wasn't sure whether it was a sound or a movement out of the corner of her eye that made her heart freeze. But the cold, murderous rage in her husband's eyes sent ice shooting through her veins. Were it not for Lamont on one side and a man she didn't recognize, but who looked to be in charge, on the other, she suspected her husband's unusual restraint might have been at an end. As chains went, however, the two men by his side seemed more than equipped for the job.

The king flickered a warning glance at Eoin before turning back to her. "What happened?"

"It was as you suspected. The garrison was very low on provisions. They were surviving on bits of grain, meat from dogs and cats, and the last of the ale. The men were—are— suffering, my lord."

She refrained from glancing meaningfully at Eoin. He had vastly underplayed the condition of the castle. Eachann might not have been suffering as badly as the others, but it was only a matter of time. Days. Her heart squeezed at the memory of seeing his pale face for the first time. She hadn't wanted to leave her son, but she knew it must be she to bring back her father's message.

"My father was not inclined to listen to me at first. But eventually I was able to convince him that there as no way out this time. He could either watch his men die or he could submit and see them live."

"So he agreed?"

Hearing the disbelief in the king's voice, she nodded. "Aye. You can send in your men to work out the terms of surrender tonight, and he will hand over the castle to you in the morning, and submit to your authority as king. But as you and I discussed, he and his men will be permitted to go into exile."

Bruce was probably relieved that he would have her father's submission without having to try to welcome his brothers' killer back into the fold. She'd expected relief, and perhaps a little exuberance. But the tent stuffed with about fifteen men—most of whom were as tall and powerfully built as her husband—was oddly quiet. The king voiced what must be the collective concern. "How can we be sure this isn't a trick?"

"You can't." She lifted her chin. "But I believe my father

was in earnest, my lord. I would not have left my son in there otherwise. If you wish, I will lead your men in there myself."

The king's mouth twisted wryly. "That won't be necessary. I do not mean to sound ungrateful, indeed I am very appreciative of everything you have done."

Margaret nodded. Suddenly, the exhaustion of the past few days overwhelmed her. "If we are finished, I should like to return to my tent. I'm afraid I haven't had much sleep the past few nights."

There was definitely a sound this time. A sharp, harsh sound of outrage that made her heart pulse erratically and her breath hitch shallowly. She didn't look in his direction this time, perhaps a little scared of what she might see.

The king nodded, and it took everything she had to maintain her dignity and not run out of the tent.

He would have caught her anyway.

She could feel his presence behind her as she wound her way through the camp. She was practically running, but his footsteps were ominously slow and even. *Thump. Thump.* Good lord, the ground couldn't be shaking. She'd listened to too many faerie tales about hungry giants.

Wasn't he supposed to be hobbling? How could he be walking so quickly with a stick to brace himself?

She knew there was no escape, but she still wished the tent had a door—preferably one with a big iron bar. Although somehow, she didn't think that would keep him out tonight.

The mouse was cornered.

She feared she was squeaking when she finally turned to face him to explain. "Now, Eoin, I know you are upset—"

Something that sounded suspiciously like a growl cut her off.

He was standing near the opening of the tent seething at her like a madman clenching his fists. Actually, he was clenching everything. Every muscle in his body seemed taut and flared like a beast waiting to pounce.

She bit her lip. Perhaps she didn't know him as well as she thought she did. He didn't seem quite as civilized as she remembered. Actually, he looked rather *un*civilized. Clearly, she wasn't the only one who hadn't slept or eaten much the past few days. Neither had he found time for a razor, although she must admit the dangerous brigand look sent a little pulse of excitement shooting through certain parts of her.

But there was no denying her nervousness; her voice was shaking as she said, "Perhaps we should save this discussion for the morning, when we are both rested and a little more rational."

Where was that brilliant mind when she needed it?

It was the wrong thing to say. He was on her much faster than a man with an injured knee ought to be. He loomed over her, threatening but not touching her—almost as if he didn't trust himself to do so.

"I don't think so, *a leanbh*. Rest isn't what I have in mind for you right now."

The dark huskiness of his voice made her shudder, leaving her no doubt what he meant.

"I thought we both agreed that wouldn't be a good idea."

"To hell with a good idea, Maggie. Take off your damned clothes because I'm about two seconds from ripping them off you, and five seconds from being inside you. If you're lucky, we'll make it to sixty before we're both crying out."

Oh dear, that shouldn't make her so hot and tingly, should it? "Eoin . . ."

He leaned closer, fixing his gaze on hers, leaving her no doubt he meant what he said. "One."

"Won't you try—?"

She didn't finish. The sound of her ripped bodice was muffled by the low groan in his throat as his mouth came down on hers.

❧

One taste of her, and he was gone. All Eoin could think about was being inside her.

He *needed* to be inside her. Needed it more than he'd ever needed anything in his life.

He kissed her like a starving man—or maybe like a man who'd spent the past three days worried out of his bloody mind.

He tore off her clothes, stripping her bare so he could look at every damned inch of her and assure himself there weren't any other bruises she was hiding from him.

When he thought of the one on her face . . .

He kissed her harder, deeper, letting the feel of her tongue sliding against his take the edge off the burning rage.

He moaned as heat and sensation drowned him. He'd forgotten how incredible this felt. How incredible she felt.

With more gentleness than he thought himself capable at the moment, he eased her down on the bed, breaking the kiss for long enough to look at her.

He muttered a curse. A fist locked around his heart and squeezed. She was so damned beautiful she took his breath away.

How many times had he pictured all that smooth, creamy skin? Those long, slender limbs? Those incredible breasts. Aye, those he'd pictured most of all. He'd pictured his hands on them, squeezing, his mouth on them, sucking, and his face buried between them, inhaling that sweet scent of her skin.

But the memories of the girl paled in comparison to the woman before him. She was a little softer, a little fuller, and even more sensually curved than before.

He didn't know whether to curse or get on his knees in gratitude. How could he blame men for panting after her? She was an enchantress with a body ripe for pleasure.

His pleasure, damn it. She was his.

And he proved it—in only a few more seconds than he'd promised.

He pulled his clothes off with marginally less impatience than he'd given hers and lowered himself down on top of her. The next instant her legs were wrapped around his waist and he was thrust up deep inside her. It was as if their bodies had come together on their own. Instinct, memory, he didn't know. All he did know was that it felt perfect and natural, as if six years hadn't come between them.

He looked into her eyes and felt an overwhelming sense of quiet. Of peace and fate.

He didn't say anything. He didn't need to. His emotions were raw and there on the surface for her to see. He loved her. He'd always loved her and always would.

The flurry of emotions that had sent him into a frenzy the past few days began to unfurl as he thrust. Slow at first and then faster as her moans urged him on.

Pressure pounded at the base of his spine like a sledgehammer. Insistent. Demanding. Hard.

Sixty seconds might have been ambitious—for both of them. The only salve to his pride was that she cried out first.

When Eoin rolled off her, he took her with him, tucking her into his side. It took a few minutes for the breath to find Margaret's lungs again before she could speak. Propping her chin on his chest, she stared up at him. "Better now?"

He lifted a brow. "Sweetheart, if you think that came anywhere near to making me feel better, you're in for a rude awakening. That barely took the edge off." His hand skimmed down over her naked bottom, pressing her closer to his leg.

His leg! She jumped up. "Your knee! I forgot about your knee. Oh God, did that hurt?"

His mouth quirked. "I can assure you the last thing I was thinking about was my knee. But it's fine." He paused, leveling his gaze on hers. "Helen's potion worked its magic."

She blushed, realizing what he was getting at. "I'm sorry, but it was the only way I could think of to prevent you from stopping me."

"By drugging me?"

She shrugged. "I knew you weren't telling me everything—which you weren't—and I knew I didn't have much time. It was only a little more than you were supposed to take." When it looked as if his temper might flare again, she added, "Besides, it's not as if you were being rational about the matter."

"With good reason, damn it." He took her chin, tilting her face to the light from one of the oil lamps. "I'll kill him."

"You'll do no such thing. He's my father, Eoin. I'm not making excuses for him. Well, maybe I am, but he isn't exactly in the best frame of mind. He hasn't eaten in days, giving all his food to his men and Eachann. I came on too strongly, telling him what he didn't want to hear, and he reacted without thought. I was more in the way than anything else."

"That's no excuse."

"No, it's not," she admitted. "But he felt so guilty about it that it helped me convince him there was only one course. Eachann helped, too. He truly loves the boy, Eoin. He couldn't bear to think of him suffering."

"What will he do?"

"Go to Ireland or the Isle of Man, I suspect. England is out of the question for a while. Edward won't be happy that he surrendered one of his most important castles." She paused, hesitant to broach the subject but knowing she must. "He wants to take Eachann with him."

His entire body went stiff. "Over my dead body."

She didn't think it wise to say that is exactly what her father had proposed.

But then a bolt of panic leapt in her chest at what he meant. "And it will be over mine before I let you take him from me."

He lifted a brow, but she wasn't being dramatic, she meant it.

Still, issuing threats wasn't going to help anything. She needed to reason with him. "You can't just take him away; he doesn't even know you, Eoin."

"I know, and I intend to change that. But I have no intention of taking him from you."

Her breath held. "What about our separate ways?"

His gaze swept over her naked body and the sheets twisted at the bottom of the bed. "That didn't exactly work out very well, did it?"

She could barely breathe. "What are you saying?"

"I'm saying that I'd like you to return to Kerrera with me and our son."

Kerrera. She stiffened at the mention of the place where she'd experienced so much unhappiness.

"It will be different this time, Margaret," he said, sensing her reaction. "I will be with you. For a while at least. The king has given me leave until my knee is healed. But even after that it won't be like last time. I will be able to return to you—to you both—more frequently. The end is coming."

She paused, not wanting to ask, but knowing she had to. "Does this mean you have forgiven me?"

He nodded, sweeping his thumb over her cheekbone as if it were the most rare porcelain. "Aye, we both made mistakes. We can't go back, but we can try to go forward."

Margaret couldn't believe it: he'd forgiven her. She pushed aside the unease and anxiety provoked by the idea of returning to the place she'd run from all those years ago. It was his home, and if she wanted to be part of his life—to give their marriage another chance—she would have to make it her home, too. For Eachann's sake, as well as her own, she nodded.

The smile he gave her tore through her heart. "Then it's settled." He drew her up on top of him. "But other scores have not been." One hand snaked around the back of her neck and the other around her bottom to draw her in. "This time you're going to help me feel better slowly. Very, *very* slowly. And it's going to take a long time."

She did, and it did.

23

***

BY MIDDAY Dumfries Castle belonged to Bruce, her father had swallowed his pride long enough to voice the words submitting to "King" Robert's authority, and Margaret had said her farewells to him under the blistering glare of her husband, who despite her pleas, made no effort to make his feelings toward the man who'd struck her less apparent.

With Dugald MacDowell vanquished, the king and his men were celebrating the victory over the last of the Scottish resistance with a feast in the Great Hall of the castle that would be slighted on the morrow. Dumfries—like all the other strongholds Bruce had taken back from the English—would be destroyed to prevent the enemy from garrisoning it again.

Given the circumstances, Margaret did not feel like celebrating and decided to stay in the room that had been set aside for her and Eachann.

Although the day could be counted a great success for Bruce and had proceeded as well as could be expected, it had been a difficult day for her. Not only had her father's virulent antagonism upon hearing that she intended to stay with her husband been difficult to bear, there was also Eachann's reaction.

A reaction that hadn't shown any signs of waning. Even after a hearty meal of his favorites—including mutton from the king's own stores and sugared plums procured by Eoin as if by magic—and a warm bath, the boy was still close to tears and, as she tucked him into bed, still asking the questions he'd been asking since he'd walked out of the castle with her father.

"But why must we go with *him*? Why can't we go with Grandfather to the Isle of Man or back to England with Sir John? I thought you wanted to marry him?"

"I did," she tried to explain, fearing she was doing no better than she'd done in the note she'd written to Sir John. She hoped he'd understood. "But that was when I thought your father had died. He is my husband, Eachann, and even were I to wish it—which I don't—I cannot marry anyone else."

The little face that was so much like Eoin's screwed up angrily. "I wish he was dead. He's a traitorous bastard, and I hate him!"

Apparently he'd learned how to pronounce the word correctly. Margaret didn't want to be harsh with her son after all that he'd been through, but she knew she could not allow these feelings to fester. Her expression hardened, imparting the seriousness of what she was about to say. "I know you are confused and upset, but wishing someone's death is a grave matter. Your grandfather was wrong to speak of your father like that, and I was wrong to allow him to. Your father has never been a traitor. He has always fought for what he believed in, even if your grandfather doesn't agree with it. It shames me to think that you would condemn a man without giving him a chance."

The face that looked up at her was as pale as the pillow behind him. He blinked, his rounded dark-blue eyes filling with tears. "But why does he want me now, when he didn't before?"

Margaret gasped in horror. "Who told you that?" As if she needed to ask. Her mouth fell in a flat line. "Your grandfather was wrong. Your father wants you very much. He stayed away because he was angry with me—for something *I* did." His eyes widened. "Your father trusted me with something, and I betrayed him by telling someone I shouldn't have. Many men died and your father was nearly killed because of it. He didn't know about you. Had he, nothing would have kept him from you."

He seemed to accept what she said, but as always he understood more than she intended. His expression turned grave. "If you did that, why does he want you back?"

She wasn't sure he did, but the boy was confused enough. "Because your father is a fair man, Eachann, and he's giving me another chance. I hope you will do the same for him."

He considered her for a moment and nodded. Margaret heaved a sigh of relief, smiling at the small victory, and bent over to press a kiss on his forehead.

Before she could wish him a good night, however, he asked, "What's a whore?"

The smile fell from her face. "Where did you hear that word?"

He flushed uncomfortably, seeming to realize he'd said something he shouldn't. "One of Grandfather's men."

"What did he say?"

He looked down at his feet under the bed coverings. "Nothing."

"It's all right, sweetheart," she said gently. "You will not hurt my feelings."

"He said you were no more loyal than a halfpenny whore." He paused. "It's not a very nice word, is it?"

She shook her head. "No, it's not. But he is wrong, Eachann. I love your grandfather and will always be his daughter, but my loyalty belongs to your father and has since I married him, just as yours now belongs to him." Divided loyalties had interfered in her marriage before; she would not let them again. "Do you understand?"

He nodded solemnly.

She smiled. "Good, then try to get some sleep. We have a long day tomorrow."

She pressed another kiss on his forehead and closed the door to the small ambry attached to her bedchamber behind her.

She startled at the shadowy figure looming in the bedchamber, relaxing when she recognized Eoin. But good gracious would she ever get used to his size? In a low voice so that Eachann wouldn't hear, she asked, "How long have you been standing there?"

"Long enough." His fists clenched. "I should have killed the bastard. How could he tell my son I didn't want him?"

Margaret didn't know; nor would she make any excuses for him. "Eachann knows the truth now. That's what's important."

But Eoin would not be so easily pacified. "Your father has poisoned him against me. God knows what other lies he's told him!"

Margaret didn't want to contemplate. "Eachann will see they are lies. Just give him some time."

"I've lost too much time as it is." She could hear the

emotion in his voice as he raked his fingers through his hair. "He's five, Maggie. *Five.*"

Margaret looked at the devastation on his face and knew she had to do something. "He cried horribly when he was a babe—and always in the middle of the night. I didn't sleep for almost a year. He would screech until my ears were ringing, and I thought I'd go mad."

Eoin frowned, clearly taken aback. "He did?"

She nodded. "Aye, it was horrible. But not as bad as all those dirty cloths."

The frown turned to befuddlement. "Cloths?"

"Aye." She shivered. "It was amazing such a foul smell could come from one tiny creature."

His mouth twisted with amusement. "That's disgusting."

"Not half as disgusting as cleaning up when his nurse-maid wasn't around, I assure you."

He held her gaze, a wry smile curving his mouth. "You're trying to make me feel better."

Her mouth quirked. "Maybe a little. But I'm just point-ing out that not everything was coos and goos, and cute little baby faces. There were plenty of days I felt like pulling out my hair. And I'm sure there will be plenty more for you to look forward to."

"Thanks—I think."

She laughed, and then asked, "Was there something you wanted? From the sounds below, the celebrating is just get-ting started."

"It is, but I wanted to make sure you both had every-thing you needed."

She smiled. "We're fine, Eoin. You don't need to check up on us. Enjoy your celebration. I know you must have been waiting for this for a long time."

Given what had happened years ago, she would not

begrudge him his victory, even if it was at the expense of her father and clansmen.

But what would become of the once proud and ancient clan of MacDowell? Eoin had her undivided loyalty, but that didn't mean she stopped loving her family.

He stepped closer to her, and she couldn't prevent the resulting quickening of her heartbeat—or of her breath.

The passion they'd shared last night only heightened her body's reaction to him. Every nerve ending seemed to flush with awareness and not a small amount of anticipation.

She'd forgotten everything. Forgotten how good it was between them. Forgotten how it felt to experience the kind of all-consuming pleasure that grabbed you deep down and wouldn't let go. Forgotten how it felt to have his weight on top of her, how it felt to have him inside her—filling her. And most of all, she'd forgotten how it felt to shatter into a million tiny pieces of bliss.

Six years of abstinence would not be sated by one night. First Tristan, and then when he'd tired of waiting for her mourning to be over, Sir John, had tried to make their relationship intimate, but it had felt wrong—disloyal somehow even to a husband she thought dead.

Ironic, given that . . .

She tried to push the thought away that had lodged in her head the night before, when she realized the difference in her husband's lovemaking. He made love like a man—an *experienced* man. With all the confidence and finesse of someone who knew exactly how to bring a woman pleasure.

Her chest squeezed. She had no right to expect six years of abstinence from him, but being confronted with the proof otherwise hurt.

He stared down at her. "I have been waiting for this day

for a long time, but strangely I don't feel much like celebrating." He smiled a little deviously for someone usually so serious. "At least not with the men below."

The gaze that swept over her body and lingered left her no doubt of what he meant. But Margaret was determined not to fall into the trap of passion again. She wanted to be close to him—not just physically—and she sensed there was something about the warriors he was with all the time that was important.

She took a step back. "Tell me about them."

He frowned. "Who?"

"The men you are always with. Ewen Lamont, Magnus MacKay . . ." She was about to say the good-looking man MacKay was always with, but then realized that wasn't exactly descriptive, as she would have had to be blind not to notice his friends were all rather uncommonly attractive. "The dark-haired warrior he's always with, Robbie Boyd, and the three scary-looking Islesmen." There may have been one or two others, but they were the ones she could remember.

Had she not been watching him closely, she would have missed the surprise that crossed his gaze before the blank mask dropped over his face. *He's hiding something*.

"What do you wish to know?"

She shrugged. "I don't know, you seem unusually close, that's all. It's odd to see men of different clans fighting together rather than with their own." She frowned; most of the men in Robert Bruce's retinue were well known— Douglas, Randolph, Edward Bruce, James the Steward, Robert Keith, Neil Campbell, Alexander Lindsay, David Barclay, and Hugh of Ross. "Are you part of the king's retinue?"

"Not exactly, although I often fight with them." He

closed the distance between them, not un-coincidentally she suspected, backing her to the most dominant piece of furniture in the small chamber: the bed. "Why are you so curious about them, Maggie?" His voice was husky as he brushed the back of his finger over the curve of her cheek. When he dropped it down her throat, over her pulse to the curve of her breasts, and leaned down closer, her breath quickened. "Do I have cause to be jealous?"

Heat roared up her cheeks. "Of course not!"

"Good. They're all happily married anyway."

"I wasn't—"

He cut off her protest with a kiss. A long, slow, thoroughly distracting kiss.

Though she suspected it was intentional, she decided to let him get away with it. She had to be patient. She wanted to know about him—about what he did—but sharing and trust would not come overnight. And in the meantime . . .

He was awfully good at distracting.

∞

The muscles in the back of his neck tensed with the sound of laughter. Eoin had to force himself not to turn around again. He knew what he would see.

Bloody hell, he thought with not an insignificant amount of irritation. Maybe they should have ridden to Kerrera after all. When Hawk had offered to sail them to Gylen on his way to Spoon Island to see his own family, Eoin had jumped at the chance to avoid the drudgery of overland travel and long days in the saddle—especially with his sore knee. By ship, the journey that could take weeks depending on the roads would be only a matter of days. Although the sea roads between Dumfries and the Argyll coast could be dangerous—and Eoin would not have chanced it on his own—with the best seafarer in a kingdom of seafarers at the helm, Eoin was confident that they would be able to outrun any trouble.

MacSorley had saved their hides more times than he could count, and Eoin trusted the brash West Highland chieftain with not only his life, but his wife and son's. But why the hell did he have to be so damned *likable*?

MacSorley was wickedly funny, could charm the habit off a nun, and never took anything too seriously. In short, he was everything Eoin wasn't. Which was why watching his son—the son who'd barely said three words to him—hanging on his friend's every word, spellbound by the big *Gall-Gaedhil* (who looked more Viking than Gael), grated. Margaret wasn't helping matters any; she was laughing at Hawk's jests just as hard as the lad, damn it.

Why was he surprised? Hawk and Margaret were two sides of the same coin. He frowned. At least they used to be. When he'd first met Hawk, Eoin had been struck by their similar personalities. But Margaret had changed, he realized. She no longer walked into the room with the brash, swaggering confidence of a pirate taking over a ship; she didn't say outrageous things or make irreverent jokes; and she dressed as fine as any English noblewoman, with her bold, dramatic locks tucked neatly and modestly behind a veil—although she was having a devil of a time with the wind. He smiled, watching her struggle to tame the red strands from whipping wildly around her head.

She was far more quiet and reserved, and although her beauty would always set her apart, she no longer stuck out like a peacock in a flock of wrens. She was the type of decorous noblewoman who would make any man proud. Which was exactly what he'd wanted, wasn't it?

Turning around, he caught sight of her face twinkling

with laughter, and it clobbered him in the chest with the force of a taber. He was a bloody fool. He'd been drawn to her precisely because she was so different—because she was so special. She'd brought out a side of him no one ever had before. He'd felt lighter when he was with her. Happier. The world hadn't seemed quite so grave and not everything so dire. His life had felt broader than the narrow field of battle.

No wonder she'd been so unhappy at Kerrera. He'd forced her into a mold of conventionality and made her feel as if she wasn't good enough for him the way she was. But she'd been perfect.

He wanted the girl he'd married back. He wanted her to be happy again. He wanted her naughty and a little outrageous. He wanted to see her hair flowing down her back and her head bent over a horse as she tore uninhibited across the countryside. He wanted her to look at him as if she couldn't wait to swive him senseless.

The way she was laughing right now made him think that it might not be too late.

But as soon as their eyes met, she seemed to catch herself. The girlish smile fell from her face and her laugh seemed suddenly more restrained.

Guilt stabbed, and he swore he would do what he could to make it up to her. "*Get your family in order*," the king had said before he left. Eoin intended to do just that.

But it would be a hell of a lot easier if he could confide in her about his role in Bruce's army. He hated keeping her in the dark, and if her questions about the Guard were any indication, her perceptiveness was going to make it difficult.

As the coast of Galloway disappeared into the morning mist, he took his turn at the oars, focusing on the steady rhythm of the blade cutting through the waves, rather than the goings-on at the back of the ship. But he could hear them.

"I have a son about your age," MacSorley's deep voice rang out.

"You do?" Eachann asked. "How old is he?"

"He'll be five just after midsummer."

"I'm already five," Eachann said proudly. "My birthday was on All Saints' Day."

Eoin's gut stabbed; he hadn't even known that.

"I should have guessed," MacSorley said, laughter in his voice. "You are much bigger than Duncan."

"I am?" Eachann couldn't hide his surprise. "My grandfather said I had to eat more or I would never grow big and strong enough to be a warrior."

"You can be whatever you want, Eachann," Margaret interjected firmly. "You don't have to be as tall as the captain to be a warrior—if that is what you want to be."

From the way that Margaret hastened to respond, Eoin sensed the lad's size was a tender spot. Was he small? Eoin didn't have much experience with boys his age, but supposed he could be. Eachann was built like his brother Donald. Donald was two years older than Eoin, but Eoin had been a head taller than him by the time they were thirteen. Donald was lean and wiry, as opposed to muscular like Eoin and their eldest brother, Neil. It had bothered Donald, too, until he'd found his strength. Like MacSorley, his brother excelled at seafaring.

MacSorley must have picked up on the sore spot as well. "Your mother is right, lad. In fact, I even know a lass who can flip me on my backside. And she has . . . more than once," he grumbled.

"She must have been a big lass," Eachann said, clearly not sure whether to believe him.

MacSorley laughed. "I'm afraid not. She's about Peter's size." He pointed to the youth, who was only a few inches over five feet and probably seven stone soaking wet.

"Now I know you're jesting," Eachann said.

"Her name is Cate and she's betrothed to a friend of mine." He paused. "At least they were betrothed until . . ." He waved it off. "No matter. She also happens to be the king's daughter."

"But the king's daughter is in an English convent," Eachann said.

"I think he means the king's natural daughter," Margaret said.

"You mean she's a bastard?" Eachann asked.

Eoin's mouth tightened. He didn't need to turn to feel the boy's gaze land on his back. Damn Dugald MacDowell to Hades!

"Eachann . . ." Margaret started.

But MacSorley only laughed. "Aye, I suppose she is. But I wouldn't call her that if I were you, or she might put you on *your* backside."

Eoin had heard about how Gregor MacGregor's intended had been trained in warfare and had managed to flip the big, always-ready-with-a-jest Viking while practicing. The other Guardsmen had been needling MacSorley about it ever since. Eoin would have given a month's wages to have seen it.

Tired of watching from afar while Hawk entertained his son, Eoin moved off the oars. He was going to see if Eachann wanted to help him with the navigation, when he heard MacSorley ask, "Would you like to hold the ropes for a while?"

"Me? Really? You mean it?"

Eoin quickly sat back down at the excitement in his

son's voice. Rough maps of the shoreline and a sun compass could hardly compete with holding the riggings.

He didn't realize he was frowning until Margaret sat down beside him. "Your friend is amusing. He reminds me of someone, although I can't think who."

Eoin hid a smile, wondering how long it would take her to figure out it was herself.

She lowered her voice. "Eachann is scared. He isn't deliberately trying to hurt you. He just doesn't know what to say. Your friend MacSorley is easier—there is nothing at stake with him."

Christ. Was he that easy to read? He didn't bother denying it. "I tried talking to him this morning before we left, but he couldn't seem to get away quickly enough."

"What did you talk about?"

He shrugged. "Nothing in particular. I asked if he had a favorite weapon he liked to practice with and mentioned that I was looking forward to his training when we arrived at Kerrera."

She didn't say anything.

"Did I say something wrong?"

She bit her lip as if debating something. After a minute, she reached a decision. Her gaze held a hint of challenge when she said, "I don't think Eachann is very interested in warfare."

Her words took him aback. "I thought every little boy was interested in warfare." He hadn't thought of anything else.

Her mouth tightened almost imperceptibly. "Not Eachann."

He sensed a slight defensiveness and guessed that like the boy's size, the subject was a sensitive one. It wasn't difficult to figure out why. Dugald MacDowell only raised warriors. But frankly, given that was all Eoin thought about—at least until he'd met Margaret—he'd assumed he would as well.

He thought for a moment. "What is he interested in?"

"Books. He reads everything he can get his hands on. He likes to build things." She gestured toward the compass. "He'd probably be interested in that. He likes to know how things work."

The beginnings of a smile lifted one corner of his mouth. Perhaps his son was like him in other ways. "The lad is clever?"

Her mouth twitched. "You could say that. He's already beating me at chess."

"Well, that's not exactly saying much."

"Eoin!" she shoved his shoulder. "That isn't very nice."

He laughed. "Maybe not, but it's true. Patience has never been your forte, but you do have other . . . uh, talents."

The meaningful look he gave her sent a blush roaring up her cheeks, but she drew up primly. "Aye, well you've never been very patient either when it comes to certain things."

He laughed again. She was right. He still wasn't patient when it came to her. They had six years of catching up to do, and he couldn't wait to get her back to Kerrera to start.

Their laughter had caught the attention of their son. As soon as Eoin's gaze met his, the little boy turned away. Eoin sighed, realizing he was going to need *quite* a bit of patience when it came to his son.

∞

Margaret was sad to have to say goodbye to the strapping seafarer. It wasn't just that she liked Erik MacSorley— which she did (she hadn't laughed like that in years)—it also meant that they'd arrived at their destination.

As the flat, green hillsides and dark, rocky seashores of the Isle of Kerrera came into view, she had to admit she'd felt more than one pang of apprehension and doubt. But any worries that she was doing the right thing had faded when she remembered seeing those two dark-blond heads bent together for the first time. Her throat still grew tight just thinking about it.

As they'd left the small island off the shore of Ireland where they'd spent the night, Eoin had taken her advice and asked Eachann if he wanted to learn how to navigate the ship. Though hesitant, their too curious son had been unable to resist the temptation of the flat piece of wood with curved marks drawn from the sun's shadow on a vertical pointer. He'd asked dozens of questions, which Margaret quickly lost interest in, but which Eoin didn't seem to mind. She had to admit it was nice to have someone else to answer Eachann's never-ending questions, with increasing focus on the minutest details, that sometimes taxed Margaret's motherly patience.

She could almost see the boy's mind working as he tried to figure out a way to improve the accuracy of the crude instrument. Eachann liked to build things. Not forts and castles out of mud and sticks like the other boys, but useful things. Things that made tasks easier for people. She'd never forget when he read about the great horologe at Canterbury Cathedral that sounded the time with bells. It used weights rather than water, and before her failed wedding the boy had been experimenting with building his own *cloc*, the Gaelic word for bell. He'd been so excited, he'd talked nonstop about it for days.

He was that way now. The difference this time was that he had an equally intrigued audience. Her mouth twisted with a smile. Maybe not an audience but an enthusiastic cohort.

Eoin had been surprised to hear that his son didn't seem to have much interest in being a warrior, but he'd recovered faster than she expected. Surprisingly, he didn't seem disappointed. Actually, as the conversation intensified, Eoin's pride in the boy became readily apparent.

She was doing the right thing. Her son needed this. A father who was proud of him—who understood him—no matter what he chose to do was worth any risk to her heart.

Buoyed by the first signs of softening in her son's attitude toward his father, Margaret bid farewell to the handsome seafarer with the devilish grin, who was eager to return to his wife and children, and held Eachann's hand tightly as they followed Eoin up the sea-gate stairs to the square stone keep of Gylen Castle, which sat perched on the cliff overlooking the sea. She needed all of that encouragement as she gazed up and saw the couple waiting to greet them. Her heartbeat quickened, and a familiar dread draped over her like a soggy plaid, the uncomfortable weight of it dragging her down.

Margaret knew Eoin had sent a missive to his parents, apprising them of Eachann's existence, but there hadn't been time to inform them of their arrival. She harbored no illusions on her own account—Eoin's parents were hardly likely to welcome her with open arms—but for Eachann's sake, she hoped they would hide their disdain.

The thought that her son might think less of her was something she couldn't bear.

Eoin was a few steps ahead of them, presumably to give his parents a quick warning, but it proved unnecessary. Lady Rignach's gaze seemed to find hers instantly. Beneath the surprise, Margaret would have sworn she saw what looked like relief before the other woman's eyes shifted down to the side. Her face lost every trace of color, and she might have slid to the ground had her husband not caught her by the arm.

The proud chief looked almost as shaken when he realized why his wife had almost swooned.

Eachann was not a timid boy, but when the two imposing figures stared at him as if he were a strange creature from a menagerie, he drew in tight against her.

Lady Rignach's fingers went to her lips. The dark eyes that turned back to Eoin were shimmering with tears. "My God, he looks just like you. I'd feared . . ."

Her voice dropped off.

Margaret stiffened, realizing what she'd feared: that the boy wasn't his.

But a few moments later, she wondered if she'd been mistaken. The gaze that met hers now wasn't filled with derision or animosity but with gratitude. "Thank you for bringing him here. After what happened, I feared nothing could make you come back."

Margaret would have thought Lady Rignach would consider that a good thing, if she hadn't been looking at her with such obvious relief.

Feeling as if she'd just stepped into some kind of faerie hole, Margaret didn't know what to say. But with her hand losing feeling from being squeezed so tight and the small body pressing against her side in danger of giving her bruises, she shook off the disquiet. "Eachann." She drew the boy forward. "These are your grandparents, Lady Rignach and Laird Gillemore, Chief of MacLean."

Eachann, looking very serious, gave them a short, formal bow, murmuring that he was glad to meet them.

Lady Rignach looked at the boy with such longing Margaret thought she might try to pull him into her arms.

Apparently, Eoin thought so as well. To save the boy from being more overwhelmed than he already was, Eoin stepped in front of him. "Should we go inside? It has been a long journey, and we are all tired."

"Of course," the laird said. "Your mother will have some rooms prepared."

"Room," Eoin said firmly. "My wife and I will share my chamber, and my son will sleep in the antechamber." If there was any doubt about her place, there wasn't any longer. Even Margaret was surprised by the leave-no-room-for-objection tone.

She quirked a brow, but his only reply was a forbidding frown, which she assumed was his way of telling her to behave.

Trying not to laugh, she followed Eoin and his parents into the Great Hall. Not much had changed in the years since she'd been here last. The room could have rivaled one at any royal palace. Fine tapestries hung on the freshly limed walls, colorful cloths covered the rows of trestle tables, and the table on the raised dais was adorned with heavily embossed silver candelabrum and other rich plate.

As it was late afternoon and the midday meal had already been completed, the Hall was relatively quiet. They hadn't been expected, so a feast had not been prepared, but Lady Rignach promised that would be rectified on the morrow. The clansmen would be eager to meet the laird's grandson. His *first* grandchild, Margaret realized. Apparently, Marjory had yet to have a child. Sensing the subject was a painful one, she did not ask any more questions.

From the little Eoin had told her about his sister and foster brother, Fin had made his peace with Bruce and was now serving as the laird's henchman. He and Marjory would live in a new tower being added to the castle, but for now were residing in a house in the village.

Margaret admitted she'd wanted to turn back when Eoin had told her of his presence on the isle that first night of their journey, but pride had prevented her. She would not let Fin drive her away. She might not be as convinced as Eoin that Fin had changed, but she was willing to try to put the past in the past.

Though she was just grateful not to have to do so right now. There were only a few clansmen gathered in the Hall, and Fin was not among them.

Without thinking, Margaret almost took a seat at the table just below the *hie burde*—the high table—where she'd so often sat with Tilda (who had married and moved away a few years ago). But Eoin drew her forward to the place where his mother was waiting at the dais. She sat between Eoin and Eachann as they took their seats on the end of the long bench. Lady Rignach looked like she was contemplating squeezing in beside them, but the laird steered her to the middle of the table.

Eoin and his father filled most of the conversation, as they enjoyed a light meal of roasted fowl and mutton, cheese, and bread. Eachann was very subdued, although he did revive a bit when a few pies and cakes were brought out for him to sample.

Margaret was laughing to herself as she noticed how he and Eoin chose the exact same plum pie and spiced cake, when she looked up and caught her mother-in-law's teary but also amused gaze. Clearly, she'd noticed it as well, and for the first time the two women who couldn't have been more different shared a moment of understanding.

Margaret didn't know what to think. She'd expected

politeness from Eoin's proud mother, but this seemed to be something more. Was she perhaps not the only one trying to put the past in the past?

It seemed so. Before they retired to their chamber, Lady Rignach pulled Margaret aside.

"I owe you an apology," the older woman said. Though over six years had passed since Margaret had seen her, Lady Rignach had not changed much. She was still an attractive woman, though she must be a few years past fifty.

Margaret was too taken aback to respond.

"You were my son's wife, and I should have made you feel welcome. I should have made you feel as if you could come to me with whatever problems you were having with Finlaeie." Her face hardened with distaste. "I *knew* something was wrong. I should have never let Marjory marry him, but she was so sure he loved her." She gave a shake as if she'd said too much and met Margaret's gaze again. "My deepest regret is that you felt your only choice was to leave. I . . ." Her voice dropped to a whisper. "I was a fool and listened to gossip. You were right, I should have trusted my son's judgment." Her gaze drifted over to where Eachann stood with Eoin and the longing there was almost palpable. "It nearly cost me my son and my grandson."

Apparently Eoin had held his mother partially responsible for Margaret's leaving.

Seeing the proud lady humbled might have once been satisfying, but Eoin's mother wasn't the only one haunted by regret. Margaret, too, had made her share of mistakes. She hadn't known how to relate to the great lady any better than Lady Rignach had known how to relate to the wild, backward girl she'd been. Margaret had stormed in here paying no heed to rules or customs. She'd done what she wanted without any thought for how that would reflect on her husband or his family.

She doubted they could ever be friends, but perhaps they could learn to accept one another. Besides, they had two important people in common: Eoin and Eachann.

"That was a long time ago," Margaret said. "We both did things we regret, but as we cannot change them, perhaps we could try to start anew?"

"I should like that," Lady Rignach said solemnly.

"Mother," Eoin said with an unmistakable note of warning in his voice. "Is there a problem?"

Margaret hadn't realized he'd come up behind her. For such a large man, he moved like a cat. It was a little disconcerting.

Before Lady Rignach could reply, Margaret put her hand on his arm reassuringly. "Everything is fine." She did not need him to rescue her, although she appreciated the effort. "I was just going to ask your mother if she would like to go with me and Eachann to Oban on Monday. I should like him to meet the nuns at the convent."

"I could take you," Eoin said, perhaps anticipating his mother's objection.

But Lady Rignach was not about to object; she jumped at the opportunity to be with her grandson. "I should be honored to accompany you."

Margaret nodded. They had a long way to go, but it was a start.

She turned to her husband and felt her heart squeeze with longing. A start. Right now that was all she could ask for.

24

MARGARET MOANED, twisting in her sleep. Her body felt so heavy, so languid. She gasped, arching, at a delicious flicker of sensation between her legs. The long slow circle, a gentle thrust, and stroking of a . . .

Her eyes popped open. A tongue!

Soft rays of sunlight spilled through the slits of the shudders, enabling her to just make out the dark-blond head of the man who'd roused her from her slumber.

Not that she was complaining, especially when he . . .

She moaned again as his tongue thrust deep inside her. So deep she could feel the intimate scrape of his jaw against her. And then he was licking her again, nuzzling tenderly—hungrily.

It felt so good . . .

Her body started to tremble. Her nipples strained taut beneath the sheets—he'd stripped her bare last night—as her back arched and her hips lifted shamelessly to his intimate kiss. Hot swirls of pleasure raced through her. She could feel the sensations building . . . intensifying.

"Oh God, I'm going to . . ."

She didn't realize she'd cried out until he lifted his head. "Privacy, remember?"

He wouldn't dare stop. "Eoin!" She looked down at him with murder in her eyes. Although it was too dark for him to see her expression, he must have guessed from her tone and started to chuckle.

"We don't want to wake Eachann."

"He will sleep through anything."

"I hope you're right because I'm going to make you scream."

He did. Cupping her bottom, he lifted her to his mouth and ravished her. Those long, wicked strokes . . .

He kissed her harder, sucking and licking until she thought she'd go mad with the pleasure.

And when he brought her to the very peak, he held her there, forcing the spasms deeper, slower, harder. She felt the release rock through her, and then explode in a shattering wave.

She put the pillow Eoin gave her to muffle her cries to good use. And when she was done, she handed it to him.

He was going to need it.

Eoin didn't realize what she was doing right away. It wasn't exactly what a man expected from his wife.

When she'd handed him the pillow and taken him in her hand, he'd been amused. Their games in the forest after they were married were a long time ago. A hand—even her hand—bringing him pleasure wasn't going to make him lose control enough to shout.

But his smile fell as the lips peppering kisses over his mouth and jaw started to trail down his chest and stomach.

They didn't stop.

What was she doing?

He stiffened, feeling something almost like alarm. The hand that was gripping him had stopped pumping and his cock was pounding.

She stopped when her mouth was inches from the throbbing tip and looked up. There was just enough light peeking through the shadows for him to make out her naughty, catlike smile.

He knew *exactly* what she was doing—and so did she.

He was holding himself so tightly he didn't realize his hands were gripping the sheets until she laughed. "I think you might need that pillow after all."

He couldn't talk. Her mouth was too close and he was so damned taut with anticipation he didn't know how much more teasing he could take before he started to beg. Before he gripped the back of her head and moved her mouth over him.

Suck me . . .

Just the thought of her warm mouth closing over him made his cock jerk in her hand and a bead of pleasure seep from the tip.

She licked it. With one slow flick of the tongue she licked and swirled the plump, sensitive hood as if he were a juicy plum.

Pleasure shot through him like an arrow. He nearly came off the damned bed. But it was nothing compared to the incredible sensation when her mouth finally wrapped around him, those sensuous crimson lips stretching to take him in. Lower. Deeper.

Oh God. How many times had he imagined this? But he'd never come close to the reality. He wanted to thrust. He needed to thrust. His body shook as sensation coiled at the base of his spine.

When he couldn't take the torture anymore of her innocent kisses, he told her what to do. He told her how to milk him with her tongue and hand, and how to suck him deep and hard.

She didn't need much instruction. It didn't take her long to bring him to the edge. He would have pulled out, but she wouldn't let him. She took him deep in her throat, coaxing the thick vein with her tongue, and he couldn't hold back. He started to come in hot, fierce, pulsing waves that tore from him in a roar of pleasure so intense, he probably could have used two pillows.

How had she known . . . ?

Eoin didn't let himself finish the question that he had no right to ask. He'd let her think he was dead. He had no right to expect fidelity from her. She'd been betrothed to another man, for Christ's sake.

No good would come from knowing or wondering. It would be better for them both if they erased those six years from memory and never spoke of it.

But it wasn't going to be easy. The jealousy and irrationality that had always been his weakness where his wife was concerned did not listen to reason.

∞

Margaret should have no complaints. The first few days at Gylen were much better than she could have expected. Eachann's natural cautiousness had eased a bit, and he seemed to be coming around to the idea of new grandparents—especially a grandmother who had made no secret that she intended to indulge him beyond all good measure.

Seeing Lady Rignach with Eachann showed Margaret a different side of Eoin's formidable mother. It gave

Margaret an idea of what she must have been like with her own children. She must have loved them fiercely, protecting them like a lioness did her cubs. Margaret coming out of nowhere, throwing her son's life in a tumult, would have been perceived as a threat. It did not excuse all of her coldness, perhaps, but it explained some of it.

With Eoin, Eachann was still reserved—if not so wary—but that lessened considerably after Eoin showed him his personal library and promised to arrange for a tutor to instruct him until he was ready for schooling. The lad's excitement knew no bounds. He'd even relaxed enough to join some of the other young boys in the yard for training one day.

The wall of animosity and suspicion that had faced Margaret at Gylen the first time did not seem so thick, although vestiges of it remained. Some of the clansmen still whispered and stared, and there were subtle reminders of her status as the daughter of one of Bruce's greatest enemies. A plaid that she'd left behind woven of wool from Galloway somehow found its way to the top of her trunk; one of the laird's "*luchd-taighe*" guardsmen looked at her whenever the word "traitor" was spoken; and another stared at her whenever John of Lorn and his rebellious cohorts were mentioned. Apparently the exiled MacDougall chief had been put in charge of the English fleet and was making it difficult for Bruce to get supplies from Ireland and France.

Her short trip to Oban with Lady Rignach and Eachann had gone about as well as could be expected. After Margaret's departure, Eoin's mother had learned the truth of what she'd been doing there and had made a substantial gift to the convent that—fittingly—had been used to set up a school for the children in the village. As apologies went, it was a satisfying one.

The most difficult moment thus far had been when Margaret had been forced to confront Fin at the feast. As he was Marjory's husband, he could hardly be avoided. But after an awkward greeting, both Eoin's sister and her husband had kept their distance. Margaret knew she had Eoin to thank for that.

Eoin's knee had improved enough for him to walk around without the brace Magnus had made for him, and he'd promised to take her riding around the isle soon.

Though he'd been locked up with his father and his men for most of the days, the nights had belonged to her. As always, their passion was explosive. They made love fiercely and tenderly, with an intimacy of which she'd never dreamed.

It was almost perfect. But she couldn't escape the feeling that something was bothering him. On the fourth morning after their arrival at Gylen she had to know. As always, Eoin rose early, before the light of dawn was strong enough to fully light the chamber. He'd already drawn on his tunic and had just finished tying the breeches at his waist when she spoke.

"Have I done something wrong?"

He turned to her in surprise. "Of course not. Why do you ask?"

She drew the sheet up around her chest and scooted up to lean back against the carved wooden headboard. "It seems as if something is bothering you." She paused. "It's been that way since the first night we arrived." She thought for a moment, the sudden realization of what it might be dawning. "Since I . . ." Her voice dropped off in embarrassment. "Did what I did not please you?"

He sat on the edge of the bed, putting the sporran he'd picked up to tie to his belt on the bed next to her. His hand found her cheek. "Are you crazed? Of course you pleased me. Could you not tell from all that shouting?"

She almost let the boyish smile stop her. He looked so handsome and relaxed, so different from the grim, angry man who'd showed up at the church four weeks ago. But she knew she was not imagining it. "Don't, Eoin. Please, don't do this again. If there is something wrong, tell me. I don't want there to be any secrets between us this time. Don't you see? It cannot work otherwise."

He drew back, his expression hardening. "Some secrets are best hidden. The truth is not always a great panacea. Sometimes the truth can hurt. Sometimes we are better off not knowing."

"What does this have to do with me? I don't have any secrets from you."

"Don't you?" He was angry now, his eyes hard and his mouth white. "Then should I ask you how you knew to do that? Should I hear about the men you've shared your bed with? Should I learn all the salacious details? Will that truth be good for me?"

Margaret sucked in her breath, staring at him in shock. He thought she'd . . .

Dear lord! What was bothering him was the same thing that she'd been trying to force from her mind. Maybe he was right: some secrets could only hurt.

But he was wrong about her. "I learned from Fin."

"What?" he exploded. "Why did you not tell me? God's breath, I'll kill him—brother by marriage or not."

She grabbed him by the arm before he could leap off the bed. "I simply meant that he told me you enjoyed that. He asked me if that's how I persuaded you to marry me." He eased back—marginally. "I've never done that to another man, Eoin."

He held her gaze for a long moment. She could see some of the anger waning. "I let you think I was dead. You were a free woman. You do not owe me any explanations."

"Perhaps not, but you shall have one. Unlike my first marriage, I was waiting until I was actually married to share a bed with my second husband. Had you arrived one day later I may not have been able to say this, but there is only one man I have ever been intimate with, and that is you."

His eyes held hers searchingly. "You don't need to tell me this. It would not change anything if you had. I would hate it, but I would get over it."

She understood that too well. "Maybe so, but it's the truth anyway. My memories of you were too strong. I was almost scared to try. I'd loved you so much." She smiled sadly. "It was different for you. You hated me."

He frowned, and then seeming to understand what she meant shook his head wryly. "Not all that different. Besides, unlike you, I knew we were still married."

Margaret didn't understand. "But you broke your vows anyway?"

"I was trying to tell you that I didn't."

"But you must have!" she blurted.

He looked at her as if she were crazed. "Why?"

"Because . . ." She could feel her cheeks flush. "Because you're so different."

At first he didn't seem to understand what she meant, but then he smiled. "I had a lot of practice."

Her heart sank, as the color washed from her face. "I thought you said—"

"Not that kind of practice. The kind of practice I taught you." Suddenly, she understood: he'd thought of her while touching himself. "I thought of how I wanted to touch you—where I wanted to touch you—in vivid detail. I practiced with you over and over for six years."

Her breath held, not daring to hope. "You never . . . with another woman?"

He shrugged, almost as if he were ashamed to admit it. "I wanted to. I hated you, and it infuriated me that I still wanted you. I tried—once. But it didn't get very far."

Margaret didn't know what to say. She was surprised—stunned—and undeniably relieved. She'd been willing to accept what she must, but she was glad she didn't have to. "I'm glad."

He shot her a glare. "It was humiliating."

"You don't expect me to feel sorry for you?"

His mouth twisted. "Under the circumstances, maybe not."

"Do you have any other secrets you want to confide in me?" She said it jestingly, but his face drew up in the blank mask she hated. The mask that shut her out.

He's hiding something.

"Like what?"

Her gaze fell to his arm, where she could just make out a dark shadow under the thin linen. "Like what you are hiding under that shirt, and why you won't let me see you without it in the light?"

He swore under his breath and raked his fingers back through his hair. "It's nothing."

"Then why won't you let me see it?"

He didn't answer her directly. Was he embarrassed? Was that what this was about?

"It's just something I did awhile back. It's a marking."

Her brows drew together. "You mean a tattoo?"

He nodded. "It was something some friends of mine did."

Was it some young man's lark? Something he now wished he hadn't done? Good lord, what did he have tattooed on himself? Her mind filled with all kinds of silly possibilities.

"May I see it?"

He drew off his shirt and she gasped—not even looking at the tattoo. Good gracious. Seeing him in the shadows was nothing like seeing him in the light. Her eyes gorged on the impressive display of bulging muscle before her. He was so big. Strong.

His chest . . .

His arms . . .

God in heaven, he was beautiful. She wanted to run her hands over every inch of those sculpted muscles, she wanted to—

He cleared his throat, clearly amused, reminding her of what she was supposed to be doing. Not that looking at his arm was any hardship. He'd bent his arm to show it to her, and the flex of muscle made her breath quicken and her body warm with unmistakable arousal.

Truth be told she barely noticed the lion rampant and strange weblike markings that surrounded his upper arm like a cuff. She did, however, notice the same words that were engraved on his sword—*Opugnate acriter*—since they were right on the edge of the biggest bulge of muscle, the sharp demarcations of which had her *quite* fascinated.

"Keep looking at me like that, sweetheart, and Eachann is going to get a very different kind of education when he walks in here in a few minutes."

She blushed. "What do the words mean?"

"It's Latin. The rough translation is strike with force."

She thought for a moment. "It's what you do on the battlefield."

He seemed surprised. "In a manner of speaking." He bent over to kiss the top of her nose. "Now, if your curiosity is appeased for the moment, I should go." He stood and reached for his sporran. "Will you hand me that?"

She picked it up, feeling some kind of small, hard object inside. "What do you have in here?"

"Nothing." He tried to snatch it from her, but she was already pulling the object out.

Realizing what it was, she held it in the palm of her hand and stared at it in disbelief.

"Bloody hell, Maggie. Can't you follow any of my rules? I told you no snooping."

She ignored the reference to his ridiculous rules (he couldn't honestly have thought she would really follow them), feeling her chest swell with emotion as she took in the chess piece that she'd stolen all those years ago from Stirling Castle.

"You kept it." Her eyes met his. "All this time you kept it."

He may have hated her, but he'd loved her, too. He'd kept a part of her—a symbol of their love—with him always.

He grumbled something, clearly embarrassed by the sentimentality, and then, as if in acceptance, shrugged and dug something else out of the sporran. "And this. I read it every time I went into battle."

She recognized the wrinkled parchment right away as the note she'd left him. Glancing at the crude writing and misspelled words, it was her turn to be embarrassed. "You should have thrown that away." She tried to laugh it off. "Or perhaps it was a reminder of the ignorant girl you mistakenly married and how fortunate you were to be rid of her."

His reaction was both instantaneous and fierce. He

took her chin in his hand and turned her face to his. "It was a reminder of what a damned fool I was. It was a reminder of the girl who'd loved me so much that she'd withstood rumor, gossip, and innuendo to learn to write and read because she thought it would please me. Because I made her think she wasn't good enough. But I was wrong, Maggie. You were perfect just the way you were, and I hate that I made you think you needed to change for me. Reading, writing, none of that mattered. It was never what was important."

She looked away, cringing at the memories. "I was a wild, backward little heathen. I don't know what you saw in me."

He forced her gaze back to his. "You were strong and beautiful and funny and outrageous and sensual as sin, and I loved you from practically the first moment I saw you."

"You did?"

He nodded. "I've never stopped. God knows it would have been easier if I had, but you are in my heart, Maggie, and that is where you will stay."

"I love you, too."

He smiled and kissed her so tenderly she just knew that this time it would be different.

25

WITH NEIL holding Tarbert Castle for Bruce and Donald serving as commander of the king's galleys, their father looked increasingly to his youngest son as his de facto *tanaiste*. As soon as Eoin arrived at Gylen he was beset by a multitude of problems that needed his attention, including the biggest one, John of Lorn, now Chief of MacDougall and would-be Lord of Argyll, who sure as the devil who spawned him was stirring up trouble again.

Eoin was sure he wasn't the only one wishing Arthur Campbell hadn't let Lorn go after the Battle of Brander four and a half years ago. Campbell—or Ranger as he was known among his fellow Guardsmen—had fallen in love with Lorn's daughter and let him flee into exile for her. Eoin could understand the conflict perhaps better than anyone (having hoped to see his own wife's father on the edge of his sword more than once), but Campbell's show of mercy had been punished many times over the past few years. If Bruce caught him again, Lorn wouldn't get a second chance.

"How can you be sure it was him?" Fin asked the

fisherman who'd come to them with the latest report. "Did they identify themselves?"

Eoin tried not to grind his teeth when his foster brother spoke but failed. For the sake of his sister, Eoin had attempted to forgive Fin for what he'd done to Margaret—he'd seemed so damned remorseful and sincere in his apologies—but Margaret's latest revelations had reignited his anger. Eoin wanted to kill him all over again, not just for touching her, but for speaking to her so crudely. He'd been having a hell of a time keeping his temper in check all morning while they gathered in the laird's solar with the other members of his father's *meinie*.

"I know it was 'im," the old man said stubbornly, not letting Fin intimidate him—which given the henchman's size was an impressive show of courage. Fin had added considerable bulk—most of it muscle—to his tall frame and had become the chief's mostly deadly swordsman. "I recognized one of the men who took my catch."

"I thought you said they were all wearing helms," Fin said sharply, obviously trying to catch the man in a lie.

"They were, but he had a scar." The fisherman drew a long line down his cheek and across his nose. "I could see it when he lifted his visor as they sailed away."

Eoin gave Fin a sharp look and asked the man a few more questions before thanking him and sending him on his way.

Though a number of his father's *meinie*, including Fin, thought they should wait for more "proof" than the recollections of an old fisherman, positing that the men were probably just Irish cateran, Eoin's father insisted on sending word to Bruce. If Lorn's men had been sighted this far north—so close to his former stronghold of Dunstaffnage—the king would want to know. When it was further decided that someone should go to Dunstaffnage Castle to see if the keeper had heard anything, his father looked relieved when Eoin volunteered.

His father was the only one at the table who knew that the keeper of the former MacDougall stronghold—Arthur Campbell—was one of Eoin's brethren in the Highland Guard. Together Eoin and Campbell would be able to deal with any threat from the man who'd once been the most powerful in the "Kingdom" of the Isles.

The meeting broke up and the warriors left to attend to their duties. Having offered to pen the note to Bruce, Eoin didn't notice that one had stayed behind until he spoke.

"I'll go with you," Fin said.

Eoin looked up, his expression a hard mask. "That won't be necessary."

"But what about your knee?"

"I'm taking a skiff, not running. Besides, it's almost healed."

"Does that mean you'll be picking up a sword again soon?" Fin said with a grin. "I've been waiting for our rematch."

Eoin gripped the quill until his fingertips turned white. Fin's "everything is fine" attitude grated on his already stretched-to-the-breaking-point temper.

"You will have it," Eoin promised darkly. Last time he'd held back, but this time he'd grind his friend into the dirt.

"What the hell is the matter with you? Does this have something to do with your wife? I've stayed away from her as you asked. I thought we were past this. I told you I was sorry. I was drunk. I didn't know what I was doing."

"How about what you were saying?" Eoin snapped. But seeing Fin's confusion and realizing Margaret wouldn't want him talking about this, he shook his head. "Just leave it."

Fin stood there a minute staring at him. "I would, but I

don't think you can. I don't understand it. After what she did, how can you forgive her? How can you bring her back here when she *betrayed* you?"

Eoin's teeth were grinding again. He knew Fin was only voicing what many others were thinking. It had taken Eoin a few days to notice the subtle coldness toward his wife by some of his clansmen. Highlanders had long memories and would not soon forget that she was a MacDowell and that she'd left him. And like Fin, a number of his father's *meinie* knew that she'd betrayed him at Loch Ryan.

"The same could be said of you, and yet here you are."

She was his wife, damn it. And his best friend had tried to have his way with her.

Fin's face reddened and something hard flashed in his eyes. "She got her vengeance though, didn't she? You weren't here, I nearly lost a bollock because of her."

"You would have lost them both had I been here."

Fin stared at him, his jaw clamped tightly as if he were fighting to hold back something. "I told you I was drunk."

Was that an excuse? Maybe he hadn't forgiven him as much as he said he had. Eoin drew a deep breath. Though he didn't owe his foster brother an explanation, he gave him one. "It was more complicated than I realized. Margaret thought she was helping me."

Fin didn't hide his disbelief. "So you trust her again?"

Eoin didn't answer; he didn't have one. "She's my wife, and the mother of my son."

Fin stiffened, although Eoin hadn't meant it as a dig. Marjory's recent miscarriage after years of not being able to have a child had been heartbreaking for all of them, but Fin had taken it the hardest. He seemed to take offense if even the word "child" or "babe" was mentioned—as if there was some implied criticism of him.

"So forgive and forget, is that it? Well, have care that the lass doesn't learn something to betray you again. What are you going to tell her about Campbell?"

Eoin's eyes narrowed. He knew Fin was curious about his place in Bruce's army and all the disappearances that he refused to explain, but how much had he guessed? Did he suspect what he and Campbell did or was it just a general question? "What do you mean?"

"Nothing. Just be careful. Her father has probably joined forces with Lorn."

Apparently it was just a general warning this time. But at others, Eoin could swear that Fin suspected the truth.

Margaret wasn't the only one hurt by Eoin's keeping her in the dark. It had affected his friendship with Fin as well. Maybe just as much as Margaret had come between the foster brothers, Eoin's secret life had as well.

And that was his fault.

Margaret's words this morning came back to him: "*I don't want there to be any secrets between us . . . It cannot work otherwise.*"

Their conversation had troubled him more than he wanted to admit. He knew she was right, but what the hell was he going to do about it? How was he going to continue to keep her in the dark about his place in Bruce's army? Secrets had torn them apart all those years ago. Were they destined to repeat the same mistakes?

Damn Bruce. How could Eoin get his marriage in order if he couldn't tell her anything? All the other wives knew what their husbands did. Did she not have a right to as well? Could he keep something that was so important to him from her?

As before, he was in an untenable position. The difference was that this time he knew it could not work. He could not leave for weeks and expect her not to ask questions. He couldn't expect her trust, love, and loyalty and give her nothing in return.

But could he trust her after what had happened? Surprisingly, he wanted to. Looking back, he realized that much like him she'd been in an impossible situation. He'd given her enough information to be dangerous, but not enough to make the right decision. Did he wish that she hadn't admitted his presence to her friend? Without a doubt. He'd been clear in his instructions, but he couldn't blame her for doing what she did—her motivations had been pure.

If anyone was to blame, it was him. He'd put her in that impossible position by not telling her what he was doing there. But his damned cousin had given him little choice.

"Let me worry about my wife," Eoin said, guilt taking some of the edge from his words. Fin had put one wall between their friendship, but Eoin had put the other. "Besides, she doesn't exactly have a way of contacting her father—if she even knew where he was."

Before Fin could reply, Eoin glanced to the doorway and saw Eachann watching them. How long had he been standing there?

"I'm sorry," the boy said. "The chief"—he'd thus far refused to call him Grandfather—"said the meeting was over. I can come back if you want to play another time."

Damn it, the game! Eoin had almost forgotten. "Nay," he said quickly—and probably too eagerly, "We are finished here."

The missive to Bruce could wait.

Fin nodded to Eoin and then greeted Eachann with a smile and cheerful hello. But Eoin didn't miss the flash of pain—and something else?—that crossed his face when he first saw the boy standing there.

There was an awkward moment of silence after Fin left, where Eoin tried to figure out what to say. He didn't want to say anything wrong or come on too strong. The lad was as skittish as a foal where he was concerned.

He wasn't the only one. Bloody hell, how could a five-year-old have him so tongue-tied?

The boy shuffled his feet, and Eoin realized he was staring. He stood and went to the sideboard to fetch the set. "Your mother said you were a good player." He tucked the board under his arm and gathered the pieces in his hands. "She said you can already beat her."

When Eachann didn't say anything right away, Eoin turned to find him apparently mulling his words. "Aye, but . . ." He let his words fall off. "She can add more sums than me in her head. I can only remember five or six. She can do up to ten."

Eoin grinned. His son had the makings of a fine statesman. He put down the board and started setting down the pieces. "I don't think your mother really ever took to the game."

Eachann met his gaze conspiratorially, and the tentative smile he gave him a moment later made Eoin's chest squeeze as if it were in a vise.

"She's too impatient," Eachann said. "And—"

"Always wants to go on the attack," Eoin finished for him.

Eachann's tentative smile turned into a full-blown grin, and Eoin felt like he'd just swallowed a ray of sunshine.

"Mother made you a set, too?" Eachann said, picking up one of the beautifully carved and painted pieces.

"Nay, I found it in . . ." *Oban*, he finished to himself,

as the truth hit him. He'd seen the set in a shop in Oban about six months after Margaret left. It was the only one of its kind, the owner had said. A priest had brought it in to barter for some goods.

That's how she'd left, he realized. He'd always wondered how she'd found the money to leave so quickly.

Eoin picked up one of the pieces, seeing every loving stroke that she'd put into it, feeling his throat tighten.

"Aye," he said gruffly after a long pause, noticing that Eachann was watching him with a puzzled look on his face. "She made it for me."

He'd just never been here for her to give it to him.

"Is something wrong?" Eachann asked.

Eoin took a deep breath and shook his head, trying to clear the emotion from his lungs and throat. But the regret burned. He wondered if it would ever stop. "Nay, now are you ready to show me what you've got? I won't go easy on you."

A countenance that was every bit as grave as his own looked back at him. "I won't go easy on you either."

Eoin grinned. "Good to know. I guess I've been warned."

After a dozen moves, Eoin realized it was a good thing, and he'd better focus if he didn't want to be trounced by a five-year-old.

∞

"The linens are changed on Fridays and washed on Saturdays," the maidservant said unhelpfully. "They'll be checked for tears and mended then."

Margaret tried to rein in her temper, but why must every request—no matter how small—be met with resistance?

She smiled. "I just thought that since I noticed a small tear in the bedsheet, I might borrow some of the thread that matches and tend to it now."

"Today is Wednesday," the woman said obstinately.

Margaret gritted her teeth, her smile faltering. "Yes, I'm aware of that."

"Is there a problem?"

Both women jumped a little at the sound of Eoin's voice behind them. He'd seemingly materialized in the corridor out of nowhere.

She frowned at him for sneaking up on her, but then noticed his expression. Putting a hand on his arm, she silently begged him not to interfere. "No," she said brightly, glancing at the flushing servant. "No problem. Morag and I were just discussing the linen schedule."

Clearly Eoin wanted to say something more, but with a furious tightening of his mouth he deferred to her wishes. He nodded, which Morag took as a dismissal, scurrying down the stairs as if she couldn't get away fast enough.

"I think you frightened her," Margaret said wryly.

"Good," he said with a dark glare down the stairwell, where Morag had disappeared. His gaze turned back to hers. "They really were horrible to you, weren't they?"

It wasn't as much a question as an acknowledgment.

A half smile turned her mouth. "I grew a thick skin. It was easier once I realized they didn't hate me—they hated that I was a MacDowell."

"You were my wife," he said bitterly.

It hadn't been enough—then. "It's better now. Your mother is making an effort for Eachann."

"And for you." He paused. "I wasn't exactly happy when I learned you had left. When she suggested that maybe it was for the best, I let her know in no uncertain terms just how wrong she was." He shook his head. "Christ, I'm sorry, Maggie. I didn't want to believe it. Hell, maybe I *couldn't* believe it."

Her brows furrowed. "I don't understand."

"I had so many things pulling me the other way, how could I have left you? I needed you to be somewhere where I thought you were safe."

So he could concentrate on what he needed to do. Strangely she understood. "It's different now," she said. "Eachann will help. We both just need to give it time."

He seemed to understand that she was asking him not to interfere. He nodded, but he didn't look happy about it.

"Speaking of our son," he said. "You were right about his skill with a chessboard. It's remarkable for one so young."

"Did he beat you, too?" She couldn't hide her delight at the prospect.

He lifted a brow. "Of course not. But I did have to pay attention."

"Which is more than you can say for me, is that it?"

He gave her a lopsided grin that would have made her breath catch, if she wasn't so outraged.

"I didn't say that."

She scowled. "But you were thinking it."

He just shrugged and his grin broadened. "He liked my chess set. Actually, he said it looked like his." He pulled something out of his sporran and handed it to her. "Does it look familiar?"

She froze, staring in astonishment at the painted figure he'd given her. It was a piece from the set she'd worked so hard on for him all those years ago. "Where did you get it?"

"In town. A priest had given it to a shopkeeper to sell. I thought it was magnificent. I can't believe you did this, Maggie. The craftsmanship is extraordinary." He took the piece—the king—and held it up, twisting it in his hand. "It's me, isn't it?"

She nodded.

He shook his head. "I should have known there was a reason the queen has red hair."

She laughed. "I wanted to make sure you knew who was in charge."

He pulled her into his arms. "Is that right?"

She nodded, and he covered her mouth in a long kiss before releasing her.

"Hmm. We'll have to see about that. You can show me tonight. But first there is someone who I think will be eager to see you."

Margaret couldn't think of anyone on Kerrera who would be eager to see her. Even when he led her to the stables and told her to wait, she didn't guess. So when he led out the big black stallion, her knees wobbled and the blood slid to her feet in absolute shock. "Dubh?"

At the sound of her voice the horse's ears perked up. She rushed forward and threw her arms around the startled animal. She murmured soothing words against his silky coat to calm him—and herself. When she finally lifted her face to meet her husband's amused gaze her eyes were damp. "You kept him?"

"Actually, Fin did." That didn't surprise her. Fin had made no secret that he wanted the animal. "He gave him back when I returned."

"You mean when the MacDougalls were defeated, and he changed allegiance to Bruce?"

He nodded, and Margaret let the matter rest. She didn't want to talk about Fin or his opportunism. She was too happy to have her horse back.

"Should we stretch his legs?" he asked.

She hesitated. "Your knee is strong enough?"

"You're as bad as Helen."

She arched a brow. "Is that an answer?"

He rolled his eyes. "It's fine. I promise to take it easy."

She held him to that.

It was a perfect afternoon. They rode to the north end of the island and sat on an outcrop of rock for a while watching the fishing boats pass on their way out to sea. For the first time, she saw the prettiness of the isle. Whenever they passed someone on the road, Eoin made a point of stopping and introducing her as his wife. With the tender look in his eye and the tucking of her hand into his elbow, he was making sure there was no doubt about her importance to him.

They were laughing as they climbed the stairs to their tower chamber to change for the evening meal—Margaret was teasing him about the suddenly sore knee that was to blame for his losing the race back to the castle.

It was Margaret who pushed open the door, and thus it was she who let out a cry with what she saw on the bed.

26

E**OIN'S BLOOD** had run cold when he'd heard Margaret's cry, but it turned to ice when he saw the reason why.

His jaw locked in wintry rage as he quickly removed the plaid—and the dead bird that had been resting on it—from the chamber. He called for one of the servants to dispose of both. He would question them all later, but first he needed to attend to his wife.

She was still pale as he entered the room. He went to the sideboard and poured her a cup of whisky. Handing it to her, he said, "Here, drink this."

She didn't argue and did as he bade. He was rewarded by a flush of color to her cheeks.

Handing the cup back to him, she laughed nervously. "At least we don't need to guess for whom it was meant."

Eoin's mouth tightened furiously. No, there wasn't any doubt. It hadn't been just any dead bird, it had been a dead raven—the symbol of the MacDowells. "I will find out who was responsible."

The menace in his voice must have worried her. She put a quelling hand on his arm, her golden eyes wide with worry. "I'm sure there is no real threat. It was probably someone's bad idea of a jest, or a way of encouraging me to go back home. But this is my home, Eoin, and I won't let them intimidate me this time. I was merely startled. No real harm was done. It might only make things more difficult."

"God's bones, Maggie. You can't think I will ignore this? Call it what you will, but someone wanted to scare you."

"Maybe so, but I am not so easily frightened." A wry smile turned her pretty mouth. "I know you too well to think you will do nothing. I'm just asking you not to over-react. You'll not gain me any friends by subjecting all your clansmen to an inquisition."

His mouth fell in a grim line. "I know where to start."

It was obvious to whom he referred. "I doubt Fin would do something so blatant."

He didn't think so either, but no one had been more discontented to hear of Margaret's return.

The incident cast a pall over the rest of the evening. Eoin explained to his parents what had happened, and they seemed nearly as outraged as he—especially his mother, who pointed out how easily it could have been Eachann who found the dead bird. Indeed, she seemed to have taken the "message" personally, and insisted on questioning the servants herself after he had finished.

His father sent for Fin and his other household guardsmen. One by one, Eoin questioned them, but most of his father's men—including Fin—had been away all afternoon patrolling the seas to the north and west. They hadn't returned until the first course of the meal.

The questioning was to no avail; no one had seen anything.

Eoin kept a close eye on Margaret and Eachann (fortunately, the boy wasn't aware of what had happened) over the next few days, rarely leaving them alone, but nothing appeared amiss. No doubt the coward had been alerted and scurried back into his foxhole.

Margaret was probably right. Eoin doubted it was a real threat as much as something to make her feel unwelcome, but he wouldn't take any chances. Knowing he couldn't delay his trip to Dunstaffnage any longer, he was debating whether to take them with him, even if seeing Campbell again so soon provoked more questions from Margaret, when the problem was solved for him. Although not in a way that would make it any easier.

Answering a summons from his father that pulled him away from training, Eoin was surprised to find Campbell waiting for him in the solar. Although the prized scout was the one known for his keen, almost eerie instincts, Eoin could tell right away that this was not a neighborly visit. The members of the Highland Guard had perfected the stone in stony, so Campbell's expression gave nothing away, but Eoin sensed his friend's edginess.

To ensure their privacy—and that what they had to say would not be overheard—Eoin's father stood guard outside the door himself.

As soon as he left, Campbell's expression turned grave. "I know you are supposed to be on leave, but I need your help."

"Does this have something to do with your father-in-law?"

"How did you guess?" he asked with dry sarcasm.

Eoin filled him in on the fisherman's story.

Campbell's jaw was clenching so hard Eoin wondered if he was second-guessing his decision all those years ago. "That sure as hell sounds like him. We've had a few reports of 'pirate' attacks in the past few weeks, as well as reports of his men in the area demanding rents from his former tenants."

Eoin wasn't surprised. When Bruce had been exiled in the fall of 1306, he'd funded his return to claim his kingdom by sending Eoin, Lamont, Boyd, and MacGregor on similar missions to collect rents from his tenants (or former tenants according to King Edward) in Ayr. At the time their movements had been aided by Campbell, who'd been acting as an informant in the English camp, much as now they relied on information from a secret source in Roxburgh Castle they simply called the Ghost.

"That's why I'm here," Campbell explained. "I need you to help me set a trap for them." He had a credible report the MacDougalls were heading to Appin—the small coastal peninsula between Loch Linnhe and Loch Creran—and wanted to be there waiting for them when they did.

The MacDougalls had a small fort on an islet just off the coast in Loch Linnhe called Stalker, with many loyal clansmen in the area. Despite Bruce's victory at Brander a few years back, and the fact that he'd made Dunstaffnage his royal headquarters in the Highlands, there were still plenty of clansmen in the area sympathetic to the former Lords of Argyll MacDougalls, who had reigned over this part of Scotland like kings for centuries. Before the war, the MacDougalls had been the most powerful clan in the west. But their ill-fated decision to support the Comyns rather than Bruce had opened the door for the MacDonalds and the Campbells.

"How fast can you be ready?" Campbell asked.

Eoin started to respond, then hesitated. *Margaret.* It wasn't just that he hadn't discovered who had left the raven, he also knew that his leaving was sure to provoke questions. Questions that he didn't want to answer—or rather, didn't want to *not* answer.

Campbell mistook his silence. "Is it your knee? Have you not recovered enough to fight?"

Eoin shook his head. "I resumed training yesterday."

"Then you are reluctant to leave your wife?" Campbell's perceptiveness had stopped surprising him years ago. "She'll want an explanation, and you can't give her one."

It wasn't a question, and Eoin didn't need to explain. He was sure Bruce wasn't the only one who didn't want Margaret to know what he did. Eoin might be ready to trust her again, but that didn't mean his brethren felt the same.

He cursed, dragging his fingers through his hair. Why the hell did everything have to be so complicated?

"I shouldn't have come," Campbell said. "You need more time. I can find someone else. Maybe Hawk . . ."

"You don't have time to fetch Hawk and be in position by nightfall," Eoin said flatly.

"I have my brothers. They and a few other guardsmen will be enough."

Eoin knew Arthur referred to his brothers Dugald and Gillespie, who served the king with Arthur at Dunstaffnage. They were both formidable warriors.

But they weren't the Highland Guard.

This was his job—his responsibility—and he sure as hell wasn't going to let one of his brethren down without good cause. A hypothetical threat and wish to avoid conflict wasn't enough. If something happened because he wasn't there, he would be responsible.

It was only a few days at most. His father would protect Margaret and Eachann with his life. And if Margaret wanted to know where he was going . . .

Bloody hell, he was going to have to deal with this at some point. It might as well be now.

"Give me a half hour, and I'll be ready."

"But what about your wife?"

"I'll figure something out."

He just wished he knew what.

❦

Not again.

Margaret stared at Eoin in shock, telling herself not to overreact. But she couldn't escape the feeling that it was happening all over again. The floor of the chamber suddenly felt as if it were a boat swaying on the ocean. Her head was spinning.

"I have to leave."

She'd known something like this was going to happen when she'd recognized the man riding through the gate as one of the warriors from Dumfries. During the siege, he'd been quieter than the others and seemed to blend into the background, which is why she hadn't noticed him right away. Arthur Campbell, she recalled Eoin calling him. He was the youngest brother of Neil Campbell, the chief who'd been with Robert Bruce all those years ago at Stirling Castle and was still by his side now.

Margaret had felt a trickle of unease slither down the back of her neck, sensing that the real world was about to intrude. But if this was their first test, it was a failure so far. She hadn't missed that he hadn't told her anything about where he was going or what he was doing. *In the dark . . .*

Eoin looked pained. "God, Maggie, don't look at me like that. I hate leaving like this, but I have to go. It's only a few days at the most. You'll be safe. My father will personally see that you and Eachann are guarded."

"That won't be necessary."

"I know you think it wasn't anything, but I won't take a chance—"

"It was Marjory." It was his turn to be shocked. He drew back to gape at her. "I was coming to tell you, but your father said you were in a meeting and could not be disturbed." Now she knew why. *More secrets.*

"How do you know?"

"Eachann saw her going into the room with a 'gift.' He asked her about it today when Marjory came to spend the afternoon with your mother working on the new tapestry."

He swore.

"Your mother had much the same reaction, although not so plainly put. I've never seen her so angry. I took Eachann from the room, but Marjory left a short while later in tears. I'm sure the incident will not be repeated."

"I'm sorry, Maggie." He shook his head, furious. "Damn it, my own sister!"

"You have nothing for which to apologize. Marjory is not your responsibility."

"I'll speak with Fin, when I get back."

"Don't. It will only make it worse. Besides, I suspect your sister's marriage doesn't need any more challenges."

Perhaps the same could be said of hers. She wanted desperately for Eoin to trust her, but maybe she was asking too much. Maybe forgiveness was all she could expect?

Would that be enough?

In her heart she knew it wouldn't. She did not need to know all the details, but he could not cut her out of half his life as he had before. Not when she knew the difference now. There was something he was hiding. Something important. But she could not force him to trust her.

She turned away. "I will see you when you return."

He grabbed her elbow to turn her back. "Don't be like this, Maggie. I want to tell you, but I can't."

She dipped her face so he wouldn't see her disappointment and hurt. "I understand."

"No, you don't," he said, turning her face back to his. "Nor should you. It's just . . . damn it, it's complicated."

She nodded, not trusting herself to speak. She didn't know whether she'd start sobbing or start hurling demands and accusations at him. But neither would do either of them any good. It would only make it worse.

Patience, she reminded herself. But how long would it take?

∞

Eoin made it as far as the dock before he turned around. He couldn't do it. He couldn't leave her like this.

It felt too much like last time—except maybe this time it was worse. He didn't have accusations and demands to fuel his anger, distracting him and helping him convince himself he was doing the right thing.

He wasn't doing the right thing. All he could think about was the hurt and disappointment in her eyes when he'd told her. A stony lump had formed in his chest, and it had only grown heavier as he'd left her standing in the *barmkin* beside his parents, clutching Eachann's hand like a lifeline. Seeing her so vulnerable ate at him. Margaret was strong, confident, irrepressible. He was breaking her heart, damn it. Just like he'd done six years ago.

"*It can't work . . .*"

She was right, if they were going to have a chance, he needed to trust her. "I have to go back," he said.

Campbell had already jumped in the *birlinn* and was readying the ship for voyage. Oddly enough, he didn't look all that surprised by Eoin's pronouncement. "Forget something?"

"Aye, to tell my wife where I'm going." The blunt admission elicited only a quirked brow from Campbell. "Do you have an objection to that?"

The other man shrugged. "Not if you don't."

In other words, Campbell trusted his judgment. Eoin knew that—they'd all had their lives in each other's hands at some point over the last seven and a half years—but somehow this felt different. He acknowledged the show of faith with a nod.

Campbell's mouth lifted in a wry smile. "Marrying the enemy's daughter isn't easy, is it?"

Eoin smiled back at him, appreciating the understanding that could only come from someone in the same position. "You can sure as hell say that again. Give me a few minutes."

He took the stairs two at a time, hoping to catch her in the yard, but the small group that'd bid him farewell on what was allegedly a short trip to Dunstaffnage had already dispersed.

He nearly ran into his father as he started up the stairs to the tower house. "Did you forget something, son?"

Eoin shook his head. "Have you seen Margaret?"

"She went to the stables. I think she said she was going to go on a ride."

His chest stabbed with a hard prick of guilt. Damn it, he really must have hurt her. He remembered riding away had been her first impulse when she'd been hurt by Comyn's sister all those years ago.

He found her in Dubh's stall with one of the stable lads, securing the saddle around the horse.

She jumped when she heard him come up behind

her. "Eoin! I thought you were . . . you startled me." He thought he glimpsed a twinge of fear in her expression before it turned to concern. "Is something wrong?"

"Aye." He told the lad to fetch the horse a carrot and give them a few minutes of privacy. As soon as the boy was gone, he startled her again by drawing her into his arms. "I forgot to tell you something."

She blinked up at him, obviously confused by his odd behavior. The light through the open window cast soft shadows across her delicate features. Her skin was so smooth and pale it almost looked translucent. "Yes?"

"You didn't ask where I was going."

Her gaze held his for a long heartbeat. "I thought it was a secret."

"It is. But I trust you."

Her eyes widened. "You do?"

He was ashamed of how much surprise there was in her voice. "Aye. I want it to be different this time." He wanted to make her a part of his life—all of his life.

"So do I," she said, the surprise turning soft with happiness.

He took a deep breath; it wasn't easy sharing things he was used to keeping to himself. "John of Lorn is making trouble again. There are rumors that his men are in the area, trying to scavenge up some coin. We have reason to think they'll target his former lands in Appin next. We're going to set a trap for them and see if we can learn what they have planned."

She didn't need to know the details, the gist was enough. More than enough. Though he was not technically breaking his promise to Bruce—he hadn't told her about the Highland Guard—he knew his cousin wouldn't approve of him telling her anything about his activities.

But Eoin intended to have a serious talk with Bruce the next time he saw him. Either he let him out of his promise or Eoin was going to leave the Highland Guard. The secret of his role in Bruce's army was too big to keep from her. She might not need to know all the operational details, but she needed to know what he was involved in.

Margaret had been right: he owed her a duty as much as he owed his cousin. Eoin hadn't made his wife a priority before, but that was going to change.

He made sure to impart the seriousness of what he was telling her. "No one not involved in the mission knows this but you, Margaret." He hadn't even told his father as much as he'd told her. "That's the way we like to keep it." The less people who knew, the less chance there was for something to go wrong.

She bit her lip, concern clouding her features. "Will it be very dangerous?"

"It's nothing I haven't done a hundred times before. I won't lie to you, there is always an element of danger, but it's greatly reduced by having the element of surprise." He smiled. "It's better to be the pirate, remember?"

The jest earned him a smile. "I thought you called it Vikings and Highlanders. Which one is the pirate?"

He grinned back at her. "Both."

She laughed, and he pressed a soft kiss on her lips. A soft kiss that nearly turned into something more, when her hands wrapped around his neck and her breasts melted into his chest. He went hard at the contact, his cock instinctively seeking the sweet juncture between her legs. He cupped her bottom, lifting her against him, as his tongue stroked deeper and deeper into the warm cavern of her mouth. But it wasn't enough. He wanted to be inside her. He wanted to feel her legs wrapped around his waist as he drove in and out.

He was a few grinds of her hips away from tossing her down on the pile of hay behind her. But Campbell was waiting for him.

He drew back—with some effort. "I have to go."

She nodded a bit dazedly, her features still bearing the stamp of arousal. Her eyes were heavy, her pupils dark, her lips cherry red and swollen, her breath uneven . . . Christ, she was going to kill him.

He started to go, but she called him back. "Eoin."

He looked back over his shoulder.

"Thank you."

Their eyes held, and the smile that spread across her face was one that he would never forget. It was as brilliant as a rare diamond but a thousand times more precious to him.

"I love you," she said softly.

A powerful warmth spread through his chest, filling him with a sense of contentment he'd never experienced before. He'd done the right thing.

"And I love you, *a leanbh.*"

A few moments later he was gone, leaving the shadows of the stable—and its opened window—behind.

27

MARGARET'S EMOTIONS had swung from despair and heartbreak to elation and happiness in the matter of a few minutes. Were it not for the danger and the worry that accompanied the revelation, her happiness would have been complete.

For the first time since the early days of their marriage, she had hope for the future. The closeness beyond the bedchamber that she craved seemed possible. She and Eoin had turned an important corner. Her patience had been rewarded, and he had confided in her. Maybe not everything—she knew there was something bigger and more significant that he was not telling her—but it was an important first step.

He trusted her, and she vowed to be worthy of that trust.

Of course, she didn't expect to have that vow put to the test less than twenty-four hours later.

She'd spent the morning with Lady Rignach and the steward, while Eachann worked with his new tutor. Margaret had been surprised to be included in the meeting, and even more surprised when Lady Rignach asked her opinion on a few purchases. Apparently, she'd learned how

Margaret had repaid the nuns at the convent for teaching her to read and write.

Margaret didn't think the proud lady would relinquish her role as chatelaine anytime soon, but the fact that she was willing to include Margaret at all showed a clear intention on her part to make Margaret feel more a part of the household. And maybe even some day, part of the family.

The person most resistant to that asked to see her after the midday meal. While Lady Rignach took Eachann to the stable to see a new foal, Marjory sat with Margaret in the garden to apologize.

Though Marjory was only a year older than Margaret's five and twenty, the past years had taken their toll. Few vestiges of girlish prettiness remained behind the lines of disappointment and heartbreak. Whether it was her marriage or her inability to have a child thus far that was responsible, Margaret didn't know. Perhaps it was both. But the proud, spoiled young beauty was a forlorn shadow.

"I didn't mean to scare you," Marjory said, her hands twisting in her lap. "I just wanted . . ." Her eyes filled with tears. "You to go away like before."

"Was it so perfect for you when I was gone?"

Margaret spoke quietly, but Marjory's eyes widened as if the words were an explosion. She stared at her almost in shock. The first tear slid down her cheek and her lower lip quivered when she shook her head. "Nay. It wasn't perfect at all. Fin never loved me. I think he married me only to be closer to Eoin. When you left, he blamed me."

Margaret pursed her mouth. "That's ridiculous. You know why I left."

It was a challenge, not a question.

Marjory nodded, the tears rolling full force now. "Aye, I saw everything—except that I didn't want to believe it.

I thought he loved me. I convinced myself that you had to have done something to make him kiss you. But in my heart I knew."

Margaret sighed deeply, almost feeling sorry for her. "Then why did you marry him?"

The other woman shrugged, her chest heaving from her sobs, and wiped away some of the tears with the back of her hand. "I thought once you were gone, I could make him love me. I thought that when I gave him a son . . ." Her voice fell off. "Fin says I'm barren, but I know this baby was a sign and next time . . ."

Margaret's heart went out to the other woman, but she feared Marjory was pinning all her hopes on the wrong thing. A baby wouldn't make her husband love her. She wasn't even sure Fin was capable of that kind of emotion. She wasn't surprised that he'd put the blame for their lack of a child on his wife either.

Marjory looked up at her. "But then you came back, and he wants you again."

Margaret shook her head. "He may have once, but that was a long time ago. I think he despises me more than anything else. He doesn't look at me like that now."

Now he looked at her as if he couldn't wait to see her gone. There was something cold in his eyes . . . She gave an involuntary shudder, but she had no intention of letting him scare her away this time.

Marjory's tear-streaked face stared back at her. "What if he's just better at hiding it?"

Margaret shook her head. "I don't think so." But whether it was true or in Marjory's imagination didn't matter. It never had. "I love your brother, Marjory. I have always loved your brother. There was never anyone else for me from the first moment I saw him."

The other woman looked into her eyes, perhaps seeing the truth for the first time: Margaret wasn't a threat. If she wanted someone to blame for her unhappy marriage, she would have to look somewhere else.

Feeling as if she'd turned an important corner with her sister-in-law, Margaret left the garden with an even greater sense of optimism for the future.

But just when it looked like she was finally finding a way to fit into her new life, her old one came back threatening to destroy all the inroads she'd made.

She was on her way to the stables in the late afternoon when she noticed a monk walking toward her across the yard from the sea gate. He wore the brown robe of a friar, and though the skies were clear, a hood covered his head, hiding his face from view. But that wasn't what drew her attention. It was the way he walked. Erect. Proud. Like a warrior, not a poor, humble churchman.

Curious, but also slightly uneasy, she looked around to make sure they weren't alone. The yard wasn't crowded, but a half dozen of the laird's guardsmen were practicing a shout's distance nearby.

Reassured by their presence, she started to greet the newcomer, who was now only a few feet away. "Welcome, Father, might I help . . ." Her voice trailed off as the face beneath the hood came into view.

Her breath jammed in her chest.

"*Brother*," her brother Duncan corrected under his breath, taking her hands in his as if in blessing. "Not Father."

Margaret was too stunned to react. She'd frozen in place.

"Christ, Maggie Beag. Do you want me thrown in the pit? Pretend like you are giving me directions to the kirk."

He released her hands, and she recovered enough to realize he'd pressed a note into her palm. Slipping it into her skirts with one hand, she pointed out the gate with the other. "What are you doing here?" she whispered.

But he was already heading toward the gate. "Rescuing you," he said in parting. "Be ready."

Margaret's heart was still fluttering wildly as she carefully unfolded the parchment in her chamber a few minutes later. The hastily scratched letters in black ink jumbled in her head. She had to read it a few times to realize that her brother and his men would be at the anchorage on the other side of the island tomorrow just after dusk to "rescue" her and Eachann and take them to the Isle of Man, where they could be reunited with their family.

Apparently, her brothers had surrendered Buittle Castle to Bruce as well and joined her father in exile. Duncan was obviously under the impression that she and Eachann had been coerced into going with Eoin.

Margaret cursed her father, knowing he was responsible for that. She wondered if Dugald MacDowell realized what danger he'd put his son in by giving him that impression—and by the problems he'd created for her. Though Margaret was moved by the risk her brother had taken to come to her aid, his showing up like this was going to make things difficult

Now, Eoin wasn't the only one with secrets.

∞

A few hours before dawn Eoin made his way up the seagate stairs. His knee screamed in agony with every step, but he didn't mind. He was damned lucky to be alive, and he knew it.

Still, he was furious. He'd barely exchanged one word with Campbell the entire way back. But he could sense the other man's question—a question Eoin didn't want to hear.

It wasn't her, damn it!

But how had it gone so wrong? Not only had Eoin's perfect plan to trap Lorn's men been foiled, they'd been the ones nearly caught in a net.

Eoin and Campbell, along with a team of Campbell's best warriors—about fifteen men in total—had been in position on the western ridge of the Glen Stockdale overlooking Loch Linnhe and the fort of Stalker by dusk after leaving Gylen. From there they could see Lorn's men land on the Appin shore and then be ready for a surprise attack when the MacDougalls made their way inland to their tenants at Glenamuckrach.

Eoin and the team of warriors had lain in wait the first night to no avail. Taking advantage of some nearby caves to rest during the day, they'd emerged at nightfall to take position for the second night.

The MacDougalls waiting for them. A hail of arrows had rained down on them from behind. The men on watch had been looking to the west, but the MacDougalls had taken a circuitous route from the east, approaching Appin overland rather than by sea. Almost as if they knew someone was waiting for them.

Five of Campbell's men had been killed in the first few minutes. Campbell had taken an arrow in the back, but the thick leather and providentially located steel studs of his *cotun* had prevented it from sinking into his flesh. Eoin had been lucky to be wearing a steel helm and mail coif, or the arrow that struck him just below the ear would have killed him.

Despite their small fighting force being cut by over a third those first few minutes, they'd rallied and fought off the attackers, who outnumbered them by at least two-to-one. The MacDougalls had eventually fallen back, but with three more of Campbell's men dead and another four wounded, giving chase was not an option.

Not all MacDougalls, a voice reminded him. He wished that voice would shut the hell up. He didn't need reminding to recall seeing Margaret's brother Duncan and at least a dozen MacDowells fighting alongside their distant kinsmen.

It didn't mean anything. It could hardly be considered a surprise that the MacDowells had joined the MacDougalls. They'd all known the MacDowell submission wouldn't last.

He and Campbell had gathered their men and sailed back to Gylen, if not in defeat then in something coming damned close to it.

How the hell had it gone so wrong? Had someone warned them? But that wasn't possible. No one had known their plan. Except for . . .

Eoin knew what Campbell was thinking—because he'd thought the same thing, damn it—but Margaret couldn't have betrayed them. Even if he thought her capable—which he didn't—unless she'd sprouted wings and learned how to fly, there hadn't been time for her to tell anyone.

There had to be another explanation. He would find it. As much for Campbell as for his own piece of mind.

His father must have had his men watching for him, as the locked gate was opened by the time Eoin reached the top of the stairs. He would have gone straight to the kitchens to rid himself of all the grime and blood of battle, but his father was waiting for him in his solar. He wasn't alone—Fin was with him.

His father's gaze swept over him, taking in every detail of Eoin's appearance. "Are you hurt?"

Eoin shook his head. Pain in the knee was to be expected, and it wasn't anything he couldn't handle. He'd fought with much worse. "The blood isn't mine."

His father nodded, his face turning grim. "From your expression, I'm assuming your trip was unsuccessful?"

Eoin frowned, with a glance toward Fin. "It was."

His father's grimace deepened. Understanding Eoin's silent communication, he explained, "Fin is here for a reason. He has some . . . distressing information."

Eoin turned to his foster brother for an explanation.

"You aren't going to like it," Fin said bluntly. "Maybe there's an explanation."

Sleeping a few hours in a cave, being ambushed, and nearly killed weren't exactly conducive to patience. "Whatever it is you have to say, Fin, just say it."

"Your wife was seen talking to a monk yesterday."

Christ, what the hell was Fin getting at? "And?"

"There was something odd about the man. I followed him into the village kirk, but he hit me from behind. By the time I woke, he was gone." From the way Fin and his father were looking at him, Eoin knew he wasn't going to like what Fin said next. He didn't. "I caught a glimpse of him before he hit me. It was Duncan MacDowell."

Eoin's expression gave no hint of the blow Fin had just dealt him, but inside he felt as if every bone had shattered, splintering into a million pieces. He remained standing by sheer force of will, but they could have toppled him with a nudge.

It didn't mean anything.

Unless it did.

❈

Margaret woke to the warmth of the sun streaming through the shutters. She stretched lazily, feeling a little bit like a well-satisfied cat, and opened her eyes.

She gave a sudden start at the man sitting in the corner

watching her, but then smiled when she realized who it was. Relief swept over her. "Eoin! You're back!" She frowned, peering at him in the shadows. "Why are you sitting there like that? You startled me."

He remained perfectly still, not reacting to her words. "Watching you sleep. You look like an angel."

There was something strange—almost accusatory—in his voice that made her skin prickle.

He stood and walked toward the bed.

She gasped at his appearance and sat up quickly. Blood and dirt were splattered and streaked all over his face and clothing. He looked like a man who'd just climbed from the pits of hell. "My God, what's wrong? Are you hurt?"

She attempted to reach for him, but he took her wrist and brought her hand firmly back down to the side. "I'm fine."

Her heart jumped. For despite his words, she knew by the intensity of his gaze that something was wrong—very wrong. Margaret was used to being caught in the hold of those dark, piercing blue eyes, but this was different. She felt like a bug under a magnifying lens, as if every move was being scrutinized. "What happened?"

"That's exactly what I want to know."

"Did you find the MacDougalls?"

"You might say that. And what of you, Margaret?" He changed the subject. "What did you do while I was gone?"

There seemed to be a purpose to his question that she didn't understand. She answered tentatively—everything about him made her tentative. He was drawn as tight as a bow—the muscles in his arms and shoulders taut and straining.

"Your mother asked for my help with the steward

yesterday, while Eachann worked with his new tutor. I think he was in heaven." She laughed, but he was oddly silent.

"Anything else?"

The question seemed innocuous, but she knew it wasn't. She tried not to think of the note that had been reduced to embers in her brazier. "I spoke with Marjory. She apologized. I think she is truly sorry for what she did."

Again, no reaction except he continued to watch—scrutinize—with unsettling intensity. Her heart started to beat faster. Did he know something or was guilt making her imagine it?

Blast her father for putting her in this position! Duty and loyalty to her husband warred with that to her brother. She wanted to tell Eoin about Duncan, but she didn't want to put her brother at risk.

Could she trust Eoin to do nothing with the information that Duncan was in the area?

She knew the answer. If she told Eoin he would be in the same position as her: caught between divided loyalties. If he used the knowledge he would betray her, but if he didn't, and Duncan did something against Bruce, he would feel as if he'd let down the king.

Margaret wouldn't put him in that position of having to choose between two loyalties. She would tell him, but only once Duncan had gone.

"Nothing else?"

Whether it was his persistence or his tone, she didn't know, but every instinct flared. Still, she didn't heed the warning and shook her head.

His eyes never left her face. "We were set upon by Lorn's men last night."

"Oh, Eoin!" She moved to her knees, wanting to throw

her arms around him in relief that he'd not been injured or worse, but he pulled back stiffly.

"I think they were warned."

Her eyes widened. "But how? I thought you said no one knew your plans."

"No one did."

It was then that she understood his cold greeting. She pulled back, looking at him in horror. "You don't think I said something?" But it was clear that was exactly what he thought. A wave of hurt crashed down on her, threatening to drag her under, but she forced herself to stay calm. "It wasn't me, Eoin. I know the danger—I would never betray your confidence."

His eyes scanned hers. "I want to believe that."

She lifted her chin. "Then do. It's the truth."

"And what about your brother's visit yesterday? The visit you failed to mention. What's the truth about that, Margaret?"

The blood slid from her face. He *had* known. Oh God, she should have told him. He must be thinking the worst. How could she make him understand? "I wanted to tell you, but I didn't want to put you in an awkward position."

He made a sharp sound. "You must be jesting. You can't seriously claim to have lied to me for 'my own good'?"

Margaret bristled at his tone. "I didn't lie to you. I was going to tell you when my brother left the area. But he's my *brother*, Eoin. I don't want to see him hurt any more than I do you. I did what I thought best under the circumstances. What would you have done had I told you? Would you have betrayed my confidence and gone after him or would you have ignored your duty to Bruce and let him go?"

His mouth fell in a flat line—clearly he didn't like her question or being put on the spot. "It isn't that simple. Nor is this about what I've done." Taking her by the elbow, he drew her off the bed to stand before him. "What did you tell Duncan, Margaret?"

"Nothing." She met his gaze square on. "I told him nothing." Her eyes beseeched him to believe her, but his expression was set like stone and just as impenetrable.

"So it's just a coincidence that your brother shows up here one day and that very night the MacDougalls not only avoid the trap we have for them, but turn it against us? A trap, I might add, that no one knew about but you."

She lifted her chin. "Someone else must have known about it, because I didn't tell him. My brother's purpose here was not to spy on you or gather information. He was here to offer Eachann and me a way to leave. He was under the impression we were not here of our own volition and might be in need of rescue."

His eyes sharpened to hard blue points. "And what did you tell him?"

"I didn't have a chance to tell him anything. We barely exchanged two words. But I would have told him that we were quite happy here and in no need of rescue." Now she wasn't so sure. "I certainly didn't share anything about where you were going or what you were planning. Why would I do that? It doesn't make sense."

"I don't know. Why don't you tell me? I've been trying to figure it out myself. Did you let it slip out accidentally? Did he threaten you or Eachann?"

"I told you that I didn't say anything. Is that so hard to believe?"

He didn't respond, but just stared at her coldly—harshly.

Margaret felt her own temper spike. She thought they'd gotten past this. But maybe they would never be able to get past it. The newfound trust she'd been so excited by had crumbled at the first test. "So is this how it's to be then? Am I to be the first one suspected whenever anything goes wrong no matter what I say? What about all those things you told me, Eoin—do they mean nothing? I thought you trusted me."

"I did—or I never would have told you my plans."

"And now?"

His mouth drew down in anger. "Now I wish to hell I'd kept my mouth shut."

She flinched, her cheeks stinging as if he'd slapped her. "So not only am I suspected, but found guilty and condemned as well?"

He dragged his fingers through his hair. "Damn it, Maggie, look at the facts. What am I supposed to think?"

"I guess it's too much to think that I might be telling the truth."

His silence was answer enough.

"I won't do this, Eoin. Not again. I made a mistake six years ago, but I wasn't the only one to blame. You didn't share enough with me for me to make the right decision. Had I known what you were involved in and had any sense of the danger, I never would have admitted to Brigid that you were there. For our marriage to work, there can't be secrets between us. I won't be half a wife. I love you, but I'm not going to live my life under suspicion. I need you to trust me. Right here, right now. Even when all the 'facts' tell you otherwise."

"Or what?" he said furiously. "Are you still issuing ultimatums? Is it blind faith or nothing? That's not the way it works, Margaret. You're my wife, not my priest."

A knock on the door startled them both. Eoin answered it, took the missive from the man who'd brought it—one of his father's guardsmen—and read it quickly before turning back to her. She knew what he was going to say before he spoke. "I have to go," he said grimly. "We'll have to finish this discussion later."

Later. It was always later with him. He never put her first. *I have to go.* Just be patient, Margaret. Stay here, Margaret. Don't ask questions, Margaret. Be a good girl, and I'll make it up to you in bed.

Well, she couldn't do that anymore. "Of course," she said tonelessly. "No doubt it's important."

He frowned, perhaps hearing something in her voice. "I won't be long."

"And if I asked where you were going?"

His mouth fell in a hard line. The answer was obvious. He wouldn't tell her.

"Don't worry," she said, not letting on that he was tearing her heart to shreds—again. "I won't ask."

She turned away, feeling an overwhelming sense of hopelessness. She loved him, but it wasn't enough. Hurt and disappointment stabbed; there was nothing more she could do. Maybe in another six years, he would realize she was telling the truth, but she wasn't going to wait around hoping that day would come.

Once again, passion had deluded her into believing things had changed. But it was no different than it had been before. He would share his bed with her, but nothing else.

She'd done everything she could to try to regain his trust, but it would never be good enough. *She* would never be good enough. She was a wicked MacDowell. The enemy and an outsider.

She was done trying to prove herself to anyone. To hell with him. To hell with all of them.

28

CAMPBELL WAS WAITING for him at Dunstaffnage. His friend had arrived home not long after dropping Eoin at Gylen to find one of the nearby villagers requesting to speak with him immediately. As soon as he'd heard what the old woman had to say, he'd sent for him.

The message had been short and to the point: one of MacDougall's men is in the village.

It seemed the old woman had a granddaughter who had been involved with one of the MacDougall warriors before he was forced into exile. He sometimes snuck back to see her when he was in the area. Last time he'd left her with a babe and a black eye, which had earned the enmity of the old woman, who was only too happy to take her revenge by reporting his presence to the king's keeper.

Eoin, Campbell, and a handful of Campbell's men had the small cottage surrounded by late morning when the MacDougall warrior finally emerged to take a piss. Caught with his pants down—literally—and without a weapon, he didn't put up much of a fight. Hours later, however, he had proved less than forthcoming in response to their questioning.

They'd left him in the pit prison to contemplate his options while they ate. But even though Eoin hadn't had a meal in almost twenty-four hours, he was too restless to force down more than a few bites. He couldn't escape the feeling of trepidation that had been dogging him since leaving Gylen.

At first he attributed it to his anger toward his wife, but the longer he was gone and the more he thought about it, the more the unease grew.

"We need Viper," Eoin said, a short while later as they waited in the guard's room for the man to be brought back up. Lachlan MacRuairi was an expert at extraction—both of people and of information.

Campbell eyed him carefully. "Anxious for confirmation? I thought you were convinced your wife let something slip to her brother."

"It's the only thing that makes sense."

"But?"

Eoin raked his fingers through his hair harshly. "I don't know. Something about it doesn't feel right."

No matter how many times he replayed the conversation with Margaret in his head, he couldn't convince himself that she'd been anything other than hurt and stung by his accusations. He'd seen her guilt, aye, but only about hiding the truth of her brother's presence from him. Of the rest she'd been adamant—*aggrieved*.

Had he been too ready to jump to conclusions? Too ready to find her guilty?

One corner of Campbell's mouth lifted. "I've always found that my instincts served me well."

That was an understatement. Campbell had become the best scout in Scotland by relying on his instincts.

"What about when it comes to your wife?"

His friend smiled. "Aye, well, they tend to get a bit confused when it comes to her. I just have to listen a little harder."

"Margaret didn't say anything to anyone," Eoin said suddenly. "I'd stake my life on it."

Campbell nodded, as the MacDougall warrior was led back into the room. "Then let's find out who did."

It was easier than they expected. MacDougall wouldn't say anything against his clansmen, but he wasn't as close-mouthed when it came to talking about the traitor who'd given information to Duncan MacDowell on Kerrera. The man had been a traitor to them before.

Faced with the enormity of his mistake, Eoin raced back to Kerrera. It was already dark as the shadow of the tower on the cliff came into view. That his instincts about his wife had been proved right was small consolation for the realization that they might have come too late.

"I need you to trust me. Right here, right now."

A mix of dread and panic fell over him. His pulse was racing, and a cold sweat chilled his skin. He felt ill. What the hell had he done? He'd been so angered by the ultimatum that he hadn't thought about what else she'd done in the past. The "or what" that he'd put to her—the fact that she'd left him, and he might have given her every reason to do so again.

∞

"Where are we going?"

Margaret looked down at the small figure walking beside her and tried to give him a reassuring smile, fearing the unshed tears burning in her eyes were anything but. "It's a surprise," she said with forced brightness.

Even in the growing darkness she could see the small frown on her son's face. "I don't like surprises."

So much like his father . . .

Her chest squeezed, trying not to think about how much it hurt. She could do this. She'd done it before, hadn't she?

"I know, but I hope you shall like this one." Turning around and seeing that the tower had faded from view, she decided they were far enough away. The anchorage point was just on the other side of the islet of Eilean Orasaig in the bay. "How would you like to see your favorite uncle?"

"Uncle Duncan?" the boy asked excitedly. "Here?" He frowned and looked up at her with a furrowed brow. "Has he decided to fight for the bloody usurper, too?"

Margaret winced, realizing the short time on Kererra had not wiped away all traces of her father's anger. "Nay. He's with your grandfather and the rest of your uncles on the Isle of Man. But he's come to take us for a visit."

He stopped, letting his hand fall from hers. "But what about . . . what about my father?"

She knelt down to face him. Over his shoulder the sun flattened on the horizon. It was almost dusk. She knew how confusing this must be to him—it was confusing to her—but she vowed she would do whatever it took to see that Eachann was not hurt by her decision. Even if it meant she had to be apart from him sometimes—God help her. "You may come back and see him whenever you wish, but I—" Her voice dropped off. What could she say? "I can't stay here any longer."

She couldn't be half a wife—even for her son. She wanted to share Eoin's life, not merely be a part of it. But the secrets between them from the first were still there.

Eachann's face drew so serious she wanted to squeeze him tight and never let him go. "Doesn't he want us anymore?"

She threw her arms around him and gave him a fierce hug. "Of course he does, sweetheart. He wants you very much."

"Then why are we running away?"

"We aren't—" She stopped, staring at him. He was right. She was running away. Just like before. Maybe they were doomed to repeat their mistakes after all. All of them.

She was trying to figure out what to say when she was saved by a dot of white in the distance. A sail. She stood and took his hand. "Come, son, we must hurry. Your uncle is here."

∞

Eoin was too late. They were gone.

He'd raced up the tower staircase to the room he shared with Margaret, only to find it dark and empty. He didn't need to look in the antechamber to know that Eachann was gone as well.

It felt like a stone wall had crashed down on him as he realized everything he'd lost. It was like the last time, when he'd come home to realize she was gone, except maybe even more devastating. He'd lost his wife and his son.

They'd fled and it didn't take him long to realize how: her brother. Eoin had been so angry about the failed trap he hadn't asked her the details of how her brother planned to "rescue" her. He must have planned to pick her up on the way back from Appin—today.

A quick questioning of the guards on duty at the gate told him he was right. The lady and the wee laddie had left over an hour ago for a short walk to the village. Not the village in reality, Eoin knew, but one of the other anchorages on the isle. There were three, including the one at the castle. The one on the northwest side opposite Oban would be too busy—even at this hour—but the one on the east side of the isle would be easily accessible for a ship of marauding MacDowells sailing down the Firth of Lorn who wouldn't want to draw a lot of attention.

The anchorage was a short walk. Twenty—thirty—minutes at the most. If they'd left over an hour ago, he knew they were likely long gone. But he had to make sure. Knowing it would be fastest to ride, he started toward the stable when someone blocked his path.

"She's gone," Fin said.

It took everything Eoin had not to kill him. Only the fact that Fin was married to his sister prevented his grandfather and namesake's fabled battle-axe from coming down across his head. But still, his hand itched to reach to his side and pull it from the strap.

Not cognizant of the imminent danger, Fin added, "I saw her and the boy boarding a ship by the dock at Bar-nam-boc."

Eoin took a threatening step toward him, his hands fisting at his sides. He'd never wanted to strike someone so badly. "And you did nothing to stop them?"

Fin shrugged, obviously mistaking the source of the threat that he was too good of a warrior to have missed. "I figured it was for the best. She betrayed you again. The traitorous bitch is better off gone with her kin."

"Don't you mean better off gone where I won't discover the truth?"

Fin's confidence slipped, but only for a moment. He did, however, straighten from his relaxed stance into something slightly more defensive. "You know the truth."

"Aye, I do," Eoin said darkly, his muscles tensing as he took a step closer.

"I told you about her brother Duncan being here on Gylen."

"You did," Eoin said, seething. "But you neglected to mention that you were the one who told him my plans. You were in the barn, weren't you?"

It was the only explanation, and the one Eoin hadn't considered when he'd been so focused on condemning his wife. Someone had overheard them. It was his fault, damn it. He'd been in a rush and hadn't checked.

Fin hesitated. He seemed to be weighing whether to lie. Apparently recognizing the futility, he just shrugged again. As if it were nothing. As if his betrayal hadn't cost Eoin everything. "Fortuitously outside the window. I saw you come back and decided to stay."

"So you spied on me and decided to betray me?" Eoin couldn't contain his rage. He slammed him up against the stone wall of the *barmkin*. "I trusted you. You were like a brother to me."

Fin's expression slipped, revealing anger and bitterness that must have been simmering for years.

"*Were* like brothers, until you married her. *Married* her!" He scoffed with disbelief. "You surprised me. With all those rumors going around . . . I never thought you would be the knight-errant type to ride into her rescue."

It took Eoin a moment to realize what he meant. "It was you. You started the rumors about what happened in the library."

Fin didn't bother denying it. "It was no more than she deserved. The lass was shameless and totally wrong for you. But you didn't see it." His mouth hardened. "But I never spied on you. I was curious, and I thought she was trying to have you send me away after what Marjory did. I would never have said anything, but when I saw MacDowell the next day . . ."

"You decided to take advantage of it, knowing I would blame Margaret, is that it?" Opportunistic bastard. Fin had done the same thing in the war. Eoin had made excuses for him, but he wouldn't do so any longer. He held him up by the scruff like the dog he was and shook him. "Men were killed. Good men. I could have been killed, damn it. All so you could take out your misguided hatred on a woman who would have been a friend to you, if you'd given her a chance?"

"Friendship?" Fin sneered, ignoring the hand that was squeezing around his neck. "I didn't want her friendship. I just wanted to fuck her." Eoin's fist slammed into Fin's jaw before the offending words had even left his mouth. Blood ran down his foster brother's chin as he smiled. "She must be as good as she looks, for her to have turned you against me so quickly."

Eoin was barely listening. He was too busy pummeling his former friend with everything he had. The face. The gut. The ribs. It took him a minute to realize Fin wasn't fighting back. He was bent over, half on his knees.

The blood was still pounding through Eoin's veins as he leaned over him, holding him upright by the edge of his *cotun*, his fist poised for one last blow. "She never tried to turn me against you. She didn't need to. You did all that by yourself when you *attacked* her."

Fin's eyes turned black with rage. "Aye, but it's cost me, hasn't it? That bitch has made me pay."

Assuming Fin was referring to their friendship, Eoin said, "So you try to have me killed?"

"I knew you and Campbell weren't in any danger. Bruce's indestructible phantoms?" Fin laughed at Eoin's shock. "Do you take me for a complete fool? Do you not think I never guessed all these years?"

Eoin stared at the man who'd been his closest friend and felt his rage dampened by disgust and an incredible sense of sadness at the loss of something that had been important to him.

He lowered his hand, knowing he couldn't kill him. But they would never be friends again. "Get the hell out of here. I'm going to get my wife and son back, and I want you and Marjory gone by the time I return."

He heard a woman's gasp behind him. He turned to find his sister staring at him. But that wasn't what distracted him. It was the two people standing beside her.

"We're right here, Eoin." The smile on his wife's face and the way she was looking at him made him wonder how much she'd overheard.

He was stunned. "I thought you left."

Her mouth curved wryly. She looked down at their son and gave his hand a loving squeeze. "Well, someone reminded me that running away never solved any problems, and that MacDowells are fighters."

"Even against pigheaded, humorless, too-smart-for-their-own-good horses' backsides," Eachann said proudly.

Margaret gasped, looking down at her son in horror. "You weren't supposed to hear that." She gave Eoin an embarrassed shrug. "I was talking to myself."

Relief and an outpouring of happiness the likes of which he'd never felt swelled over him. He grinned. "Obviously louder than you realized."

So focused on his wife, Eoin didn't see the threat until too late. Beaten and bloodied, Fin lunged toward Margaret.

A flash of silver flickered in the torchlight.

Oh God, he had a blade!

Eoin cried out a warning, but it was too late. Fin

snaked his arm around her waist and held the blade to her throat. "You already robbed me of a son, now I'm being cast out—"

Fin's words were cut off as his eyes widened in horror. A moment later he dropped to the ground, landing with a deadly thud. Only then did Eoin see the hilt of his sister's eating knife sticking from the back of his neck.

29

IT WAS EVENING before Margaret had a chance to speak with Eoin alone. He had to tend to his shocked and traumatized sister, while Margaret did her best to ease the fears of their son, who'd nearly witnessed his mother's death before seeing his aunt's killing of his uncle.

She knew it would be some time before the events of the day were forgotten, but warm milk, a butter cake with sugar and cinnamon, and lots of hugs had gone a long way to soothe the boy's distress. Eachann was sleeping peacefully by the time Eoin entered their chamber.

A look in the direction of the antechamber was his first question.

"He'll be fine," Margaret answered. "I'm not sure he understood exactly what was happening. Frankly, neither did I."

Eoin looked exhausted, wearily removing his weapons and tossing his *cotun* on a bench before sitting down on the edge of the bed opposite her chair before the brazier. "How much did you hear?"

"Enough to know that you were coming for me." She looked over at him, her eyes wide in the firelight. "You realized I was telling the truth?"

"If I had been thinking rationally, I would have realized it earlier. But thinking rationally and you have never gone very well together." He explained what had happened when he'd reached Dunstaffnage and Fin's part in it.

"How is Marjory?"

Eoin shrugged. "In shock, which is to be expected. But I think it is something of a relief. She understood the depths of Fin's resentment and bitterness better than we did. She lived with it every day and wasn't surprised that it manifested in violence. I still thought of him as the friend I fostered with, but the war, time, and disappointments had shaped him into a different person."

"I can't believe he hated me that much." She repressed a shiver, and then frowned, recalling what he'd said to her. "What did he mean, I robbed him of a son?"

"I think he must have put some of the blame for his failure to have a child on your knee."

"Yet he told Marjory she was barren." She bit her lip. "Do you think it's true?"

"I suspect it was more in his head than in reality. I think you were an easy target for his rage."

"He blamed me for coming between you."

He acknowledged the truth with a nod. "Which was wrong, as we would have grown apart anyway."

She gave him a long look, arching a brow. "Because of the Phantoms?"

Eoin's mouth twisted. "You heard that, did you?"

"Is that why you never told me what you were doing? Are you really part of Bruce's infamous Phantoms?"

He heaved a heavy sigh. "I made a vow of silence. It wasn't just me I was protecting but the others as well. But I was planning to tell you after I spoke to Bruce."

It was the piece of the puzzle that finally made

everything fit together. This was the big secret he'd been keeping from her. No wonder.

"The men at camp. The ones I asked you about." He didn't confirm or deny, but she'd already guessed. "I knew there was something strange about all of you! But I never imagined you—" She stopped, staring at him accusingly. "I should have known you would sign up for the most dangerous job. No doubt you've been right in the forefront of everything. You could have been killed. I should be furious with you. But . . ." She looked up at him, her eyes suddenly filling with emotion.

He tipped her chin with the back of his finger, tilting her face to his. "But?"

"But I'm very proud of you."

He smiled broadly—and a little too smugly. "You are?"

She shoved his chest. "You don't need to look so pleased with yourself. I didn't say I forgive you."

He took her hand and lifted it to his mouth, pressing her fingertips to his lips in a timeless romantic gesture. "But will you?" He held her gaze to his. "I'm sorry, Maggie. I should have known that no matter how bad it looked, you wouldn't betray my confidence. I did know, but it just took me a little while to realize it."

She nodded. "I think I can see now why you felt you had to keep me in the dark. It is dangerous." She thought about it a minute. "I guess I'll just have to trust you to talk about what you can with me. It was never about the details. It was about being a part of your life and feeling like I mattered."

He looked floored. "Of course you mattered. You were all I thought about, you were what I was fighting to get home to, you were what kept me from sinking into the darkness of war. Without you nothing else mattered." She must have shown her skepticism because he laughed. "If you don't believe me, ask Lamont. He can attest to my less-than-sunny disposition the past six years. Without you"—he paused—"the world was darker. You were my light."

She smiled. "That's sweet."

He looked appalled and glanced around, as if worried someone might have overheard. "God, Maggie, don't say things like that—especially around Hawk."

"Who?"

He didn't hesitate. "MacSorley."

She understood. "War names! Do you have one, too?"

"Striker."

She recalled the words on his arm. *Just something some friends and I . . .* "The tattoo?"

He nodded and changed the subject. "What made you decide to come back?"

Her mouth quirked. "I think Eachann has come to like it here. He didn't want to go, and I realized when I thought about it that neither did I." She paused. "I didn't want to keep making the same mistakes, and I intended to come back here and knock some sense into that supposedly brilliant mind of yours."

"Not always. Remember, I told you once when it came to you I wasn't smart at all."

Their eyes met, remembering that day long ago when they'd fallen in love, married, and consummated that love (not necessarily in that order) all in one rainy afternoon. She smiled up at him through watery eyes. "I wish it hadn't taken seven and a half years to figure it all out."

He drew her into his arms. "Me, too. But we have a lifetime to make up for it." He grinned. "Starting right now."

She smiled, letting him carry her to the bed. "Maybe you're pretty smart after all."

EPILOGUE

❦

Garthland Castle, Galloway, February 15, 1315

EOIN DIDN'T WANT to be here. The memories were too sharp, the pain too fresh, the ghosts too vivid. Eight years wasn't long enough to forget. Hell, a lifetime wouldn't be long enough to forget. But he knew how important it was to Maggie to come home, so he'd agreed to return to the place of so much death and despair.

He gazed down at the fiery-haired bundle in his arms and felt an overwhelming sense of gratitude. He was damned lucky, and all he had to do was look at the faces of his family to remind him. Margaret's, his now seven-year-old son's, or the fifteen-month-old redheaded cherub's in his arms who, if her toddlerhood was anything to judge by, just might be the death of him in a few years.

"Here you are," Margaret said, coming into the room behind him. "I should have guessed." She bent over, her own fiery locks tumbling over her shoulder. She'd dispensed with the veil and was much more the unabashed, take-no-prisoners young girl he remembered. "She looks so sweet when she's sleeping, doesn't she?" she whispered softly. Their eyes met, and she grinned. "Almost makes you forget what she's like the rest of the time."

He grimaced. "Almost. The little tyrant threw one of the chess pieces out the tower window again this morning."

Margaret attempted to hide her grin—unsuccessfully. "Let me guess? The bishop again? She shows an appalling lack of respect for your game."

"And for churchmen," Eoin said dryly. "Wonder where she gets it?"

Margaret put her hand on her swelling stomach. Their third child would be born in the summer. If it was a boy, Margaret was threatening to name him after Viper, whom for some God-only-knew reason she'd taken a liking to. "Perhaps you will be luckier with the next, and Eachann will find some new competition."

He gave her a hard glare. "He only beat me one time. I told you it was an aberration."

Their eyes met and they both started to laugh. It hadn't been an aberration. Eachann was almost eerily bright. A problem solver, Eoin called him. He was convinced the lad would invent something great one day. "It's a boring child's game anyway," he said. "Or so I've been told."

She laughed, took their daughter from his arms, and set her back down on the box bed that had been provided for her. "Come," she said. "Marsaili will watch over her."

"Like she watched over you?" Eoin lifted his eyes. "God help me."

He rubbed his upper arm when a fist socked him. "Ouch!" he said. "That hurt."

"Good," she replied primly. "But as one of Bruce's fabled warriors, I would think you would be a little tougher."

"Didn't you hear? The war is over. Now I'm just the keeper of a royal castle at Sael."

She made a sharp scoffing sound. "And *tánaiste* of the MacLeans." His father had made it official a few months ago. Eoin knew how unusual it was for a third son to be named as heir and had been honored. "Besides," she added shrewdly. "I saw you huddled with Erik and Lachlan earlier. You don't fool me. I know you're up to something. And I'll have it out of you later."

He lifted a very intrigued brow. "And how do you intend to do that?"

"I have my ways," she said smugly.

She sure as hell did, and he couldn't wait till tonight when she inevitably brought him to his knees. So many things had changed between them, but the passion burned just as hot as it had all those years ago. Hell, thinking about how he'd woken to the feeling of her bottom pressing against him insistently this morning, maybe even hotter.

He followed her down the stairs, through the Hall, and out into the courtyard.

"I thought we could walk," she said.

He nodded, and they started toward the gate. He looked over his shoulder, and she must have sensed his thoughts.

"They'll be fine," she said. "Duncan will take good care of them while we are gone." He must have made a face, and she shook her head. "Don't forget, we are all one big happy family now."

Although Margaret's brother had made his peace with Bruce after the end of the war and been made keeper of Garthland Castle in return, Eoin being the guest of his former enemy still took some getting used to. But he knew how important it was to Margaret to be here, especially after the death of her eldest brother in battle last year. Her father still stubbornly refused to accept Bruce and was fighting in Ireland.

"How can I forget? You've reminded me every day for the past six months to try to get me to agree to come here."

She squeezed his hand, suddenly serious. "Thank you. I know this hasn't been easy for you, but I wanted to do something."

A short while later when they arrived at the loch he discovered what she meant. He turned to her in surprise. "You did all this?"

She nodded, her eyes roaming his face uncertainly as she tried to gauge his reaction. He was stunned, and then incredibly moved by what she'd put together.

His brethren stood along the edge of the water, flanking two men in the center. The first wore a crown, and the second a bishop's mitre: King Robert the Bruce and the most important churchman in the country (and Bruce's longtime ally), William Lamberton, the Bishop of St. Andrews. Behind them, the calm waters of the loch were filled not with the red that he'd seen last time he'd been here, but tiny white flowers. Snowdrops, or as they were known due to their use at Candlemas, Our Lady's Bells.

"There must be thousands of them," he said aloud.

Margaret shook her head. "Seven hundred eighty-four. I counted every one."

Their eyes locked in shared understanding. His throat tightened at the significance. Each flower represented a man who'd died as a result of the failed mission at Loch Ryan eight years ago today.

"It's time, Eoin," she pleaded. "It's time to let them rest in peace."

He nodded. She was right. It was time to say a prayer for the men who'd died here, and let go of the ghosts of the past—all of them. He would never forget what had happened here, but he'd forgiven Maggie, maybe now it was time to try to forgive himself.

"Thank you," he said, his voice tight. He squeezed her hand, fighting back emotion. "I love you."

She gave him one of those smiles that rivaled the sun. "And don't you forget it."

He never would. With a nod, Eoin let his wife take his hand and lead him forward where his friends waited to help him bury the past forever.

AUTHOR'S NOTE

THE CHARACTER OF Eoin is loosely based on John Dubh MacLean, who was the third son of either Gilliemore or Malcolm MacLean and the grandson (or great-grandson) of the famous Gillian of the Battle Axe, who is considered the first chief of Clan MacLean.

John Dubh (Black John) fought with his father and two brothers for Bruce. His mother, Rignach, was said to be a relation of Bruce's. One theory—and the one that made the most sense to me—was that she was a daughter of Neil of Carrick, and thus a half sister to Bruce's mother, Marjory.

The MacLeans were shown favor by Bruce after the war for their loyalty, with John Dubh being named keeper of the royal castle of "Sael" (Seil Isle?), his brother Donald named as commander of the king's galleys, and his brother Neil also named keeper of a royal castle, this one probably Tarbert. Unusually, however, despite having two older brothers, John Dubh is named chief when his father dies. No explanation is given, but the idea for my brilliant strategist was born.

John Dubh's two sons, Hector (Eachann Reaganach or

Hector the Stern) and Lachlan (Lachainn Lubanach or Lachlan the Cunning/Wily), are the famous progenitors of the two branches of MacLeans/Maclaines. As readers of my *Highlander Unchained* might remember, they will also cause endless name confusion—a recurring problem for me—by providing the first name for countless generations of chiefs. It will be over three hundred years after John Dubh before the Duart MacLeans have a chief who is not named Hector or Lachlan.

John Dubh is said to have designated his lands of Lochbuie for Hector, and Duart for Lachlan. The MacLeans grow further in importance when Lachlan marries a daughter of John MacDonald, the first Lord of the Isles. Hector, interestingly, marries Christina, a daughter of the MacLeod of Harris. Those of you who have read *The Chief* might be smiling right now; I know I couldn't help but wonder whether this Christina was a descendant of Tor and Christina. I love when fact and fiction serendipitously intertwine like that.

As with most of the books, I take a lot of inspiration from genealogical charts. There is always tons of great fodder in the notes. Although citations are sometimes thin, and there are usually discrepancies, it's often the place I find information that I can't find elsewhere. Case in point was when I was trying to figure out where the MacLean lands were *before* the war (after they are associated with the Isles of Mull, Tiree, Coll, and Morvern and Lochbuie on the mainland). They were generally thought to have been from Lorn, as vassals of the Lord of Argyll, but it wasn't until I came across a genealogical record for "Eoin Dubh Mac Gilliemore" (John Dubh) that I found a reference to Gylen Castle on the Isle of Kerrera as the place of his birth. Since Gylen Castle was a MacDougall castle, this seemed to fit.

This same record also provided the inspiration for the character of Fin, as the notes refer to an attempt by the MacKinnons (formerly MacFinnons) to kill John Dubh's sons, making the clans, not surprisingly, hardened enemies.

Finally, a few genealogical charts had Eoin possibly married to a Comyn, providing my inspiration for the wife who is the daughter of the enemy.

The character of Margaret MacDowell is fictional, but Dugald/Duegald MacDowell/MacDowall/Macdowyl/Macdouall/Macdougall (these are just a few of the many ways his name is spelled) is said to have had eight sons. As is usually the case, there is no mention of whether he had any daughters.

MacDowells claim descent from original Gaels who came from northern Ireland to Galloway in the eighth or ninth century, and recent DNA studies seem to support this (www.scottishorigenes.com/content/medieval-ethnicity-map-scotland). Like their Balliol and Comyn kinsmen, they were blood enemies of Bruce. And like the MacDougalls, who were also kinsmen to the Comyns, the MacDowells would prove the biggest and most consistent thorns in Bruce's side during his long struggle for the throne.

Bruce forces MacDowell to flee to England sometime in 1308–9, where he is listed in the public records on April 8, 1309, as being "hated by the enemy" and given "the manor of Temple-Couton in York" by King Edward II for the residence of his family. But Dugald is back in Scotland again a few years later occupying the important Galloway stronghold of Dumfries.

By far the biggest thorn that Dugald stuck in Bruce was the disaster at Loch Ryan on February 9, 1307 (six days earlier than I have it). Readers of the previous books will know that this is not the first time Loch Ryan has been mentioned (i.e., *The Hawk*, *The Hunter*, and *The Arrow*), and when you think about how devastating the battle must have been, it makes Bruce's unlikely comeback even more incredible. After being forced into exile for almost five months following his failed bid for the throne in 1306, which saw one brother and numerous friends killed and his wife and family imprisoned (some in cages), Bruce gathers enough men to make his big play to retake the kingdom, and by most accounts, a large portion of his forces are wiped out before they can get beyond the beach at Loch Ryan thanks to Dugald MacDowell.

The exact numbers are impossible to pin down, but most historians seem to put the forces at Carrick under Bruce's command at a few hundred (what I call the northern prong of the attack, featured in *The Hawk*), and the forces at Loch Ryan under his two brothers' command at somewhere between seven hundred and nine hundred.

There were eighteen galleys at Loch Ryan, of which only two managed to escape. A medieval galley probably had eighteen to twenty-four oars, which at two men per oar is consistent with seven hundred to nine hundred men total. The large majority of these men, perhaps as many as seven hundred of them, were Irish. Some of the captured, like the Irish kinglet Margaret witnesses, were summarily beheaded, while others—like Bruce's two brothers—were taken to Carlisle Castle in England to be executed by Edward. Thomas and Alexander Bruce were hung and beheaded after being "drawn at the tail of horses" for eight miles (BruceTrust.co.uk/places-events.html). Their heads were then put atop the gates of the castle as a rather grotesque medieval warning.

So from what I can tell, Bruce had maybe twelve

hundred men when he attempted to retake his kingdom in February 1307. Of those, possibly as many as eight hundred are killed immediately at Loch Ryan. He lands at Carrick with his few hundred men, and along with the survivors of Loch Ryan, he has around four hundred men left to retake a kingdom. You can see why I said that Mac-Dowell dealt him a devastating blow. I can't imagine how even the most devoted of followers could have given Bruce much of a chance after Loch Ryan.

For his service to the English crown at Loch Ryan, MacDowell is said to have received a knighthood, silver, and an English heiress (the daughter of Hugh de Champagne) for his heir Dougal, who will later die at Bannockburn in 1314.

John Comyn, the murdered Red Comyn's son (and Margaret's erstwhile suitor), also dies at Bannockburn.

The siege of Dumfries Castle lasted longer than I have it in the book—possibly six or more weeks—with the occupants being starved into submission. That Bruce allowed Dugald MacDowell to surrender Dumfries after he'd handed over his brothers to Edward for certain execution is pretty impressive, demonstrating the lengths Bruce was willing to go to unite Scotland. Of course, as with John of Lorn, Bruce's forbearance isn't rewarded, and it isn't long after the surrender that MacDowell is fighting against Bruce's forces again on the Isle of Man. MacDowell suffers defeat there as well and is forced to surrender to Bruce for the second time in a handful of months. Again, however, Bruce allows him to go free.

MacDowell will stay in the English service until his death sometime in 1327–28. He will be succeeded by his second son, Duncan, who continues the family habit of fighting against Bruces. In the 1330s, Duncan will raise forces a few times to attempt to bring the Balliols back to the throne.

The difficulty Bruce must have had in bringing Galloway to heel is apparent even to visitors today. The area is remote, not easily accessible, and definitely off the tourist beaten path. I have visited most regions of Scotland, and Galloway definitely has a distinct feel to it, where very little of the outside world seems to penetrate. One can only imagine what it must have been like seven hundred years ago.

Whether the MacDowells were any more "barbarian" than the other clans, I can only speculate, but given the remoteness of Garthland Castle in the farthest corner of the Rhins of Galloway, it seemed plausible that Margaret might appear a little wild and backward to the nobles at Stirling.

Gallowegians themselves had an early reputation from the medieval period as being the "Wild Scots of Galloway," for holding to their ancient customs and laws, as well as for their fighting ability. They were reputed to have held the right to lead the van of Scotland's army in early military engagements, such as the Battle of the Standard in 1138. Sir Walter Scott summarizes them like this: "Some historians say they came of the race of the ancient Picts; some call them the Wild Scots of Galloway; all agree that they were a fierce, ungovernable race of men, who fought half-naked, and committed great cruelty upon the inhabitants of the invaded country" (Scott, Sir Walter, *The History of Scotland, Vol. 1*, Edinburgh: Adam and Charles Black, 1864; p. 26).

Although not codified as they were in Ireland, the influence of the ancient Irish Brehon laws in Scotland seems clear up until about the eleventh century (when feudalism was introduced after the Norman conquest of England),

and in Galloway perhaps until the thirteenth century. Evidence of the old mote-hills "courts" upon which the Brehon lords dispensed justice are still scattered throughout Scotland.

One of the most interesting (and succinct) summaries I've read about the Wars of Independence was in Wikipedia: "In many ways, the Scottish Wars of Independence were just a Galwegian civil war, with the Bruces the successors of Gille Brigt mac Fergusa and the Balliols the successors of Uchtred mac Fergusa" (http://en.wikipedia.org/wiki/Galwegian_Gaelic).

Although an oversimplification—English overlordship and rule was at the center of the war—there is a lot of truth to this. We think of the wars as the Scots versus the English, but it was much more complicated than that, and as I have mentioned before, much of the early flip-flopping of Bruce, Comyn, and so on, can be explained by looking at who was on the other side. The English were often cast in "the enemy of my enemy is my friend" role. Do I think Dugald MacDowell had a great love for Edward of England? No. But he hated Bruce more.

As I alluded to briefly in the novel, the two warring factions in Scotland were descended from two sons of Prince Fergus, Lord of Galloway: Uchtred (Balliols and Mac-Dowells) and Gille Brigte (Bruces). Gille Brigte killed his brother Uchtred in a rather heinous example of fratricide by blinding him, castrating him, and having his tongue cut out.

Perhaps this murder set the tone for the hatred that would break out between their descendants more than a hundred years later?

With regard to medieval marriage, readers of my previous books will know that this is a subject that has dogged me repeatedly. It is very difficult to try to determine how the "rules" (canon laws) were applied in real life and how common something was—for example, clandestine marriage. It seems that a statement of present intent was all you needed to have a valid medieval marriage. In other words, the "I take thee" vows that Margaret and Eoin spoke would have been enough alone—even without consummation. A statement of future intent (such as a betrothal agreement) and consummation, however, also made a valid marriage. But, as the rules were likely just as confusing to the medieval participants as they are to this twenty-first-century former attorney researcher, I decided to err on the side of overdoing what was required. What would a wedding be without consummation? This *is* a romance, after all.

Last, the Abbey of St. Mary's mentioned in Stirling is now called Cambuskenneth.

For more, including pictures of many of the places in the series, please visit www.monicamccarty.com.